Muscle

by

John Davies

Copyright © John Davies 2020

All rights reserved. No part of this publication
may be reproduced, stored in a retrieval system, or
transmitted, in any form or by any means,
electronic, mechanical, photocopying, recording or
otherwise, without the prior permission of the
copyright holder.

This is entirely a work of fiction. The names,
characters and incidents portrayed in it are the work
of the author's imagination. Any resemblance to
actual persons, living or dead, events or localities, is
entirely coincidental.

Saturday night at the Hive was quieter than usual. The club was only half full and Frankie put that down to being the last week of the month. Bank balances were starting to run dry before pay day. Next weekend, the club would be packed, as working men and women, flush with cash, rushed out to let their hair down, to get some release at the end of the working week.

Frankie had done the same thing himself, back when he used to earn a wage working in factories and warehouses and on building sites around the city. He'd been paid weekly back then and could remember getting his pay packet on a Friday, a little brown envelope full of cash, back before they paid directly into his bank. Frankie remembered the feeling it gave him, collecting his wages from payroll. Holding that little envelope of cash made the working grind worthwhile. He'd been paid minimum wage back then, but that didn't stop him from going out on a millionaire's weekend, hitting the pubs and clubs, getting drunk with his friends, trapping off with a woman at the end of the night, maybe even going back to her place if she was up for it. Back then, he'd thought as far as his next pint and no further. Come Monday morning, he was skint, waiting for pay day again.

Frankie had moved on since then. He was making a lot more than minimum wage now. He was never skint on a Monday, not anymore. But he still looked back on those times with a smile. They were good times, simpler times.

Frankie walked around the main dance floor. There was nothing much happening. It was an hour before closing time and the atmosphere in the club felt relaxed and calm. Frankie nodded to Chris, who was standing by the cocktail bar, keeping a casual eye on the group of lads slamming down shots, and then headed down to the main door to see Steve.

Steve was standing outside, even though it was unlikely that anyone else would be coming in for the last hour. "Is it home time yet?" he said.

"Not long now, mate," said Frankie. "You on a promise or something?"

"I'm just bored."

Steve was one of the biggest bouncers Frankie had on the crew, six foot four and eighteen stones of muscle. It was no secret that he'd had a little help in that department, but Frankie didn't judge, as you took any advantage you could get when you were working the doors. So Frankie didn't mind if some of the lads were on the gear. He didn't touch the stuff himself, though. Firstly, he couldn't stand needles. And more importantly, he didn't want his bollocks shrinking.

"Head back in," said Frankie. "You can try your luck with Emma again."

Steve made a face. "Nah, she's stringing me along. I know her game."

"Or she knows yours," said Frankie and as he spoke, his eye caught movement in his peripheral vision. A car was coming down the street towards them at speed, engine running at high revs. The rear window was down and a bulky, shadowy figure was hunched in the back seat. The car skidded to a halt in front of them and a double barrelled shotgun was thrust out of the rear window. Frankie shouted, "Get down!" and he and Steve threw themselves to the ground. There was a flat crack and the shattering of glass. Frankie heard manic laughter as the car screamed away in first gear.

Frankie lifted his head, looking as far down the street as he could with his chin stuck to the concrete. He looked over at Steve. "You okay?"

"Yeah.... Yeah, I'm fine." Steve let out a shuddering breath. He looked embarrassed. "You?"

"Yeah."

They both stood up. Frankie's legs trembled with the aftershock of adrenalin. The street was quiet again. Frankie looked behind him, to see what the damage was. The neon sign above the door had been taken apart by the blast. What was left of it was littered across the pavement.

"Did you see who that was?" said Steve. "The fucking cunt."

It was more of a statement than a question. Steve knew who'd pulled the trigger, just as Frankie did.

Warren Kelly.

"Come on," said Frankie. "Let's get inside."

2

Rachel, behind the reception desk, was waiting for them. "What happened?" she said. "I heard a bang. Was there an accident?"

They had been standing just outside the spot covered by the camera above the main door, so she hadn't seen their dive to the pavement. Frankie didn't see the point in worrying her. "Some little scrotes," he said. "They shot out the sign with a catapult."

"It made a hell of a noise," she said.

"Tell me about it," said Frankie. "They must have used a ball bearing or something."

"Little bastards," said Rachel. "Those things can take someone's eye out."

Frankie nodded and Steve grabbed a broom to sweep up the debris from the shattered sign.

No one else in the club had heard the shot over the music. The police didn't show up, so it appeared that no one out on the street had witnessed the event or had cared enough to call the law if they had. Frankie was grateful for that. It was one less headache for him to deal with. He found Chris, took him to one side and gave him a heads up on what had happened.

"Jesus, Frankie, are you all right?" said Chris.

"Yeah, yeah," said Frankie. "He wasn't aiming to hit, the prick. But we need to watch ourselves, just in case."

"This is getting out of hand."

"You don't have to fucking tell me," said Frankie. He gritted his teeth, and took a breath. He hadn't meant to snap. "I'll sort it." He patted Chris on the shoulder. "Soon be home time," he said, forcing a smile.

Even though there was less than an hour to go, the rest of the night seemed to drag by. Frankie was tired. He just wanted to get home, collapse into his bed and go to sleep. The fatigue he felt was one of the after effects of the adrenalin surge he'd had earlier. Closing time couldn't come soon enough.

As the final drinkers were shown out and the bar staff went about stacking glasses into dishwashers, Steve took Frankie to one side.

"You need to sort him, Frankie," said Steve. "You need to find out where that cunt lives and put both barrels through his fucking kneecaps." He was almost spitting out the words and was shifting from side to side on the balls of his feet. Frankie could tell that he'd done a line or two of coke. "I can get hold of a shotgun anytime, just say the word."

"You need to chill out, Steve," said Frankie.

"Fucking chill out? We were fucking shot at! And you don't want to do anything about it?"

"I didn't say I wasn't going to do anything about it. But I ain't gonna do his legs, it ain't worth it." Frankie would have taken great pleasure in doing Warren's kneecaps, but the risk wasn't worth the reward – if Frankie got caught for it, he wouldn't see the outside of a prison cell until he was ready for his pension.

"You wouldn't have said that a few years ago," said Steve. "I'd have been trying to calm *you* down."

He was right. A few years back, Frankie would've been straight out the door, gun in hand, and he wouldn't have given the consequences a second thought. But things had changed. He'd changed.

"Yeah, well, like you said, that was then. I'll deal with Warren, don't you worry."

"Just be sure you do. You're the fucking boss. You've got to be seen to be doing something. He's had enough fucking chances. You can't let him keep taking the piss. You'll end up a fucking laughing stock."

Something must have flashed in Frankie's eyes. Maybe a glimpse of the old Frankie, the hit first and fuck the consequences Frankie, because Steve backed up a half-step. He held his hands up, palms out. "Sorry, Frankie, I don't mean any disrespect by it. I'm your mate, you know that. But it has to be said."

Frankie nodded. "Don't worry about it," he said. "Go on, get home. Try and settle down. We'll talk about it tomorrow."

They parted on a handshake. Frankie left shortly after, once the club manager had locked up. He walked back to his car with his head on a swivel, even though he didn't expect any further attacks. If Warren had wanted to do him an injury, he'd have taken a better shot earlier. No, tonight's attack hadn't been about causing harm. It had been about causing a scene, about putting on a show. It was all part of the game.

3

Frankie got home a little before three o'clock. He was still restless. He took a beer from the fridge and sat in front of the TV, hoping that the sports channel highlights would slow his mind down. After half an hour, he decided that he should at least try to get some sleep. He went upstairs, took a quick shower and slipped into bed as quietly as he could, so as not to wake Chloe. She groaned and rolled over, but didn't stir.

Frankie stared into the darkness of the room, images from that night running unchecked through his head. He closed his eyes and forced himself to breathe slowly, trying to push the thoughts from his mind.

Finally, after what seemed like a whole night's worth of worry, he drifted off and fell into a restless sleep. His dreams were fractured and disorientating, full of shouts, jostling figures, and gunshots.

4

Frankie woke up just after seven. He was an early riser by habit, even after club nights. Chloe was still asleep. Frankie eased out of bed, pulled on a T shirt and headed downstairs.

He lived in a four-bedroom detached property, in one of the quieter areas of the city. The house was bigger than he actually needed, but Frankie saw it as somewhere for him and Chloe to grow into, if they decided to have kids.

He was in the kitchen, drinking a cup of coffee and watching Sky Sports when his phone rang. It was a number he didn't recognise.

"Hello?"

"Hello, granddad. How're you this morning?"

The sound of Warren's voice brought on an adrenalin rush worse than last night's, like a depth charge of acid in his gut. *Thank fuck I haven't had breakfast*, he thought and immediately felt stupid and cowardly and embarrassed. His hand, holding the phone, was trembling. His legs felt hollow and shaky. *Get a fucking grip*, he told himself. He felt gutless and weak. *Man the fuck up*. He took a breath through his nose and swallowed once before speaking.

"You've got some nerve calling me, boy," he said. He was relieved to hear that he'd managed to stop the shakiness in his legs from reaching his voice. He sounded strong. He sounded steady. He sounded fearless.

"Just seeing if you was all right, you know, after last night," said Warren. "Must've given you a bit of a fright, especially at your age."

"It'll take a bit more than a stray shot to bother me, Warren."

"You hit the deck quick enough though, didn't you? I'm surprised you didn't put a hip out. You couldn't get any lower. I thought you was gonna start digging." Warren laughed. He sounded like a dog coughing. "Yeah, you looked bothered enough from where I was."

"And where was that, Warren? In the back of the fucking car as it sped off?"

"Easy, old man, don't be getting feisty now. You'll have a heart attack. I wouldn't like that. Wouldn't be no fun in that."

"You want some fun, Warren, you come down to the club. Me and you can have all the fun you want."

"I don't think so, man."

"I didn't think you would. Straight up stuff's not your thing, is it Warren? You like your little shoot and scoots, don't you? Like doing things mob-handed, when you've got some back up. But you can't man up and do a real man's work, can you? I'd be surprised if you can even take a shit on your own."

"I could fucking take you, you old cunt."

Frankie laughed. "Easy, Warren. Don't be getting *feisty*, now."

"Fuck you, Frankie, you're yesterday's news. You're too fucking old to be part of the scene. Your time's coming."

"Really? You'd better start getting some target practise then, if you want to do a better job than last night."

No response. Frankie could hear Warren breathing on the other end of the phone. "What's the matter, Warren? Run out of things to say? Haven't got your little posse with you to help you with your big boy words?"

"This ain't over, old man."

"That's original." Frankie gave an exaggerated yawn. "You know what, Warren? If you were this big, hard man you seem to think you are, if you had anything about you, anything at all, you'd meet me for a straightener, and we could put all this to bed once and for all. No more tit for tat crap, no more hit and runs. Just you and me, no tools, no rules. But you haven't got the balls, have you? And me? I've got better things to do."

He cut the call.

He put the phone down and looked at his hands. They were shaking. He clenched them into tight fists. The adrenalin was churning around inside him with nowhere to go, no way out, no release. He took a few deep breaths. That felt better. The sick feeling started to ease.

"Who are you talking to?"

He looked up to see Chloe coming down the stairs, still in her pyjamas, hair all over the place. She looked as if she was still half-asleep, but that was Chloe. She'd never been a morning person.

"Morning, babe. I was on the phone." He flicked the kettle on. "You want a cuppa? Kettle's not long boiled."

"Who to?"

"Say again?"

"I said, who were you talking to?"

"No one important." He dropped a tea bag and two sugars into a mug.

"It's quarter past seven on Sunday morning, Frankie. If it couldn't wait until later, then it must be important."

"It's just some stuff with one of the clubs." The kettle clicked off and Frankie poured in boiling water. "Nothing to worry about."

"Whatever."

"What's that supposed to mean?"

"It means, if you don't want to tell me, don't tell me." She took the mug from him and took it over to the fridge to put in some milk.

"What have you got the hump about?"

"Never mind." She turned and headed off upstairs.

Frankie watched her go in silence. What was all that about? He shook his head and went back to his coffee. She'd probably just got out of the wrong side of bed. She was like that sometimes, a bit moody if she hadn't had enough sleep. She'd be all right later.

He'd been with Chloe for two years now. He'd met her at a club called Fever, where he'd been head doorman. She'd started chatting him up while he was watching the dance floor. He'd shagged her a week later, and they'd started going out a couple of weeks after that. At twenty eight, she was more than ten years younger than him. When they'd gone back to the club one night as a couple, Shelly, who was one of the barmaids at Fever and roughly the same age as Frankie, had looked at him like he was a dirty old man. Frankie put it down to jealousy, plain and simple. He'd had the odd snog and fumble with Shelly a couple of times after work but had blown her out when she'd asked him on a proper date. Shelly wasn't his type, not for going out with anyway.

Chloe was a team leader at a call centre, but in Frankie's opinion, she should be earning a living as a model. Blonde hair, long legs, nice tits. She'd had a boob job last year. Just to make them a bit perkier, she'd said, when she'd told him that she wanted to have it done. Frankie hadn't objected. He was a breast man, always had been. He had paid for it as a birthday present. It had cost him nearly five grand, but it was money well spent, worth every penny.

He liked the looks Chloe got from other men when she walked down the street. He liked the looks he got from those same men when they saw she was with him. Looks that said, *Nice one, mate. Get in there.* Looks that said, *You lucky bastard.*

He felt lucky, too. There he was, nearly forty, with a girl like her on his arm. And she could do a few things in the bedroom, too. Or the living room. Or the car. She was always up for it.

But things hadn't been as good in that department recently. Take just now, for instance. The way she'd come downstairs, hair all tangled, tits straining at her pyjama top, she was a gorgeous, scruffy mess. Any other time, he'd have taken her straight back upstairs and shagged the arse off her. But that was before all this shit with Warren and his little crew. He'd kept it from her, like he did with most of the stuff that happened at work, but it was wearing him down, stressing him out. And it was having a knock on effect in the bedroom. He was sure she'd noticed, even if she hadn't said anything.

His phone beeped with a message notification. He picked it up. It was from Warren.

NXT SUNDAY 8AM @ THE ARCHES LETS SORT THIS.

Frankie felt the adrenalin trickle through him again. He nodded to himself as he sent the reply.

You're on.

A few moments later, Frankie's phone beeped again with another message.

DONT 4GET 2 BRING A WHEELCHAIR

Frankie smiled despite himself. The prick. He just had to have the last word.

He rang Steve and brought him up to speed.

"Fucking brilliant," said Steve. "You'll tear his fucking head off." He laughed. "You want me to be your second?"

"I wouldn't ask anyone else."

"Are you training?"

"The usual."

"You need to work on your hands. I've heard he trains at that MMA gym over the river, so he's into all that grappling shit. You need to finish him before it goes to the ground."

"It won't matter what he's into when I'm biting his nose off," said Frankie, but the bravado in his voice rang hollow in his ears.

"That's the spirit," said Steve. "Anyway, I'm off back to bed. Let me know when you want me to hold the pads."

"Okay. Take it easy."

"Laters."

Frankie hung up. He rubbed his eyes. He was tired. The four hours' sleep he'd had wasn't enough. He needed to get some more, or else he'd be in no fit state to start training. He switched off the television, dumped his mug in the sink and headed upstairs. He could hear Chloe moving around in the bathroom. He padded past and went into the bedroom.

He drifted into an agitated sleep. In his dreams, he was working the door, but the location kept changing. Sometimes he would be outside a nightclub, other times outside places from his past: the factory where he used to work, his old secondary school, a video store where he used to hire out VHS tapes. He told a man he couldn't come in. The man protested and the dispute quickly turned into an argument and in the next moment, they were fighting. The man's face was a waxy, formless blob, and Frankie's punches were comically slow. It took every ounce of effort to even lift his arms and he felt sickeningly, terrifyingly weak. No matter how many times Frankie hit him, the faceless man wouldn't go down.

Frankie woke up confused and sweating, his heart hammering away in his chest, his fists clenched.

He was scared.

5

The rest of the day was a typical Sunday. Frankie hoovered the living room and tidied up the garden, while Chloe loaded up the washing machine and cleaned the kitchen. Like many other working couples, their jobs meant that they were busy during the week, so they often spent the weekends catching up on housework.

Frankie didn't mind. Maintaining his home gave him a sense of pride and reminded him of how far he had come. He'd left school with basic qualifications and he'd done his fair share of low-paying, manual jobs, scratching to get by. Now he had his own house, his own business and money in the bank. He didn't lead an extravagant or indulgent lifestyle, but he didn't watch every penny, either. He had a good life, one he'd worked hard for, one he worked even harder to keep.

Later, after the jobs were done, they took a walk to their local pub for a carvery lunch and a few drinks. Chloe was back to her usual self, chatty and smiling. Whatever had been bugging her earlier seemed to have been forgotten. They talked about nothing in particular and laughed often, like couples comfortable in each other's company often did.

Afterwards, they walked back home holding hands and spent the rest of the day on the sofa, catching up on a Netflix serial that Chloe had discovered.

For most of the day, Frankie had managed to put aside his troubles at the club. But as afternoon moved into evening, those worries began to slowly intrude, creeping in from the edges of his mind and filling his head like a thickening fog.

Sitting there, stretched out comfortably on the sofa in his nice house with Chloe by his side, he was no longer thinking about the things he had achieved. He could think only of the things he stood to lose.

6

On Monday morning, he started his training.

He didn't have long until the fight, so his regime for the next six days would be about maintaining and sharpening what he already had. Frankie kept fit out of both necessity and habit. He'd been into sports as a kid and along with rugby, football and cross-country, he'd done judo and boxing after school. The other pursuits had dropped away over time, but the boxing had remained, and Frankie had had several amateur fights in his early twenties. In time, those competitive fights had stopped too, but he continued with the training. He lifted weights, he ran, he jumped rope, he pushed himself through conditioning circuits, and worked out on the heavy bag.

Steve was right, Frankie did need to work on his punching. The heavy bag was good for power, but Frankie needed to sharpen his speed and accuracy, and for that he needed to put in some time on the pads. He'd arranged to do a session with Steve at the gym tomorrow, so today he decided to do some roadwork, to keep the cobwebs out of his lungs and run off some of the tension that had built up inside him since last night.

He took a familiar route through the local park. He stopped at various points along the way to do press ups and squat thrusts before running on again. He pushed himself hard, his breath coming in heavy gusts, his legs burning as he sprinted.

He thought about Warren. Warren Kelly was from somewhere in the north west and had headed south to make his fortune selling cocaine, ketamine,

MDMA and ecstasy. Frankie didn't know what had brought him down here, but he assumed Warren had relocated to avoid the attention of the local police, other criminals, or both. Warren was supposedly a bit handy, but he had a rep for carrying out mob-handed home visits, crashing through his enemy's front door in the early hours, accompanied by his crew of dead-headed lackeys, and pouncing on his unsuspecting victims as they were still rubbing the sleep from their eyes.

Frankie owned a security firm that supplied guards for live events and building sites, and doormen to several clubs, pubs and bars in the city. It was all legitimate, but when you took away the administrative tasks that came with running a company, the bidding for contracts and the book-keeping, the submission of tax returns and accounts, what Frankie did for a living was simple.

He provided muscle.

A lot of things had changed since Frankie had first started out, but when it came to drugs in the club, things were done a certain way. Drugs and nightclubs went together, it was as simple as that. They always had and they always would. And the bouncers running the doors would always have a hand in the drugs business, regardless of schemes like SIA licencing. The way Frankie saw things, it was about maintaining a measure of control. So, for a small fee, he allowed a select group of local dealers into his clubs and made sure his lads turned a blind eye as they went about their business.

When one of Warren's dealers was caught selling in the club Frankie was responsible for, he had his stash confiscated and, because he made a fuss and took a swing at one of the bouncers, got a kicking for his troubles.

That was how it had all started.

There were a couple of tit-for-tat attacks. Ryan, the bouncer who'd given Warren's dealer the beating, was ambushed on his way to the club a week later, ending up in A and E with a shattered cheekbone, broken ribs and a collapsed lung. In retaliation, Frankie and Steve had found one of the culprits, inflicted similar injuries, and had thrown a broken arm into the bargain.

Shortly after that, another pub Frankie was looking after had its windows put in. Several customers had been badly cut by flying glass.

Then things had escalated with the drive by on Saturday night.

It wasn't the first time Frankie had been involved in something like this. He'd been working the doors, on and off, for over twenty years. He'd been beaten, cut, stabbed, glassed, clubbed, and even shot at before. He'd been involved in feuds with other violent men. He'd felt fear and pain and doubt. But every time he'd taken whatever had been thrown at him, gritted his teeth and fought his way through it. Every time, he'd come back stronger, tougher, harder.

But this time was different. Frankie didn't know why, but this thing with Warren was getting to him. He wasn't sleeping properly. He'd started to dread going on the door. And of course, there were the problems in the bedroom. He'd managed to keep up the front with the lads on the door, managed to make sure he looked strong and sure for Steve and the boys, but inside he felt like something was slowly eating away at him, gnawing at the iron that had once ran through him.

He had to get that iron back.

He ran faster.

7

Back at home, Frankie stretched off and ran the shower. Chloe was on the late shift this week, and was still in bed. He looked himself over in the mirror. He was thirty-nine this year and was still strong and fit at a solid fifteen stone. He could spar with the best of them down at the gym. His stomach muscles were still rock solid, but now there was a layer of fat over them that he just couldn't shift, no matter how many rounds he did on the heavy bag or how far he ran. He was all too aware of the signs of age now. The lines on his forehead, the crow's feet around his eyes, the loose skin at his neck. And the hair, how could he not notice the hair? It was sprouting out of places it never had before. The tip of his nose, his ears, across his back. The toll his life had taken was etched on his body too. The scars from the knives and broken bottles. The dented and buckled knuckles, misshapen and disfigured from countless fights.

Looking at himself, he was suddenly tired. He wondered how long he had left in the game, how long he could keep forcing his body to keep up the pace, when all it wanted to do was slow down. Yeah, he could hold his own and he had experience on his side, but there was always someone younger, someone stronger, faster or more violent.

He knew that one day he'd meet his match.

Why was he still doing it? He owned the firm and he made a tidy packet supplying the bouncers to the clubs, even without the cut he took from the dealers. He didn't have to do the doors himself – so why did he? Was he trying to prove something? If so, what?

That he could still cut it? That he was still the top dog?

Who was he trying to prove it to?

To Chloe?

To the rest of the lads?

To himself?

He didn't know.

He pushed his thoughts to one side and got into the shower.

He was washing his hair when the cubicle door opened and Chloe stepped inside. "Room for a little one?" she said.

She stood behind him and wrapped her arms around his chest, her breasts pressing into his back. She kissed his neck and rubbed her hands across his chest and sides. Her hands slid down his stomach to his groin. She stroked his balls and soaped up his cock. He grew stiff and hot in her hand. She squeezed him tight. "Mmm, that's better," she said. "I was starting to wonder where he'd gone."

He turned and kissed her, pulling her tight against him. Her hand kept working at him, moving faster. Frankie was so hard it hurt. It felt good. *She* felt good. The strength of his desire took him by surprise. He'd forgotten how much he wanted her. He spun her around, bending her forward. She gripped the cubicle door with one hand as he pushed himself inside her with a grunt. He fucked her hard, getting as much pleasure from watching his cock move in and out of her as he did from being inside her.

He felt better about himself with every thrust. Yeah, he was nearly forty, but here he was, fucking a woman ten years younger than him, who wanted his cock, who wanted *him*.

He wasn't too old. He wasn't past it. He still had it.

He was Frankie Collins. *Frankie fucking Collins*.

Who the fuck was Warren Kelly?

Warren Kelly. His mind latched onto the name like a dog to a bone and wouldn't let go. His thoughts were suddenly filled with everything that had happened over the past few months – all the shit at the club, the shooting, the straightener next week.

He tried to concentrate, tried to force his mind to take hold of the here and now – him and Chloe, how good it felt to be with her, inside her – but he found his purchase slipping and the present tumbled away. Rushing to fill its place came all of his worries, all of his fears, until he couldn't see anything but Warren's grinning face, mocking him.

His cock began to wilt. He buried his face in her neck, trying to immerse himself in her, trying to think only of her, to feel only her. It didn't work. His erection sagged. Chloe made a noise, a mixture of confusion and disappointment. He ground to a jerky, pitiful stop and slid out of her, soft and limp.

"What's the matter?" She turned around. "Frankie?"

"Nothing," he said. He couldn't look her in the eye. He opened the shower door and stepped out.

"Nothing? You call that nothing?"

"I've got a lot on my mind, that's all." He grabbed a towel and pressed it to his face, digging the heels of his hands into his eye sockets. What the fuck was wrong with him? He took a deep breath. He turned his back to her and started to dry himself.

"Yeah? What sort of things?" She was out of the shower now, still wet. She pulled on a towelling robe. "Who is she?"

"What?"

"I said who is she? Who are you shagging?"

"I'm not shagging anyone." He laughed, hoping she'd see how ridiculous her accusation sounded.

"Don't fucking laugh! You used to have my knickers off if I did as much as bend over to get something out of the fridge. You haven't touched me in weeks and when you finally do, you can't keep it up, even when you're inside me. You must be getting it from someone else."

"There is no one else. Chloe, please, don't do this. I'm not in the mood."

"You never fucking are!"

She pushed past him and stormed out of the bathroom. Frankie thought he saw tears in her eyes. He heard the bedroom door slam.

He wrapped the towel tight around his fists, twisting it into a knotted rope until his forearms burned. His cheeks were hot and his eyes were wet and burning. He wanted to cry. He wanted to scream. He wanted to smash something up. He looked down at his flaccid cock. Even his own body was betraying him. He imagined Warren, imagined how he'd laugh if he could see him now. Impotent and useless, unable to keep a hard on, unable to satisfy his own girlfriend.

Frankie's chest swelled with molten rage. He was going to bury that prick on Sunday. He was going to smash his face into the back of his skull and grind him into the fucking pavement. He'd do such a job on him, that the bastard would wish he'd never left whatever shit hole he'd come from, never come south, never crossed Frankie, never been fucking born.

Then Frankie would return home, a brave and valiant warrior, bloodied and weary from battle, and in the aftermath of his victory, he'd take Chloe to the bedroom and fuck her until she couldn't stand.

He dropped the towel and sat down on the toilet seat. He put his head in his hands and tried to hold back the tears.

8

The rest of the morning with Chloe passed in an uncomfortable near silence. They spoke only in short sentences, about nothing of any substance or meaning. Yesterday's domestic bliss seemed so very far away.

Frankie felt like an intruder in his own home. He did his best to keep out of her way. When she left for her shift Frankie was relieved to be alone.

He thought about Sunday.

The arches were just outside of the city centre, on a derelict industrial estate, where the main train line to London ran over a disused car park. It was tucked out of the way, at the end of the estate. It was one of those places that you wouldn't stumble across by chance, that you didn't arrive at without intention. Frankie had fought three straighteners there in the past.

A straightener was a simple thing. A fight between two men. No weapons. The rules of what you could do could vary depending on what had been agreed by the combatants, but the ones Frankie had fought had been 'anything goes.' The fighters could have someone with them – usually a close friend, ideally with some fighting prowess of their own – to act as a second, making sure there was no foul play and that no one else jumped in. The fight would last for as long as it took for one man to be beaten, or to surrender. And once it was done, whatever argument had led to the fight ended with it.

Frankie thought about Warren. From what he'd seen of him, Frankie guessed that he was maybe six or seven years younger. He was bigger too, weighing in at around eighteen stone, most of it muscle. Frankie wasn't overly worried about Warren's size – it didn't matter how many weights Warren pushed, he'd never be able to grow muscle on his chin – but the MMA stuff Steve had mentioned gave him pause for thought. He'd watched the fights on the sports channels and those blokes could do it all, they could kick, punch and grapple. Frankie wasn't worried about the kicking – he didn't have any intention of giving Warren any space to kick. Frankie had been brought up in boxing gyms, so he'd keep the fight at punching distance, where he was at his best. But Warren might be dangerous if the fight went to the ground. Grappling was the one thing Frankie had no real training or experience in. He could put a rough and ready choke hold or arm lock on a scrote at the club, but that was it. Those MMA fighters though, they could do all sorts of shit on the ground, fold you up like a fucking piece of origami. That skill, combined with Warren's weight and strength, would give him the advantage there. Still, there were no rules on the street. If Warren laid hands on him wanting to wrestle, Frankie would bite his face off and dig his eyes out of his fucking skull.

Frankie's plan was to keep the pressure on. He would hit Warren early, hit him hard and fast, keep going for the jaw, keep going for the chin, keep going for the knockout. If he couldn't get that, then he'd do as much damage as he could to Warren's face. He'd break his nose and make it hard for him to breathe. He'd cut his eyebrows and blind him with his own blood. He'd hammer him with body shots, go for his short ribs, where no muscle could grow, to wind him, to break those fragile bones and drive the splintered edges into his lungs until every breath he took felt like he was inhaling broken glass.

Warren might have the size and he might have the training.

But he didn't have what Frankie had.

Frankie had too much to lose.

9

On Tuesday, he met Steve at the gym.

Frankie got there early, so he could use the heavy bag before working the pads. He'd been coming to this place for years. It was an old school gym, dominated by a boxing ring that had seen more than its fair share of battles. Various punching bags and speedballs hung from the rafters and one side of the gym was lined with dumbbell racks, barbells, medicine balls and benches. Most of the equipment was old and shabby but Frankie preferred it to the polished chrome and bland sterility of most chain gyms. He liked the atmosphere. He liked the smell of the place. He liked the history held in its walls, the stories of struggle and hardship, of victory and defeat, of facing and overcoming weakness. It reminded him of the first gyms and boxing clubs that his dad had taken him to, all those years ago.

There were a few other lads training. Frankie knew most of them by sight and a few of them by name. Many of them knew him by reputation. He exchanged nods and a few greetings as he walked through to the changing rooms.

Back out in the gym, he started with the skipping rope, his footwork light and agile for a man of his size. Ten minutes later and nicely warmed up, he pulled on his gloves and worked the heavy bag, putting together simple combinations, lefts and rights, crosses and hooks. Working on power, driving his whole body behind each shot, feeling the solid, satisfying impact of a punch well thrown and imagining Warren's face collapsing like an empty beer can under each blow.

Steve arrived ten minutes later. He was dressed in tracksuit bottoms and a fitted t shirt, the material stretched tight across his shoulders and chest. He watched Frankie move around the bag. "Nice," he said. "You need to watch that right shoulder, though – you're dropping it."

Frankie drove a three-punch combination into the bag and stepped back. His vest was dappled with sweat and he was feeling good.

Steve grabbed a set of focus pads and they moved to one corner of the gym. Frankie hit the pads, working on accuracy and speed, chasing the pads as Steve moved around, drilling them with hard, fast shots. Steve coached Frankie with a mixture of encouragement and criticism, all of it seasoned with a heavy helping of piss-taking.

"Fuck's sake, you punching or tickling me?... Better... That's good... What was that? I've had harder kisses... Fucking hell, my gran hits harder than that, and she's dead... Good... Again... Good."

Frankie trained with a focus he hadn't had for years, not since he was a young man, hungry to carve himself a reputation as a fighter to be reckoned with, eager to make a name for himself as a man to be feared.

As he trained, Frankie noticed some of the other guys watching him work out. It was more than normal curiosity. They were taking more interest than usual.

Frankie felt the pressure of their scrutiny, knowing that they were observing him with a critical eye, assessing his technique, his speed, his power. Measuring him up.

Steve was aware of it, too. He punched a pad hard into Frankie's shoulder and hissed, "Focus. Come on."

Frankie channelled the anxiety into his punches, whipping them in, his gloves hitting the pads with vicious snaps. If they wanted a show, he'd give them a show.

They worked out for an hour. By the end of it, Frankie was covered in sweat, his arms heavy, spent. Steve clapped him on the back. "Good work there, Frankie. Those punches are feeling strong."

Frankie stretched off. He nodded his head towards the other blokes in the gym, the ones who had been watching him earlier. "So, the word's got out."

Steve nodded. "It never takes long. Bush telegraph, and all that."

Frankie grunted. "What are they saying?"

Steve was silent for a moment. "Don't matter what they're saying when you're punching holes in that cunt's head on Sunday morning."

Frankie didn't like the way Steve had paused before speaking. "What are they saying, Steve?"

Steve pursed his lips and breathed out heavily, the way he always did whenever he was about to give Frankie the no-shit truth. Frankie valued his counsel. Steve was one of the few people who would give him the hard truth, no matter how uncomfortable it was. That was the measure of their friendship. That was the measure of any friendship amongst men. Friends could give you the facts you needed to hear for your own good. Hurt feelings didn't come into it.

"Most of them are saying he's gonna do you," said Steve. "They're saying if you had a chance, you wouldn't have left it so long before sorting it out."

Frankie nodded once. He'd half expected something like that. But it still stung to hear it, and his gut twisted at the implied insult. "What about you?" he said. "What do you think?"

Steve looked him straight in the eye. "I think they're right, that you've left it too long. So you need to step up and do what needs to be done. Fucking bury him." He flicked his head in the general direction of the gym, the other men training, the outside world. "You know how it goes. People need to be reminded of how things stand. So come Sunday, you need to show them who's fucking boss, that you're not to be fucked with. Show them what's what."

Frankie nodded. He would.

He'd show them.

10

He spent the rest of the day at home, sorting through the various administrative tasks that came with running his business. Paperwork, invoicing, making phone calls to arrange cover. He used the smallest bedroom as a makeshift office, where he had a simple desk, chair and laptop arrangement. He'd never been one for sitting behind a computer, but he got by. He'd come to accept it as part of running his business. But he still preferred being out there, with the lads.

He'd been thinking about what Steve had said. Was he right? Were the others right, all those spectators and critics, watching from the background? Had he let things with Warren slide?

He thought back to the one time that he'd seen Warren, in the flesh, not long after the trouble had started. It was just after Frankie and Steve had done over one of the guys that had hospitalised Ryan. Frankie and Chloe had been out in town, having a meal and a few drinks with Pete and Aimee, a couple who lived on the same street. They had a table at the window, looking out onto the busy square lined with pubs and bars and restaurants. Frankie remembered laughing at something Pete had said, then glancing out of the window as he sipped at his beer. His eyes were drawn to the bar across the street, and the gaggle of people drinking in the outside area. Standing with a couple of other men, chatting to a group of young women, was Warren Kelly.

A wave of adrenalin rose up to meet the beer Frankie had just swallowed, crashing around his gut in an acid squall.

A wild rush of thoughts sped through his mind in a matter of seconds. There he was, Frankie's enemy, standing less than fifty yards away. Frankie could go out and confront him. Give him a choice – draw a line under it and end hostilities, or go for it, right there and then, one-on-one.

But he was with Chloe and Pete and Aimee, people who had nothing to do with his work on the door. Frankie saw the different parts of his life that he purposely kept separate on a sudden collision course. Until a few seconds ago, he had been enjoying a nice meal and the company of friends, his woman at his side. Now that other part of his world had intruded, and it unnerved him.

Then there was Warren. The sight of him had triggered something that went beyond the normal fight or flight response, something that bit at Frankie deep inside.

He turned away from the window and back to the conversation. He told himself that he wasn't going to confront Warren because he was out with Chloe and their friends and he didn't want to cause a scene and ruin their night. It wasn't fair on them.

But inside, he knew he was fooling himself.

Looking at Warren and imagining going up to him had filled Frankie with real fear.

Now, sitting in his home office, he wondered if things would have been different, had he faced up to Warren that night. If he hadn't made excuses to justify his cowardice.

A similar thing could happen on the doors. Frankie had seen it with several of his lads. It had happened to Frankie too, back in his early days. He'd see the trouble coming, see the signs, see it building. The belligerent drunk, making a nuisance of himself, stumbling around and pissing everyone off, just as likely to be the victim of violence as the perpetrator. The toxic couple, playing out their private drama in public, needling each other, winding each other up, the verbal abuse inevitably moving to the physical. The violent thug, daring someone to hold his gaze for a moment too long, to bump his shoulder, to laugh at the wrong moment, anything for an excuse to kick off. Frankie would see it all, could recognise the story and the characters, knew what was going to happen before the action took place.

And then it would reach a certain point where he knew that it was time to get involved. Knew that he had to take action and get in there quick if he wanted to nip trouble in the bud.

But he didn't.

Instead, he waited. He watched as even more of the drama played out. Because a part of him was hoping for the best to happen, for the situation to somehow resolve itself, for the troublemakers to get bored or leave of their own accord, for it to all go away. On that occasion, for whatever reason, he just didn't want the trouble. He didn't want the strife.

But he'd learned that the best never happened. That the trouble never went away on its own. And this thing with Warren was just a further confirmation of the facts: that you always had to take action.

11

Chloe got home a little before nine o'clock. Frankie had made a chilli. He was a fairly decent cook, providing it could be done in a wok, a casserole dish, or the slow cooker.

They ate at the dining table in the kitchen. Frankie opened a bottle of wine and poured Chloe a glass. He took a bottle of water from the fridge for himself.

Chloe looked at the bottle in his hand. "Not drinking?"

"I'm giving it a rest this week." He was off the booze, now he was training. He wouldn't touch any until after the straightener.

"What's brought this on?"

Frankie shrugged. "I just don't fancy it."

She raised her eyebrows and held his gaze for a moment longer than necessary.

"What?" he said.

"Nothing." She turned away and took a sip of wine.

Frankie knew exactly what she was getting at. A queasy feeling of shame and humiliation slid through his gut. He gritted his teeth and turned his attention to his meal.

Chloe told him about her day. She'd worked at the call centre for several years. She'd been one of the top sellers when she'd been on the phones and now that she was team leader, she'd replicated that individual success with her team. Her call centre was like any other workplace, with its own cliques, internal politics, and conflicts. Frankie listened as Chloe updated him on the latest squabbles amongst the managers and although he nodded and made comment, he couldn't help but find the office dramas trivial and pathetic. Disputes that could have been resolved with an honest, face to face conversation were conducted via emails to third parties and dragged out over days and weeks. It sounded like those who had been slighted then held grudges and sought petty revenge when they could, usually by throwing someone under the bus in a staff meeting. Frankie didn't get it. He didn't understand why they just couldn't be up front and move on.

Would he be able to move on, though, if he lost the straightener with Warren? The unwritten rules said so. Those rules said that he would have to accept his defeat, his loss of face.

And then what? Where would that leave him?

He'd be remembered as a loser. All those previous victories, all those past glories, they wouldn't matter, not one fucking bit. He'd be defined by his loss to Warren, marked by it, tainted forever. He'd be hollowed out and diminished, trying to hold on to the fragments of his shattered reputation.

He couldn't have that. Couldn't accept defeat.

He *wouldn't*.

Meal finished, they loaded the plates into the dishwasher and Chloe headed upstairs to shower and change. Frankie settled down to watch some television. Chloe came back downstairs a little while later, her hair up, wearing a pair of pyjamas. She kept one eye on the television and the other on her tablet.

"That film's out this weekend," she said. "There's a showing pretty much every hour."

"Huh?"

"The film you wanted to see." She tilted the tablet screen towards him. "Shall we go on Saturday?"

"Yeah," said Frankie. "We can go to one of the earlier showings."

"I thought we could go to one in the evening, go for a meal afterwards and a few drinks."

"I don't want to be out too late this Saturday."

"Why not?"

"I've got some stuff to do on Sunday morning."

"What stuff?"

"Work stuff."

"On a Sunday? What's so important it can't wait until after the weekend?"

"Stuff that needs sorting," he said.

She gave him a look but said nothing further. Although he never told her about that particular side of his business, she wasn't entirely unaware of it. It was easier for them both to not discuss it, for Frankie to gloss over the reality of his work and for Chloe to ignore it.

They lapsed into silence. After a while, Chloe put her tablet down on the side table and stood up. "I'm heading up," she said. "You coming?"

"I'll be up in a little while," he said. He looked back at the television.

Chloe left the room. He heard her moving around in the kitchen for a moment before heading up the stairs.

Frankie stared at the television, hardly paying attention to what was happening on the screen.

He'd stay downstairs until Chloe was asleep. He couldn't face another episode of impotence. He didn't even know how his own body was going to react anymore. He felt like a coward, hiding downstairs to avoid his girlfriend's touch.

For a moment, he had thought about telling her what was going on. Just talking to her, letting her know exactly how he was feeling and how it was affecting him. But that filled him with as much fear as the prospect of another shameful sexual failure and he knew he couldn't do it. He couldn't sit in front of her and spill his guts.

And Chloe wouldn't want him to, not really. No woman would, no matter what they told men about the need to communicate, to share, to open up. Frankie could see it now, could imagine telling her about all of his worries and fears and insecurities and then looking into her eyes and watching the respect she once had for him fade away with every new disclosure.

There was a chance – Frankie had to accept that there was a chance – that he could lose to Warren and that he'd lose respect, out there on the street.

He couldn't lose it at home, too.

12

Frankie spent the rest of the week focused on his training. He worked the pads with Steve again. He felt fast and sharp, light on his feet.

After that, they put on gloves and headguards to spar. They kept it light but mimicked the way the fight might go, rather than sticking rigidly to Queensbury rules.

Steve moved around, dodging, slapping Frankie's punches away, smothering his attacks and wrapping up his arms, trying to frustrate him.

When he got Frankie in a clinch, he trod on his toes, butted his head into Frankie's chin, elbowed him and threw in low blows. He swung Frankie around, tried to trip him, tried to turn it into a wrestling match, forcing Frankie to punch his way out of trouble, to get his shots in before Steve could get a proper grip on him. Frankie held his own. It gave him the confidence to know that he could handle Warren when the gloves were really off.

He put his problems with Chloe to one side. He had more important things to worry about. He had his reputation to keep. Warren was trying to take it away from him, and without it, what was he? Chloe wouldn't want him then, would she? When he had nothing. When he was a laughing stock. When he'd let this usurper take his crown.

Once Warren was dealt with, he'd get things back on track with Chloe. He'd be better, then. He'd be back to his old self. He'd take her away, go for a holiday in the sun. Majorca, maybe. Or perhaps one of the Greek islands. There, they could both relax and unwind. They could drink all night and fuck all day, put all this shit behind them.

But that was for later. All he could think about for now – all he could allow himself to think about – was the straightener.

So he trained.

13

On Friday night, he was working at the club.

In some ways, things were getting better. He was more physically confident after his week of training. In that respect, he felt like himself again. The old Frankie. The strong Frankie. The Frankie with iron running through him.

He was in the back office, having a break, when his phone rang.

"Hello, granddad."

"What the fuck do you want, Warren?" said Frankie.

"Just ringing to see how you was. I hear you've been training for our little get together. You wanna watch yourself, getting all exerted and that. You wanna watch your heart. Ain't good for someone your age."

"Don't you get tired of the sound of your own voice, Warren? Cos I do. This shit might've entertained the muppets up north, but it just bores me. You're a fucking joke."

"And you're old news. You ain't got what it takes to run your patch. You're past your sell by date. And Sunday's when you get taken off the shelf. When I take what's yours. Your clubs, your patch, your rep." Warren barked a laugh. "I might even take your bitch, give her a taste of what she's been missing. How did you manage to get a piece of that?

Must be a charity thing, like Help the Aged. She's got some nice titties on her, ain't she? She likes showing them off on her Instagram, don't she? All those low-cut tops. All those crop tops she wears down the gym. And those tight leggings, mmm-mmmmm.... I reckon she's advertising. Putting herself on the market for a proper man, someone who can keep up with her. I bet she's nice and tight, too. Don't worry, I'll stretch her out..."

"The only thing you'll be taking is a fucking trip to intensive care, you fucking –"

Warren laughed, a hyena's cackle. "Sounds like I hit a nerve there, Frankie boy. See you Sunday – give Chloe a kiss from me, tell her I'll see her soon."

Warren cut the call.

"*Cunt.*" Frankie's knuckles were white, forearm muscles bunched tight as he gripped the phone. It took all of his self-control not to throw it against the wall.

Back on the door, Frankie's thoughts spiralled wildly. What the fuck had Warren meant with that stuff about Chloe? About her getting what she'd been missing? He knew that Warren was just gobbing off, firing wild and scoring a lucky hit. Frankie knew that Warren didn't know – *couldn't fucking know* – about his problems with Chloe, but it didn't stop him from imagining the two of them together.

Talking about his failure to perform.

Laughing at his inability to satisfy her.

The pair of them fucking, Chloe screaming Warren's name as he made her come in all the ways that Frankie couldn't.

Someone tried to push past him into the club, snapping him out of it. Frankie put his arm across the door, blocking the way of a young man who was weaving unsteadily on his feet. "Not tonight, mate," he said.

"You what?" said the man. He looked to be in his early twenties. Not much more than a kid really. Slack mouth and wide, glittering eyes. He wobbled as he stood in front of Frankie.

"I said, not tonight, mate," said Frankie. "You've had enough."

"Don't be like that," said the young man. "Let us in."

Frankie blew out a hissing breath, feeling his patience slip its leash. He wasn't in the mood for this fuckwit tonight. "I said no, are you deaf or what?"

The young man's face twisted into a grimace of belligerence. "Don't fucking talk to me like I'm a bit of shit."

"On your way," said Frankie.

"Who the fuck do you think you are?" he said and jabbed Frankie in the chest with a pointing finger.

Frankie nutted him square in the face.

It came right up from his toes, through his legs and hips, all fifteen stone projected through the top of his head and straight into the little bastard's nose. The man dropped as if his legs had been cut out from under him, crashing onto his back. Blood splashed over his mouth and chin. Those closest to the front of the queue let out a collective gasp of surprise. Frankie followed him down, grabbing his throat with one hand and punching down with the other, over and over. Red spots danced in front of his eyes.

He was sick of this, sick of people taking the piss. This little scrote. Warren. Chloe, even. All of them, taking him for granted, thinking he was a soft touch, someone to be ignored and laughed at and pitied, someone who could be walked over and taken advantage of. No fucking way. Not now, not tonight, not ever.

The red spots jumped into the air. It took him a moment to realise that they were flecks of blood, spritzed through the air by his fist.

Strong hands grabbed him by the shoulders. A thick arm wrapped around his chest, pulling him away. The young man rolled himself into a ball, clutching his face. "That's enough," said Steve, walking backwards and taking Frankie with him. "Calm down – do you want to get nicked?"

"Little fucking prick, I'll fucking kill him –"

"Calm *down*." He pushed Frankie up against the wall and held him with a meaty hand, leaning all his weight into Frankie's chest, pinning him there. Steve turned to look at the young man, who was propped up on one elbow, spitting out blood. "You – get up and fuck off, before I let him go. Go on – get lost."

Frankie tried to squirm out of Steve's grasp as the young man staggered to his feet, but it was a token effort. The young man tottered off, and when he was safely out of range, turned round. "You fucking arsehole," he shouted, pointing at Frankie. "I'll fucking be back for you. You're dead."

"Whatever," said Steve. "Just keep walking."

"You're dead! You're a dead man! Wankers!"

"Yeah, yeah," said Steve.

The young man spat blood on the pavement and lurched away, shouting to himself. "Fuckers! You're dead! Dead!"

Steve watched him disappear around a corner, out of sight. He turned to Frankie. "What the fuck was all that about?"

"I told him he wasn't coming in, but he had to push it," said Frankie. "I've had enough of people taking the piss."

"Yeah, well, save it for Sunday. And you need to remember where you are." Steve pointed a thumb at the CCTV camera above the nightclub door. "You'd better sort the hard drive, in case he comes back with the law."

"I don't give a fuck."

"Frankie, as a mate, I'm telling you – go and sort it."

Frankie felt suddenly deflated, post-adrenalin fatigue kicking in. He took a deep breath. He nodded and headed into the club.

As he walked up the stairs to the office the reality of what he had just done hit home. What had he been thinking? He'd never lost it like that before, especially not in front of witnesses. He just hoped nobody had filmed it on their fucking phones. He swore to himself. *You stupid bastard.*

He deleted the CCTV footage and told Steve he was going home. He was no good on the door tonight, not when he was so fired up.

No good. No good on the door. No good in the bedroom. Seemed like he was no good to anyone.

Sunday. On Sunday he'd show them all.

14

On Saturday he did nothing. No training, no work at the club. He told Chloe that he didn't fancy going to the cinema. She surprised him by telling him she'd made other plans anyway and was meeting friends in town for some window shopping and a few drinks. Frankie nodded, told her to enjoy herself. The jealousy and suspicion he had felt last night after Warren's phone call was gone, replaced with a numb indifference that bordered on self-pity. If she did cheat on him, who could blame her?

Alone in the house, he spent the day thinking about the impending fight, playing and replaying every strategy and move over and over in his mind. By noon, his head was spinning, filled with a chaotic cycle of blood and violence, like a video nasty stuck on a loop.

He started to worry, struggling against thoughts of failure. What if Warren beat him? The possibility wormed its way into his head, where it curled around his brain and grew fat on his fears.

He's stronger than you.

He's bigger. Younger, fitter.

You're going to lose. You're going to lose, and everyone is going to hear about it.

He's going to show you up for what you are, a weak old man, past his prime, living off his old rep.

Everyone is going to see you for the fraud you are.

The fear of defeat twisted through his gut. The terror of losing it all sat on his chest and squeezed tight.

He just wanted it to be over.

15

Sunday morning came around too quickly.

Frankie stood in the living room, waiting for Steve to pick him up. He was dressed in his fighting gear. Loose fitting tracksuit bottoms, T shirt, and boots that were light enough to move in, but sturdy enough to do some damage. He had a hooded top on to keep himself warm and was wearing a groin protector to guard against kicks. He'd made himself a cup of coffee half an hour ago but had managed to drink only a few sips. His stomach was churning with anticipation.

Chloe was upstairs, still in bed. They were still talking, and they even had a laugh now and then, but their lives had gone in separate directions when it came to the bedroom. Frankie had continued to avoid going up to bed at the same time as Chloe. If Chloe went up first, Frankie would say he had some work to do on the laptop. And if it looked as if Chloe was going to stay up, Frankie would tell her he was tired, head for the bedroom, and feign sleep when she finally came up. She didn't push it or challenge him and that was perhaps what saddened Frankie most of all. It was as if she'd given up on him.

Steve's car pulled up to the kerb outside.

It was time.

16

The journey to the arches went by in a tense silence. Steve knew to stay quiet and leave Frankie alone in the last moments before the fight. For Frankie, it was too late now for thinking or for planning. It was all about getting his head into the zone. When the fight started, he had to be committed – no doubts, no fears, no second thoughts. When it started, he wouldn't have time to think about the club, his rep, Chloe, the consequences, or anything else but beating Warren, whatever it took.

They were early. Steve parked up under one of the railway arches, driving carefully over the broken concrete. Frankie got out and started to swing his arms, skipping lightly, warming up the blood, getting the adrenalin flowing.

Ten minutes later, at eight o'clock, a 4 x 4 trundled over and stopped ten yards away. Frankie felt his adrenalin spike, spurting down his legs like hot water, hollowing them out. He took a deep, calming breath through his nose.

The doors opened and Warren and his second, a short, thick-set man in jeans and a leather jacket, got out and walked towards them. Frankie kept his eyes on Warren. He looked bigger than Frankie remembered, heavier looking, more solid. He was dressed in loose workout pants and a tight singlet. His shaved head was glistening, and as he got closer, Frankie could see that he had smeared his forehead and eyebrows in Vaseline. He smirked at Frankie and gave him a wink.

Steve stepped forward to Warren's second. "You clear about the rules?"

"My man's happy that anything goes," said Warren's second.

"Same here," said Steve. "No fucking picking up bricks or anything. Any of that shit happens, it gets broken up. Okay?"

"Got it."

"Once it starts, it keeps going until one of them's knocked out, gives up, or can't defend himself," said Steve.

"Let's just fucking get on with it," said Frankie, pulling off his hoodie.

"You heard the man," said Warren.

"Show your hands," said Steve.

Frankie and Warren raised their hands, turning them palms out and then palms in.

"Okay," said Steve. "Let's get it done."

Frankie slotted in his mouth guard, clenching his teeth hard against the plastic. Steve leaned in close, grabbing the back of Frankie's neck and digging his fingers in, getting Frankie's blood up. "Rip his fucking head off."

Steve and the other man stepped back, giving Frankie and Warren space. Both men raised their guards and started circling.

Now the fight was on, Frankie felt calm and focused. There was no time for worry or fear now. No time for thoughts of failure or consequence, of win or lose. There was just the here and now. Muscle and will.

Frankie kept his eyes focused on Warren's chest, so he could see as much of his body as possible, watching for tell-tale signs like the twitch of his shoulders or the shift of his hips. He flicked out a jab to find his range. Warren let it come, slipping his head to the side.

Frankie jabbed again, stepping forward at the same time and letting his jab fall short so Warren didn't notice he had closed the distance. He jabbed once more and then immediately came over the top with a big right hand that caught Warren on the cheek, staggering him. Frankie felt a surge of elation to see the bastard's legs go and followed up with a left that clipped Warren's jaw.

Now, keep hitting him, don't give him a chance to recover, take his fucking head off, go!go!go!go!go!

Frankie stepped forward with another right hand, a hook, aiming for the hinge of Warren's jaw just beneath the ear. Warren ducked and covered, and Frankie's fist bounced off his shoulder. Warren drove a punch into Frankie's gut. Frankie saw it coming and managed to shift his hips back and brace his abs, but it still hit him like a sledgehammer. As Frankie stumbled back a step, Warren skipped forward, leg whipping out, his shin slamming into the outside of Frankie's thigh. Frankie went numb from kneecap to hip and his leg buckled. He staggered, tried to right himself, and stepped straight into an overhand right.

His head snapped violently to one side and the mouth guard spun away. Bright light flashed in front of his eyes and a murky darkness seeped in from the edges of his vision. He fell to his knees. He lunged forward desperately, wrapping both arms around Warren's legs, tucking his head in against his hip, holding on tight. Warren punched down on Frankie's back and shoulders, trying to free himself.

Frankie's senses returned. He drove an uppercut into Warren's groin. Warren bellowed with pain, and Frankie punched him again, missing this time, his fist glancing off Warren's hip. He grabbed hold of Warren's balls, fingers gripping tight through the thin material of Warren's workout pants. He squeezed as hard as he could. Warren hissed and moaned through gritted teeth, both hands instinctively grasping Frankie's wrist, trying to pull him off. Frankie held on. Warren punched him in the face, once, twice. Frankie fell back, losing his grip.

Warren kicked out, catching Frankie in the ribs and knocking him flat. He raised his foot and stamped down. Frankie took the blow on his forearms and caught the foot. He hugged it tight to his chest and rolled over hard. Warren wobbled and toppled over, landing next to Frankie on the rough concrete.

Frankie was still holding on. Warren kicked out with his free leg, catching Frankie's cheek with a glancing blow. Frankie pulled himself up Warren's body, scrambling on top of him, taking more punches. He felt something crack in his face and tasted blood. He got his hands to Warren's head and dug his thumb into his eye.

Warren thrashed his head and got his forearm under Frankie's chin, the bony edge crushing his windpipe as he levered Frankie up and off him. Frankie felt Warren shift beneath him, twisting his torso to bring his knee and shin against Frankie's hips. Warren twisted again, scissoring his legs, and Frankie was flipped onto his side, Warren rolling with him to come up on top. Frankie rolled onto his stomach, trying to scramble away, and immediately realised his mistake as Warren jumped on his back and snaked his right arm around Frankie's neck, clamping it tight in the crook of his elbow. Frankie managed to tuck his chin in and get his right hand in front of his throat. He struggled to his knees, flailing at Warren's arm with his free hand, fingernails gouging his skin. Warren wedged his left arm over the back of Frankie's neck, pushing down with his hand on the back of Frankie's head, locking the choke on.

It wasn't a perfect choke, but it was good enough. Frankie felt pressure build in his head. He tried to pull Warren's arm away with his right hand and windmilled wildly with his left, trying to find Warren's face, searching for an eye to gouge, an ear or lip to grip and tear. His lungs burned with lack of air, and his head became heavy and woolly as Warren's choke hold slowly cut the blood supply from his brain.

Through blurring vision, Frankie saw Steve, seemingly standing miles away, his face a rictus of rage and fear and savagery. Steve was screaming at him, fists clenched, but Frankie couldn't hear what he was saying over the sound of the blood rushing in his ears.

Darkness burst in thick blooms in front of his eyes. Frankie could feel unconsciousness reaching out for him. Part of him welcomed it, wanted to turn towards it with open arms and let the darkness wrap itself around him. He could slip away into oblivion and that would be the end of it.

The end of the fight.

The end of the feud.

The end of all the trouble.

The end of all the conflict and the stress and the worry. The end of having to appear strong when he felt weak. The end of keeping up a front when it was all he could do just to hold himself together. The end of the constant pressure to perform, to keep pushing, to keep his contracts, his clubs, his position, his rep.

Would it be so bad? To let go now and let go of it all? To give it all up. To be something else. To be someone else. To lay down the burden of being

Frankie Collins. Chloe would still love him. Chloe would still want him.

Wouldn't she?

Just let it go. It's not worth the fight. It's not worth the pain.

Then, in the distance, he heard a hundred dogs barking. The sound grew closer, clearer, and he realised it was Warren, laughing in his ear.

"It's over, granddad."

Something exploded deep inside him. Something red and violent and full of furious rage. It surged up, battering his doubts aside, crushing his weakness underfoot.

He wouldn't let it go.

He wouldn't give it up.

He was Frankie fucking Collins.

With a strength he didn't think he had, he reached back and grabbed the back of Warren's neck with his left hand. He flexed his body forward and pulled hard, heaving Warren over his shoulder. Warren's grip came loose and he landed on his back by Frankie's knees. Frankie dragged air into his lungs, feeling suddenly light-headed as the blood rushed back to his brain. Warren was already scrambling for a better position when Frankie drove a fist into his nose. Warren's eyes rolled back in his head and Frankie punched again, the same place, feeling Warren's nose collapse under his knuckles. He punched once more, crushing the nose flat.

Frankie straddled him, kneeling on his shoulders and punched him again and again and again, pounding down with both hands into Warren's face and jaw. His fists grew slippery. Pain shot through his hands, but he didn't care. Warren twitched and shuddered under every blow, his face breaking into a formless, bloody mess. Frankie felt detached, remote and distant from it all, as if he was watching the action from somewhere far back inside his own skull.

"That's enough, that's enough, it's over, it's over!" It was Steve, pulling him away. Frankie let him, falling backwards into his arms, his body flooded with relief.

Steve helped him to his feet. Frankie looked over at Warren, sprawled on his back, broken and ruined. Warren's second was bent over him, talking to him, holding his head, trying to get a response. Warren twitched, his body hinging suddenly from the waist. He spasmed with a violent shudder and fell back to the ground and was still.

"That's it," Steve shouted at Warren's second. "It's done. You tell that cunt when he wakes up. It's done. It's over."

Steve led Frankie away, back to his car. He bundled Frankie into the passenger seat and jogged back round to the driver's side. As he started the engine, he glanced over at Frankie with a grin. "You fucking did him," he said, his voice soaring with savage glee, "you fucking did him good and proper." He laughed and threw the car into gear.

As they drove away, Frankie twisted in his seat to look back at Warren. His second was talking frantically on his phone and Warren was still on his back. He didn't seem to be moving.

Frankie wondered if he'd done permanent damage.

He wondered if he'd killed him.

He realised that he didn't care.

He'd won, that was all that mattered.

He'd *won*.

17

They went straight back to Steve's house. Frankie stripped off and Steve bundled his clothes –

tracksuit bottoms, boots, underwear, the lot – into a black bin bag. He went out to dump them while Frankie took a shower, washing off the blood and sweat and grime, letting the hot water soothe his aching and battered body. He dried himself off gently and assessed the damage.

At least two of the knuckles on his right hand were broken. His nose and cheekbones were swollen and painful to the touch, but he didn't think anything was broken. It hurt to swallow and his throat felt swollen, his neck pinched and stiff. His face was a patchwork of bruises and cuts. The adrenalin had worn off now, and he could feel every injury. He patched himself up as best as he could with plasters, dressing strips and tape from Steve's bathroom cabinet.

He would heal.

Steve came back and found Frankie some spare clothes. The T shirt swamped him and the tracksuit bottoms were baggy and too long, but they were good enough to get him home. Steve fetched some beers from the kitchen and they sat in the living room, Steve chattering excitedly about the fight, like it was a film he'd watched. Steve gave him a look, his face full of concern and said, "I fucking thought he had you at one point, I really fucking did." Then he burst out laughing.

Frankie laughed too. His throat hurt, but he couldn't stop.

He sat back on the sofa and let the beers go to work on him. He felt relaxed. He felt happy.

He felt like his old self.

18

Steve dropped Frankie off at home a little after eleven o'clock.

Chloe was in the living room. She was still in her pyjamas, her lazy Sunday morning attire. When she saw Frankie's face, she said, "Oh my God, what happened to you?" He thought she was going to cry.

"It's nothing," he said. "Nothing to worry about. Not anymore."

He sat down on the sofa next to her. She reached out and held his face gently, turning his head one way, then the other, inspecting his wounds. Her touch felt good.

"It's okay," he said, and kissed her, long and deep, feeling the old passion come back, untainted by worry or fear. They stayed like that for a long time, just kissing, holding each other close. The pain faded away. His chest swelled with need, like a sudden tide. He got down on the floor and pulled her to the edge of the sofa, kneeling between her legs. She lifted her hips, pushing her pyjamas down to her knees, her eyes on him all the time, hungry and bright. He pulled her pyjamas down to her ankles and yanked down his own trousers. She guided him to her and he slid inside. He gave a long groan that came from somewhere deep inside.

They fucked urgently, hungrily, pulling each other tight and close and deep. All of Frankie's worries and doubts were gone. He felt as strong and sure of himself as he ever had. The iron was back. He was back.

He came with a shout of joy and triumph.

They stayed there on the sofa in a loose tangle of limbs for a long time. Frankie didn't want to be anywhere else.

He was *back*.

Thursday night was quiet. Frankie stood out on the main door with Steve, listening to him chatter on about the new car he was thinking about buying. Frankie nodded and made the usual noises you made to show that you were listening to someone, even if you weren't really paying attention.

In the two weeks since the straightener, he hadn't heard anything more from Warren. As far as Frankie could work out, he'd fucked off to some other area of the city, maybe even left entirely. Frankie didn't know and didn't care. News of the straightener had spread amongst those who had an interest in that sort of thing. Frankie's rep had been cemented. Warren's had crumbled to dust. There was no more trouble.

In those two weeks, Frankie had taken some time to think about everything that had happened, about how things could have been. In Frankie's world, your rep only went as far as your last fight. There was always someone else around the corner. There would always be another Warren. It was only a matter of time before he came up against somebody who would beat him.

And then what? Shuffle off, out of the game, a has-been? A used-to-be-a-somebody?

No thanks.

Not him.

Not Frankie Collins.

He'd leave the game on his own terms. He'd go out with his rep intact.

So tonight was his last night on the door.

He'd still run the firm. But the front end stuff, the confrontations and the fights, he'd leave that to younger men.

He'd spend his nights at home. Things were good with Chloe now. Everything was back to normal in the bedroom. Things between them were better than they'd ever been.

"I'm going to grab a brew," said Steve. "You want one?"

"I'll have a coffee, ta." He looked at his watch. "Make it a good one – it's the last one you'll make me on this door."

Steve shook his head and disappeared inside.

Frankie rolled his shoulders inside his jacket, stretching his back. Part of him would miss it. He thought about the times he'd had on the door, the lads he'd known. The scrapes he'd got into. The fear, the laughs, the camaraderie.

He caught movement in the corner of his eye, pulling him from his memories. Someone walking up fast, coming from just behind his shoulder. He turned, ready to tell whoever it was that the club was closing in the next half hour, that they weren't letting anyone else in, when something punched him hard in the chest. His whole body went numb. His ears registered a flat clap.

As he stumbled backwards, he saw the gun. His hand went up in a feeble attempt to knock it away. There was another flat clap and something slammed into his stomach.

He fell onto the pavement and he saw the face behind the gun, partially hidden under a hooded top. A young face, red and angry. Eyes wide and wild, shining bright with a mixture of terror and rage. A misshapen nose, recently broken. A familiar face, a face Frankie knew from somewhere.

"I fucking told you," the face was saying. The face was shouting but to Frankie the sound was muted, as if his ears were packed with cotton wool. "I fucking told you I'd be back. Not so fucking big now, are you?"

The gun clapped once more.

Frankie didn't feel the impact. He didn't feel any pain. He didn't feel anything.

Not like this, he thought.

It can't end like this.

But deep inside, he knew that he would die here. He could feel himself sinking.

Falling.

Fading.

He tried to conjure up a pleasant memory, a good feeling, a warm thought. He tried to picture Chloe's face, tried to remember how it felt to hold her. But the images slipped past his mind's eye too fast, too fast for him to focus on. He tried to slow them down, to grab one and hold it tight.

He wanted something to take with him into the darkness.

The End

Printed in Great Britain
by Amazon

40721547R00056

VISA
Wives

Radhika M.B.

VISA
Wives

Emigration Experiences of
Indian Women in the US

EBURY
PRESS

EBURY PRESS

USA | Canada | UK | Ireland | Australia
New Zealand | India | South Africa | China

Ebury Press is part of the Penguin Random House group of companies
whose addresses can be found at global.penguinrandomhouse.com

Published by Penguin Random House India Pvt. Ltd
No: 04-010 to 04-012, 4th Floor, Capital Tower -1,
M G Road, Gurugram -122002, Haryana, India

First published in Ebury Press by Penguin Random House India 2016

ISBN 9788184007862

Typeset in Goudy Old Style by Manipal Digital Systems, Manipal

Printed at Manipal Technologies Limited, India

www.penguinbooksindia.com

This is a legitimate digitally printed version of the book and therefore might not

To

My Ammumma

Contents

Introduction

'Oh my God!' I screamed.

My husband had just told me he had to move to the US. In four days. Impending travel had left us hanging in the air for the past few months. My husband works in the IT industry, and his H1 visa had been approved six months ago. Delay in his actual travel had put us in a bind for all these months.

'What are we going to do?' I exclaimed as I hugged him tight, reality suddenly hitting home. Our beautiful Chennai apartment would soon become history. And so would the proximity of the extended family scattered in different suburbs of the forever-summer metro city. Mixed emotions. Would this nomadic life—of job postings and shifting to new cities every few years—never end?

'Four days!'

So many things to do . . . How would I manage after he left? Wind up a whole home, deal with phone connections, gas connection, pack all the books and clothes, dispose of or pack away and store the furniture—all for a project that would probably not last long.

The moment my husband got his visa, I knew I was soon to be a dependent 'visa wife'. True, I was on a low-health phase then which got in the way of my work, but this moment ruined any hope of reviving my career. Why did I agree to the move?

Could I actually back off? Or was it pre-voyage jitters? Maybe this is just a phase.

'It's only for nine months, this project,' he explained.

Maybe I should stay put. But before I could figure out my own thoughts on the matter, he had informed our landlord that we would move out.

Two days later, he was in his father's former office in Bengaluru, to purchase a suitcase from their Central R&D organization's 'dry canteen'.

The retiree father's moment of pride had arrived, after years of surviving the frustration of watching colleagues' kids head off to the US for studies, reach academic heights, some of them even turning scientists at their alma mater, while his own kids lagged behind in India.

'He is heading to the US,' his dad repeated to friend after friend as my husband went red with embarrassment.

'But I could not take away that moment from him. I had no right to do that. He was so proud to show me off!' he explained to me later.

Two years later, when we visited India from the US, he talked of my dad showing him off too, as 'the son-in-law who lives in the US'.

What makes entire families still look at America as *the* place to be?

For someone like me, who would rather simply visit the US than live there, the run-up to D-day was a confusing phase. It was hard to accept the sudden change, but somewhere deep inside me, a part of me looked forward to the trip, while yet another part worried about the future and what to expect from it. A million thoughts ran through my head all the time, warring against each other, till I didn't know what to think any more.

Forty days later, I took a snapshot of my family and relatives at the Chennai airport, their smiles trying hard to mask pangs of grief.

And turned into a visa wife overnight, over-flight.

Little did I know, much like the thousands of women who immigrate to the US, what the move to America really meant.

Year after year, numerous flights—via the Middle East, Germany and England in the western direction, and via Singapore, Hong Kong, sometimes Tokyo, in the eastern direction—fly across the world, carrying Indian engineers and allied professionals, all heading to the US as skilled workers. Their spouses, women like me, follow suit. I say that women follow their husbands because the number of men following their wives is negligible. Despite our qualifications that make us eligible to work, we become dependent visa wives, by rule.

Whatever the backstory, the transition to a new country usually spells unlimited trauma. This book chronicles that journey, into this trauma that is not discussed much, and unravels realms of pain and hope, to explore invisible feelings.

~

Immigrant history related to the Indian diaspora has been discussed over and over again. Endless debates rage on the question regarding why Indians should head overseas at all rather than serve their own country. In the din of it all, and in an era of 'reverse brain drain', it is a fact that the American dream continues to draw its believers.

As early as 1886, Anandibai Gopalrao Joshi received her MD and became India's first woman physician, after graduating from Women's Medical College of Pennsylvania. Her journey to make it to the US was an uphill climb. She was motivated by the loss of a baby to disease, and she had the support of her husband. Sadly, she did not live long enough to see her medical degree put to use.[1]

Did any Indian women arrive on US shores before she did? Or soon after? My research was not so fruitful. But considering that India's Punjabi agricultural workers moved to the US's western region and to Canada in large numbers by the mid-nineteenth century, one might wonder if some women made it with them. Going by the hostility faced by such workers who were engaged in lumber mills and in building railroads in the West, it's highly improbable. The history of early mass Indian immigration to the US is full of racial oppression and exclusion. Indians faced bloody riots too. It was young men of famine-hit Punjabi homes who escaped to the US so that they could earn a better livelihood.[2]

Before this, a few hundred traders had landed on the east coast at Boston. The earliest recorded Indian immigrant landed on America's shores in the year 1790. They are believed to have settled down to trade in Indian goods and spices and married local American women of African origin and integrated into their communities. The question of Indian women making it to this continent then is again nil.

It was not until much later that any presence of Indian women was noted on the west coast. There is mention of Indian women who came as wives as early as 1910. Anti-Asian sentiment was so strong that when the fourth Indian woman arrived in the US, newspaper headlines read, 'Hindu Women Next Swarm to California'.[3]

During the years of exclusionary laws for Asians, family reunions were not allowed, causing Indian men to marry Mexican women in California. Such families have been documented enough. Only by the 1940s were families of immigrant Indian men allowed into the US. By that account, Indian women really mass-migrated to join their husbands then on, as well as during the 1965 reforms.

The trend continues to this day—of women joining their husbands—despite the rapid strides that Indian women have made in varied disciplines. Some women who arrive today do so as students. Some arrive as skilled workers with H1B visas themselves. Largely though, the arrival of women is for family reunions, and to fulfil the familial ambitions of the men working in the US.

It is this mass population from India that the likes of Sarika, Bindhu and I joined. What happens to women who arrive on dependent visas? Sarika Prasad and Bindhu Rahul were qualified engineers who had been working in their respective cities. I had worked for about ten years before moving. A few others I know moved right after marriage. And none of us knew what it was like to survive the first two years and more, with no jobs in hand, with the culture differences of the new place and the utter lack of family support.

~

Mine was a generation that grew up in a neighbourhood of parents (most of them scientists and officers) either grooming their kids for 'studies in the US' or getting daughters married off to American grooms who were considered 'prize catches'. Those who could not afford either looked on in envy.

Going to the 'States' was more fashionable than ever before in the 1990s.

In the throes of the IT boom, Bengaluru in the 1990s teemed with youth armed with degrees in computers and engineering. They would soon fly off—to Singapore, to the UK, to the US.

'America is in an Andhra guy's genes,' proclaims Sairam, speaking of the obsession his peers and family nurtured. Sairam detested it initially—how his mother's American uncle continued to enjoy fame in the family for decades—but American Parker pens and HB pencils marked 'Made in America' used to be his prized possessions during childhood. He remembers when, as a teenager, an aerogram from America had arrived at a neighbour's home with some chewing gum stuck to it. He had got half of it. 'They treated it like Tirupati *prasadam,*' he laughs. Soon, he found himself swept up in the wave of IT professionals immigrating to the US. Their common underlying quest: 'What the hell was this America about?'

His wife did not dream of America at all. 'I hated those America alliances,' says Sarika, about her 'groom-hunt'. Like Sairam, she was a qualified engineer, but raised to be a 'good girl' ready for the marriage market. The last thing she wanted was to leave her parents and move to a foreign country.

She ended up being a dependent visa wife too.

Lakshmana Rallapalli says he was not really seeking a ticket to Stamford, Connecticut, when his Bengaluru firm sent him there in the mid-1990s. He had made trips to Singapore through work before the US opportunity landed on his lap. 'It was a coincidence. I thought I'd work for a couple of years and return. Prospects in software were not great that year in Bengaluru. And demand for software professionals in the US was so high they would train people in India and send to the US. Before 1995, the IT industry did not open up much. Many universities had not started computer science courses till the mid-1980s.'

It was a crumbling Bengaluru of the late 1990s and the first decade of the 2000s that prompted some to want to escape the city. It is probably this thought of escape from other Indian cities too—Hyderabad, Gurgaon, Chennai, Mumbai and Kolkata—that drives many to seek a life abroad.

'Bengaluru's traffic and pollution got on my nerves. It was too much to bear,' remarked Bindhu, catching a break from work in Bay Area, California. Bindhu is my classmate from school with whom I reconnected while writing this book. An ace student, she obtained her bachelor's in engineering from a regional engineering college.

In 2002, Bindhu returned to Bengaluru, her home town, after a fresh-out-of-college stint at Panjim in Goa. She soon tired of it all, though. The city's rhythm is addictive, its beehive buzz alluring, and we fall for it despite our complaints about pollution, traffic snarls, crowds and getting caught up in the rat race. But for a chunk of each city's denizens, escape proves a romantic alternative. An introvert by nature, Bindhu preferred the beauty and quiet of landscapes elsewhere to the bustle of Bengaluru.

Bindhu's friends who shifted to the US after studies triggered in her the desire to move to America herself. When the groom hunt began, she accepted the process of her parents finding the right match for her. She wanted someone like her.

On Bindhu's wish list was that, like her, the groom be from the IT industry so he would 'understand the demands of my profile, that it meant working late into the night, sometimes during weekends. My profile needed occasional travel. I wanted him to accommodate those little changes. Bengaluru and the US were fine. We ran out of options through traditional marriage bureaus, so I registered on a matrimonial website.'

Bindhu, an otherwise reticent girl, soon found herself chatting with a prospective groom in the US. He had lived there for six years. For three months, they chatted online and on the phone. Her father realized that his priceless girl had found her man. Bindhu met her future husband for the first time at their engagement. Four months later, she got married at Idukki, Kerala—and flew to Boston immediately after.

Most Indians moving to the US to study and work are men. Qualified women moving to the US or any other western country to study or work are much fewer in comparison, though parents are slowly warming up to the idea. A son relocating to join a dollar-earning 'pardesi bahu' (daughter-in-law living abroad) happens too, but such instances are few and far between.

It's why Anamika Mohanty from Balasore, Orissa, was surprised when she landed her Los Angeles on-site opportunity, and her husband encouraged her to travel on the H1B visa. 'His logic was that since he could not make it to the US on his own, I should take the opportunity. I battled my own doubts. We were married for two and a half years and were employed in different Bengaluru firms. He was a Bengali settled in Orissa. Ours was a love marriage. I did not want to leave him behind. But we had bought a house—with a sixty-lakh-rupee mortgage, and I had borrowed money from my parents too which I had to return. Financially, it made sense to take the H1B opportunity.'

Anamika's own H1B journey was not easy. She was jittery about having to live alone. However, it is not like she was the first woman who was making it alone. She did hear of other girls on H1B who were heading to the US.

Revathi Arun Kumar from Atlanta, Georgia, talks of how her sister, who was in the US on an H1B visa many years ago, attracted a tall list of grooms. 'These men were only motivated to marry her because it would be the easiest way for them to get to the US,' she says. 'Luckily for her, we found her a wonderful husband who had studied in the US and was also working there.'

~

A quick check on the current decade's migration trends: Mid-2013 numbers by the Migration Policy Institute based in Washington DC, note that as many as 20,61,000 migrants in the US were from India. The institute based its data on the findings of the UN Population Division in the article titled 'Indian Immigrants in the United States'. According to the report, 'There are 14.2 million Indian migrants worldwide; after the United Arab Emirates (28,52,000), the United States (20,61,000) is the second-most common destination. Other popular destinations include Saudi Arabia (17,62,000), Pakistan (13,96,000), Nepal (8,10,000), and the United Kingdom (7,56,000).'[4] The overall growth rate of the Indian population in the US was 105.87 per cent between 1990 and 2000, according to the US Census of 2000.[5] The Indian population in the country grew by 130 per cent, ten times its national average, as per Wikipedia.[6] Such data clearly points to the phenomenal IT-workforce migrant population's relocation to the US in the last two and a half decades. This is mainly because India is the largest recipient of H1B visas, sought by American firms for Indian IT majors. So India's IT industry is today the largest contributor to the India-to-US migration. The United States is the second most-sought-after country, after the UAE, for Indians to migrate to.

H1B is a non-immigrant visa. The H1B legislation as such came about in 1990, in the US, when it was passed under the Immigration and Nationality Act, section 101 (a) (15), and allowed US-based employers to temporarily employ foreign workers in specialty occupations.

A chunk of H1B visas are also given to the pharmaceutical industry and professionals like nurses, graphic designers and artists, biologists, chemists, economists, physicians and surgeons. But the IT industry benefits the most from H1B visa allotment. Some get allotted to those joining a few universities in America too. The yearly cap of H1B visas is, as we know, 65,000, with an additional 20,000 approved for high-skilled workers with advanced degrees. In the last few years, applications have far exceeded the quota, and so a lottery system is now used to grant visas.

A CNN report noted that the number of H1B applications hit a record high in 2015, with 2,33,000 applications filed by 'foreigners'. India, on an average, bags two thirds of the total H1B visas allotted, so one can imagine the numbers that would have formed a portion of this figure.[7]

All the same, each year, H1B arrivals in the US check into hotels for a couple of weeks, look for apartments in the vicinity of their workplaces, apply for their social security number (SSN), and settle in before they begin making efforts to bring their families over. If they are married, their spouses either fly in with them or follow them soon enough. Among other H category visas are H2A, H2B and H3 visas. H2A Visas are meant for temporary agricultural workers. H2B is meant for temporary or seasonal non-agricultural workers. The H3 visa is issued for trainees or special education exchange visitors.

~

An H4 visa, otherwise known as a 'family reunion' visa, allows the spouse and children to join the relative working in the US, but does not permit them to apply for a job. A dependent-visa spouse is not eligible for an SSN. So much so that if the spouse wants to get a driver's licence in some states, she or he must go to the Social Security Office and get a denial letter for the SSN to apply for a licence at the Department of Motor Vehicles (DMV).

H4 visas are not the only dependent visas, although they are the most popular. Among those eligible for work permits is the J2 visa for families of J1 visa holders—those who get placements in the US through exchange programmes. An L2 visa is given to families of L1 visa holders—managers and executives of companies outside of the US who have obtained a transfer to the US branch of the company. The F2 visa is given to spouses of F1 visa holders—otherwise simply known as the student visa. These are all dependent visas. Rarely do women arrive on the K visa—a fiancée visa. While J2 and L2 allow spouses to work through EAD, or the Employment Authorization Document, F2 does not.

~

This book focuses largely on the issues of new H4 arrivals, but I have also touched upon the issues of dependent F2 visa holders and of EAD-eligible visa wives who become dependent by circumstance. Some women move to the US on B1/B2 visa and later become H4 visa holders. Some arrive on the J2 visa, and may end up homebound because of motherhood, health adjustment, absence of close family for co-parenting, etc. Still others arrive on F1 visas and get married to an H1 spouse before their Optional Practical Training period or OPT period (when they are allowed to work in the US after the completion of their courses) ends, hence obtaining an H4 visa.

Effective 26 May 2015, the US Department of Homeland Security extended the eligibility for employment authorization to certain H4 dependent spouses of H1B non-immigrants seeking employment-based lawful permanent residence. This is now popular as the H4 EAD rule. It means that H4 spouses (mostly women), whose H1B spouses are on their way to being granted the Green Card and have obtained the Form I-140 that is part of the Green Card process, are allowed to apply for jobs by applying for EAD. Conventionally, the EAD is provided to dependent spouses at a much later stage in the Green Card process.

What is Form I-140? This document is an immigrant petition for foreign workers in the US, used to petition the U.S. Citizenship and Immigration Services (USCIS) to classify workers as eligible for an immigrant visa based on employment. It is usually filed by employers on behalf of their employees.[8]

The reform by the Obama administration effectively aimed at helping H4 women become eligible to work grabbed headlines for spirited lobbying by several people for immigration reforms. It allows thousands of high-skilled women, who joined their husbands, often leaving their well-paying jobs behind, to work. An H4 EAD holder can belong to any field, not just the coveted STEM (science, technology, engineering and mathematics) fields. A person who gets an H4 EAD need not necessarily work for it to hold good. She or he can also work with multiple employers. As long as the spouse is eligible to stay in the US on his/her H1 visa, the H4 EAD is valid.

The reform is new, surrounded by rules and confusions, as in any other law. Its biggest concern is that women need to wait a few years till the I-140 stage in their spouse's Green Card or Lawful Permanent Resident process actually comes through. And it is the first few years that prove crucial for their mental health and the overall outlook of their life in America, influencing their willingness to stay or leave. Their first few years could be productive years after all.

How many companies would actually file a petition for their H1B employee's Green Card? In any case, the woman's position is determined indirectly by her husband's employer in addition to the USCIS. Companies control who they find 'eligible' for the lawful permanent residence status, and who they do not. The reform is significant, but a small step in the long journey towards an equal opportunity world for the women who join their working husbands in the States.

What is the socio-economic impact of such a reform, especially on the institution of marriage? Traditionally, H1B holders, with an eye on a double-income household, look for brides in the IT industry or the field of medicine. If they want their women to remain housebound, they opt for women from other fields or those who are less educated.

What happens in the world of women who fly on dependent visas? When an American assignment opportunity knocks at the door, women often convince themselves using these arguments:

'How bad can it get?'

'I can use it for a break from work.'

'I need to spend time with my kids. And I'll apply for an H1B myself soon.'

'I'll study.'

Chances are that the family and extended family may suggest this too. In some cases, they could prevent the woman from joining her husband in the hope that the son does not settle down in the US.

An alternative argument is: 'It's so far away. Can you really cope?'

~

Each woman who boards that US-bound flight has a story to tell, endless tears she has dealt with, and a battle at hand—adjusting to a new lifestyle. Sometimes, it's also a mind bursting with ideas relevant to the workplace she left behind—something she needs to silence in the emptiness of her new home and jobless life. And face an inner war of identity.

While the statement that 'life in the US is not a bed of roses' sounds like a cliché, it is true. Not all that exists in the vast country is about the 'good life'. For a start, you struggle with a new system of life. You wonder day after day if moving across continents was the right thing. During your phone calls home, you want to hide from your worrying family the facts of your struggle. So you tone down the hitches, and say all is good. You try hard to communicate excitement about the new place instead of your overarching fear of being sent back home by bullying bosses. After all, for your family back home, you just became a bona fide rockstar they can gloat about.

Families desperate to find NRI matches seldom understand the challenges their daughters will face during their drastic move into vastly different time-zones.

When free-spirited Radha Kumar was asked by her father if she would marry a cousin they had in mind, she refused. Her family was 'not so conservative, but not so liberal', in her words. Parental rules for college included no smoking, no alcohol, no drugs, besides the regular 'good girl' rules. After a futile groom hunt, she agreed to marry her cousin. Radha had barely finished her graduation when the opportunity to experience work life flew out the window with the alliance. The cousin she married worked in Seattle, Washington.

'I got married and came to the US with my husband the following month. It was not a "dream come true" match, because I did not have any US fantasies. My friends drooled over it, though. I thought going to the US was like travelling to Delhi or Mumbai. Little did I know what it actually meant!'

Her story repeats itself in conversation after conversation about alliances in the US. If you land a US groom, you are expected to view it as a 'fairy-tale' match. So any trouble you have after you set foot in the new continent gets brushed aside as an 'adjustment' issue. The best of your friends and cousins burn with envy even though you might be drowning in helpless tears.

The woman, an individual in her own right, with a mind of her own, faces the bitter truth—that the law of the land will not allow her to work (and earn a living for herself) on the visa she is travelling on. She gets reduced to the role of a caregiver, financially dependent on her man, even as she pines for her country, its relative freedoms, her family, her ex-colleagues and everything else with an ever-pervading sense of hopelessness.

1

Outlining Dreams

Late 2011.

'How can you travel to New York all alone?' I poked at my husband.

'Why? Did you want us to go together?' He was surprised. It was the first time I had openly admitted to wanting to see New York City. I had never dreamt of living in the US. Probably, the urge to explore new places and countries remained in me and was being rekindled at the opportunity at hand.

'I won't see much of it. Will wait till you come,' he promised.

Wow! New York! I was actually going to see that city!

Rewind to about a decade back. New York was the backdrop of Karan Johar's film *Kal Ho Na Ho*. Manhattan stood out in all its magnificence in the story of love and letting go. Not in my wildest dreams had I seen myself walking the city's streets then. I wanted to make it big at work. It was the pressure-cooker phase of my twenties—when 'cooked me with their concern' over my tying the knot, and stress levels ran high.

A year after I watched *Kal Ho Na Ho*, an uncle came up with an 'NRI proposal' at a cousin's wedding. 'Who is this guy?' I wondered then. 'Some random NRI with an America nameplate hanging around his neck?' Soon, I walked up to the uncle and politely requested him to call off the groom hunt. 'Do you have someone in mind?' he asked earnestly during a follow-up phone chat. 'No. But what if I say "yes" to this match and end up finding my man in the run-up to the wedding?' Blasphemy.

Six years on, long after I had outlived my infamy in family circles, I sought the same relative out at another wedding. This time, it was to introduce the man I had found. It was a happy conversation, warm and perfectly timed. Call it coincidence, but my husband was ready with his H1B visa to go to the US.

A few days after that wedding, I was due for the most anxiety-ridden interview of my life—my own H4 visa interview at the US consulate. Life in the US had come chasing me after all. How much I had scoffed at property-hunting, cash-rich NRIs and their 'do-gooder' pomposity! I was on my way to being labelled an NRI myself.

Usually, bride-hunting H1B grooms brandish their visas to land the 'homely', 'cultured', 'not forward-thinking but willing to adjust to America' girls. The America alliance is loved, loathed and envied. Imagine the price tag—parents who made those umpteen sacrifices for sons can now reap the benefits in the form of dowry and a trophy bride. They only need to show the 'US groom' business card to the bride and her family.

Some ethically evolved H1B, L1 or J1 holders refuse dowry. No compromises for Bollywood-style, grand weddings, though. The process is simple: a three-week trip to India, sometimes one week, pick your earthling to serve you and give birth to your children, and get her to fly back with you in celestial vehicles—little or no relevant questions asked.

We are familiar with advertisements for H1B visa holders seeking brides. 'Educated boy employed in an IT firm, looking for a fair and cultured girl from a good family'. The demand is for a 'homely girl', 'fair girl', 'good-looking girl', 'girl with good values', 'caring girl', one that is from an 'educated family' and 'respects elders'.

~

'Every other ad would talk of a "fair girl". I have been dusky all my life. These ads were really like shopping orders— appropriate height, probably weight too, the word "caring" thrown in an ample number of times . . . They looked for a "Telugu" girl—the language turned into an adjective. I speak Telugu at home, but I speak a lot of English and Kannada too. Where would that place me?' says Madhuri Sharma, who went through the groom-hunting phase fifteen years ago. She found her partner through a matrimonial site, moved to London and then shifted with him to the US. 'Not much has changed over the decade,' she says. 'Choices in matrimonial ads and as such groom hunts remain the same.'

For grooms, the questions range from 'What is your package?' and 'Do you have a house and car?' to 'What are your savings?' and 'Any other property?' These become catchphrases for parents looking for the 'suitable boy'.

A friend once fumed at such ads on websites. 'What is it with girls?' he said. 'Every girl wants me to "have a sense of humour" in her ad, as if my job in life is only to make her laugh.'

He did not spare the men, either. 'They say "habits *illa*" (Kannada for 'no') in their ads, as if none of us have any habits.' The reference is chiefly to smoking, drinking, or addiction to drugs, sometimes with an added emphasis on the boy having only 'clean habits'. Whether they brush their teeth on time or not, or throw their wet towels and underwear carelessly around the house, or know to make their cup of tea, or have slept with many women, is a mystery in such ads.

Do matrimonial ads give any signs of possible abuse by men or if they have an appetite for violence? Never. How can they, when the alphabets U, S and A beat any other punchlines to sell the suitable boy?

Seldom do proud mothers think that their darling America-resident sons may not be sought-after all the time by Indian girls and their parents.

Madhuri knew that if she married a guy working in the US, she would end up as an H4 wife of an H1B visa holder. She had a choice—between an H1B holder who was a dream alliance, and another great match who was a UK resident. Her choice was easy—the UK guy. She is happy with that decision. 'European countries make good use of the talent available. Working in London was the best option,' she says.

Revathi remembers the US groom frenzy among her classmates in college. 'The parents of a few of our classmates (girls) strongly believed that doing MCA or post-graduation in general was one of the things that a US groom would look for. Career prospects were not really as much the motivating factor behind choosing these advanced courses as the US groom prospect was. Once married, they got packed off to the US with their respective spouses.' Unlike many other women, Revathi chose her own partner, a Bengaluru-based man, and the US was not on the cards for a long time.

When Sarika's parents lined up grooms for her, they went for boys from the same caste. A key factor in the accept–reject game was dowry. Sarika rejected some 'good' alliances during the 'let the boy and girl talk' ten-minute sessions. After each such rejection, she got busy defending it to relatives who could not understand how she 'rejected such a good match'. No US guys of course.

'Some guys demanded high dowry. One such "educated" guy from the US wanted my dad to buy an apartment for him in Madhapur, Hyderabad. The apartment cost would be Rs 30 lakh. My dad's dowry budget was Rs 5 lakh. My dad also reasoned—what was the point in giving that guy an apartment if I was not around in India to live in it? The whole process of grooms coming home to see me was new for a start. It was not easy. We went through fifteen such alliances.'

A US-based groom alliance often comes with strings attached, like the apartment that boy wanted from her so that she would leave her family behind, cook and clean for him, take care of their kids, but not live in it.

Chandrashekar, a boy of marriageable age with a work visa, opted for a 'homely' bride from his village and was happy for a while. When finances took a hit, he felt that he had made a mistake. She cooked, cleaned and took care of him. But what about that extra income?

'I wish I had married that engineer girl, even if she did not bring dowry. She would have worked,' is a common regret among such men. For long, the debate has raged on in feminist circles about the need for women to get paid for household work, which they sweat at every day. People like Chandrashekar feel envious of the relatively better lifestyle of their peers, forgetting the enormous amount of work women put in to keep their households running.

Sarika's parents resisted US-resident alliances for a long time. When the groom list shortened considerably, they relaxed their criteria to include US grooms. Sarika was an engineer who worked at a firm owned by her father's acquaintance. Dowry hikes for US grooms made them edgy, but they were willing to stretch. A few lakhs more and she would be 'settled in America', would she not?

When Richa Jain's relatives suggested an alliance for her, the thought of a US-based groom did not cross her mind. But her would-be partner was on a US stint. The two agreed to the match, but it was understood that he would have to return to the US after a few months. Richa was employed in Bengaluru, and enjoyed her job. The two liked each other, and got married.

'It was not certain that he would return to the US, although they hinted at the possibility. So we kept our options open. We booked an apartment in Bengaluru (to own). I quit my job only once we had the tickets in our hands.'

The man she married was a distant relative. Compatibility was not an issue, in spite of the match being an arranged one, brought over by relatives. The difficulty was in having to give up her job before she moved to San Francisco. What made her decide to fly, leaving it all behind? Richa put in her papers hoping that they would return to India in six months. She planned to rejoin her company once she returned. The US was simply too far from India. 'It is easier to travel from Dubai, Malaysia or Singapore to India.'

Richa lived in Cupertino, California, for about two and a half years before she returned to India, having become homesick in spite of enjoying the company of friends and travelling to places. Travelling to the US was fine by her, and so was living in the country. But it came at the cost of not having her immediate family around. She opted out.

Sarika and Richa both travelled to the US thanks to partners who were in the country because of their IT-industry-related jobs. Sarika's husband finished his master's at Alabama and sought a job there itself. Richa's husband was educated in India, and had moved on to work there.

Both the girls wanted to continue with their jobs. Sarika had to put in her papers a few months before her wedding. She did not know when she would return at all.

And then there are women like Anamika Mohanty who made it on their own, on H1B visas, a feat not many women manage to achieve. Men with IT jobs that I speak to insist that it is less likely their managers would push for a woman employee to head to the US. The presumption that the woman may head to the US only to return in a few months (because of family pressure in the most cases) is a big deterrent. Rather than give a woman employee an H1B opportunity (who they think is risky investment for all the money they would spend on her visa), they would prefer to invest in a man for the same job,' says an IT insider, on condition of anonymity. Others say that men tend to stay on longer, thanks to support from their families back home, which means more returns on investment for the companies.

'Managers are open with this bias,' says Anamika. 'They think that if the husband pulls the strings, the wife who has gone on an H1B, even if it's just for a few months, will return to India. Some think, "Why should both the husband and wife earn so much?" Such managers are usually people who have wives who are not working and who only look after their home and kids. They think that we do not need an H1B petition. They openly tell us this.'

Anamika did not really think her H1B petition would be approved when she submitted her documents. But come it did. Validating her opinion is a mid-level IT decision-maker: 'Companies do file an H1B if the woman is not married. Or if women clearly state that they have no constraints in travelling to the US despite having a husband and kids. If the husband is already in the US and the wife needs an H1B, she is the best candidate.'

Aruna Raman made it to the US in 2003 on an H1B. She arrived at Long Island, New York, and remembers stepping out of the New York airport and hailing a cab to Holiday Inn. As someone responsible for herself, she had to take care of herself. She did not know anybody. She was very conscious of herself because it was a short official trip. She did not want to order anything expensive at her hotel or buy things for herself because she was not sure that the company that sent her would reimburse the money on return.

Years later, she returned to the US, this time on an H4 visa—as the spouse of an H1B visa holder. Her husband, Vikram, had lived and worked there for six years, had set up his rental home after a lot of struggle and had reached his current position after many hardships. Now things were settled for both of them. For once in her life, she took a step backwards from her active role as a contributor to family income and caregiver. She wanted to be taken care of by someone.

When Shyla Sen's parents found her a man to marry, she had her own apprehensions about him being based in the US. She got married after waiting a whole year. 'The newspapers were full of stories about fraudulent marriages in the US, where boys got married in India because of parental pressure, only for the girls to discover they were already married in the US. Every magazine or newspaper would have such a story. So before we okayed the match, my cousin who lived in the US went to meet my fiancé.'

She had to wait for her own H1B visa to be processed. She decided to head to the country on her own work visa. She waited another year after getting married till her own H1B petition was approved, so she could join him. It certainly meant a long-distance marriage for a while. But Shyla says she connected with her husband the best among the boys she met, and decided to jump in.

In that season of distrust for NRI grooms, Shyla's was a leap of faith. She insists on thorough enquiries about NRI suitors who head to India seeking brides.

What would it be like, on the other side of such enquiries? In our first year in the US, conversations during grocery rides with my husband's bachelor colleagues would often turn towards marriage.

One bachelor friend, a shy Telugu boy, revealed how he had a tough time convincing the relatives of prospective girls that he was not fake. They would ask him intrusive details, putting him off. Some days, a colleague or other office staff would get random calls from the families of prospective brides. The soft-spoken eligible bachelor was at his wits' end, more so because such families were highly reluctant to let him call their girls on phone or video chat with them. 'They either stop calling me after my request or delay talks.'

Boys like him face the effects of the antics of cheap men who exploit women and their families. Philandering, alcoholism and substance abuse have almost become the buzzwords associated with eligible NRI bachelors.

His roommate avoided marriage for years. The reserved roommate (let's call him Subramanian) put high premium on personal space. Once, Subramanian got hospitalized, and had to be taken care of for many days. Something changed. With no family around, the youngster found it so depressing that he decided to find a companion, whatever it took.

'If the girl does not agree to come to the US, I will shift my job to India. Everything depends on her,' he told us. What he saw happening to his friend because of all the lack of trust among Indian parents prompted him to travel to India, meet people face to face, be upfront about himself and spend time with the prospective brides for the big decision, rather than do the three-week fly-in-fly-off-with-a-bride exercise.

He sought a 'work-from-home' option at his company, sold his prized possessions, a two-wheeler and his car, and got ready to fly to India. To his bad luck, his company went through a shakedown that year. His job was safe, but the company backed out of his 'work-from-home' incentive. His India plan fell apart. He was crushed. He had not as yet applied for his Green Card, so he was relieved that he would be able to bring his wife with him to the States without much difficulty.

His parents insisted that he then do the short trip. When a girl he fell for through the alliances accepted his proposal, he thanked his stars. She agreed to move to the US with him, and his joy knew no bounds.

Vijaya Shetty was a well-paid employee at an IT major, doing well at her workplace, when she developed affections for her colleague. The two were great friends. He flew to the US to study. A few weeks into his culture shock phase, he realized he had fallen in love with her, and confessed. She had feelings for him too. Their overseas courtship began. Time passed and they grew more certain about getting married to each other. It was understood that he would stay in the US for a while after his studies. Vijaya had three options apart from applying for an H1B herself: move to the US on the F2 visa as a dependent of the student husband, get herself an F1 visa, or move in with him after he got a job, on an H4 visa.

She spent two years trying for her H1B visa before she mulled over the other three options. 'The H1B cap opens every year on 1 April. That is when most consulting companies have candidates lined up. I had reached out to two of them through online forums. At my company, there was no option of coming on H1B visa because it was not doing well. They were not sending anyone to client companies overseas. That year, as many as 2,50,000 applications were filed for H1B. This had happened after many years. I lost in the lottery. It meant that I could not join him by the following October. It was frustrating.'

She did not give up. The experience made her wiser, and the following year, she applied through four different companies. She checked on many more forums and gained more insight into the H1B process. They all charged her $1000 each as legal fees, which meant more than Rs 50,000. The H1B season again had a lot more applications. She lost in the lottery. Again.

'It is super frustrating when you have the skills, the qualifications, you have done the homework, you have companies willing to sponsor you, but only because of the mechanism of the visa, you must give up. It was throttling my ambitions. If I went to the US on an H4, what would I do in a different country with no family and no friends? I am not into hobbies, I am not creative. My fiancé knew it too, that I would do better on a work visa. I gave up the H1B chase and decided to study so I could join him.'

A disheartened Vijaya changed track. Her next goal was enrolment in a university and the F1B visa. Her goal was to join her fiancé in the States, whatever it took. Her love for him egged her on.

While Vijaya put everything aside and decided to study again for love, Rani Kant was never interested in moving to the US. When she got married in 2006, she was still in her first year of college studying law at Patna, Bihar. She got married after her exams. Five days after their marriage, her husband had to leave for the US on a project. She was crushed, despite having known of his impending travel beforehand. And scared. True, he went off on a note of prosperity. But she was a bride for God's sake! Her husband, Kant, was based in Chennai then and sent on an H1B visa. He soon readied the papers for her H4 visa. A few months later, the time came for her visa interview at the Chennai US consulate. He travelled from the US to Patna to pick her up for the interview at Chennai. She refused. 'I put my foot down and told him that if he wanted to live with me, he could return to India. I would not set foot outside the country. How could I? Till then I had not stepped outside of Bihar. And suddenly I was expected to leave the country. I was terrified of going to a strange place and dealing with strangers. My father was not keen on letting me go either.'

Rani's husband, Kant, was in a sticky position with his company on the matter. It had spent a great deal on his visa. If he refused to head back to the US on the assignment, they would pressurize him to quit the job. He quit—to save his marriage. The couple did make it to the US after a few years when another company filed for his work visa. And her own career in Indian law went out of the window with the move. She was registered with the Bar in Patna, but had no chance to practise. The couple had two kids by then.

Factors surrounding intercontinental relocation from India are not just marriage. Kant's H1B petition was subject to the decisions made by his bosses at the IT firm, the project that he was attached to and the client company based in the US. Other determinants were children, their schooling, their health, the health concerns of their parents and parents-in-law, their fears of losing the kids to another country and its foreign culture and, most importantly, finances.

The 'let's go' decision primarily takes into account the husband's career growth factor. It is mostly presumed that the woman must step back so that her family's financial position improves, or that the husband's CV prospects thrive. Covert pressure on her to quit an existing job and become a homemaker takes the form of subtle changes in the behaviour of the family, the in-laws and people ranging from the milkman to the landlord, once word goes out about the possible move to the States.

One can note the change in the way the landlord talks, note the pointed queries by an apartment complex watchman doubling up as a real-estate agent ('How long are you planning to stay there?') or the chatter about who must stay with you if the husband travels first. Or who must take care of the kids in his absence. A woman's life begins to be seen as revolving around the husband's physical presence.

Let us then look at how the men who mostly travel get chosen. And get to know the bosses who have a say in the husband's US-move decision.

In the cubicles of IT companies at Bengaluru, Hyderabad, Chennai, Gurgaon, Mumbai, Kolkata and other cities, an interesting mix of factors plays out when an IT firm manager files the H1B petition for a team member. Assuming that the client company is US-based and in need of a resource, what goes on in the mind of a decision-maker?

H1B workers I spoke to did not want to be named for obvious reasons. Over coffee, a friend opened up: 'Usually, people who have been performing well over the previous one or two years and are liked by the boss, the project manager, get to file H1B petitions. In my office, the boss would offer it to the team's best performer. If the best one refused, he would offer it to others. Half the time, employees do not want to travel because of family constraints. Often, companies that file H1 petitions make you sign a bond. They spend about $3000 on your application, and cannot risk your quitting. So they make you promise to pay that amount if you resign. Bonds serve as a mental block for some people. They do not sign up.'

By norm, the selection of an employee for overseas assignments is need-based. A client company asks for a particular 'resource' that they cannot find in the US. If the Indian company has the 'resource', it provides the same. Otherwise, it goes out into the market, recruits someone for the profile, and files an H1B petition immediately.

A senior-level decision-maker in an IT major told me that the choice of an H1B worker in the Indian company is almost always based on his communication skills and rapport with the boss. 'As a management level guy, I would look at an H1B worker as an investment for the company. If I invest in a person, I expect a higher rate of return, longevity of the employee in my company and use the "reward and recognize" strategy. Only if the employee has been loyal and useful for the company in the long term does he deserve to go to the US. At the realistic level, though, you see that it is linguistic favouritism, same home town association, same state preference and being in the good books of the boss that actually work in your favour if you want to apply.'

One would love to believe that work performance mattered. But as this IT insider put it, companies would rather use their best-performing team members offshore, read India, than send them to the US, or anywhere else for that matter.

'Work hours in the US, even for Indian companies, are lesser than in India. It is possible to extract more from the employee if he is based in India. Instead of the best performer, the average performer who can market himself well goes to the US. To understand and implement what the US clients say, you need someone with a lot of exposure to his company's processes and the outside market. A team boss would need someone who can talk well and promote your company.'

Sindhu Venugopal wanted to travel to the States on her own, and her IT company's boss agreed too. The hitch: her project did not have an on-site assignment option—at least not in the US. Her husband worked in another firm and his company backtracked on filing his L1 visa that year. 'They told me that the L1 visa rejection rate was high.'

The company filed his H1B petition the following year, putting them in a spot. What would happen if the visa got picked up? Should the wife quit the job? Should the two live across continents and wait for something to click for her so that she could travel? If he moved to the US for whatever time it was allowed, their plans to expand their family would suffer.

~

Indians also arrive on the B1 visa. It is a visa provided to individuals from countries other than the US, to travel for conferences on specific dates, scientific, professional or business conventions, settle estates, negotiate contracts, participate in short-term training and so on. The B1 visa is temporary and valid for six months. It may get extended up to one year if the B1 arrival gains visitor status, with enough proof that there was no prior intent to do so.

Revathi, who calls her transition to the US a staggered one, arrived on a B1 visa during her first visit. She was the assistant manager in a multinational company in Bengaluru when her husband moved to Gurgaon, Haryana, to a smaller firm that sent him to Philadelphia on a B1 visa. He stayed there for three months. The client company liked his work, and he was comfortable too. The firm decided to process his H1B visa so he could work long-term. When he returned to India for two weeks, the couple attended the visa interview for his H1B visa and her H4 visa. He returned to the US. She stayed back. She felt no need to hurry up and pack her bags. She loved her job.

She was not scared of the lack of familiarity with the States. She had visited the west coast once for work. It was the current uncertainty that she had to deal with. Would he like his job? What if he did not like it? She continued to work, so that it would give them a buffer to decide. He visited home every three months. Her career was going 'fabulous'. After more than a year, 'I decided it was time to call it quits and start to rebuild our marriage together.'

When Sathya Srinivas decided to follow her husband to the US, she weighed her options. For three years post marriage, her media career didn't seem to be going anywhere, partly because of their move to other cities, the post-wedding blues, and mostly because her ill health left her an emotional wreck. Physically, she had come to depend on him a great deal. Their debts piled up. He was desperate for professional growth. Should she decide to stay back, she would have to depend on her aged parents, or settle into the joint family of her husband's parents. The two options were far-fetched. She and her husband had a lifestyle a lot different from that of their elders. How could she bear to live away from the one nursing her back to health?

Her career was almost ruined already. Why not let him thrive? By the time she finalized her decision, his visa was stamped. And she braced herself for the tedious procedure of getting her own visa.

2

Facing the Interview

Morning traffic raced by on the Gemini Flyover as the queue outside the US consulate in Chennai grew longer.

The blistering late morning sun made people in the queue wipe sweat off their hands, forehead and neck every once in a while. Vanitha Shashi tried hard to remain calm. It was the spring of 2000—in reality, summer in Chennai. A turmeric *mangalsutra* thread (one of the wedding ornaments worn by married women in India as a symbol of their marital status) adorned her neck, its two tiny gold bowls new and shiny.

Every few minutes, she wiped beads of sweat off her forehead and neck. Vanitha had worn more wedding jewellery than was her wont, to project a 'bridal look'. The henna on her hands was still fresh. What she was not prepared for was the twenty-five other girls wearing similar turmeric threads, waiting in the queue clutching their bundles of documents.

Within the secured walls of the building, she awaited one of the most important exams of her life. She had often appeared for interminable examinations, but this one would, it seemed, seal her fate. Was she eligible to travel to the US at all? Vanitha wished her husband was with her at that time. On their phone call the previous night, he had assured her that she would be granted the visa, and that she should not worry. Her father was with her, though, which was a solace. Things had not been going well at her in-laws' home in Hyderabad. They seemed to be very unhappy with her husband, and he was not around to face their ire—she was. They resorted to taunting her for things her husband had done or not done, long before she had even entered his life.

Now, standing in the queue, she wondered if those taunts would play havoc in her head during those crucial minutes at the counter. Her visa application was not for H4, but F2. She would be the dependent resident of a student, as her husband was then pursuing his PhD. Vanitha also wondered if they would send her application into the visas mantis, given her husband's subject of study—physics.

The visas mantis is one of the many forms of security clearance, or security advisory opinions (SAOs), put in place by the US government—to grant or deny a visa to certain visa applicants, mainly used for individuals hailing from countries suspected of sponsoring terrorism. If a visa mantis SAO request is raised by the consulate, an investigation request is sent out to various federal agencies in the United States to inquire into the individual's case for possible espionage, terrorism, and illegal export of technology outside the US. A visa cannot be granted to the applicant unless a satisfactory response is received from all the agencies investigating the case. It can delay one's visa by a few days or weeks, and it is impossible to expedite an individual visa process once the request has been raised. No one had given Vanitha tips for the interview. She was worried, though she tried to not show it. 'What if the documents are not good enough?' Her husband's stipend was all of $1200 then. What if the officer decided that the amount was not enough for two people to live on?

After submitting her documents, she awaited her turn at the interview counter. She saw two other girls with new turmeric threads get rejected. 'It looked like they did not understand the questions. When my turn came, I understood what they were saying because I used to often watch American television series and was familiar with their accent.'

A common tip handed out for the visa interview is to make eye contact with the interviewing official. Common errors on the passport must be rectified before the interview, which includes the change of the surname in the case of newly married women.

'One must maintain a polite distance from the people ahead in the queue,' says Manasi. 'When you go to a departmental store too, you maintain a distance between yourself and another person, unlike in India.'

The usual American greeting is, 'Hi, how are you?', to which the reply is simply, 'I am good. How are you?', followed maybe by a remark on the weather, but that does not happen in a visa interview.

Manasi insists that it is essential to be honest at the interview. 'Even if you have a petty theft in your records, it is better to admit it.'

Manasi's name had the initial 'G' in the birth certificate. During the run-up to her interview, she discovered that her birth certificate, issued by a nursing home and not the municipal corporation in her city, was not valid. 'For the municipal corporation to issue a birth certificate, the nursing home would have to transfer their certificate to the corporation with the details. And then, the corporation would issue it.' To her dismay, she discovered that the nursing home had shut down.

An alternative was to have her birth certificate validated by a judge. When she went to the court, the judge was away on vacation. There was no option but to wait for the judge's signature, and then re-apply for the visa with complete documents. Even though Manasi eventually did get her visa, the whole process took her four months.

If you are a new visa applicant in India, you will learn through the course of the process that the two-mile-long traditional name that your elders bestowed upon you can be a botheration. Usually, such long names that contain the names of fathers, clans, villages of yore, or cities of present, are simply morphed into alphabets that are placed either before or after our names.

In fact, the diversity of our languages allows for consonants such as p, k and m to be paired with vowels such as a, u and i, to read Pa, Ki, Ma, which are shorter versions of the surnames that prelude or follow given names. Not so in America, where the concept of first, middle and last name reigns.

When my husband and I filled out our passport applications, little did we know about how the rules of names play out.

'Should I write my initial in the surname section or the first name box?' I asked him sheepishly.

I still cannot remember what he said. But in the next half hour, we had an argument about which website said what.

Says Manasi, 'Your name, if misspelt in the passport, will stay so in all the documents that follow in the US. You also need to be prepared to be called by your first name by everybody. Most times, it is the initial in your Indian name.'

So, if your name is B. Manasi, where the 'B.' stands for 'Belgaum', you will be called Belgaum instead of Manasi if you enter Belgaum as your first name. So the correct thing to do is to make Belgaum your surname while filling in the passport application. The same applies to your father's name, family name or your mother's name. If your name has more than one initial, keep Manasi as your first name, Belgaum as your surname, and the other initials as middle initial names—for example, Manasi X.Y.Z. Belgaum.

In effect, it is also essential that your passport corresponds with your name in the birth certificate. Women who apply for their passports ahead of visa interviews, or at any other time in their lives, need to keep in mind that even if they do not intend to travel abroad, and instead want to treat their passport as another document of identity, such differences in name usage get invariably dictated by the norms of the West.

A few people make the mistake of not giving a surname. Or writing their given name in the blanks provided for surname. The US consulate states that if you do not state first name or surname, your first name gets printed as FNU or First Name Unknown. This could make things difficult when you apply for a driver's licence, and also when you become eligible to apply for an SSN.[9]

~

The one question that ran through Sathya's mind before her visa interview was: 'Why should our Indian names be influenced by Western usage?' A part of her protested against the hegemony. On the one hand, she knew some villagers who had no idea of their family names or even their right age, and had spent a happy life without being sure of such details. On the other, here she was trying to get her name and age right to the letter and proving it as well. Naturally, her irritation was palpable.

Ahead of her H4 visa interview, she memorized the basic details about her husband, his role in the company, and made sure to carry a set of her wedding pictures—what the instructions called the 'fire ceremony'. She was not happy with the quality of the photograph that accompanied her application. She looked bloated, dejected, lost and scared as she stared at the camera, her face pale like that of a ghost.

Her husband had not travelled to the US by the time of her interview. And the copy of his stamped visa showed the officer that.

'Good morning,' the officer greeted her.

'Good morning,' she said. Looking back, she feels she should have said, 'How are you today?'

He asked her for her documents, which she promptly handed over.

He checked them, and asked her the expected question.

'What is your highest qualification?' She had a post-graduate diploma, but her husband had told her it was not valid in the US.

'Bachelor of Arts.'

'What is the name of your father-in-law?' he asked.

She gave him the right name.

'What is your husband's date of birth?'

She told him the date, slow and clear.

Her husband had given her a useful instruction: 'Ask them to repeat the question if you cannot understand something. They will repeat it for you.'

'Do you have your husband's payslips for the last one year?'

This was something she was not prepared for. His payslips had not been mentioned as a part of the essential documents list, but were required now as a result of his not having left for the States yet.

She could not make head or tail of what the official said after that. She could not fathom his accent any more.

He kept the I-797, the client letter from the US company inviting her husband, and returned her passport.

Sathya's heart sank. Not taking the passport meant rejection. He handed her a blue sheet of printed directions and wrote a number on it. She did hear something to the effect of additional documents. It all happened so quickly that she had already left the counter before she came to her senses.

Confused, she approached another official in the waiting room.

'I got this sheet. Do you know what it means?'

The lady said she was not allowed to talk to applicants. She was obviously conscious of the surveillance cameras.

'Come on! This is a genuine query. I only need to know what this is!' Sathya's thoughts screamed inside her head, even as no words spilled out. This was a rejection.

She quickly stepped outside, feeling entirely responsible for the situation. Her husband would not be able to travel. Calling him from the nearest payphone, she wailed as soon as he answered, 'I got rejected. They gave me a blue sheet and the passport too!'

'Don't worry. It's not a rejection. They just need additional documents,' he tried to calm her down, though his tone relayed apprehension.

The couple discovered later that the sheet was actually the 221G form that said that the consulate has been unable to issue the visa under Section 221(g) of the Immigration and Nationality Act (INA). The form further said the applicant must submit the marked documents required at the US government designated agency before a stipulated time.

The form comes in blue, green, pink, white and yellow, depending on which city the applicant's consulate is located in. The applicant is supposed to follow the instructions on the slip and drop off the additional documents demanded at the agency's drop box along with the passport. It is essential to not contact the US consulate about it; they will get in touch with you on their own.[10]

Sathya had to cancel some travel plans as a result of the delay. When, after three weeks, her passport came home with the stamped visa, she rejoiced. 'Half the battle won,' she thought.

Sathya was a city-bred, well-educated girl, who was quick to research things she did not know about, and usually got the hang of the way things worked fast enough. There were plenty of girls out there applying for visas who did not understand basics such as the qualifications of their spouse.

Neha Thomas, who got married as per the Hindu as well as Christian ceremonies, used the certificate provided by the church for the visa interview. She was asked if she would be interested in working in the US. She replied in the negative. If she had said 'yes', her visa would have been rejected.

Bharathi Verma knew what her husband's designation was, and his role in the company. She was armed with the client letter and other relevant documents, and felt confident when her token number was called. She was excited. She would finally join Hareesh. Their one-year separation had been nothing short of an ordeal. 'The officer asked me why it took me so long to join my husband. I said I wanted him to settle down. At this, the officer's tone assumed caution. He asked whether I knew that if my husband was not being paid properly by his employers, we could report it. I did have hints about my husband's state, but I was not bothered about it. I simply replied yes.'

Bharathi tells me that she is not sure whether she should have said something about Hareesh being treated like an errand boy by his employers. Little did she know that things would turn so bad that she would be unable to visit India for three years.

Armed with the wisdom gained from what she went through, her advice is, 'Be very thorough with documents.' Years later, for her H1B visa approval, she not only took a letter from the client but also clicked pictures of her client's office and of the cubicle where she sat. 'It's okay to over-prepare,' she says.

A friend who travelled to many countries before finally relocating to the US had a perspective on the visa interview experience which was coloured by his numerous visits to various embassies.

'By the time you reach the visa interview counter, they have already decided whether to approve your visa or reject it. It is often not in your hands. It is their targets for the day or month that matter. You need to be confident in your body language, precise in answering questions, and leave the rest to God.'

When Rupashree Biswas was applying for her L2 visa, she was relieved that she would finally be able to get a job. It had been a roller-coaster ride till then. She was eight months pregnant when her husband's Kolkata-based firm told them that they could send the couple together to the US. But the catch was that the on-site assignment would last only six months. The thought of travelling with him to an unknown country in her condition, and then giving birth in the US without her family being around, was daunting. Still, she attended the visa interview with him, and everything went smoothly.

Soon, their tickets were booked. As the actual date of the journey drew closer, her then seemingly unimportant worries morphed into monsters of fear. She opted out of the journey three days before they were to travel, not willing to risk her own health or that of her baby.

By the time she once again stood in the interview queue for the L2 visa, two years had passed. She had lived in India, away from her husband, all this time. She consciously did not nurture hopes of working with a small child, even though she was a lecturer in Kolkata at that time. The move would make her a dependent in the foreign country, despite being eligible to work. She had braced herself to be the family nurturer. If a job opportunity happened to present itself, she would gladly embrace it.

She was instructed to not take her baby along—just the photographs would suffice. Her documents included her child's as well. The obvious question was how long she had stayed in the US. She spoke about not having gone at all because of her baby. She was questioned about her husband's position in his company and her own educational qualifications.

Her husband had asked her to call him up as soon as the interview was over. The normally reticent Deepan was overwhelmed with joy when he realized he would be reunited with his wife and child very soon. Countless hours of video chats had not been able to make up for the lack of physical proximity with his family.

3

Are We Going or Not?

The months before Rupashree got her treasured L2 visa renewed were filled with self-doubt, helplessness and sorrow.

Should she have discouraged her husband from taking up this project in the US?

Rupashree mulled over her decision the day he left, her hand gently caressing her belly. The run-up to their moment of reckoning had been difficult enough. She had opted out of the journey at the last minute. Rupashree had been working as a lecturer when her pregnancy had prompted her to take a break. Deepan had hoped that he would get called for the project in the US well before Rupashree's second trimester began.

The timing had been awful.

A lot happens in the run-up to an impending travel call for a project abroad. It can keep families on edge for months, and the would-be visa wives oscillate between the ifs and buts and don'ts of it all. Their neither-here-nor-there status can impact crucial family decisions such as the marriage of a sibling, a loved one's surgery, or long-awaited purchases that must wait because you do not know if you will leave India or not.

When Rupashree got her L2 visa stamped, she did not have to make crucial decisions on home purchases the way other women heading to the US did. She and Deepan lived with her in-laws. Their furniture belonged to his parents. Problems of furniture disposal and the like were ruled out as a result.

Rupashree's primary fears were about the impending birth. Her baby was already making its presence felt—kicks, uneasiness, swollen legs, hormonal ups and downs. She got flustered, annoyed and confused easily. Would she be able to manage without Deepan? How could he miss such an important event in their lives? But another part of her reasoned with her—she would be able to follow him to the US eventually.

Three months after Deepan left, Rupashree's sleepless nights had begun, feeding her baby every two hours, cradling him, changing his diapers and longing for a few hours of peaceful sleep. She was juggling the baby's routine as well as Deepan's phone calls, timing her life around US time zones and the baby's waking and feeding cycles. Mostly, she was annoyed. It bothered her that she had to stay awake not just for her baby, but also to get a few minutes with her husband on the phone. He was not there for the birth of their son. There was no excuse for that.

'He offered to come on leave for three weeks for the delivery. I was not prepared to see him go at the end of those three weeks. I told him, "Come back for good, or do not come at all." I had a caesarean. I needed my husband every day. His own agony was no less. He saw our son during our video chats, but he was desperate to hold his baby. I was not depressed that he was not with me. I was angry.'

To compound her misery, visiting relatives would repeat the same question: 'When will Deepan return?'

An emotionally distraught Rupashree would cry into the wee hours of the morning. She knew she would head to the US some day, to the warm embrace of her husband. She knew she would be allowed to work, and that her motherhood would not give her the time to do so. Something told her that her qualifications might not work in the new country. But those were things to worry about later. All she wanted, at the moment, was her husband by her side.

The pendulum phase—of deciding whether to move or stay put—is as knotty as it gets. Couples who have to relocate face a predicament similar to Rupashree's. For many working women, the choice is often between asking their companies to sponsor a visa, or giving up their jobs, or dealing with their spouse's absence. Women often find that any choice they might make is subject to a mountain of social obligations.

Kaushalya and Prakash Anand had gone through their own post-marital glitches and a honeymoon phase ruined by job schedules. They were working in companies located at opposite ends of the city, so the only time they spent with each other was on weekends. Obligations to attend family events and visit their in-laws who lived in another part of the city strained their relationship further.

Prakash cleared his visa interview and waited for his project call in the midst of cut-throat internal politics in his team at the IT major he worked for. Her dilemma was bigger. She did not want to put in her papers. Her employers had given her no hope for an H1B till then. His L1 visa had been rejected the previous year. And now, he had no clue when, if at all, he would be called to relocate.

'I had no option but to stay back and work. Financially, it made more sense. My in-laws did not want Prakash to travel to the US. They were not happy, but not sad either. They believed in horoscopes and expected him to travel. They just did not want it to happen. Apparently, the horoscopes predicted that I would travel on my own H1B visa. My parents were against my joining him. They felt it would be risky to give up my job for his short-term assignment.'

During this time, Kaushalya only shopped for basic grocery items that they would consume quickly. All other purchases were put on hold. Kaushalya had badly wanted a sofa for their living room, tired of hand-me-down plastic chairs. Her husband believed that he would be leaving soon and placed an embargo on all purchases. They were excited. And nervous.

Another thing put on hold was the decision to have a baby. 'We could not plan a baby yet. But I had so many

questions running in my mind. What if he went away
for a long time, and my visa was rejected? What would
happen to our plans to have a baby? What would family
elders think about me? What would society say if I did not
conceive? People might think we were so busy planning
our finances that we could not be bothered about building
a family. And even if my H1B visa came through, I could
end up in a different American city. How could we plan
a child then? What would happen if I opted for an H4
visa? We would become a single-income family. How long
would it be before I could work again? Where would my
baby be born?'

For men, a US job posting demands a single choice:
'Will I go, will I not?' For working wives, the dilemma is,
'Should I quit? Should I not?' And if they have children,
another facet is added: 'Should we travel together? Should
we wait?'

Aruna quit her job four months after her marriage,
even as her husband's visa was being processed. Those
months prompted her to review their way of life.

'You begin doubting your decision. I implicitly trusted
my husband. But you start questioning the situation. I
was never someone who fell back on faith in God. This
was about having faith in the idea of faith. You realize
that not everything is in your control. You can place all
pieces of your life correctly, in perfect symmetry, and they
may still not align.'

Shyla, too, felt she had lost control over her life during
the year it took for her to move to the US to be with her
husband. She was often asked questions like, 'So when

is your husband going to pick you up?', 'How is your job going?', 'Are you in touch with your in-laws?'

She spent the honeymoon phase of her marriage video-chatting with her husband for hours. 'My parents would get irritated when I would be on the phone with my husband. I was missing him. We were newly married, longing to be with each other. And the visa situation had put us in a quandary. I would not say it was a major problem. But my parents did not approve of their routine getting disturbed because of my phone calls,' says Shyla.

At work too, Shyla was going through a bad phase. She had not spoken about leaving the company. But her colleagues and bosses had come to her wedding. They knew the groom was from the US, and this was enough to impact her position at her office. Her own prospects of getting an H1B visa were nil. During appraisals, she got a low rating. Heartbroken, she tried to reason with her bosses. They gave her the cold shoulder. They would not say it, but it became obvious that they did not think she would stay for long at the company. Shyla regretted inviting them to her wedding.

The decisions about a move are not career-based alone. They often involve social obligations. It is assumed that a woman should be with her husband. In social circles where long-distance marriages are an accepted norm, the woman finds it easier to stay on in India long after her husband has moved. In other circles, when social pressures become difficult to handle, the move to the US becomes the woman's only escape route.

For Bindhu, it was an easy choice because she wanted to move to America. Sarika, on the other hand, did not have a choice. Her husband was on an H1B visa, but he obtained it while living in the US, after his optional practical training period of seventeen months. She was getting married to a US resident. It was expected that she would join her husband shortly. What she was not prepared for was how her life would change overnight after moving in with her hostile in-laws.

In sharp contrast was the situation of Anamika Mohanty, whose husband was the one who took the backseat and let her make a career choice for them both. Their plan was that she would work a few months at her new location, he would try to get an H1B visa through consultants, and if that did not work out, he would join her on an H4 visa. Either way, Anamika was simply not sure what her future would be like in a country without the feeling of security that she had in her own country, in the proximity of her family.

Aanchal Tripathi's husband, Sandeep Tripathi, first made it to the US on an H1B for three months. At the time, it did not make sense to Aanchal to leave her job as a biology teacher in a school near Gurgaon. She had a hectic schedule—tuitions in the morning and evening, school during the day, cooking before and after tuitions. Her in-laws babysat her son for her.

She decided to wait it out. Over the next two years, her husband would visit the US on different projects. Aanchal wanted to travel to the US, to be with her husband for a short while, but could not get any leave. The couple finally took a call based on their son's education. 'I wanted to educate my son in the States. My dream was that my son should study in the best school in the world. So giving up my job was a small sacrifice.'

Preeti and Pravin's move from Hyderabad to San Jose was also affected by their daughter's requirements. Only, they decided to leave her with Pravin's parents till the end of her academic year. It was a tough decision. But if Pravin went alone, not being used to living alone, he would struggle to take care of his meals and other necessities. Also, the couple had never had the opportunity to spend uninterrupted quality time with each other during the nine years of their married life, which being alone at this time would provide. Their eight-year-old daughter was too attached to her grandparents to mind being left behind. Leaving her with them for a few months would help the child prepare mentally for the move.

The weeks after Sathya's visa interview were vexing for her and her husband, Surya. Their visas were ready but his project call had not come. They had to find a way to dispose of their furniture. But if he did not get the call, and his visa tenure expired, they would have to stay back. They would be left with an empty house. If and when the call came, she hoped they would have enough time to pack up everything and dispose of the rest. Some friends advised her husband that a visit to the 'Visa Balaji' temple in Hyderabad would help. He dutifully paid obeisance.

The real reason for the delay was because the on-site opportunity had been dangled in front of him like a carrot by his company to entice him not to quit his job.

He had been made to sign a bond that would not let him change jobs.

Perpetually in this waiting mode, Sathya listed out things that needed to be discarded. She started writing to friends living in the US about what had to be done before leaving India.

'Don't worry about the move. Take it slow, one step at a time,' wrote in a friend.

Seriously? Sathya looked around her home—a bed to give away, a computer to wrap up, tons of books, a whole kitchen-full of utensils, a gas connection, her own phone connection, crafting supplies, clothes, paraphernalia at the pooja altar, the refrigerator, washing machine, air conditioner, toiletries, TV, living room furniture. Even thinking about it was exhausting. Another friend talked about how some places have Indian stores, so necessities would be within reach in most cities.

· 'Get your four-wheeler driving licence,' chirped another friend. Should she really be learning to drive when there were more important things at hand, and a whole house needed to be packed up? For the moment, all Sathya could do was to avoid buying more Indian clothes. She could carry her wedding sarees. And maybe stick to bare necessities . . . wait, what should she take to the new country?

'Buy shoes.'

'Buy some Western casuals.'

'Get your masala *dabba*.'

Her friends chimed in with suggestions, and Surya came home day after day, sullen, with no word from his bosses about his US assignment.

4

Baggage and All That

The minute you decide to move to the US is when you begin to live on two continents instead of one.

You do all you can to shut shop in your home country. You throw away excess baggage, surrender your telephone connection, say your goodbyes and board that flight. But can you shut off, discard or pack away memories, good and bad, from your mind's inner sanctum? Can you imagine making an instant switch from your mom's idli breakfast to pancakes?

A yearning for home is a universal phenomenon. Anyone from anywhere who moves to another part of the world feels pangs of grief. The trauma of transition peaks when you must sweep a lifetime of memories under the carpet, and make new ones.

It is very tough to push away memories that find a physical form in the furniture you own, the schoolbooks that you hold to your chest, in the two-wheeler that's a symbol of a first job's sweat, in greeting cards you stashed away, or diaries you wrote in for years. What if that repository of memory is your grandmother's heavy iron mortar and pestle to crush spices, or your mother's granite grinding stone? Letting go is hard. In the moments and months before you board that flight, 'letting go' feels like a buzzword that should be reserved for sanyasis, not you. How does one simply move on?

You suddenly must discard your books, kitchen utensils, tools of trade and relics that are a part of your daily existence, home décor that you agonized over for days on end. It is not as if we live in boxes. We live in spaces we nurture and which nurture us. We live in our memories. We live among the security of people's love. We live in the din of ambient noise—stray dogs barking, the sounds of squirrels and crows squabbling among trees, vehicles honking in high-traffic neighbourhoods, doorstep vegetable vendors calling out their wares. We hoard material goods more for their sentimental value than their utility. Such keepsakes become a bother as the time of departure draws closer. We cannot carry them all.

The biggest dilemma, as Manasi, who moved to the US years ago, puts it, is, 'How can one pack an entire life and household into two suitcases with a 50-pound weight allowance?' Also, things you may think are important in India will not be important in the US—for instance, your pooja paraphernalia. Where will you put it if you don't have a pooja room? 'I was going on a fiancée visa, which meant I was moving in with another family. Since my parents had moved in with me in India, I left behind everything for them to use—my SIM card, furniture, utensils, everything,' she says.

'From my cartload of albums, I had to choose a set of pictures of my daughter and me. I mainly took clothes and some books which were precious to me. I came to the US in summer, so I had to buy winter clothes afresh. Winter clothing is so different from south India where you can manage the whole winter with a shawl! I had to buy winter coats, shoes, gloves, headgear, accessories—an entirely new wardrobe!'

When you are packing, those two suitcases can symbolize a dilemma of an entirely unimaginable kind— the possible tug of war with your parents-in-law, or your mother, if she wants to pack her home and sentiments, and even with members of the extended family who might want to have a say in what clothes you should take. Sentiments run high and can turn the household into a battleground. Questioning glances when you do not tuck in extra items of worship and careless remarks like 'Why did you buy so many items for your house?' all make you want to scream.

Try justifying your wedding shopping for the house, and the money spent on indulgences essential to building your perfect home—if you want to risk a fight just before leaving. If you have the reputation in your family of making your own decisions, it might be possible to deflect such interference somewhat. But you will still be scrutinized when you least expect it.

Packing a suitcase is also a tug of war between the man's 'pack light' instructions and the woman's 'pack the home because you will need it' instinct. 'I missed my bike the most,' says my husband, who left his two-wheeler behind for his brothers to use. In reality, what most men miss the most are their mommy's meals!

Not so for women. When Kaushalya set up house after marriage, she was very particular about the quality of furniture, décor and utility of space. She had lived in many cities before getting married to an engineer in Delhi. In spite of her mother-in-law's objections, she managed to have her way in decorating their home. When the time came to pack up for the States, she wept because she had to leave it all.

When it was time for her husband to leave, she focused her energy on packing his suitcases. The weeks before his departure were marked by not just their own arguments, but also the unsolicited advice that was handed out by her parents, his parents and their relatives, even as they were debating tough decisions like her quitting her job if nothing worked out. Prakash had bagged a California project that would complete in six months, after which his parents wanted him to return to India. They believed that if Kaushalya did not quit her job, their son would be more inclined to return home after the project.

Every piece of advice was loaded with the hope that the trip would be 'temporary'. The thought of their son moving away was too much for them. Kaushalya was fed up with having to tailor her journey based on their fears. She understood their old-age woes. She just did not want them to play out their insecurities over her boxes. She considered staying at a friend's apartment, or at a hostel for the period that he would be gone. But then, family and extended family would take over her life in the name of care.

Kaushalya wanted to be with Prakash. After two years of bliss, she was keen on a baby. How could she explain to the elders that she wanted a baby, that she would find it hard to do without her husband, or that she wanted to experience life in the US? Prakash supported her, which eased her worries to a large extent. She could quit or stay as per her wish. Her boss granted her leave on loss of pay so that she could relocate for a few months. But he wanted her to wind up her current assignments before her long leave, delaying her own journey to join her husband.

For two months, Kaushalya lived alone even as she packed her bags. Every workplace break left her calculating what to shop for and how to keep her purchases discreet to avoid arguments at home. Every day, a new item would pop up as a must-buy. Another would be struck off the list. Her shopping list was long. For a start, she had packed her husband's boxes with clothes, chutney *podis* (sachets), toiletries and medicines with their prescriptions. She had thrown in utensils—a small pressure cooker, some ladles and cooking bowls. A friend had forewarned her that without a car, his shopping trips in his Los Angeles suburb would be limited.

Kaushalya timed her own departure to the US such that she could travel back with him after her leaves were exhausted. She spent a great deal on cosmetics and Western clothes.

'I stashed away my suitcase that had my inner-wear and prayed that my in-laws would not open it when they came to help me pack. It would have been too embarrassing if they had seen my expensive lingerie. What if my mother-in-law wondered aloud why I needed so many, or such expensive ones?'

She had a reason to buy lots of clothes. Friends had warned her that in the absence of a maid coming to wash clothes, laundry would happen once a week. So a large stash of clothes was a must.

As for the furniture and furnishings, her parents-in-law had arrived at a decision. 'Don't pack up. If the need arises, we'll do it.' It was a decree. Prakash had to pay rent for the apartment even for the months that he was away. Should he stay back in the US and land another project, his parents were willing to hire movers and packers, transport some of the luggage to their own home in Hyderabad and cart away the rest to her parents.

To the penny-pinching Prakash, though such expenditure felt wasteful, he decided to obey his parents. For Kaushalya, it took the burden of winding up the house off her head. But she had now lost her say in what she could do with her household items. She did not know that another option could have been to pack up all the stuff and house it in warehouses.

Her suitcases had turned into a mini-home, despite all the hassles. Her logic was simple—to avoid costs in the initial months, when transport to the nearest stores would cost a fortune, they needed many things. She would not compromise on her husband's traditional meals. And so went in small pressure cookers, plastic storage boxes, masalas, ladles, spoons, steelware and the like. Her US-based friend egged her on to carry basic stationery—staplers, paper clips, sheets of paper, a pair of small scissors, markers, post-its and ball pens—to keep things handy for a start. 'Don't believe your husband when he says everything is available in the desi stores here,' her friend advised. 'Your needs are different from his.'

When Manasi had moved out of her home in Bengaluru, her aged parents had moved into her fully furnished apartment, but eventually moved out to live with her siblings owing to their old age. Today, after about seven years, she has a project in hand. 'The house has been empty with all the stuff under lock and key for some time now. I will need to clean up and maybe sell it,' she says.

Another family bought a three-bedroom apartment during their short, two-year break in Mumbai after staying for many years in California. Just before they moved back to the US, this time to Oregon, they simply moved all their belongings into one of the three bedrooms, locked it up, and rented the rest of the house as a 2BHK (two-bedroom-hall-kitchen). The girl's parents made a few trips to her place to check up on it. After about two years, they tired of making such trips. The room is probably still locked.

Married couples, even if they have set up home for a few months before departure, find it a mountainous task to move when they do not live in joint families. It gets complicated with kids around. The packing phase leaves homemaker women vulnerable—they must draw favours from relatives, friends and parents, and cope with the guilt of burdening their near ones with the task of safekeeping.

A newly married Bindhu moved in with her husband a few weeks after her wedding. Her biggest worry was what to take with her for her new home. Her husband told her they would be able to purchase everything in Boston. 'I believed him!' she laughs at her innocence. 'We did not carry much because he said he had everything. Once I arrived at Boston, though, I was scampering for supplies, mainly groceries. The nearest Indian grocery store—Patel Brothers—was a forty-minute drive from home. And American grocery stores do not stock Indian food.'

Today, after over a decade of living and working in America, she says that had she known what men's concept of packing was, she would have tucked in a few spices and other things.

Kaushalya, on the other hand, was well-prepared. She had thought that plastic storage containers for the kitchen she would move into were far-fetched. But one look at their empty apartment, and she wished she had carried more. Prakash, who was starved for her home-cooked food, was relieved too.

Vanitha faced a bigger packing predicament. Her husband had left her with his parents after their wedding-in-a-jiffy sixteen years ago. Packing involved their whims more than her needs. She was to join him in Alabama barely a month after the wedding. 'There were what I would call "luggage fights". My mother-in-law had to have a say in everything that was packed. I did not protest. They were too orthodox to listen. Had I said anything, I am sure they would have started crying, and made it look like I was denying them their basic rights, or that I was torturing them by going against will. So I had to simply put up with whatever they did. There was a lot of friction between my husband's parents and another elderly couple, my husband's uncle and aunt with whom he shared a close relationship. I packed my choice of wedding sarees and jewellery. But there were other clothes—they selected my dresses, even the colours, saying that since I was dark, cream and green would look good on me. The memory of those comments about my skin colour in the middle of the packing, hardly a few days after I got married, still rankles.'

Vanitha says her parents paid for her travel purchases, not her husband or her in-laws. She travelled at a time when pickles were still allowed in hand luggage. She carried about 10 kg of different varieties of pickle—mango, *methi* (fenugreek), gongura, tomato, *imli* (raw tamarind), among others. Masalas and chutney podis were part of her luggage too. You can no longer pack pickles that way. If you are able to scrape through the arrival airport's customs officials without a hitch, consider yourself very lucky. But chances are that pickles will get shoved aside when they open your boxes. I know of someone whose packets of home-made pickles were poked by the authorities, causing oil to seep out and spoil brand new clothes in the suitcase.

Rani, who was unsure about how long her husband would have to stay in Delaware, moved most of her belongings to her mother's place in Patna before the family moved, along with their babies. 'They were expensive items—good quality furniture, furnishings, clothes. If we try buying them again, I doubt if we will get that quality,' she says.

Motherly sentiment reaches fussy heights during the momentous occasion of suitcases being packed, says Rani. Her mother wanted to put loads of worship items in. She arrived a few weeks before the festival of Makar Sankranti. 'She wanted to pack *til* barfi (a sweet made of jaggery and sesame seeds) and dahi *chura* (another dish made of curd) to ensure that we could celebrate the festival with authenticity. It was very hard to turn her down. My priority was the kids' food that we would need for the first few weeks before we could shop for other items. My mother managed to send the sweets and other things later through some relative who was travelling to New York. She would not give up.'

Of course, today, everything is available and there are lots of options, but often one does not know what to prepare for. What if we couldn't visit the grocery store immediately? What if the kids didn't like the food options available and started crying for the food back home? An anxious mother wouldn't take a chance with her kids.

The one item that no one wants to leave behind is the 3-litre or 1-litre pressure cooker. *Breaking News*: pressure cookers are available in the US! Indian stores stock them. But they are nothing like the little one you use in your Indian kitchen. Families travelling with children are forced to choose their kids' food items and clothes over such seemingly essential items.

Today's women are used to getting 'must-pack lists' by experienced relocators off the Internet. Such lists do lessen some amount of stress. Yet, each one's requirements are different. They depend on where in India a person comes from, their gender, age, profession, family needs and constraints and personal habits, among other things. I spent some hours online looking at others' must-pack lists, and ended up getting more confused.

Rina Datta did not carry any food, spices, Bengali tools, 'not even cookbooks', when she moved to New York ten years ago. Her boxes had few clothes and sweaters, gloves and hats, even though they were travelling in December.

'It was stupid,' she recalls. 'Because we landed in a place filled with Indian colleagues, and birthdays every weekend, when everyone else came dolled up in sarees and suits.' The mother of two has moved across many cities in the US due to her husband's work. She still wonders how people could arrive with thirteen suitcases in tow—grinders, kitchen vessels, 'the whole rigmarole'.

'I am glad I did not. Indian stores carry most of the stuff I need. On our visits to India, we still do not bring back a lot, except tea and sweets.'

Rina's mantra—willingness to adapt right away. She probably would have done the same if she moved to any other continent on the globe. Eventually, over the months, she bought Indian kitchenware from local stores. But after all these years, she says that an idli stand is the only authentic Indian item in her kitchen.

～

Going by the experiences of Kaushalya, Rani, Bindhu, Rina and others, one realises that the primary hindrance that towers above cooker and spice considerations is the uncertainty of project tenures, and the impending return to India.

Bosses in IT companies do not tell the work visa traveller if the posting will be long-term. Their commitment is based on the overseas client company's temporary requirement, which might be for a few months only. Further stay is subject to the next project, the part of the US it is available in, and visa renewal or extension after arrival in the country.

I will mention books here, the biased book-lover that I am. Not many of the women I spoke to admitted to being in love with books, though some did admit it—albeit a little sheepishly. During a work visa move, it feels far-fetched for women to expect their husbands to lug along the treasured book collection over to the US.

I found it hard to talk openly to my husband about packing the books. Other 'important things' needed priority. So, I housed them in large storage trunks at my grandfather's dilapidated two-room home in Chennai. On a visit, I briefly pulled them out to air them. This proved costly. Hiding among the tiles of the roof was a rat that got at the wick of an oil lamp. It probably carried the lit wick around, and before we knew it, it had set fire to the house, gutting my books, and everything else that was in there. It was traumatic for us. 'Thank God they had surrendered their gas connection. It would have been an even greater disaster otherwise,' my mother said to the neighbours and passers-by who were helping out. If only I had access to commercial storage then!

India has a huge nomadic cyber workforce that travels, bag and baggage, to other countries. It's surprising then, that an ancillary storage industry did not take off all these years, despite amazing market potential.

'Why have you not moved beyond the Delhi area?' I asked Pooja Kothari, director of StoreMore, a company specializing in personalized storage, based in Delhi-NCR. This firm stores your personal belongings in boxes for a fee. The company even arranges for doorstep transport of your personal belongings.

For my own selfish reasons, I wish such businesses boom. No obligations with relatives. No placing extra burden on parents, siblings or friends for extra space. No risk of a crumbling structure that may end up in a fire.

Who are their clients at StoreMore? Pooja speaks of that universal sentiment that we book-lovers nurture, and rightly so.

'Often, we are approached by people who want to store their books. People are emotionally attached to books. We have clients who inherit homes, and need to move in their things for a while. Many others travel abroad to UK, Australia, US, mostly for assignments of different tenures. When you go, you go for six months, eight months, and the trip sometimes gets extended. Packers and movers usually run out of or from warehouses. They only keep things for a few days.'

The company caters to the Delhi-NCR region, and plans to expand to other cities. It even resells your goods if you wish. With the number of people moving to other countries rising each year, it is not without reason that women like me hope for more such options to crop up in our neighbourhoods—one such space for every city, suburb, town and village.

Manjali Khosla set up Self Storage Warehouse Pvt. Ltd after returning to India from North America. She started the company out of a personal need. 'When I first arrived in India, the only option was to put stuff in my mother-in-law's basement or rent an apartment (which would be too expensive). While surfing the Web, I found no self-storage site in India, which to me was as shocking as not knowing what is basmati rice. The only option was StoreMore, and I did not want my stuff in a box in a warehouse. Other such warehouses said, "Madam, don't worry, we are here for you, it is 100 per cent safe," etc., etc. I have heard that too many times in India. It does not mean anything. Further, storage area prices changed according to how rich they thought I was.'

At Self Storage, you get a walk-in closet large enough to hold different items of all shapes and sizes that you can access whenever you want, and where the safety of your possessions is guaranteed. A majority of the clients at Self Storage are NRIs who travel to India every few years for a few months at a time. Some are overseas clients.

'Please expand your business. More cities need this!' I urge these women. I gave away a whole lot of my treasured possessions on a recent India trip, and sent another chunk of them to the *kabaadiwallah* (local scrap dealer).

A survival tip I learnt: When things do not really work out on the storage front, let go. Click a picture of that item. And let go. On days when you miss those prized possessions far too much, open that folder in your phone or computer and browse through the pictures, replaying the memories till you fall asleep.

5

The Flight—to a Dot on the Map

Sathya and her mother-in-law eyed the long queue at the check-in counter from the waiting lounge at Chennai airport's departure terminal. Given the security measures across airports, Sathya was surprised that this airport still allowed families inside. Surya had finally got the project call from Chicago four days earlier. His flight was due in three hours. He had stepped out with his father and brother to grab some coffee.

Sathya and her mother-in-law's feelings were chequered at this point. Sathya struggled to accept the fact that she would not see her husband for a few weeks—she who depended on him for her every little need. How could he just leave her? Her in-laws were reluctant to help her. They merely agreed to take some of her furniture. Any help from them in winding her home up was a pipe dream. Her mother-in-law was lost. On one hand, she feared that she would never see her darling son again.

On the other, she beamed with pride that he was going overseas.

After all, she had been frequently taunted, and could barely forget the indirect jibes about back-bencher sons. And now here he was, proving his mettle, ready to take off to the US. His wife would move with him. But it was she, his mother, who had nurtured him all these years. It was she who should be headed to the US. What would he eat? How would he survive? It was not as if Sathya was a great cook. Her kitchen skills were mediocre.

When you catch a flight to any destination in the US, from the time you bid an emotional farewell to your loved ones and push your luggage trolley towards the airlines check-in counter, to the time you finally step out of the airport terminal in a foreign country, there are moments—mundane and dramatic—that stay with you for life.

Soon, Sathya would be at the departure terminal, waving goodbye to her loved ones. Would she be able to keep her tears in check, or would she bawl like a little kid she had just seen, who hugged his uncles tight and refused to let go? If she had a baby, would her husband expect her to travel alone?

For thousands of women like her, airport departure zones are more than starting points for a flight—lofty, alluring, but cold, and staffed with courteous airline personnel, who only utter well-rehearsed sentences, clearly conveying that they mean business. Since most visa wives travel alone, their husbands having left earlier, the ordeal of international travel, with all its complexities and norms, is more than a regular challenge. It requires a lot of courage.

This airport seemed to be the last link connecting Sathya to her home and everything she had known so far. How would she be able to snap ties? Should she still decide to stay back? Board that flight and you cannot come back. How would the journey turn out?

It was still summer in the US when Kaushalya joined her husband there. She knew her in-laws were still furious with her for choosing to leave them to join Prakash. Her parents too tried to reason with her. 'Why do you want to throw away your career?'

She fought hard to suppress her tears in the cab. What a day! At the office, she had worked all morning to finish pending work before leaving for her six months' leave. Her colleagues were buzzing around. She thanked her boss in her head a million times. If only he had pushed for her on-site opportunity, though.

She checked her list of documents one last time—her valid passport stamped with the H4 visa, Form I-797 which was actually her H4 visa petition approval, photocopies—of her husband's H1B visa and his passport since she was travelling alone, copy of his Form I-179 which was his H1B visa petition approval, an invitation letter by the client company inviting Prakash to work in the US, her own company's No Objection Certificate for her to travel to the US because she was still employed. She also had a letter from Prakash's company, validating her as Prakash's wife, even though she was carrying their original marriage certificate. Why take chances?

When she stepped out of the door of her rental apartment she turned back to take one last look at her first home after marriage. 'Bye, baby! I will miss you,' she whispered.

That day, she had worn a pair of jeans paired with a casual top. It was the first time she had worn Western casuals in her in-laws' presence. By the time their cab slowed down at Indira Gandhi International Airport, Delhi, her entire family was in tears.

For Sarika, the thought of leaving her parents behind was too much. They all accompanied her to the airport to see her off. She was angry at having to leave her country at all. Her mother-in-law's nonchalant rejection of her during their recent war of words was still stinging. When her husband had insisted that her parents pay for her visa, she realized she was not sure if she should trust the guy she had married.

One look at Shamshabad airport's vastness and she shuddered. Till then, her journeys outside home had been limited to bus journeys to office and back, and before that, to the college she studied at. She rarely went out, except occasionally with her cousins. Here she was, clutching her bundle of documents, with her husband's million instructions echoing in her head.

Sarika managed to maintain a cool façade, while going through one of the toughest moments of her life. She was leaving her parents—for good. Her throat felt choked and her hands felt numb and lifeless. Everything felt eerie—almost surreal.

By the time Sathya arrived at the airport, well in time for her departure, she was exhausted. The past few weeks had been chaotic. Trips to the doctor to ensure she did not carry her cough and cold into the flight, along with winding up the house and cleaning up the apartment, had left her with no time to so much as glance at her appearance. 'All these years, he managed the show. Suddenly, he wants me to take charge!' she had complained to her cousin.

It was midnight. Her flight was at 3 a.m. Was she carrying all the right documents? Would she be able to call up Surya from the transit airport? After the confusion at the visa interview, she had to be careful. A part of her wanted to escape from it all. She took a picture with her family and cousins before bidding them goodbye. They all managed to hold themselves together somehow, and so did she.

Kaushalya's flight to Los Angeles was routed through Singapore and Tokyo. At Changi Airport, Singapore, she looked around, and was thrilled to discover a beautiful indoor hanging garden, complete with palm trees and a picturesque ceiling. It was almost like stepping into another world. She could lounge there all day. A mini-tram was moving between terminals with luggage. What a contrast from the IGI airport at Delhi! True, they had tried to make the Delhi airport world-class, but this was a different level of beauty altogether.

'Even the toilets had vases with fresh roses. If we tried that in India, people would steal the roses to gift to their loved ones. I was not sure if I would ever come to Singapore again. So I bought jade jewellery worth $70 as a souvenir.'

A layover airport can turn into a nightmare even for experienced travellers, subject to delays, clashes in flight timings, confusion due to lack of signage or guidance or one's understanding of the same, and flight cancellations. No one knows these travails better than the to-be visa wife, who must navigate her way through them, often all by herself, and be in time at the right departure gate. Kaushalya was less worried than most visa wives because she started to treat the journey as an adventure, and partly because her transit airport was a grand tourist spot with endless attractions to interest her. She recalls how fascinated she was, what a pleasurable experience she had while travelling, and how the thought of visiting tourist spots in the US had helped her look forward to the trip.

In sharp contrast, Sathya's layover was an ordeal. She got off at Heathrow Airport in London, where she needed to wait for four hours for her next flight. She had to navigate a real-life maze of moving walkways, escalators, a terminal train, and finally the lounge. Any query to the airline and airport staff about directions to her next terminal was answered with the same, cold sentence: 'Please follow the purple signs.'

'Are these people robots?' she fumed to herself. 'Can they not be more warm and helpful?'

The lounge was huge, and dominated by a Starbucks cafe. 'So this is Starbucks!' she thought. It was 2011, years before Starbucks made its entry in India. Back then, it was that luxury coffee chain one only heard of in the media. She spotted other Indians and noticed that, unlike her, they all wore Western clothes. She suddenly felt out of place. Every few minutes, she ran her hand instinctively over the pocket of her backpack where she had kept her passport and documents. 'Be very careful. Keep checking your items. Do not leave things here and there,' her husband had warned her repeatedly. She felt tired of being scared and perpetually on high alert.

Though Revathi had travelled to the US earlier on a B1 visa, mixed emotions now filled her as she absent-mindedly scanned the crowd of strangers. She had had to leave her job behind. It was a new feeling—one that she was unable to comprehend. Was it fear? What would her equation with her husband be like after all the time they had spent apart? she wondered.

Scenes flashed by in front of her eyes—her parents, with their tearful smiles, as they bid her farewell; various moments of success and failure at work, tying the knot with the man she thought was the love of her life. She did not want to watch movies on her flight. She simply closed her eyes and let the drone of the airplane drown out her thoughts.

Sarika somehow managed to get through the transit airport without trouble. She was in a trance. A battle raged inside her head even as she flitted between sleep and wakefulness. Was she really on a plane to the US? Was her husband, Sairam, a monster? What awaited her in the new country? Was she headed for a disaster?

It suddenly occurred to her that she was alone. Her thoughts went back to what had happened in the months preceding her wedding. Her uncle had died tragically. The good daughter that she was, she did not dare dream of a

Prince Charming while she was growing up. She obeyed her parents and said 'yes' to the man they chose for her. She went out of her way to prove she was their 'little girl'. She wanted to protect their name in family and society. She was strong and brave. She would protect their honour and fight the world for it.

'Do you need to order something?'

Sarika's reverie was interrupted by her co-passenger's query. He was from her city, and on his way to America on an assignment. He struck up a conversation, and soon she was sharing her one big fear with him. Would she be turned away at the Port of Entry in the US?

'He told me I had over-prepared. There was no need for all the documents my husband had forced me to carry,' she recalls ruefully, unhappy at the memory of the stress she went through.

A sense of foreboding had plagued Vanitha too when she was on the way to board her flight to Atlanta, Georgia, seventeen years ago. Halfway during the flight, someone had tapped her on the shoulder. To her horror, a bottle of pickle, in her hand baggage stashed in the overhead bin, was dripping oil. The gentleman sitting right underneath it bore the brunt of her folly. His shirt was stained. She apologized profusely, nearly in tears. Luckily, he took it kindly. Even so, the embarrassment was too much for her to bear.

Usually, a window seat is a luxury for a woman travelling such distances. It doesn't make much of a difference when you are up in the air because all you can see are blankets of clouds for hours on end. It's only when

the flight takes off or lands, or when you can spot the
ground below mid-flight, that it matters. Sathya looked
out of the window often during her journey. Back in
India, clouds of various heights and shapes drifting past
had always inspired her to write down her thoughts, and
she would happily pull out a paper and pen and jot down
poetry or reflective articles.

Three hours into the flight, the pilot announced they
were forced to return to London because of a technical
snag. They were then flying over the Atlantic Ocean.
Sathya froze in fear. Would she sink and drown without
a trace? Unease gripped the passengers, even as placating
announcements were made and the crew sprang into
action. Soon enough, another announcement informed
them that once in London, a different flight would be
organized for the passengers to continue their journey.

Once she had landed at Heathrow, she managed to call
her husband for a minute, her throat still choked up with
fright that had made her wonder if she would ever talk
to him again. The airline had distributed compensatory
food vouchers to the passengers, but Sathya struggled to
find something vegetarian to eat, eventually settling for
a banana, an apple and a bottle of water. A few hours
on, now on the substitute flight, Sathya's heart leapt to
her throat again as the plane wobbled uncertainly, hit by
turbulence. The seatbelt signs blinked on, but there was
no announcement this time. Were they going to crash?
Why were the other passengers so calm? They were again
over the Atlantic Ocean. She tried catching a wink of
sleep, but couldn't.

Pooja's story was different. Even before they got married, Pooja's fiancé, Pratik, booked tickets for the two of them to fly together to the US. He had heard his friend and his wife's bitter experience when she travelled alone, and didn't want Pooja to go through that. Although Pooja was a smart girl hailing from the metropolitan city of Mumbai, Pratik did not want to take any chances. He understood that she would have her hands full, dealing with the trauma of leaving her family behind.

Their wedding, like any other Indian wedding, had had its share of drama. The two had travelled to Chennai, six hours away from their hometown, to catch their flight, and then had to check in three hours prior, as per norms for international flights. The nine hours before their flight actually took off to London seemed like eternity to Pooja and Pratik. Pooja was calm as she said her farewells. The couple was so tired they fell asleep the moment they settled down in the plane. When she woke up, they were flying over a desert—dusty sands that stretched to the horizon. Suddenly, she started missing her father, and felt restless. The enormity of her move hit her now. She became desperate to talk to him. Pratik asked the crew for details about where exactly they could find pay phones at the transit airport, and discussed with her the few things they had to do as soon as they landed. Their layover time at London was forty-five minutes. When the plane landed, they were alert and waiting, and stayed ahead of the remaining passengers. 'I planned in my head how to go about looking for the phone booth and rushed there. He rushed in another direction to the nearest foreign currency exchange counter and got me some pounds. Fast enough, I spoke to my dad and felt relieved.' Pooja acknowledges that such an exercise would have been near-impossible had she been alone.

When the time came for Rani to travel with her three-year-old and eleven-month-old girls to the US, it was unthinkable for her to travel by herself. Her husband Kant flew down to Patna, and the family took their flight to New York together.

Kant took care of the elder daughter during their journey, while Rani focused on her toddler, fed her once in a while, cradled her to sleep and held her when she cried. Travelling with babies was not easy. But having the father around made things easier.

Vijaya flew on an F1 visa. She was a student, getting ready to join classes in a week. The difference—she was a bride too. Between naps on the long flight, Vijaya reflected on her struggle for the past two years. However, that wasn't the only thought that filled her head. She pondered over the future—she would have to dive right in, from the word go, to be a student and wife simultaneously. The next two years would be about so much more than assignments, lectures and research.

6

That First Feeling

Any visa wife will tell you how the very nanosecond you step out of the airport on foreign soil is a memory that stays with you for the rest of your life.

I can remember in graphic detail, for instance, the dim yellow lights, the cold air that hit my cheeks, the emptiness outside the airport, the shock of actually getting clearance from the luggage scanning area, to stepping out into the city outside, the confusion about what time of day or night it might be in that new world outside the airport . . .

If you think your journey from India to the US was the longest flight of your life, the journey from your flight seat to the airport's arrival lounge where your loved one may be waiting, or where you will take a cab, will seem longer still. The big wall between you and the rest of America was inside the terminal. It was called the Port of Entry, which decided whether you would be allowed to step out of the airport to live with your loved one, or sent back home without letting you get a glimpse of your waiting family.

Glimpses of landscape as you step out of the airport are your first ever impressions of the land. First impressions are lasting, even if your thoughts evolve over time. By this point of time, your body clock has gone awry, and your mind and heart race in anticipation of what is to come. You can calm yourself by focusing on working out the logistics, and observing the differences in everything around you from what it is like back home.

Vijaya and her husband, who were travelling together, were exhausted by the time they joined the immigration queue at the airport. They were in for a shock when he was pulled aside for a random check. Vijaya waited with bated breath as her husband was asked questions that ranged from why he had travelled to India after his master's from one city and entered the US now through another, why he was landing in a city so far from his original destination, and so on. The couple had separate visas—he had H1, and she had F1.

They had landed at Newark, New Jersey, and were headed for Durham in North Carolina. They missed the connecting flight that afternoon and had to take the evening flight instead. Consequently, they were unable to pick up the keys to their new apartment from the leasing officer, which left them with no place to stay that night. Luckily, Vijaya's husband's friend picked them up at the airport and invited them to stay with him at his bachelor pad for the night.

'We got home-cooked food and a warm welcome from my husband's friend and his flatmates. In our apartment, we would have been in an empty house with nothing to do,' she said, opting to see the silver lining instead of the grey cloud.

Aruna landed on Valentine's Day in 2003, in Brooklyn, across the East River from the Big Apple. The difference between her and millions of other visa wives was that she was on the coveted H1 visa. Her perception of the trip, and her thoughts on arrival were very different. Jet-lagged, she took a cab from the airport to her hotel. The new place did give her some jitters.

Three years later, Aruna landed at Pittsburgh, her new home, as a newly-wed, with a feeling of déjà vu. Her husband's uncle lived in Pittsburgh, so there was someone to pick the couple up from the airport. Aruna was elated. It was a form of escape from the responsibilities that dogged her at home. The anonymity that Pittsburgh, and the US in general, would give her, was comforting.

Eighteen hours after she bid adieu to her parents and in-laws, Pooja was surprised by the long queue at the Port of Entry. She was weary after the long flight, but having her husband by her side was a relief. 'I got busy watching people of different ages and nationalities. Their hairstyles were all so different! I like hairstyles of different kinds,' she remembers.

Pooja was familiar with American accents, having worked at an American company in Mumbai. She felt confident about being able to answer the Port of Entry officer's questions.

'Do you know that you are on H4 and you are not allowed to work?' the lady at the counter asked her.

'Yes,' said Pooja.

'Yes,' came from her husband too.

'I did not ask you; I asked her,' the officer snapped at him. The two were, however, let go without further ado.

Outside the airport, the newly-weds got a warm welcome from his cousin's family. As they were driven from the airport to their would-be hometown an hour away, she was struck by the cleanliness outside the airport, but much more by the chill in the air and the fall scenery. 'We had landed at about 5.30 p.m. It was dry all around. Trees had no leaves. No greenery. People back home talked so much about America and its greenery. Was all that an exaggeration?' she remembers wondering. A winter arrival in America's north can jolt you, especially if you are not used to the cold.

When Sarika saw Sairam waiting for her, holding a bunch of flowers, she did not quite know how to react. Inside her head roared a million thoughts and questions: 'Is he really my "husband"? Is he the one I must spend my life with?'

She was in a daze. In her mind, she was still in Hyderabad, flitting between a scoffing mother-in-law and her parents who probably felt wronged. Her grief was compounded by her guilt at not having been able to mourn her recently deceased uncle. She wanted to cry her heart out, but her tears were stuck in her throat. And here she was, about to begin the next phase of her life with a stranger.

Others in the arrival lounge were busy greeting their loved ones with hugs and smiles. Sairam, the stranger, was standing patiently, holding a bouquet for her.

He smiled, happy that his bride had arrived at last. She was in a different world, though.

Sairam had heard of brides blushing at the sight of their husbands. He hoped she would be happy after having spent some quality time with his mother for the past two months. After all, his mother had wanted to know the new bride better before packing her off to her son. His mother knew what was best for him. And he hoped that his wife would have learnt some homemaking skills by now. He knew the wedding did not go as it should have. He had lost his cool a couple of times too, but then, 'such things happen during weddings', he justified to himself.

'The luxuries of our new home will make her happy,' he tried to placate himself. This was a fairy-tale marriage for a girl brought up in the protective confines of a joint family. Her colourless face jolted him. When she smiled, it was forced, not the smile that had greeted him effortlessly when he had first met her. Her eyes wanted to tell him something. He gave her the flowers and took her luggage cart. Throughout the two hours it took them to reach home, she hardly spoke a word.

He had expected her to chatter on. She was not interested in anything. She was exhausted. Clean roads, speeding cars on the highway and open skies, they all flitted by as she remained in her reverie.

Sathya was the last to join her immigration clearance queue. She had to use the bathroom, and was yet to fill up her I-94 form that the crew had given her on the flight. 'If you want to kill me, let me see my husband just once,' she had bargained with God during the turbulence a few hours before.

A brush with possible death mid-air numbs you for a while at least. And so Sathya walked to the officer's desk with lowered confidence. She missed the customary greeting because she did not know it.

That was not how she greeted strangers in India. She assumed the officer would treat her the way Indian officials did, with minimal eye contact and an authoritative tone.

'How do you greet people in your country?' he asked condescendingly. Was it fatherly?

She folded her hands and showed him, 'Namaste'. It occurred to her later that he might have just been annoyed that she did not say, 'Hello, how are you?'

He found her unapologetic 'Namaste' amusing.

'Why are you here?'

'I'm here to join my husband.' She could not avoid a smile. It was shameless glee. Was she being stupid? Damn those mid-air frights.

'You carrying any seeds? Or rice?'

'No.'

'Is this your first time in America?'

'Yes,' she smiled again. A friend had coached her to say things like, 'I want to do some Christmas shopping' or 'I want to travel to "so and so" places'. She had forgotten it all.

He directed her to place her hands for biometric printing. He wrote down a date on her passport after stamping it and said, 'Welcome.'

'Thank you,' she chirped. On her way out, she quickly peeked at her passport for the 'date' that had been stamped on it. She noted with relief that it was valid for her husband's duration of stay.

Before she could rush out into her husband's arms, she had to collect her heavy luggage. Her suitcases had been pulled off the conveyor belts, and were waiting for her when she arrived. She could not lift them, and hoped to find helpful fellow Indians. To her horror, she realized she would have to pay for a trolley! The train of trolleys was chained to a pay machine that had slots. For the first time in the whole journey, her dollar currency came handy. Four dollars. She converted it into Indian currency in her head, multiplying by fifty.

'Two hundred Indian rupees to use a cart!'

A staff member helped her use the machine by inserting her currency notes. A passenger came to her rescue by lifting her suitcases onto the trolley.

On her way out, a woman security officer stopped her. An elderly Indian couple ahead of her had also been stopped, but then the elderly are always suspect, with their penchant for carrying pickles and grocery items, she thought.

'What do you have in your luggage?' she was asked by the woman. No smile, no frown.

Tips from her friends ran in her head. 'Walk confidently. Do not fumble with your words when you answer queries. Be calm.' 'Cooked food is always allowed, just like processed food.' She had not carried her homoeopathic medicines as she could not find a doctor's prescription for them.

'I have clothes, medicines with their prescriptions, and cooked food, because my family was worried about my food,' she rattled on.

'What kind of food?'

'Idlis,' she said.

'What is idlis?'

'It's made with rice flour and is a steamed dish.'

'Flower?'

'No, flour as in F, L, O, U, R,' she spelt it out for the officer. 'Do I need to get it scanned?' she added, confidence personified.

'No, you can go. Have a happy stay.'

Things that mid-air frights can do!

Sathya raced out with her trolley before anyone else could stop her. She spotted Surya and ran to him. He was quick to greet her, but didn't give her a hug. He was with a senior colleague who had given him a ride. When the gentleman excused himself to make a call, the two hugged tight. All their tiffs and tears melted away. She had nearly lost him, had she not?

Running into her husband's arms was what Revathi did too, when she landed at Atlanta.

'Finally made it,' she thought upon landing. The arrival airport was a frenzy of activity and everyone was in a hurry to get somewhere. Post-immigration, having collected her baggage after an interminable wait, she finally began walking towards the exit. It was late in the evening. The winter cold sent chills down her spine. Her eyes desperately looked for her husband, Arun.

'It felt like I was meeting him for the first time all over again. I felt so emotional to finally be with him. Yet, I also could not shake off the uneasy feeling of having left behind a part of me in India,' she remembers.

The cold is the first thing most women notice when they arrive in winter. The period from the end of September to December is officially called 'fall'. Try convincing a fresh-off-the-boat arrival (FOB is an accepted acronym among immigrants) about it. If you arrive in the months of January or February, you will be greeted by the sight of snow. Imagine being a snow-starved desi who gets a white welcome when you step out of the bland artificiality of the airport, where there is no traffic, to add to your sense of wonder.

Vijaya talks of how, after having lived in congested Bengaluru, she found Durham in North Carolina a village in comparison. 'A smaller city, with vast expanses of land, limited bus transport, shopping complexes spread far apart, no people on the streets . . . ' She remembers how in Bengaluru she could go from anywhere to anywhere by simply hopping on to an autorickshaw, or her two-wheeler.

'If I had landed in a city like New York, it would have been a different first impression of the country,' says the software techie who moved to Seattle, Washington, thereafter.

New York, Manhattan to be precise, is a different world. In New York City, streets remain crowded till late in the night. It is where you would be least likely to feel lonely. For an Indian, used to packed Indian cities, New York feels like home the minute one sets foot in it. Its jutting skyscrapers, traffic, trains, taxis, parks and a multilingual and multicultural population make the transition less traumatic, though the cost of living is astronomical.

Most of us don't get to be in the Big Apple, however. A chunk of the Indian population settles down in towns peripheral to big cities. A larger chunk moves to towns that simply have no big cities near them. A city-dweller would squirm at the thought of moving to a smaller town in India because everything suddenly gets more difficult—access to public transport, good hospitals, social occasions, concerts, products, necessities such as water and electricity, and the 'big-city dweller' label.

Not so when you move to this side of the globe. Smaller cities and towns here have their own share of warmth. Like India, transport is left to the affordability of individuals in the US when it comes to smaller towns. But the roads are good. And the traffic law-abiding. IT, pharma and biotech majors do not shy away from setting shop in small towns, especially if it means tax incentives and a cheaper workforce. Walmarts and Targets, Pizza Huts, Walgreens and Dunkin Donuts usually exist not far from home if you are a town-dweller. While individual brands of stores might not be available everywhere, there is no dearth of convenience and grocery stores, medical stores and coffee shops irrespective of the town or city you are in. The dynamics do change in the villages, but in a country heavily oriented towards car ownership, it is unlikely that you will find villagers with no personal transport of their own.

Lack of heavy traffic on roads is initially disconcerting for migrants from India, but what is even more shocking is when you hardly find any multistorey buildings unless you are in a metropolis. You wonder why the traffic is so orderly, why the places look so desolate, why the buildings look so boring, why it is all so silent. You will at least be able to notice skyscrapers if you land at New York, LA, or maybe Chicago.

Suddenly, those smells, smoke, sounds of fights with autorickshaw drivers are what you want around you. Look out of the car window, and you will thirst for vehicles other than cars and trucks. Autorickshaws that flood our metros and become India's souvenirs or even the two-wheelers that are omnipresent in India are simply absent here. Do these people even know what a scooter is? You cannot help but wonder.

'This country has no smells. Strangely, even *hing* (asafoetida), which is so basic to our kitchen, does not have its smell here. Fruits that you buy at the store have no flavour,' says an exasperated Alladi Jayasri. She did not miss India in the beginning. On her first visit to a local grocery store the evening she landed, she was fascinated to find some Indian vegetables. Beans, peas and greens are commonly available at your regular American grocery store. The difference is that you visit grocers once a week to stock your refrigerator, which is something a newcomer from India finds hard to do, habituated as he or she is to neighbourhood shopping and doorstep vendors. Jayasri also realized she could not just drop by at a cousin's place near her Basavangudi home in Bengaluru any more. Visiting friends in the new country meant calling up in advance and making plans.

Orderliness can feel cumbersome when you've lived in chaos for a long time and are used to mayhem. The luxury that you chased till now and suddenly found becomes perplexing.

7

The Shock Begins

Arrival in an alien land can entail a certain amount of shock. Sarika, for instance, has blocked out the memory of those first few months in the US. When asked about that time, her anger rises with each passing minute as she begins to narrate what happened.

When Sarika reached Sairam's apartment, it felt like it belonged to another world. She felt as if she had been torn away from her joint family household and transplanted into a claustrophobic, one-bedroom home. It was a basement apartment with a bedroom that had one small window. She felt like throwing up.

She had given up her job, her parents, her city, her neighbourhood, her cousins, her friends, for this 'new life'? There was silence all around. Did human beings not exist in this place? Why did it resemble a graveyard? She felt her throat choke. The new reality was too difficult for her to deal with. She wanted to rush back to Hyderabad, hug her mother and cry.

'Culture shock' was a term coined during the 1960s and has since been repeated in cinema, soaps, magazines and all sorts of other media. The Oxford Dictionary defines it as 'the feeling of disorientation experienced by someone who is suddenly subjected to an unfamiliar culture, way of life or set of attitudes'. The term has become an empty cliché unable to convey the kind of hellish experiences that accompany the phenomenon.

Culture shock was spoken about in the past, yes, but larger immigration debates did not attach the words to immigrant women as much as they should have. As a dependent visa wife, you do not understand the real meaning behind those two words when you hop on to the flight after tearful partings—or even when you step out at the airport in America. You do not understand you are going through 'shock'. It is depression, really, because of the overwhelming reality of empty surroundings, the horror of silence—at home, outdoors, on the road, even in public places. It is the realization that you must live with that silence for god knows how long. The true meaning of 'culture shock', depression and similar terms dawns on you when you have survived the phase and are out of it.

Lugging her monstrous suitcases through the building's walkway after 10.30 p.m., Surya cautioned Sathya to be as soundless as possible. She was surprised to find her husband take extra care to not make noise. A little dog barked next door, probably disturbed by their movements.

It was cold outside and she was grateful to be inside their new apartment. That was when she noticed the carpeted staircase, a tingling feeling under her feet.

'This will take some getting used to!' she thought, delighted. The floor rug stretched wall to wall, everywhere. They called the mezzanine floor their second floor, and the ground floor was actually a basement.

'Get used to these,' said Surya, smiling away, gleefully showing her the hall and dining area, plus the little kitchen with a life-sized window. It was a two-bedroom apartment. The hall had a huge French door too that opened into the balcony. She was excited, and chatted away about her flight, the mid-air fright, her fear that she would not meet him ever, her unusual confidence at the Port of Entry, the food and people on the flight. He told her how heartbroken he had been when she had called from Heathrow after her plane's emergency landing.

When she woke up sometime during the night, she found her husband in tears. 'They may send me back soon. They won't let me stay I guess,' he said. 'But why?' she was concerned. His new bosses kept threatening to pack him off if he did not work well. He was dedicated to his job and good at it too. She assured him it would all work out. Even though she didn't want to go back to India, she assured him that if needed they would go back home happily.

When she woke up next, it was late morning.

'My friend's outside the building. He wants to come over,' said her husband.

'Don't bother to tidy the place up,' he added in response to the panic in her eyes. The friend came in and they spoke for a few minutes. She ran to the kitchen to try and organize some coffee. Where was the coffee powder? The fridge looked like it could hold a house. She heard the door shut.

'Why were you so curt with him?' she asked her husband.

'He stood outside the door and said, "I want to meet your wife." How should I have reacted?'

'Is he married?' she asked.

'Yeah. But his wife is in India. She's from a village and too young for him.'

Sathya's hopes of a potential friend fell like a wicket.

Aruna's first few days at her husband's friend's home in Pittsburgh brought her face to face with the realities of her new life as a visa wife. Her husband had to go to work the very next day.

'So what will your husband take for his dabba?' her host, the friend's wife, asked her. 'That was when it hit me that now I had to worry about my husband's lunch,' says Aruna, a dazed bride then.

It was not just the newness of Pittsburgh that was disconcerting. Her own position in life had changed.

Most brides, however emancipated they are and however liberal their husbands might be, face the reality of needing to cook during their first week of marriage. Going through that realization for the first time in the US, on a dependent visa, can make you feel as if you have been enslaved.

In the absence of immediate family, Aruna would look at storage boxes on her friend's kitchen shelves for an idea of how many she must buy for her own home. 'How did she know how many spoons to buy? How did she calculate the number of boxes? How did she know what and how much groceries to buy?'

One morning, in her new apartment, Aruna called her husband with a peculiar problem. She could not figure out which remote was meant for what. She was no stranger to technology, but she grappled with the newness of it all. It was not India where she could knock on the neighbour's door for a cup of curd. 'In a new situation, even a TV remote becomes a big problem!'

In the first few weeks post-wedding, Indian brides grappling with the newness, and expectations, of post-wedding domesticity feel the need to prove themselves at things they have never done before. These first few weeks in the US are also when another painful reality hits hard. If you are on the East Coast, you must wait for morning so that it is night in India to make your phone calls. It dawns on you that you cannot call your parents up so frequently during the day because they are in a different time zone on the other end of the planet, and your afternoon is their midnight.

Aruna's major problem was the ubiquitous TV remote, which she found nerve-wracking. 'With about four remotes for the TV, I could not figure out how to use them. I had to call my husband to figure them out.'

What is the big deal about a TV remote? Look at it this way—a woman gives up her family, her life, her financial stability and everything she could call her own, to follow her husband to the very country she earlier visited as a 'high skills worker', and is doing all she can to be the kind of woman she has never needed to be—the homemaker. The new home is her life's new jigsaw puzzle that she must hold together by fixing the right pieces in the right sequence. The new arrangement keeps her on her toes—housekeeping, cooking, cleaning, decorating, stock-taking, playing host, playing the *bahu*. Her dependent loneliness eats into her confidence. One's mind is so dazed taking in everything that a TV remote's annoying buttons can be another big challenge for the day.

On the second day of her arrival, Sairam drove Sarika to Virginia to meet her college friend and cheer her up. She had spent a long time the previous night clutching a photograph of her family and crying.

The trip to Virginia would give them a breather, or so Sairam thought. He hoped it would give her a chance to feel at home with her childhood friend. Sarika sobbed all the while she was there about losing out in life. By the time they started driving back to Delaware, she started talking gibberish and threw up in the car. After a minute or so, she fell unconscious. She remembers being carried into a hospital and waking up once in a while when she would become violent. Whenever she saw her husband or spoke to him on the phone, she went ballistic, demanding that her parents be brought to her. When her parents tried to calm her down on the phone, she was suspicious they were someone else pretending to be them.

Sairam was confused. He had done her no wrong. Why was she treating him like he was the bad guy? What was happening to her? He knew that if his family came to know about her condition, they would label her insane and fight with her parents. He was not willing to risk telling his parents the truth, but he was forced to keep her parents in the loop. He did confide in his brother, who was studying in another city in the US.

Even if she survived this illness, would their marriage survive? Should something happen, he would be blamed for her plight. His future suddenly seemed uncertain. Should he send her back home? Or stand by his wife? Now was not a moment of choice. He wanted her back in his life. And he decided to do whatever it took to ensure this.

For five days, Sarika was on sedatives. He slept in his car on the first night. The following nights, he stayed with a friend. Sarika would not eat hospital food, insisting that she would only eat food cooked by her mother. He tried to get her to eat food from Indian restaurants, but she refused. Five days later, she calmed down. She was kept under observation for a week more. In the medical records, her condition was described as 'Post-Traumatic Stress Disorder'.

Sarika returned to playing the role of a newly-wed wife, and began visiting an Indian psychiatrist. She thought she was adjusting. Soon, however, her homesickness came back to haunt her. She started to feel suicidal.

Sairam often took her to nearby tourist spots. But it did nothing to boost her spirits. Neither did the constant support of their Indian neighbour who tried her best to match the taste of her mother's cooking. Anti-depressants prescribed by her psychiatrist made her so drowsy that she slept all day. Intimacy with her husband was out of the question. She could not forgive him for all the drama that happened at their wedding. She did not feel particularly comfortable with the psychiatrist she went to either.

The one-bedroom apartment suffocated her. She wanted to go home immediately. For her husband, it was a tough call. He had already made two trips to India in a span of eight months. He could not send her alone. The following Thanksgiving, he travelled with her to India, with no certainty of her return. He took her to a psychiatrist in Secunderabad, fixed her appointments and returned to the US.

Of course, not every visa wife experiences the kind of trauma that Sarika did. The stress of transplanting can kill perfectly healthy plants, and here we are talking of educated women who were used to living their life the way they preferred, liked their jobs, and who were expected to adjust immediately to a country so foreign from theirs, in conditions controlled by others.

Kaushalya was over the moon when she arrived in the States. She did not know that it was because she was in the honeymoon phase of the 'culture shock bell-curve'. She was excited. She went about setting up home, happily arranging the plastic boxes she brought from India to store groceries. She found a way of washing large milk jars and using them to store lentils and flour, all stacked horizontally on the kitchen rack. Every evening, her new friends from the apartment community would turn up to chat. To her shock, a neighbour complained to the management about the noise levels of these impromptu chat sessions.

One evening, her husband's colleagues, an Indian couple, invited them to something they referred to as a 'management programme'. They offered them a ride too, saying the programme would be an excellent opportunity for them to explore since she could look for work. When Kaushalya and Prakash reached the venue, they realized the trap. It was a direct marketing company and they had been set up to be recruited as salespersons. She was hurt. She did not think people would exploit their circumstances, especially their newness. Kaushalya and her husband wriggled out of the event with some difficulty. It taught them not to trust people based solely on the country of their origin.

When Shivani arrived in Portland, Oregon, as a new bride, it was to an unfurnished apartment and a nearly empty kitchen. Her husband soon drove her over to a Safeway grocery store where she read the price tags of vegetables with horror. Converting them into rupees gave her the jitters about surviving in the country.

Over the next few days and weeks, her husband took her to the same chain because he trusted their quality. 'I was naïve. I asked my husband, 'Is the US full of Safeways?' The only places we ventured to outside home were grocery stores because we needed supplies,' she says.

Often, spouses like Shivani's do not realize that their wives need to be eased into the new lifestyle. In her new apartment, Rupashree's advantage was a lovely view of the skyline. Her baby kept her busy. With the arrival of fall, the Kolkata lass had difficulty adjusting to the temperature outside her home. Her new neighbours seemed friendly, but her husband had told her to maintain a distance from them. She hardly stepped out unless it was to shop for groceries. The couple did not buy a cot or 'bed with a mattress', as it was called locally. They preferred to sleep on the floor, and got new quilt-style bedsheets called 'comforters'. Their bedroom was empty but for the bundle of pillows and comforters.

She spent the first three months by the floor-to-ceiling window, holding her baby, looking out to the sky, to the horizon, and sometimes below, looking for signs of life in the parking lot outside her home.

8

A New Life

The most common question that yet-to-fly H1B visa holders ask their friends in the US is, 'How much do I need per month in order to sustain myself?' The question is really prompted by people's need to save every dollar earned and spend as little as possible. 'Do not come with that attitude,' we usually warn our friends. 'It makes it all the more difficult to survive.' But we have discovered that a person determined to clear debts back home or send money for a dear one's treatment will not be deterred.

After they arrive, our friends do ease up on travelling to new places in the new country, even if they calculate every small expense. The newly arrived visa wife wants to set up her new home. She may want new friends. She may look forward to doing many things she could not in India. Reality soon hits her in the form of logistical difficulties, a spouse who is still steeped in the taboos of the motherland, with ill health and unfriendly weather at times thrown in. A sociable woman might find herself suffering from social anxiety. When there are children to give her company, her situation is slightly better. But innate fears of a new place are natural and a visa wife must experience these.

As the weeks rolled by, the vista views from Rupashree's bedroom window ceased to excite her. She slowly adjusted to her new life with her baby in tow. She does not recall being depressed, but she was lonely. She longed for someone Indian, someone familiar, someone she could feel safe with. She longed for companionship. Her husband's arrival was the most welcome part of her day. With the winter timings for daylight so different from her days in Kolkata, it was night by the time he came home.

She took solace in the fact that her L2 visa permitted her to work. She did not know American English but was willing to learn. Yet, leaving her child in a day care centre was out of the question. She calculated the costs, and realized that most of her salary would go towards day care. Ever mindful that her man had come here to earn and save money, she took care to not spend much on herself.

Companies usually pay relocation expenses to skilled workers with families so that they can set up home, which new arrivals either use as a deposit for their rental apartment or save up. Finances in the initial months are used to set up the basics, with no clue about how long one may actually stay put in the new place.

Outside her apartment building, Rupashree noticed a huge trash bin. It did not stink, and neither would dogs and other animals scavenge there. One of her husband's colleagues quipped that they should look for treasures outside the garbage bin. If people wanted to discard their furniture without putting them in thrift stores, they simply left them at the garbage bin. It was considered perfectly fine for people to pick up furniture left by a bin.

Every time Rupashree spotted a discarded piece of furniture outside the bin, she would drag it home up two storeys. She wanted to support her husband by making every effort to save money.

Rani's two children would keep her busy during the day. She had never wanted to come to the US, so it was a matter of 'how many days more before we can save up enough to go home'. She made sure her children video-chatted with her family. Her mornings flew by on the phone and video chat. When the kids slept in the afternoon, Rani experienced pangs of loneliness and fear. Sometimes, she would hear ambulance or police sirens but did not have the courage to step out and check.

Sometimes she would wake up her elder child and say she was scared, unable to take the silence. The little girl understood. 'Don't worry. I won't sleep,' she would tell her mother. Rani knows today that it was silly. She still wonders how a four-year-old understood her predicament.

Women like Rupashree and Rani often live away from the traditional desi hubs of shopping, such as Devon Avenue in Chicago, Oak Tree Road in New Jersey or Artesia in Los Angeles. Such places make them feel more at home and lessen the shock of leaving their homes behind. If tucked away in some faraway town with no transportation, the possibility of meeting friends is dim, especially in winter.

'The first winter is hard,' is an oft-quoted phrase. 'Please ask her to be patient. When spring arrives, she will have many friends,' my husband's new colleagues told him. I was a snow-starved Indian then, and dreamt of being surrounded by white—on top of homes, cars, roads, trees, everything on the path.

When it actually snowed, I went crazy. You are lucky if you have a friend or spouse who understands that madness. Bharathi cannot forget the dream world that the first snow of her life brought her. 'I ran out in half-sleeves when the first snow came. It was so exciting!' says Madhusmita Bora who was a student of journalism at Chicago then.

Not everyone is that excited by snow. When Rani and Kant arrived with their children, they were greeted by snow everywhere. 'Not a single soul on the roads. Snow, snow, snow. I had no one to talk to!' Snow isolated Rani, she felt.

It was Sathya and Surya's wedding anniversary on a cold winter day. Sathya wanted to buy something for her husband as an anniversary gift. She had some dollars in hand. Stepping out was impossible and she was too scared to walk a mile to the mall in the cold. So she found two local florists' numbers on the Internet. It was 5 p.m. The websites said she must place orders a day in advance. She kicked herself but still tried.

One florist asked her for a credit or debit card. She had neither. No cash transactions, he was adamant. The other florist told her it was too late to deliver. She did not have Surya's credit card details. She had never felt the need till then.

It struck her then that she was not 'credit-worthy'. She was still coming to terms with not being eligible for an SSN—only a Tax Identification Number. It was a far cry from the days when she had worked in a managerial role.

Sobbing, she splashed some cold water on her face. Thankfully, the absence of a car did not mean she could not look her best for her anniversary. An Indian woman in the apartment community did basic beauty routines like threading and waxing at home. She would not style people's hair, cut or wash it, thanks to limited equipment, but was still a godsend for the Indian women of the community.

That evening, Surya and Sathya invited Surya's senior colleague and his wife out for their anniversary dinner. When they were dropped home, the lady pulled out their gift from the trunk of the car: a blender. To that she had added a set of utensils and storage bottles, all washed and ready to use, for her groceries. They had often taken Sathya and Surya for grocery shopping, and were aware of the limited resources the couple were managing with. Sathya was overwhelmed at the kind gesture. That moment made her value every little gesture of kindness she had taken for granted back home.

Surya was still being bullied at work with threats of being 'sent back to India'. They micro-managed his work and did not guide him into the move. Confidence personified in India, liked by his bosses, colleagues and clients alike, the situation was getting to him here where he was doubted and judged at every step.

Why did they move him here in the first place? 'They had to show on record to the authorities that they hired someone for that position,' he said. He was a 'formality'. They used him to train another colleague, an employee, in project management. 'Try getting out of the H1B status as soon as possible,' a friend advised. 'Look for another job. It's possible to transfer the visa,' was another piece of advice.

Prakash noticed an odd occurrence in his office in California. His non-Indian colleagues would leave by the evening but the Indian colleagues would stay on. Was it work pressure? Was it voluntary? He could not tell. When he moved to another city in the northeast, he bore the brunt of long hours. His bosses were Indian, and as exploitative as bosses back in India.

Such a situation is sure to impact family life. Sathya wondered if her husband's job was a veiled, politer form of slavery, or just a kind of cut-throat work culture. Either way, she was worried.

She could not trust anyone. Her efforts to befriend the neighbours had not worked. They barely returned her greetings. Her body was behaving oddly too. Her periods were delayed. 'It's because of the winter. When summer arrives, they will regularize,' assured her mother. Thanks to their VoIP phone subscription, she would at times make calls to her parents, cousins, aunts and friends. But in her own milieu, she developed a sort of social anxiety. Unable to talk to anyone, she would spend hours watching the kinds of films she would have otherwise baulked at. She played old film songs in Hindi, Kannada, Telugu, Tamil

and Malayalam, and binge-watched Indian TV serials
online. At times, she even missed the pollution.

Mahalakshmi, a self-assured bride, was much younger
than her husband, Anand, but gifted with maturity well
beyond her years. She often called and had video chat
sessions with her family in India. 'People got fed up after
a while and stopped taking my calls. They were avoiding
me,' she said. Mahalakshmi was no attention-seeker. She
loved her relatives and took a while to figure out that
some people in her extended family were cutting her off.

'They were jealous. They hated me for having a
"fairy-tale wedding" with a US-based groom. It was what
they had hoped for for their own children.' She was
struck by disbelief. She had not even wanted to move to
the US. Anand promised her that they would return to
India in two years. She was being a dutiful Indian wife
wherever she was. It did not matter that she was a train
ride away from Manhattan, or that if they got bored, the
couple would head to Times Square. She would have
probably gone to the movies back in Mysore if they
lived there. 'It was not as if I lived in a palace! I am just
a normal wife.'

Though she stopped chatting with those in her family
who had cut her off and immersed herself in her new life,
the separation pangs were difficult to bear. She felt betrayed.

Once spring arrived, Rupashree did not wait too long
to embark on her 'make friends' mission. She tucked her
little one into a stroller and went out for long walks. If she
spotted anyone who so much as smiled in her direction,
she greeted them and began chatting. She chose not to

step out with her husband, though. 'It is a headache to go on a walk with him. He will not spend more than two minutes talking to anyone, and will insist on getting home quickly.' Deepan was reserved. He took his own time to get close to people. Rupashree soon found herself a set of friends—all wives of her husband's colleagues.

Kaushalya had barely settled into her life in California when Prakash's project was downsized and he had to look for other options. They shifted to Vermont, which was in the northeast of the country and a three-hour difference away from California.

The very idyllic setup of a hut-shaped home surrounded by snow, with snow-laden trees all around, was something she had dreamt of for long. The moment that she peeked out of her hotel window on arrival was, however, not a happy one. Such a scene in real life startled her. Tears flowed down her cheeks. She felt lonely. No human beings were visible around that house, or on the road. Hardly any vehicles could be spotted or heard, one in fifteen minutes maybe. Her heart sank.

What she did love was the view from the deck, its cosiness, and the pine trees around. It was quieter than her California apartment community. She and Prakash soon faced another problem, though. 'I would hear someone banging a stick on my floor. It was an old man who lived downstairs. Walking with heavy steps caused his roof to vibrate.' The couple had to tiptoe around their home. Sometimes they forgot, and if he was home, he would use his stick on their floor to order silence. One evening, they had children over. They panicked. The children jumping around did invite their elderly neighbour's wrath. Their guests heard the stick rap on the floor too.

On their wedding anniversary, they planned a party. Kaushalya baked some muffins and took them to their neighbour. The man who opened the door was Caucasian, probably in his sixties.

'Hello, here is something for you.'

He accepted her gift.

'We are here to apologize for the noise,' said Kaushalya. 'We are organizing a party but will try our best not to make a noise. Hope it won't be a bother.'

'I am not such a bad guy,' he said. He lived alone. As is customary in America, he did not invite them in, but explained that his job in the timber business required odd hours, and he had lost some fingers in an accident. In that fraction of a second, the couple understood his frustration. They invited him to the party, which he excused himself from. 'Don't worry, I will not bother you,' he assured them.

One can understand from the different stories of these women that visa wives react differently to their new lives in the US. The air, the people, the roads, transport, products, homes—everything elicits a different response from every person. For most newly arrived women, their landscape shifts from the chequered and asymmetrical concreteness of their crowded cities in India to the monotony and loneliness of American towns. The pressure of population does not exist, with the exception of downtowns in large cities. Since manpower is expensive, there is a greater dependence on doing things oneself with the help of machines. Shopping, too, is product-specific. For grocery, drive to one store, for clothes, drive elsewhere, and so on. Some women interestingly find the absence of ambient noise, intrinsic to our cities, disturbing.

What is pleasant is to receive smiles and polite pleasantries from passers-by. There is a sense of language where emotions are carefully controlled.

Television is a go-to comfort for many lonely visa wives. Sathya, who loved watching American series back home, found that many of her favourites were no longer on air in the US. She realized that TV shows in America were telecast according to 'seasons'—some were beamed in winter, others in summer. The best-made shows were crime series. 'These people have too much of an appetite for crime,' she thought. The real surprise came in the form of weather channels that felt like non-stop disaster movies.

'It is so scary to watch them! It feels like you must expect a disaster around you any time,' Neha said. In her first year, Neha and her husband stuck to the basic cable connection with limited channels. The cable–Internet–phone package bills were too pricey. Neha had also heard that in the second year, cable TV firms hiked prices. Cable and Internet together cost them about $40 a month. This was the first decade of the 2000s. And it was in addition to the $120 a month for their calling card expenses. Neha, an avid news-watcher, observed, 'The way news is presented is so different. In India, the person interviewing gets way too much importance. As for the biases, they are similar to those in India. If one channel overtly supports Republicans, another goes with Democrats.'

Most Indian women prefer watching Indian serials. This presents itself as a huge market for some entertainment media firms that tailor packages accordingly, for Indians and people from other countries. The alternative is direct-to-home television, currently a rage in India. Some Indians prefer to buy streaming devices that work out cheaper, such as Chromecast and Roku.

For all the entertainment options available to them, basic problems of loneliness and alienation persist in the lives of visa wives. 'I want my mother. I want to go home,' wailed Kaushalya to her friends soon after shifting to Vermont. Prakash's H1B visa was in for an extension. Leaving the country even for a short vacation was risky. She had no choice but to wait it out. Meanwhile, she put in her papers at her job in Delhi. Extreme cold gave her cramps. Her back ached. She missed sunlight and took to swallowing Vitamin D tablets to sustain her through the weeks she was 'snowed in'.

Shivani Gupta became pregnant within a month of arriving in Portland, Oregon. The Coimbatore girl had neither settled into her marriage nor found her way through the culture shock phase. She was not prepared for anything—not the US, nor life after education. The couple was excited about the baby, though. 'I was paranoid about being childless. Friends who got married earlier were still struggling to have kids, even after as long as five years. I thought, "Let me have a child. I am going to be on H4 visa anyway."'

What she was not prepared for was the nausea and other health issues that lasted the entire nine months.

She went through the pregnancy, hormonal changes, restlessness, depression and weakness all alone. Her husband worked long hours, leaving her to fend for herself through the day. When her mother came to be with her twenty days before her delivery, she was relieved. 'My mother had to go back two months after my baby was born. I was exhausted. My baby slept at night and rarely during the day. I would have to sit with him on my lap the whole day. I was baby-sitting 24/7. I would cry endlessly. I often did not know why I was crying. Long after, I understood it was post-partum depression.'

Shivani's health woes were not limited to her pregnancy. Her body took time to adjust to Portland weather. 'I was allergic to carpet fibres, pollen and other such materials. I had allergies and cold throughout my pregnancy. I suffered for more than eight months after my pregnancy too. I could not go out for walks. It was very cold.' She longed for the physical presence of family, even if she video-chatted with them often. Her only wish today is, 'Let no girl who comes here go through what I did.'

On rare days, she would remember having been an emotionally stronger person in India. Since most of her new friends had jobs, their conversations almost always involved work. She would often get irritated when her new friends doled out advice like 'pick up a hobby', 'learn painting'. And the one she hated the most: 'Why have you not learnt driving?'

9

No Car, No Life

How you commute is a fundamental indicator of your local culture. It is indicative of a lifestyle, routine, the people you deal with, the paths you take to your destinations, and the routes, vehicles and timings you prefer.

It was the first fortnight after Bharathi's arrival at Chicago. On the weekend, her husband, Hareesh, was invited to a two-event-get-together by his employers, who were also his relatives. They had a stall at a fair, which he agreed to man on one of the two days, hoping to spend the other day with Bharathi.

His employer-relatives had tried to prevent him from bringing Bharathi to the US. She was shocked at the way he had been exploited with the promise of a 'good American life'. Still, they attended the fair. Afterwards, they had to attend a party organized by the same relatives in a nearby town. The hosts had them dropped at a traffic intersection and asked them to wait for another ride. The couple did as asked, and waited for a whole hour. Highway traffic whizzed by. 'We felt so lonely and helpless!' recalls Bharathi. In those harrowing minutes, Bharathi felt they were at other people's mercy. Her skin burnt as much with the heat as her cheeks flushed at the humiliation she felt.

An hour later, Hareesh, fighting his own guilt, helplessness and anger, called their hosts, who did not pick up. It dawned slowly that this was a deliberately delivered slight because he had stood up for himself.

Hareesh resolved to build their life in the US on his own that afternoon. Bharathi, too, decided to find a job, a sponsor for her H1B visa, and just not give up. The couple went home courtesy another colleague. The next evening, they went to the nearest car showroom and bought a car with money Hareesh had saved for health emergencies.

Thousands of families that arrive in the US on work visas soon discover the indispensability of cars. Sadly, America's public transport networks are limited to large cities. And thousands of families work or live out of the smaller cities, sometimes dotting a 100-mile radius outside large cities. In a country that places no premium on public transport, Bharathi's experience showed her how not having a car makes you a have-not. No car? Sorry, no life in the US.

Learning to drive spells freedom in the States—freedom to go to the grocery store and buy vegetables; freedom to decide what to cook for a meal; not having to beg your husband for a ride to your hobby store; not having to depend on friends for a ride to your gynaecologist.

'I miss being able to step out and hop into an autorickshaw,' says Jayasri, sitting in the cosiness of her study in Virginia. She is comfortable in her space, and is not in a hurry to learn to drive a car either. But the memory of navigating the huge city of Bengaluru without depending on family or friends, compared to the problems of commuting in the US, makes her pine for home.

Cars are loved and loathed, inextricably linked to one's status, held up as a symbol of having 'arrived', by the aspiring middle class. You will notice how the size of a small car in the US is a lot bigger than a small car in India.

In my sixth week after arrival in America, I clicked a picture of my friend's Virginia home porch and car park, where my husband and I sat on a sunny yet cold morning.

When I posted the pictures online, a comment flew by.

'Car, car, car, *yelli nodidru* car,' said a friend and fellow journalist. (*Yelli nodidru* translates as 'wherever one sees'.)

'India *nalli aache ogakke cheppli beku, illi* car *beku*,' a distant cousin commented from Arizona. ('In India you need slippers to go out of the house, here you need a car.')

It is what hits you on your first day as a visa wife—cars of all sizes, all bigger than in India, except for the odd two-seater and convertible, on bare roads. Through your initial months, the car is what decides your lack of mobility, lack of freedom. It can drive you mad. It is what makes that enemy of an autorickshaw driver or taxi driver from home seem like a dear friend.

America's transport system was built for cars, not mass transport, although transportation was initially meant to ease travel for large populations. In and around New York City, though, the sanest thing you can do is leave your car behind and ride the subway. Thousands living in nearby cities ride into New York City and back every single workday. The New York Subway is a spider's web that needs some mastering. It thrives below the ground. Over the ground, a Manhattan workday can be chaos unlimited, with no place for the thousands of cabs, cars and buses that crowd its roads.

The story repeats in Washington DC, Chicago, San Francisco, Boston, San Jose, Philadelphia, Miami, Cleveland and a handful of other cities. But the US has under 300 cities with populations of 100,000 or more,[11] which means that in all the other cities, in the absence of most forms of public transport, people use cars.

There are approximately forty-seven Indian cities with a population of over 10,00,000, and over 200 cities with a population of 1,00,000. India has lesser area than the US, and is highly populous. But transport options are varied, often problematic, yet mostly available. Step out of home, walk to a bus stop, or hop into an autorickshaw. Major cities have local train services. Smaller cities have buses and now, app-based cab services.

Cars were not necessities when we grew up in the 1980s and 1990s. For most visa wives and their husbands, buying a car was a dream. But in the US, not having a car can complicate friendships. Sindhu and Venugopal lived in the suburbs of Chicago. Venugopal's friends, mostly bachelors, were more than happy to help them out with grocery rides. In return, Sindhu would often invite them over for home-cooked dinners. When they had to shift to Maine, Sindhu struggled. She found company in a family that lived above her apartment.

The girl, Varada Rao, was her age, from her part of India, and well-connected in the city. She had had a simple rural upbringing, and was friendly and brash, homely and honest. The two shared stories from their lives. The catch was that Sindhu preferred to be on an equal footing, while Varada expected more from her since she was the one who 'had the car'. She expected Sindhu to share dishes that she cooked, help out with cooking and cleaning when she (Varada) had get-togethers, and even get two identical pieces of anything that Sindhu liked. After all, was she not doing Sindhu and her husband a favour?

Soon, Sindhu grew tired of Varada's growing demands. When she refused to comply on a couple of occasions, Varada let her irritation be known through offhand remarks like, 'You need to buy a car soon.' Sindhu knew it was time to learn how to drive.

At times, the husband is already driving a car by the time the visa wife arrives. Bindhu's husband, too, had a car and pushed her into driving after her first six months in the States. She cleared her driving test in the first attempt, which her friends told her was huge. And then came the real test. Her first tip for any visa wife who wants to learn driving is, 'Don't learn from your husband.' A husband teaching his wife means a fight. She is sure to end up in tears and he ends up getting her an ice cream or flowers to calm her down. It could mean war at home.

'They yell at you, get frustrated, and you fight too, but they teach,' reasons Archana Gopal about her own experience of learning from her husband.

Bindhu explains the 'how' of these car-learning fights.

'Husbands decide they know driving the best. Women make mistakes when they drive. Husbands point those mistakes out a lot. When the husband starts telling her off, the wife's ego is hurt. Fights ensue. For two people who both think they are right, it can be a tough situation.'

Bindhu and her husband were still trying to understand each other. She was grappling with the nuances of driving. The traffic was orderly, a welcome break. Drivers stuck to speed limits and followed rules. Traffic signs varied, though. On the highways, speed limits were at 65 miles an hour. Moreover, she was still conditioned to drive on the left of the road.

Shyla had her own challenges when she learnt driving. 'We would drive at nights when there was less traffic. I had no sense of driving at all. If the speed limit was 45 miles on a road, I would drive at 35. Besides, right turns are sharp and quick in the US. I would slow down a lot while turning. My husband would yell, 'If you drive like this here, there will be accidents. You will get a ticket.'

When the time came for her test, she was tested by an inspector of the DMV. 'Everyone told me he was too strict. I flunked.'

Bharathi's resolve to win it all in the new country prompted her to prepare so thoroughly for her written test that she scored 100 per cent. It was enough to floor the DMV officials who gave her a licence on the spot, with no practical test. It took her a long time, though, to get used to the speed limits of US roads and highways .

When Madhuri arrived from the UK, she was still getting her head around the 'driving right' mode of the new country. She was a pro at driving on the left and had a valid driver's licence from the UK. And so, the day she relocated to the US, her husband persuaded her to drive from Connecticut to New Jersey for a conference. 'I had a vague idea of the driving system in the US. I was used to doing the obvious while driving—turn right when I wanted to go right and turn left when I wanted to go left. Interestingly, the jughandle turns that exist only in a bunch of US states, including New Jersey, caught me by surprise. I had stay put in the right lane and go around the loop to turn left.'

Madhuri was confident about being able to drive solo on that long drive. She had her car documents, phones, credit cards, map with directions and some cash. 'By the time I got my head around jughandle turns, I hit the toll plaza where I had to pay 20 cents. I had no choice but to drive into the coin lane. We had not yet got our 'EZ pass'. My frantic rummaging through my bag and glove box to find a coin annoyed people lined up behind me. Non-stop honking tensed me up. To my embarrassment, a gentleman obviously dressed for work walked to the coin collection basket and threw a 20 cent coin in it. He was so furious he did not even make eye contact. I was relieved when the barrier was raised and I could escape.'

A fact that most of us are ignorant about is that the US allows people from other countries with a valid international licence to drive for one year after arrival, provided their licence is in English and the name on it is the same as in your passport. Some states accept the International Driving Permit (IDP) along with the driving licence, and some accept a valid driving licence issued by the foreign country where you are resident. It helps to call the local DMV upon arrival to check the rules that can differ from state to state. Learning to drive a car is an essential rite of passage in the US.

A friend learnt driving for the sake of her toddler son who had to attend kindergarten. Since they had only one car, she had to depend on ride-share. 'Usually, it happens that mothers of other kids in the same school do this to earn extra money. We must keep the teachers posted and introduce the ride-share drivers in advance. Any child's mother is not encouraged to ride along, since space is money.'

An important lesson for Indians: Follow the rules. Do not dream of bribing your way to a licence.

Manasi had been driving for about a year when, one day, she noticed a police car follow her and ask her to stop. The red and blue lights coming on in a police car is a signal for the driver to stop the car, place their hands on the steering wheel and wait for the official in uniform to come and give orders. She spotted a parking area ahead and parked her car at the lot. She lowered the window.

When the cop walked to her car, her hand was on the steering wheel. She wished him and asked, 'How can I help you?'

'The cop was polite. He asked me why I did not stop the car immediately. I told him I was looking for a parking lot, which was true. He asked me, 'Do you know why I stopped you?' And I said, 'No'. He said my car's registration had expired. It was confusing. And a bit of a surprise. I really did not know about renewing the car's registration annually. The cop understood. my predicament, but still gave me a ticket. I had to pay $25, but he said it would not go into my driving record. Probably that has to do with the procedures they follow.'

The cop let her off lightly because she was honest. Still, she was shaken. A cop had never apprehended her before. She was shivering as she dialled her husband's number. 'I don't want to drive ever again,' she sobbed. Her husband calmed her down and brushed it off as a minor incident.

Manasi relates this to possible experiences with cops in India. She is equally fascinated by how people driving their vehicles follow traffic rules even when there are no cops around—stopping at signals, stopping at the 'stop' sign, pausing to look for other vehicles and giving way to pedestrians.

When a school bus ahead of you flashes a red light, or its 'stop' arm is out, all vehicles around it need to stop at a safe distance. The country also takes drunk driving seriously. Driving under the influence (DUI) of intoxication attracts multi-year sentences, hefty fines and even the revocation of the driver's licence in many cases.

For visa-holder Indians, a DUI arrest could mean hell. It could affect your immigration status and hurt your path to naturalization in the country. If you have been drinking, do not drive.

Typically, as an H4 visa holder, you are expected to prove your credentials with the driver's licence from your home country, driving history so that your record in your home country can be checked for traffic offences, and two document proofs aside from the passport. A rental lease agreement, bank statement and marriage certificate to prove that you are indeed the spouse of the H1B holder, are also needed.

As an H4 arrival, you are not entitled to the SSN. You would need to apply for it at the Social Security office, and get a denial letter. With all other documents, you will need to take the denial letter to the DMV. You will then be allowed to take the written test.

Sathya had gone through the grind and obtained her driver's licence in Washington. But her husband lost his project there and the new client company was in New Jersey.

Before she went to the DMV there, she was given the mandated list of documents to take, which she did.

'Where's your husband? The H1 spouse?' asked the official checking her documents.

They demanded that he be present physically to prove she was his wife. 'They claimed it was a well-known fact. A driver's licence is not a passport or a security document. I have a valid visa, my original marriage certificate, his H1B documents, and still they demanded to see him as if

I were a criminal! In an instant they reminded me that I was an H4 and nothing without an H1B standing beside me.'

Sathya's husband was unhappy about having to take off for a few hours hardly a day into his new project. His wife was an engineer like him, and had worked at an IT major in India. Here, her existence boiled down to not just a marriage certificate and H4 visa, but his constant attendance to prove they were a couple.

Sathya did not have to take the written test again. But the licence was tied to the validity of their H1B visa. 'Our visa was to expire in February. They gave us a three-month buffer. The licence would expire in May. The catch was that when companies file for extensions, the process takes about five to six months. So, for a few months, I would be left without a driver's licence.'

Sathya's baby was due in a few months. She had every reason to dread the no-car situation.

Not having a car plays on the culture-shock-battered psyche of a visa wife. At the mention of a grocery ride, you go mad with the 'to-buy' list. You hyperventilate, hoping you missed nothing on the list. And that everything you need will be available at the store. You become a compulsive grabber at shops. Each trip to the store sets you off on a marathon race, to quick-fill your basket or cart. You simply do not know how soon you will be able to return to the store. So grab. Grab the veggies. Grab kitchenware. Grab bathroom supplies. Grab furnishings.

'Finish it quick. We can't make them wait,' the husband orders.

His rule: finish your vegetable hunting, packing and billing before your hosts are done. For no reason should you keep them waiting.

Reserve ride requests for emergencies alone. If you have needs such as buying that much-needed winter coat or clothes, make sure to buy only from the stores that the ones with the car decide to take you to. Forget quality. Forget choice. Just be glad you got that ride.

It does not help if your spouse's friends are bachelors who are scared of women's 'window-shopping'. It's worse if the friends have kids because their lives would be planned around their kids. Sometimes, it is just easier to live in a bus-accessible apartment community, even if the place has other cons like not very good apartments or a record for home break-ins.

10

A Product for Everything

America never ceases to surprise me.

It has the big concept about everything—big boxes called big stores, big monotony, subtle surprises beyond that monotony, products for everything in life, innovations galore, at times making you squirm with its consumerism, but mostly sucking you in with its creativity. You will become familiar with it during your first few rides out of the confines of your apartment.

Sathya remembers feeling like a Lilliputian looking up at America's many Gullivers. Only, those Gullivers were buildings, roads, bridges, food, sometimes people, and everything in between. Vanitha really liked the vastness of large chain stores that allowed her to take a walk in them during the harsh winters. She loved not having to cram in with others, unlike the supermarkets in Hyderabad. Vanitha spent her pregnancy months at her favourite big store, less for shopping and more for warmth and long walks. Window-shopping can act as a balm for a wounded soul, she discovered.

The biggest put-off in my initial months was the monotony that defined America's shopping areas—large boxes devoid of aesthetics or the smoothness of design. I would long for the bustling shopping zones of my old home in Mumbai—their cacophony of colour and displays of seasonal goods. Walk into a general store in America, and you find white shelves, a roof that resembles an airplane hangar, bright lights and no hovering shop assistants. The range of products is mind-boggling, mostly manufactured in other countries. Have we not seen enough of the 'Made in China' tag?

In the weeks after her arrival, Sathya noticed a bunch of fliers tucked into her postbox (called 'mail box'). She pulled them out and wondered why the stores were spending so much on ads. 'Looking at those $2.99 and $3.99 ads for vegetables, I naturally calculated them against rupees, and gave up wanting to use them.' She found discount coupons for specific products. A pharmacy ad-book, for instance, had photo-printing coupons, and was selling clothes, sometimes toys and cosmetics. She remembered how medical stores in Hyderabad had boards that read 'medical and *kirana* store', and smiled.

I, too, find coupons handy while buying beverages, aerated drinks and canned goods. Coupons, online and offline, from local department stores, fetch you deals in plenty. My favourite are craft store coupons.

Kaushalya found the absence of house help a big pain. To her delight, each trip to a large store would lead to the discovery of products that made it easier for her to do household chores by herself.

A refreshing departure from the 'only new' attitude ingrained in the shopping mindset of us Indians is the 'used goods are good' attitude one sees in the US. Sindhu managed to set her home up with vintage-style sofas from a local thrift store in Maine. She got herself a faux-plant, side tables, old paintings, all at throwaway prices she would not have dreamt of in India.

Buying a used product is not seen as a sign of poverty or lack of prestige, but as your resourcefulness and thrift—an appreciable quality in the land of spending. For the H1-H4 lot, it is mere necessity. With the uncertainty of a longer US stay looming large even before they set foot in the country, buying used cars, furniture and tools becomes the most viable option. It's why you would gladly accept the gift of an old dining set, or pick up a piece of furniture you spot at a dumpster. It is why you would not mind buying something off Craigslist.

Another necessity is food—and locating an Indian store if you want your favourites from back home. Radha, who craved Indian vegetables in her Seattle home, jumped for joy when she found frozen versions at the local Indian store. She was put off by their 'lack of taste', but was willing to adjust. 'The only things you can't find at Indian stores are your mom and dad. Everything else they manage to stock,' she muses.

She battled in her kitchen with frozen coconuts and drumsticks for a whole year! Indian foods are not a rarity, thanks to the teeming Indian communities in most areas. Radha was delighted to find fresh vegetables such as *hara chana* (green chickpeas), peas, gherkins, *dosakai* (cucumber), *pudina* (mint leaves) and *avarekai* (flat beans).

The country's frozen food culture ensures that your Indian store stocks frozen versions of most vegetables, even hard-to-find ones like *kanda* (elephant yam), apart from the ubiquitous Indian dishes like *vindaloo* and *idiyappam*.

The popularity of hubs—like central New Jersey, neighbourhoods in the Bay Area, the suburbs of Los Angeles, Devon Street in Chicago and North Decatur in Atlanta—transcends their cities and extends to neighbouring states as well. Central New Jersey in Edison-Iselin and Jackson Heights near Queens (New York) are popular destinations, for instance, for Indian shoppers from Delaware, Pennsylvania and Connecticut.

A former student, Namitha, from the Pennsylvania State University, would visit Oak Tree Road in Edison-Iselin every few weeks along with her dorm-mates. They would take a two-hour ride to have a sumptuous meal at an Indian restaurant, and then spend a couple of hours shopping for groceries and clothes before riding back. It was a picnic of sorts to get over their homesickness.

Indians are a population fed on festive discount sales by everyone—from silk saree showrooms and electronic stores to big supermarkets advertising deals. We are slowly catching up with the idea of discount coupons that will fetch a price reduction on a particular product. Product influx in American departmental stores varies from season to season, much like the shopping seasons in an Indian city. If Mumbai's neighbourhood stores come alive with colourful umbrellas at the onset of monsoon, *chaniya cholis* before Navaratri and fancy lanterns before Diwali, expect something similar in American stores, albeit somewhat toned down.

Sathya noticed during her first two years in the US how stores had the Thanksgiving season, Christmas season, Valentine's Day season, St Patrick's Day season, spring–summer madness, back-to-school season, Halloween and so on. Each season had its range of products. Before summer, she spotted bicycles, styrofoam ice-kegs, folding chairs, umbrellas, flip-flops, sunscreen lotions, sunglasses and a host of beach products. She also noticed colours defining not just the turn of season, but also shopping seasons—red and green during Christmas, green for St Patrick's day, an assault of red in the run-up to Valentine's Day, deep oranges, black and other fall hues ahead of Halloween, colours of the American flag before their Independence Day on 4 July, cherry blossom colours during spring, beach hues for summer and so on.

Despite the all-pervasive consumerism around seasons and festivals, a rhythm exists, in sync with their spirit. Acts of charity are also encouraged during seasonal holidays.

My favourite festival in the US is Halloween on 31 October, when children land on one's doorstep for trick-or-treating. It is usually about a hundred of them who will knock, over a period of three hours, dressed in an array of costumes. Make sure you have tonnes of chocolate, known as candy in this country.

The weeks following Halloween and before Thanksgiving are when shopping turns into a national frenzy. It's the start of a season where millions brave storms and flight delays to be with their loved ones across the continent. It is when cooking that prized turkey becomes a host's symbol of familial togetherness. It is also when the toughest of retail contests begins. 'Who profits more from which sale?' Typically, Thanksgiving and Christmas sales decide if consumer product companies thrive, survive or shut down.

'Did you stand in the queue? Did you witness that madness?' my friend asked me eagerly after our first Thanksgiving outing. 'I did not. My husband did,' I said.

It was 12° C at 9 p.m. Our friends drove us to the electronics store, where the queue stretched a few hundred feet. Entry was regulated. My husband offered to stand in the queue, chivalrous as always. We needed to buy some much-needed gadgets—a laptop, a TV, a room heater and anti-virus software. I waited at the entrance of the store to walk in with him, but was so cold after five minutes that our friends put me back in their car to stay warm.

Black Friday 'Doorbuster Sales' start in time to ruin family dinners for both buyers and sellers. The day after Thanksgiving Thursday is called Black Friday, which is when stores announce heavy discounts. Typically, these stores must open on Friday morning, but over the last few years, they have advanced their store opening times, say, from 5 a.m. Friday to 6 p.m., or midnight, Thursday. Many now open on Thanksgiving Day, a controversial move.

Store employees spend their Thanksgiving away from their families, managing crowds at the store. For shoppers, it turns out to be that hold-on-for-dear-life chance to buy deal-worthy products, often after waiting a whole year. When I joined my husband in the queue, I got chatting with the guy ahead of us. 'You should have seen this queue two hours back. It was bad. People were fighting to get in.' He was walking in a second time to return the tablet computer he had bought. A 6 p.m. doorbuster sale sees shoppers queueing up outside stores a few hours before, so they can grab the first lot of products on sale.

Unfortunately, my husband's forty-five-minute wait in the winter chill at the electronics store led to a $150 medical bill due to a cold he caught that evening. That day, though, we came upon products we had never seen before—dehumidifiers, humidifiers, room heaters, home security systems, telescopes, cleaning robots, camera tripods, X-boxes, GPS devices, electronic safes, activity tracking bracelets and smart watches, among others. I loved those dehumidifiers, and wished Chennai had them.

The product deals discount season can extend to Christmas and beyond. January is when Christmas products become available at marked-down prices.

In India, Malini Dey was a cautious shopper. She knew she had to be smarter than the stores in order not to get cheated. If they were suspicious about customers, she was equally sceptical about their genuineness. When she started shopping in the US, she did her usual cross-examining of clothes, mainly the ones she found at sales and clearance areas of stores. Months later, she realized that clothes in US stores go to clearance not because they are damaged, but because they could not be sold and the outlet needs to clear their shelves for the next range of seasonal products.

Sindhu once walked out of a store red-faced. Her friend, who she was with, had gone back to the store to return a product purchased on a deal. The cash-counter personnel returned her money in cash, but fell short of change less than a dollar, on an amount of $20. Her friend insisted on getting the dollar back. 'It may not make a difference to you. It matters to me,' her friend went on, unnerving the woman.

Sindhu, who had often returned products too, thought her friend was going too far. 'I understand one must save money, but after so many shopping trips to that store, my friend was fighting for less than a dollar. It was embarrassing.'

'Why do you keep the products you buy? You can return them to the shops after using them!' said an Indian friend when I was a new arrival. I was shocked. I cannot do that, not ever. Probably, I would have a different opinion of her advice in a gift economy. I later discovered that such consumer behaviour makes Indians notorious in a system that is relatively more consumer-friendly. The fact that one can easily return products that one is not satisfied with, should by no means be misunderstood by dollar-savers as giving them the leverage to use products and then trash them at a store's 'returns' counter.

Imagine trying such a thing in India. Ever tried as much as touching and feeling an SLR or an expensive tablet at an electronic goods store in an upscale city mall? 'We don't realize that in American stores our transactions are closely watched,' my husband told me later, upset by this freeloading attitude displayed by some of our peers. Such deeds feed the biases the local population has regarding immigrants who do not respect their norms. Biases ultimately do form a basis for hatred. Need we say more about hatred and what it leads to? Every country has its systems. It is good to adhere to local norms whichever country you are in.

Vanitha remembers buying a cassette player for her father-in-law in Hyderabad. When she asked for a product warranty, she was told, 'There is no guarantee for life. What guarantee can I give you for a product?' The product in question was manufactured by a renowned brand and at that time cost Rs 3000—a princely amount. 'You get what you pay for in the US, compared to India, where I am less sure about the quality of a product,' she says.

Aruna has more or less readjusted to her life in Bengaluru after the initial hiccups of a returnee, but nothing in the world can make her give up 'made in USA' dark chocolates. Often, her only request to friends who visit from the US is a pack of dark chocolates. It comes second to her love for chocolate-coated blueberries and cranberries. Her other favourite is the slow-cooker.

Aruna took to cooking and baking during her stay at Pittsburgh, and loved the patient, low-temperature preparation of dishes over long hours in the slow-cooker, in contrast to the speed-cooking pressure cooker. To her delight, her dishes turned out well. Conventional electric cookers have timers for slow-cooking too. Aruna swears by her American gadget.

During a beach trip, my husband and I chanced on a product we never knew existed. It could be likened to a large toothpaste tube cap, with two thick pins protruding from its flat wide base. It was a 'corn holder'. The only 'corn holders' I knew of were the pale green husks that steamed or roasted cobs from roadside carts came wrapped in. Who would ever think that corn, a staple in America, would need such pins and not husks for holding!

A list of such innovative products found in America would run on for miles. Aruna is delighted at how a lot of thought is invested in the design of each product, to make it as convenient to use as possible. Creative products are innovated and marketed well.

My inventive kitchen favourites include tea-infuser pots, aroma diffusers and wire shelves that you can insert under the kitchen shelf. Organizing products like over-the-door hangers with hooks to hold daily-wear shirts, aroma infusers that you can get for as little as a dollar, wire racks and multi-purpose, heavy-duty hangers have all been saviours in empty apartments.

A recent discovery were cleaning robots, that have not had a great start in India, but serve as tiny power machines that vacuum home floors. They would be especially useful for elderly people. A quick thought goes back to ageing parents who are afraid to hire domestic help, or get anxious when their maid does not turn up. I secretly wish such products become widely available in India.

The one thing many of us cannot understand is how processed and canned foods get consumed in such huge quantities. The weekly coupon mail is full of enticements for canned goods ranging from pickled vegetables to packaged meat, and sodas with monstrous sugar content. No doubt they are bestsellers at grocery stores.

Mercy Baker, who is from Goa and moved to the US after marrying her American beau, says there are two aspects to American food—quickness and convenience. Mercy loves her life as a homemaker in the country. American eating habits, however, disturb her. 'If only Americans put more thought into what they ate, the healthcare picture would be a lot different. Cancer is so rampant in this country, it is just like catching a common cold. It is all directly related to food. Americans are only 2 or 3 per cent genetically disposed to cancer, and that too can be reversed by eating right,' she rues.

So when you spot a shelf full of mayonnaise varieties, canned soups, canned vegetables, even pasta and spaghetti, a wiser decision would be to move over, to the section with fresh vegetables and ingredients that need to be cooked. Most Indians find canned products enticing despite them being unhealthier than their other food choices.

Rupashree, the young mother, was thrilled when she visited baby stores in the US because of the array of baby food that you can pick off the counter and feed your little one. The number of choices for cereals, too, is something Indian moms have never seen before. They would have, at best, bought cornflakes and oats. 'I had not seen people feeding banana to kids. But out here you get so many different varieties of banana foods for babies! Besides, there are juices, dry fruits and other foods especially made for children,' says Rupashree.

She also likes the wide variety of toys available. 'Toy stores are huge, and safety standards of products for kids are high.' On a trip to India, I found Chinese-make toys at local stores, which did have warnings about the toy being a choking hazard, but the quality was a lot cheaper than those one can get in the US.

Of course, the extent of a visa wife's retail therapy depends on how much her husband is willing to spend. Shopping trips are often peppered with questions like, 'Do you really need that?', 'We just bought it last month!', 'Be careful about how much you spend.' A common refrain among my friends is that their spouses will follow them to each aisle and put things back from their shopping carts, saying, 'We do not need it.'

Some of the biggest fights my husband and I have had were because I sought solace in buying 'hobby items' like jewellery pliers, patterned paper, craft paints, duct tapes, marker pens, paintbrushes, beads, jewellery findings, crochet hooks and the like, in the hope of staying sane. And his financial intelligence shone in the aisles of superstores.

One day, I warned him to stay in the car while I shopped at a dollar store. Just as I was getting the items in my cart billed at the counter, he showed up, and I snapped, 'Why did you come? Go back to the car.'

A sheepish smile made it clear he could not help himself. With the cashier smiling at our exchange, we finished paying. And our argument continued all the way to the car.

11

Home and Outside[12]

Stepping into an American home exposes the Indian woman to a whole new world—and a concept of space that she did not comprehend before.

Sarika had moved from her crowded colony in Secunderabad to the blandness of beige and white in her new one-bedroom home in Delaware. She was devastated. Its silence and smallness made her feel claustrophobic.

Kaushalya fell in love with her new apartment in California because of its airiness, smart utilization of space and the fact that it overlooked a swimming pool. Anamika was, in contrast, the H1B arrival who wanted to find a home where she wouldn't need to spend much. She looked for a shared apartment, but felt trapped at having to share it with a foul-mouthed colleague.

Their new spaces—homes, surroundings, lifestyle—made for confusions and queries in these women's minds, coupled with agony over what they had had to give up.

What is the meaning of space? We grow up with clinical definitions for the word without understanding what it means. The Oxford English Dictionary defines space as 'a continuous area or expanse that is free, available, or unoccupied'. The same dictionary also says that 'space' is 'the freedom and scope to live, think and develop in a way that suits one'.

A persistent question for dependent visa wives like Sarika, Kaushalya, Neha, Manasi and thousands of others is how to fit into this alien space, its culture and consciousness? How does one find a sense of home in surroundings that are so dramatically different from 'home'? How does one accept this new space? Will it take away one's identity? How does one accept the new country as one's own?

Space, like time, is a divine subject in the Vedas. For mortals like us, it is about the homes we live in, the offices we work at, our cities, towns and vehicles. Or, the time we want away from the daily grind. Space is about what you, the visa wife, can do or are 'allowed' to do, especially when Mr Husband turns extra-possessive and excessively worried about your forays outside the home.

'In India, the concept of space was non-existent. Everyone was literally in your face. Having lived away from India for over a decade, I clearly understand now what space means,' says Madhuri. 'There is physical, mental and sometimes spiritual space too.'

Like most visa wives, Madhuri grew up seeing large families living in two-bedroom houses. She was used to the designated play areas in her gated township and organized tree avenues in her city neighbourhood. In contrast, her summer vacations at her native village were spent with about a dozen kids and their parents under a single roof. They played in the calm, natural environs, accompanied their uncles and father to the river every day to fetch water and learnt how the household worked without realizing it. Personal space at home was something she never thought of, which is why she found 'availability of space' a revelation when she moved to England. Today, after many years, she has an appetite for it too.

Jungian analyst and anthropologist Manisha Roy, who has spent decades outside India, has something similar to share. 'The sense of space is part of the new experience of being in another culture. I personally take this as a challenge. The idea of private space almost does not exist in India. Perhaps it has to do with overpopulation, among other factors, and often because of the joint family system and community living that formed a part of Indian culture. After forty years of living abroad in many countries, I personally came to value personal/private space and try to find it whenever I visit India. But, for a few weeks there, I can also adjust to its absence.'

Before my Ammumma's home was sold a decade ago, a bunch of cousins revelled in its inner world—spacious interiors and exteriors, a thatched veranda, a backyard with a well and a host of trees and plants. Today, that period feels like a magical dream lost in time. We did not have our own separate rooms; instead, we would all be bundled up together in a room or two. The house gave us privacy and protection without our being aware of it.

In its place now, an apartment building has sprung up. Spaces that we grew up with in India have mutated over the decades, wiping out green and bringing in grime. They shrink, shriek and make us want to escape.

Aruna spent her first few days in the States reflecting on how her space had shifted from an office cubicle on a large floor to the silence of her rental apartment. When she watched her first host work at housekeeping, the unfamiliar rhythm caught her eye. What does it take to maintain a kitchen, and a home?

She was negotiating a new space—physical in the form of her new home, its surroundings, her new city, and personal as a wife and homemaker. She had to deal with being resident in a country where her identity was tied to her marriage to an H1B visa holder.

Over time, I have negotiated the American space with a lot of hesitation, partly because the culture shock hit me hard, and partly because of a husband who became over-protective. I could never stop comparing the country I had left behind with the country that I was living in. Weighing the two situations becomes an almost subconscious activity.

In Chennai, on a long visit two years after I had left, I watched our neighbour chat with my mother on her way to pick up sun-dried laundry from her rooftop. Women in my neighbourhood lean over compound walls and gates, and can talk for hours about everything under the sun. Not so in America, where a home rarely gets fenced. Lawns and lines mark boundaries. Fences, if needed, get used to cover a home's backyard.

We, the desi *betis*, bahus and professionals, grow up between invisible fences. Rules exist for all of us who arrive on American shores—unwritten, unspoken, and many times spoken and eulogized, as solid as fences—that put you through pain if you dare cross them. Your connection with the new space depends on your new home, your husband's workplace environment (read bosses, colleagues and their spouses), the number of Indians and their friendliness in the new community, neighbours and their approach towards immigrants like you and so on. For women on H1B visas, their space spans their new workplace and its challenges, their cubicles, the competition, colleagues, bosses and work hours, besides the challenge of surviving new roommates.

Anamika and her friend got a raw deal from a colleague who forced them to take her on as a roommate and breathed down their necks during the stay. 'It was like living with a tiger in the room,' says Anamika.

Imagine having a roommate who thinks she owns a shared rental apartment and nit-picks on upkeep every single day. Anamika escaped to friends and strangers, visited places and tried her best to stay out of her room for as much as possible.

The *pardesi* (foreign) home, the American one, most often says, 'You wanted space? You got it. Enjoy'—complete with silence, emptiness, solitude, frustration—the whole lot. What can four walls and a carpet possibly do to your mind? You discover exactly what when you bawl like a baby for no reason. You know it when you hate the maple trees outside your window and yearn for gulmohurs, coconut trees and hibiscuses.

You fight your fears and put on a brave front for that weekly video chat or call to India, so as to feign that everything is all right. When an elder asks you if you are managing to do your regular pooja (read: 'being a good girl'), you want to fling your laptop or phone into the trashcan. What do they know what a box made of four walls and a floor does to you?

Savouring the newfound space minus everyday scrutiny does not save you from taunts, however, that can reach you all the way from India. When Vinod held his wife a little more intimately than he would have done in India, and put a picture up on social media, all hell broke loose. His jealous cousin complained about the 'indecency' to his mother, who picked up the phone and gave Vinod's mother, her sister, a lecture on how she better control the new bride. Vinod's mother in turn called him up and demanded an explanation. She personally had no problem but was stung by what she had to hear in the bargain. Vinod fumed—who were those people, who knew nothing of their struggles, to judge them based on a photograph? The photo spoke of their love, and he was in America, not India. His wife tried to pacify the warring mother and son. To keep the peace, she 'apologized' to her mother-in-law.

Negotiating the process of assimilation in an alien culture while having to please the vastly different world back home often proves to be a gruelling task.

When Vanitha and her husband moved cities, they discovered that rents would be two thirds of his post-doctoral income. The couple could not find studio apartments in the vicinity of his university either. Their option was to rent a two-bedroom apartment in their name and sub-let it, and their leasing office would look the other way.

Their new flat-mate was a student. They had two bedrooms and a common kitchen. 'I did not mind sharing the accommodation. It worked for us because I adjusted a lot. My husband was keen that I cook for the student too. He always expects me to make sacrifices. That can get taxing,' says Vanitha.

Sathya's husband Surya's colleague pursued him for a few days for permission to share their apartment. 'I will lie in a corner of your home,' he pleaded.

Sathya was perplexed as to why the colleague would not bring his wife over. 'They got him married to a college-going girl from his village. She is still studying. There is no way he can bring her here,' Surya told her. Sathya wondered if the colleague was really looking for home-cooked meals under the ruse of sharing an apartment. She had made it clear even before they moved that she was not up for such arrangements.

She reminded herself often that not having someone to share her apartment was a blessing. Even though they had a one-bedroom apartment as opposed to the two-bedroom one that she had wanted, she was grateful that it was hers alone.

One of the things Sarika found disconcerting about her home was the inability to feel the floor under her feet. 'After getting used to cement floors, tiles and mosaic under our feet in India, now there was this carpet.' Her kitchen floor was made not of tiles but of vinyl stuck on wood. Her bedroom had closets—not shelves. An Indian rental home's shelf is either an extension of the wall, built with cement, or fixed with a granite slab. Some shelves protrude proudly in living rooms, and function as showcases or bookshelves. Our other storage places are steel almirahs in bedrooms.

Steel almirahs hide away saris, expensive shirts, cash, jewellery, silverware, all nestled between naphthalene balls and satin fragrance sachets. And on top of the almirahs, we love to dump empty suitcases, cardboard boxes and old gifts.

In contrast is the American closet—built-in and walk-in.

'Closets in these homes are bare. We are so used to having shelves back home in India. Here, there is no scope for organizing in the closet,' says Manasi. She is voicing the thoughts of many visa wives who take a while to get over the 'How am I supposed to keep my clothes in this?' feeling. Closets are usually carpeted like the rest of the room. A closet has a single slab at a height above your shoulder with a metal rod running beneath it, for hangers. This slab is for your foldable clothes, boxes, or inner-wear. All the remaining clothes are supposed to go on the hangers.

Somewhere near your new home's main door is another closet. In parts of the US where winters are severe, this closet is meant to hold winter coats, scarves, shoes and caps. An entire industry thrives on closet organization—hanging shelves, clothes boxes, innovative hangers, wire-shelves that can be fixed to the closet wall, shoe-holder racks and the like. And you thought simple slabs could fix it! So different from the saree–blouse–underskirt-influenced steel almirahs of India that can hold a hundred folded pieces, Western closets take time to appeal to your sense of storage.

Manasi initially also found it hard to get over the absence of a pooja room. An American home rarely has a designated space for an altar, putting devout Indian householders in a fix. You may figure out in your head which part of the walls or their corners you might convert into a makeshift altar, but it might be difficult to reconcile mother's advice to find a *vaastu*-compliant spot with nothing heavy above, and instructions to light a lamp and offer food every day, with your new home's layout and the challenges it presents, especially the smoke detector which effectively banish any hopes of lighting *agarbatti*s (incense sticks).

Apart from the space within the home, how must visa wives engage with the people they encounter outside?

Begin by asking yourself these questions: Do you mix freely with neighbours? Are there any forms of non-acceptance that you notice?

As Jayasri discovered, personal space and privacy are highly valued in the US. When you visit anyone, make sure to call them up, rather than drop by unannounced, which is in stark contrast with the way our network in India functions. Back home, it was still acceptable for relatives to drop in from some other city unannounced. It was also perfectly fine if as a kid you stood outside your best friend's building and yelled his name to call him out to play, instead of going up to his or her floor. It was certainly not acceptable for a bachelor in your neighbourhood to want his privacy. You heard such people being labelled 'not amiable', 'self-centred' and so on.

One look out of their apartments and visa wives would realize that not one of their neighbours stepped out of their homes unless it was to get into their cars. Though people smiled and greeted each other, it still felt like they lived in their own insulated shells.

Individual space is supreme in America. So much so that knocking on your neighbour's door when you please is frowned upon. When Sathya and Surya moved to their Delaware apartment, they did a traditional milk-boiling ritual. Sathya had carried her pocket camera over to take some pictures and dutifully mail them to her parents, in-laws and relatives. Before their new friends dropped by, the couple would ignite their gas stove to 'inaugurate' the kitchen. Unfortunately, they had no matches or lighters. As they would in India, Surya knocked on a neighbour's door upstairs.

'Am extremely sorry to bother you,' he said. 'We are new and need to get the stove started. May we please borrow a lighter?'

The guy who opened the door was annoyed. 'Look, I will help you this time. But don't think you can come knocking on my door always, okay?' He brought his lighter over, started the fire, and left without as much as a smile. Sathya and Surya were shaken. It was their first ever experience with neighbours in their new home. It put them off interacting with neighbours for the following six months.

In a space where Sathya and Surya were trying hard to 'fit in' and stay in the good books of locals, that first encounter was a blow. They subconsciously used it as a marker for things to come. A few weeks later, the community's handyman shifted in next door. He would chat with them from across the door, offer help with repairs after office hours and showed genuine curiosity about all things Indian. Despite the distance he maintained by not inviting them over, which a friendly neighbour in India would, he helped Sathya get over the fear of neighbours.

In those early days, she found a unique source of company—squirrels. They would drop by at her balcony door for the peanuts she fed them. 'You're feeding them kilos!' remarked Surya one day. She got defensive. She saw them more than she saw people. It was their hunger that drove them to her door. And it was her desperation for company that made her offer them peanuts every day.

She would feel cheated sometimes. After their tummies were full, the squirrels would run off with some peanuts and hide them around a tree. 'They know banking, these sly little fellows,' she would think.

She yearned to see some crows, with hardly any luck. Sometimes, though, there would be strange clicking sounds that would startle her. 'Because of the silence around, such sounds can be frightening. When you are alone at home, your heartbeat races and you wonder if there's an intruder in your home.'

Sathya and Sarika understood, at different times of their stay, why they heard strange noises in their apartments. It was squirrels scratching the doors and windows, and at times in the heating, ventilation and air-conditioning (HVAC) system.

Manasi remembers how her visiting aunt carried a plastic mug with her wherever she travelled in the US, across flights, trains, cities and homes, to use during bathroom visits. For Sarika, the difference was a shocker. How can the bathroom not have a bucket and mug? Her new home's bathroom hardly had any semblance to the bathrooms she had always used. She found it tougher when they visited friends. Everyone was so used to wiping themselves with a roll of tissue!

A huge challenge Sarika faced in her new American home was not being able to wash clothes and dry them. Some homemakers take to hanging washed clothes, especially innerwear, on bathroom towel rods. This might make not only for malodorous undergarments but also the risk of water dripping from them seeping to apartments below. Somewhere near or inside the bathroom is a 'linen' closet which is a tinier and narrower version of a shelved cupboard, but sits in the wall. We might want to store our sarees and salwar-kameez sets into it, but a linen closet's conventional use is to store bathroom towels, soaps and the like. She was also surprised by the method of cleaning her new home. The carpeted floors had to be vacuumed, as opposed to sweeping and swabbing.

Outside the home, you will find an abundance of space. In smaller cities and towns, there are no teeming crowds that elbow their way to work or back. You do find traffic piled up on highways during peak hours on workdays, though. As you step out of your home, you can turn into a frightened puppy. Be sure to smile at people. Most Indian women find it difficult to smile at strangers because they have been conditioned to believe that their smiles might be misconstrued as an invitation. It is not so in America.

For us, non-smiling Indians, smiling at strangers needs some getting used to. We've lived in a culture where smiling is treated with suspicion, particularly for women. So, afraid of being judged, women become careful about projecting themselves as a 'good girl', in a way that is socially acceptable. In America, if you do not smile at passers-by, it might be seen as impolite. The 'good girl' bow-your-head bit does not work.

'Come on, why didn't you smile? She smiled at you. Be courteous,' my husband would chide me on a walk if I had got lost in thought and not made eye contact with an approaching stranger.

'Hi, how are you?' and 'Hello, how do you do?' are greetings that you must use while talking to your doctor, or the person manning a store's cash counter or a toll booth.

This is a norm, and must become a natural response for you while interacting with others.

Watch your step while walking outside. No talking loudly while in trains, buses, or at a doctor's clinic. No gossiping aloud in your neighbourhood. When you go to any public place, or are standing in a queue, always be mindful of the distance between you and the individual in front of you, even if it means chanting 'privacy, distance, privacy, distance' in your head!

· As Manasi puts it, the consciousness of individual space sets in not when you set foot in the US, but much before that—at the US consulate in India. 'You do not fall over people when you are at a bank or a ticket counter,' she notes, having taken some time to get used to it. It's something you notice in most public spaces in the US—the ticket counter at the bus stop, railway stations, government offices, your local diner, in any space where people congregate.

If you want to take a walk in your neighbourhood, take care not to peer into other people's homes out of curiosity, or stare.

'In our neighbourhood, there is a small pond which I find calming and beautiful. But we don't hang around it,' says Jayasri of her community in Virginia. 'A few apartments overlook the pond. We have to be particular about not intruding into their personal space by walking past their windows.' Her hope of walking by the pond dashed by privacy considerations, she couldn't help but remember with nostalgia those unannounced visits by her uncle back home in Basavangudi, Bengaluru.

Apartment communities in towns near major cities are a welcome break from the cramped towers of cities. Spaced out, well-planned, they usually have sidewalks with lawns. You might not be able to walk to the grocery store, but you can take a walk in your neighbourhood and make friends. You'll be surprised to find people receptive to greetings and small talk.

America is an individualistic society in contrast to India's collectivist culture where the individual matters little in a highly networked society and is expected to sacrifice personal needs for the needs of the collective. This collective could be family, extended family, friends, teams, communities, caste and so on. In the new country, personal space is guarded with zest.

'Don't these people like to have fun? Aren't they lonely?' New arrivals from the other half of the world take a while to figure it out.

A month or so after arriving in the US, Sathya asked Surya if they could invite his boss, a friendly American woman, home for dinner. She craved company, and since Surya had known his boss in India too, she felt a connection.

'It doesn't happen like that! She won't come home!' he protested.

'But why?'

'If she invites you home, it means you are as good as family. People don't invite others just like that. The same applies to us too,' he explained.

Why did she have to think ten times before inviting someone over? Did she have no hopes of assimilating?

12

Boxes, Kitchens and All

Sathya's new kitchen was small. She had thought kitchens in the US were all open-plan, going by what she had seen in films and magazines. She was surprised that her new apartment did not have one like that. She was also disappointed at the lack of a fireplace—made redundant by centralized heating. She had always dreamt of a day when she would have a home with a hearth.

The kitchen serves a primal need of human beings. It is the site of agony, ecstasy, food, culture, love, hate and desire. In America, kitchen aesthetics are far removed from Indian kitchens. Walk into any supermarket's home décor section, and you cannot miss the accessories that insist that 'the kitchen is the heart of your home'.

Mercy was awestruck by her new kitchen. She was poised to become a full-time homemaker. The new kitchen was in contrast with the modest Goan kitchens she was used to. She also found that kitchens function differently in American homes. The concept of a woman spending most of her time cooking and cleaning does not exist.

Mercy says, 'Most American homes have a decent-sized kitchen. Even if they are small, they are well-equipped. An American cannot survive without a dishwasher, chimney, microwave, toaster, blender and multi-purpose food processor that can chop veggies, knead the dough, blend, slice and so on. These were a lot of gadgets for an Indian girl.'

The American kitchen is as much a new world, waiting for the visa wife to discover it, as is the country. To her, the kitchen presents an alluring maze of boxes and gadgets. After all, the kitchen is an inevitable focal point which they engage with, with disdain or delight. Some women love cooking so much they spend their entire day by the stove, churning out dishes, learning new cuisines and giving them their signature twists. Others enter the kitchen grudgingly after marriage, badgered into cooking by the 'good bahu' expectation.

The kitchen and a woman's identity are somewhat tied to each other. Patriarchal societies expect women to master it as if by magic, regardless of cooking ability and interest. On the contrary, women have a push–pull equation with kitchens. Gender equality debates have long centred on kitchens and their symbolism in women's lives.

As for the Indian kitchen, people who run them are soldiers who use their innovative might, turn spot survivalists and run the show from morning till night—making morning coffee or tea, breakfast, brunch, lunch, evening tea or coffee, snacks, dinner, and then cleaning up, washing the utensils, managing the fridge, preparing for the next day, and so on.

Mercy discovered the American kitchen after churning out delectable Goan delicacies from her basic kitchen in Goa. She observes the difference between Indian women and American women vis-à-vis their kitchens. 'In India, a woman cooks to nourish, sustain and exist, as compared to an American woman who cooks on a day when she feels she absolutely must cook. It could be because she feels like exploring her culinary talents, or trying something new. It might be that she feels like making something for the family. There is a lot of information out there which tries to get people to eat home-made meals. But I think it would be a real miracle if Americans were convinced to stop eating junk food and cook every day.'

American kitchens have undergone a great deal of change over the last century. And yet they stand in vivid dissimilarity to desi kitchens.

Sathya was enamoured of her new kitchen and how it could hold so much despite its small size. She felt guilty for being able to enjoy this luxury while her own mother toiled away at her rental home, battling water scarcity and power shortages. Her mother might not send her father off to a jungle for firewood, as her grandmother did, but they were busy chasing their gas cylinder supplier every month.

Given that background, it is no wonder that Sathya's first reaction to her new kitchen was, 'Wow!' Where were the convoys of ants that dotted the walls and the sly lizards that she hated? There was no iron grill on the kitchen window. The sink tap did not go dry when the water supply was off or drip precious pearls away through its faulty valve when the supply came back. It gave her a choice of hot and cold water instead. Water was available 24/7.

In India, she always had an extra-large vessel of water handy for those dry-faucet hours or days. She felt the kitchen to be the most inviting part of her new American home, like thousands of other visa wives. But then, its sink was shallow. The laminate sheet that wrapped her kitchen slab felt temporary. She longed for the solidity of the granite slab she was used to. Like her new home, her kitchen felt make-believe too.

All these triggered bittersweet memories—the magnetic aroma of *pakodas* that drew her into the kitchen on a rainy day, the decor-devoid range of *dabbas*—plastic, steel and aluminium—on those open shelves, the grime on the wall behind the gas stove.

Sathya loved the four-burner stove in her new kitchen and noted the other fixtures with appreciation—a dishwasher, an oven, a pantry, a chimney, vent fans and a fridge so large she could fit into it easily.

Having travelled to and lived in sixty countries around the globe, Madhuri's favourite kitchen remains the one at her grandparents' home in Andhra Pradesh. 'We always had food to eat in the village kitchen. I never relate a good kitchen with good food and a big kitchen with large quantities of food. At times, I have stayed at a friend's mansion but felt hungry because they never had enough food, or it was not cooked well. In my grandmother's house, it was the most basic kitchen and yet all of us were always happy.'

In her American kitchen, Madhuri loads her dishwasher as she talks of her grandma's makeshift kitchen that had a wood-fed stove, known as *kattala poyyi*. Her current kitchen is a large, L-shaped one with a dinette, cabinets and gadgets of all kinds.

The village kitchen had chunks of wood for the stove brought by the men of the household from the jungles. Madhuri's grandmother would cook on a fire. It was a skill only her grandmother was a master at—she knew how to use different types of wood, how much to fill the *chulha* (earthen stove lit with wood or coal), how to blow the air just enough to stoke the fire. 'It is not like an electric stove, where you adjust the flame. You really needed to know how to cook by stoking the fire.'

Younger women in that household were not expected to cook. Their job was to clean, peel and chop the vegetables. 'Nothing came out of cartons and tins. It was not being pounded, ground and baked. It was simple. You boiled it, steamed it or fried it. They would get fresh vegetables from the farm. Meals comprised rice with vegetable curry, or chapati with vegetables. They would boil rice, and if they had ladies' fingers, instead of cooking them separately, they would poke the ladies' fingers into the rice mid-way, so the vegetables steamed with the rice.'

Cut to the American kitchen—everything hides in cabinets, a culture that developed in post-war homes. You pine for those kitchens, covered in soot, that flaunt every dal and vegetable possible. Probably when you spent time there, all you dreamt of was a modular hi-tech kitchen, minus the sweat and heat.

Kaushalya was awestruck when she saw pictures of her kitchen before she actually took her flight. 'There was a four-burner gas stove. I always wanted one for the amount of cooking I do. It was a dream come true!' Homes in the US get piped gas, and not all homes have gas connections. A chunk of them work on electric stoves. Piped gas eliminates the need for the gas cylinder that the Indian middle class worships like gold. An Indian kitchen would collapse without a gas cylinder. Unlike the gas cylinder beneath your two-burner gas stove, the four-burner stove-top has an oven beneath it.

Kaushalya grew up in railway quarters in Bihar. 'During the monsoons, we had to keep vessels under our kitchen's leaking roof. Because there were insects like cockroaches, caterpillars, grasshoppers and also lizards and snakes in the pipes at times, we always had to cover our food. There were visiting cats too that came around hunting for food, and loved to taste any left unattended. My grandfather then fixed a mesh on the kitchen window. Those kitchens had a lot of storage space in the form of an attic. In spring, dry mango leaves would fall into the kitchen from the roof through the chimney. And the home would get flooded during the rains.'

Kitchens in her relatives' homes, by contrast, 'felt posh'. 'They were well-planned and airy. Their sinks were fixed with cement.'

For someone fond of cooking, Kaushalya yearned all her life for a good kitchen. She was so enamoured of this fantastic kitchen that she indulged her husband with a variety of dishes and hosted dinners within the first month of her arrival. She thanked her stars for a piped gas stove.

Shifting from induction stoves and two-burner stoves to the coil stoves of the US can be a bit tricky though.

'Switching to coil stoves was my biggest struggle. The coil electric stove (known popularly as electric heater), was what we used fifteen years ago! Even my mother laughed when I told her,' says Aruna. In India, coil stoves are a thing of the past. We use them when cooking gas runs out, or limit them to lesser tasks like heating water or boiling milk. Today's trend is induction stoves, and all those flat-bottom vessels that come with them.

Making good rotis and *phulkas* (a lighter, more puffed form of roti) is a challenge on the coil stove, as is cooking *baingan ka bharta* (a usually spicy brinjal dish). How Kaushalya missed turning the brinjal by its stem, watching it char to blackish-brown and spicing it up!

The luxury of an American kitchen does not mean it is devoid of safety precautions. In fact, safety is more of an issue because of the flammable nature of wood—the primary material used in building. Multitasking pros beware. Do not dream of taking a quick shower while a dish simmers on the stove. The entire building can burn down if you leave your cooking unattended. There are smoke detectors, but by the time they are triggered, it might be too late. So, when you cook, stay in the kitchen. If you bake, you have the luxury of a kitchen timer or stopwatch. Kitchen fires and fireplace accidents bring down entire neighbourhoods in America.

Manasi tried her hand at baking a cake for her husband at a hotel once. With no manual at hand or prior experience, she simply put the batter in a dish and turned the heat on. She was clueless about pre-heating the oven or timing it. The result was not a charred cake but a fire, causing the hotel's kitchen to go up in smoke. It set the smoke alarm off and fire engines arrived in no time. The fire was thankfully a minor one.

To think of it, my grandmother hardly worried about anything catching fire when she lit a twisted sheet of newspaper over the gas stove flame, and walked 20 feet to her backyard chulha in the morning sun to heat up bath water in a huge copper pot for us kids.

Our grandmothers and mothers struggled with woodstoves, kerosene stoves and the like before the gas stove brought them relief, followed by the coil stove, the induction stove, microwave and the electric cooker.

Many homes in the US have a 'food crusher' in the sink. It is really an electrically powered garbage disposal unit installed under a kitchen sink, between the drain and the trap. Such units came into existence in the 1930s. They shred food waste into small pieces, to ease their passing through plumbing along with the waste water.[13]

An object that confuses Indians unfamiliar with its real use is a double crate housed in a big container tucked near the sink, below the counter. Kaushalya thought it was meant to store utensils. I thought so too when I first saw it. Kaushalya diligently used its shelves to store her kitchenware, and pulled out its spoons crate and placed it on her counter-top. Visa wives often found themselves challenged by this gadget, which is actually a dishwasher. Newcomers usually spent much time gawking at the box. Now dishwashers are becoming common in Indian households as well.

When she finally got to know what it was, Kaushalya wondered if it was possible for utensils to get thoroughly cleaned without actually scrubbing them. She finally learnt how to use it properly at a hotel where they had checked in for a holiday and soon became a pro at it—loading the heavy utensils on its bottom rack, light utensils and smaller ones on the top rack, and fixing the dishwasher pod in the little shelf on its door before turning the machine on.

Sathya's husband, however, refused to let her use the dishwasher for nine months after their arrival. 'Waste of water. Waste of electricity. We hardly have any utensils. Stick to washing by hand,' he instructed. She was still interested in learning how the gadget worked. When Madhuri learnt about it in London, she had to figure out the mechanics of the machine for a start. 'There were times when I inverted things and they did not get washed. I was not sure where the water was coming from—the top or underneath.' Like most women, 'trial and error' helped turn Madhuri into a fan.

The other ubiquitous 'box' in American homes is the refrigerator. What's new about a refrigerator? Refrigerators have been part of Indians lives since the 1980s, when new owners showed them off as status symbols. In America, it's the size of refrigerators that catches you off guard, causing the visa wife to think, 'What do these people eat that they stuff their fridge like this?

The utility of the fridge in an American home is much more than in Indian households. With the high consumption of frozen foods and ready-to-cook meals, the American refrigerator is more or less your pantry, storing your meals for the next one week or even a month. Standard American refrigerators measure anywhere between 1–3 feet wide, 6 feet high and 2–3 feet deep. Freezers are a lot larger than the milk-packet-plus-ice-tray ones that we are used to. American motels and hotels normally have a refrigerator and sometimes microwave in their rooms, even if located in far-flung corners.

Kitchens are activity centres in American households, and go beyond activities of cooking and cleaning, especially with kids around. The fridge door turns into a gallery of 'been there done that' travel and décor magnets, school schedule sheets for the kids, and their pictures.

Kitchen space dynamics vary in America too depending on their location. Some apartments have no full-fledged kitchens, but kitchenettes meant for occasional cooking. By habit, Americans grab a coffee-to-go, breakfast-to-go, eat lunch at some diner and sometimes make a light dinner at home. Such people are usually working couples with no kids, or single people whose work lives and travel dominate their lifestyles. Other families stick to couponing for restaurant meals and grocery purchases.

When an Indian family, with its cultural culinary baggage, moves into such an apartment, the result can be amusing.

Anand Iyer was a bachelor when he moved into an apartment close to Manhattan. The 1960s building and its units had gone through many renovations, and he had a kitchenette, not kitchen. Being in the proximity of New York, this apartment was a replica of those in Brooklyn and Queens. When Anand got married and brought Mahalakshmi home, she was faced with a culinary challenge. The kitchenette had little storage space. A foot between the four-burner gas stove and the fridge was all she had for pre-cooking preparations. There was no pantry for grocery and utensils. The couple converted their living room closet into kitchen storage. They bought a makeshift dining table for chopping vegetables.

The newly married couple had to play musical chairs with the chopping board, colander and steel utensils in order to cope with their meals-thrice-a-day lifestyle.

Aruna's kitchen was similar. 'It was like playing chess all the time. I did not have a dishwasher. When we had company, and the first time ever that we got fifteen people home, I was nervous the whole day, wondering, "Where will people put their plates?".'

Anand and Mahalakshmi did not mind the chess-board character of their love nest, nor the absence of a dishwasher. The couple's biggest nightmare was rats, so much so that they resorted to mousetraps.

When the couple had a baby girl, they discovered that she wanted to turn on the gas stove's knobs. 'Gas stoves in India are placed high on the kitchen slab, so kids cannot reach the knobs easily. We have the option of turning the gas cylinder knob off, which takes care of safety. American stoves pose a challenge,' Anand said. One way around this is to fix a 'child gate' to the entrance to the kitchen, which they couldn't because theirs was a kitchenette tucked into the hallway that connected the bedroom and living room.

Kitchen layouts differ depending on the size of apartments, but standard American homes have an eat-in kitchen, with a nook for breakfast. In some states, apartments get built so that the kitchen and living room have separate entrances. Kitchens may also get placed closest to the parking lot, or garage, to help unload groceries from the car.

Some of Aruna's best moments were in her American kitchens. When she visited a friend whose home kitchen had a door to the yard, the friend would put a kettle on the stove and settle down to chat with her at the eat-in dining table. Kids would come into the house through the kitchen.

For Aruna, the kitchen morphed from a mechanical place to a cosy place for bonding over a chat. At her own apartment, she developed a special relationship with her neighbour who cooked well. The two Pittsburgh women would cook some dishes and leave them at each other's doorsteps. Such gestures helped the two bond in a unique way.

When she joined her graduation classes, Aruna's fellow students often had potluck lunches. 'I was apologetic initially of how my food looked. Once, I had invited four friends, and everything I had cooked looked yellow that day. I was justifying, "Everything is yellow, but all the dishes taste different." At the graduate school, I met people who cooked for fun. Cooking finally looked like an activity to bond over. It sets off sharing of experiences on culture. It was no longer a symbol of enslavement. It got creative. Cooking was liberating. It was no longer about a sad housewife, but getting together of people. Potluck lunches were when people started looking at cooking as a trigger point for childhood stories.'

With reluctance, women begin to experiment with American dishes, adding an Indian touch. Bindhu recalls how if she had known to make American dishes, she would have fared a lot better in her kitchen in her early months.

Thanks to America being the veritable melting pot, women like Bindhu and Aruna were exposed to other cuisines. The country is home to people from around the world—Chinese, Koreans, Filipinos, Mexicans, South Americans, Canadians, Europeans, South Asians. Availability of these cuisines at affordable prices puts them at ease, encouraging them to take those baby steps. Experimenting with them in your new kitchen gives you a high. Says Mercy about her own tryst with cuisines, 'Moving here deepened my curiosity regarding other cuisines. The more I read and learnt of how other people around the world eat, the more I yearned to cook their food. Kitchens in America are so well-equipped. So why not cook?' An important thing to note here is that while in India everything gets Indianized, so you have Indian Chinese and Indian Italian, in the US, a lot of emphasis is placed on the original taste, so one actually gets to try truly exotic dishes with never-before-tasted flavours and fragrances. It can be unnerving at first, but is actually a food connoisseur's delight once the tongue begins to distinguish and relish different combinations.

Indian women are delighted with another gadget they find in the American kitchen—the oven. 'When you use those knobs, some magic happens,' says Aruna, whose husband showed her how to use it. 'There is this immigrant tendency towards thrift. I thought, "I will bake. But what if it gets burnt and wasted?"'

It took her a month to move on from 'gingerly baking' to full-fledged baking. And it was only a whole six months later that she plucked the courage to take home-baked ·brownies over to a pot luck. 'Baking is about precision, unlike cooking, where you can cover up your mistakes. I bake simple things. Most people take to baking when they go to the US.'

Kaushalya started by using her oven to store vessels, oblivious to the dangers of storing anything in an unused oven, and later to set curd quicker during winter. She bought ready-to-bake cake mixes and diligently followed the directions. When her husband's colleague came by with a home-baked chocolate cake, she was quick to ask for recipes, and soon tried a variety of cakes.

An American kitchen is not just about its gadgets. Mercy notes that it is really about quickness and convenience. Madhuri, too, likes the American kitchen's gadgets. 'If I asked my husband to manually peel, cut and chop an onion, he would not be eager to do it. If there was a machine for it, he would use it. Since we bought a juicer, he volunteers to make the juice. There's literally a gadget for everything. We've a can opener, bottle opener, tons of cutters to cut vegetables. It's the fun aspect of using gadgets that gets my husband into the kitchen.' Her own favourites are an electricity-free plastic chopper bowl and a manual press juicer, both bought from India.

'Just the fact that I get my husband to work in the kitchen is something people back home would not accept. It is not a done thing,' she observes. 'Here, everyone in the family does their bit in the kitchen.'

Not all families can afford fancy gadgets as soon as they arrive. When it comes to managing home and kitchen spaces, husbands can overdo their penchant for thrift. Add to it the complex situation of 'here today, there tomorrow' for visa-dependent families, and investing in new gadgets becomes a bone of contention. Initial projects that bring families to the US could be for a month or a few months only. If the family gets serious about moving to the country, they brace themselves for the H1 holder getting the boot after a few months. Such situations can influence how you run your kitchen.

Rupashree's kitchen sported spartan essentials for a long time. 'There's no need to have too much stuff when we know we can return any time. If his visa gets extended, we'll stay. Otherwise, we're planning to just save up some money to buy an apartment. And then leave,' she convinced herself. Though a part of her longed to stay, the practical part of her decided to accept the circumstances. Her son, who she brought to the country as an eight-month-old baby, kept her on her toes. Not having kitchenware within his reach meant lesser worry. 'Having less utensils does mean washing them often. But it keeps my kitchen clean,' she explained it away. Some months later, when her husband's visa got extended and it became clear that they would stay on, she finally began populating her kitchen. Two years on, she finds her kitchen too cluttered.

During the initial two years, her husband's constant reminder was, 'Buy what you need. If you don't need it, think twice.' Husbands are prone to saying things like, 'Do not waste vegetables', 'Do not buy so many vegetables' and 'We don't need so much milk.'

Often such remarks border on control. Overt and covert statements to the tune of 'save the dollar, save the pennies' create a feeling of insecurity in the minds of women already burdened with the culture shock battle. Rupashree accepted the roving nature of her husband's job. She was willing to go the extra mile in the interest of her son's future—by moving places, incorporating thrift, not spending too much.

Rupashree and Deepan have an active social life and often host pot lucks and meet up over dinners. She feels the pinch of not having a maid to help her unlike in India, but takes it in her stride. She does not mind making food for thirty people on her own instead of ordering party trays.

13

Soul Curry for Sanity

The rare morning sun shone through her kitchen window as Shivani stirred the sambhar. She chopped coriander leaves and used a knife to push them into the steaming stew. The sun was out after many days of rainy weather. Elsewhere, Willamette River's waters gleamed while Portlanders meandered to offices on its bridges. Shivani poured some sambhar into a bowl and placed it against the light to take a picture of it on her smartphone.

She jotted down the ingredients on a post-it slip, covered the steel bowl on the stove and opened her laptop. It was the omnipresent sambhar, the recipe for which is available on hundreds of blogs and websites across the Internet, but she knew hers was different. She felt brave enough to post its recipe on her blog.

Shivani was still new to the city and its suburbs. She had no idea about a cooking blog despite being an avid

Internet user. She was just out of college when she got married to a process engineer from a computer chip firm.

A few weeks into her marriage, her husband walked into the kitchen one evening and began tightening the lids of some containers, saying, 'You have not closed the lids properly.'

Shivani calls her husband a perfectionist whom it is difficult to deal with about everyday matters. The idea of writing a blog came from him. When she did not show interest after constant persistence, he gave up. 'Do it when you are comfortable.'

Despite misgivings, Shivani decided to take the first step. Her husband was thrilled and helped her set it up.

It had been a few weeks since she had started out. A reader had tried out her halwa recipe and said it was good. Shivani looked at the sambhar pot on the stove. She smiled to herself. The walls were bare; the furniture looked alien. Gone was the homeliness of her maternal home. Her attempts at taking walks on her own were still a struggle.

Reading the comments on her blog made her feel less lonely. Someone read what she wrote. Her work made a difference to someone. On another day, a friend of a friend wrote to her saying, 'Do not think no one reads your blog. We read it and like it.'

'It was like a tonic to my confidence,' she said.

Shivani finally had something to think about other than the past. She joined an international network of food bloggers by default when she stepped into the blogging

routine. It threw interesting situations at her in the real
world too.

'Once, a friend made a good dessert. I kept asking her
for the recipe but she wouldn't give it to me. It dawned
on me later that I was nagging her. Till today, she has not
shared the recipe. I eventually read about it at the library.'

Shivani's tryst with the kitchen was inevitable. Her
marriage to an NRI, who was physically absent for most
of the day, had thrown her into this life of domesticity,
something she had known she would end up with but
was never quite prepared for. Cooking and feeding her
husband became a given. Oregon's new landscapes and
air were a journey yet to be embarked upon. It would be
a while before she mustered the courage to talk to her
neighbours comfortably. Another world out there put her
at ease, for now—virtual, and probably less judgemental
about her existence.

There is something about cooking in America,
enforced or by choice, that transforms many visa wives
into food bloggers. 'It is a good way of easing into your
life in the US,' says Jayasri, whose own love for the history
of food prompted her to start her blog—Rasam Nirvana.
In her blog, Jayasri writes not just about cooking, but
also about other aspects of living in the US that catch
her eye. 'When you go to the market, you see vegetables.
You touch them. You feel them. The experience of
shopping for vegetables is the same as it is in India. But
in India, the vegetable vendor comes to your house. Here,
you go the market. There you bargain with the vendor.
Here, nobody bothers you at the market. You cannot ask

another person anything. As Indians, we want to talk to people.' The need to talk to people is big for us when we come here.

Jayasri had worked at a daily newspaper in India before shifting to the US. She found writing a blog post liberating and very unlike filing a news story. This is true for many journalists who have moved on to other occupations and adapted to freestyle writing. Blogging is different from news reporting just as it is different from Facebook or Twitter posts. Food blogs have some of the highest hit counts among niche blogs, driven as the traffic is by the primal need to satiate hunger. 'As a writer, I don't find fulfilment in writing the blog,' says Jayasri. 'It is just a fun thing to do. I do not go into deep, philosophical reflections while writing my blog. I don't expect it to do anything dramatic to my daily life.'

For Shivani, though, blogging fetched its rewards by helping her release bottled-up emotions. Her mother-in-law, who was passionate about reading and writing, and her sisters-in-law who lived in the US too, all loved her blog. Her own parents were elated that their daughter was able to gain a foothold in her new life. Her father became her unofficial public relations officer. 'Wherever he went, he would talk about my blog. Some people would get my email id from him and write to me.' At her husband's office too, people followed her blog. She felt proud about doing something nice. In a more unconscious way, she was able to hold herself together. 'I told myself, "You are not the only person in this world and not everyone is out to say bad things about you."'

Shivani stopped blogging after a while. She felt that in his enthusiasm to get her to perfect her blog, her husband was interfering too much with her style of writing. Constant critiquing made her feel conscious and watched, and she was not willing to listen to his suggestions after a point. The arrival of her baby boy kept her busy. Today, she is a super busy mom. Yet the memory of those blogging days that gave some validity to her existence lightens her mood.

It's one thing to cook a dish, but quite another to master it. It takes time and perseverance. Blogs are such. Feed them and they stay alive. Leave them and they could vanish into online oblivion. Blogging takes consistency. It takes a lot of hard work to get noticed. Nivedita Subramanian started her blog, Panfusine, not out of the need to connect in the new country, but as a potential 'project' for a business school application for when she returned to work after her daughter turned a year old. 'The person handling the NYU (New York University) orientation session suggested the keyword 'recipe' and I began by writing a post for the technique I had been using for years. It took off from there.'

Her blog has thrived ever since. She recalls not having any time to even put any thought into her impending move to New York City from Cape Town, South Africa, where she was working night and day to finish her master's thesis in biomedical engineering.

After handing in her thesis she had two weeks to get home to Johannesburg, pack and leave. She reached New York and suddenly felt homesick. She pined for the beautiful city she had left behind. At her university, she had moved on to another area of academics—neuroscience. Luckily, the pressure of catching up with the new subject kept her from getting too lonely in the crowded Big Apple.

The need to give voice to her culinary experiments rose more out of her disappointment with 'how South Indian cuisine was under-represented in the world and stagnated by a lack of assertive presence even within the Indian perspective.' She fretted about how, technically, South Indian cuisine 'does not exist from a historical point of view, since it was never influenced by wars and conflicts.'

Nivedita's culinary experiments gathered steam. 'I started by tweaking classic recipes for a more universal audience without compromising on original flavours and tastes,' she says. Panfusine soon became her passion. She consistently tried new recipes, gave an innovative twist to traditional ones, poured her energy into it.

'From my five years' experience in the "blogosphere", I am inclined to divide food bloggers into two categories— those that blog for search engine optimization (SEO), page hits and revenue, and those that blog for the sheer joy of creating new recipes. I am the latter kind. A strong USP is critical if you are in for the long haul. Not counting the unscrupulous lot who blog only for the attention (these are usually the ones who tend to ignore basic copyright rules and blogging etiquette), there are plenty of bloggers who produce recipes weekly without fail, but at times, quality takes a backseat. True recipe creation is hard work, and the biggest challenge comes from within. There is an addictive sense of wanting to best yourself, to outdo that awesome creation you came up with last week.'

Malini started her blog in 2009 more as an online recipe box. She had learnt to live in a strange land, from scratch. She was no cook before getting married. 'My mother tried to teach me domestic skills before marriage. After marriage, when I would tell her on the phone that I made *puran poli* (sweet roti made using jaggery and chickpea flour for filling), she would get shocked.'

'You did not even know how to make chai properly. How did you learn *puran poli?*' her mother would ask, aghast.

'I learnt from a cookbook.'

Malini's sister-in-law, who had recently moved to Canada, wanted to learn cooking from her. Phone calls were expensive those days, a decade ago.

'Why don't you put your recipes on a blog? It would be easy for me to access,' she suggested. The timing was perfect. Malini was on maternity leave after the birth of·her second child. She had some time on her hands. She immediately started her blog. Her ability to network with fellow Indians, her enterprise and her willingness to learn pushed her ahead. Her friends were her critics and fans alike.

Malini's strength was simple daily fare. And she let the cuisine keep her grounded while learning several other world dishes. Feedback kept her going. 'I did not start it for traffic or popularity's sake—I blog for myself, not others,' she insists. Her true test is when her kids eat what she makes without fuss. 'If they make faces, I don't post the recipe or picture on my blog.'

Her food blog became akin to a rope she held on to desperately when she became a victim of rumour-mongering and boycott in her own friend circle in America. 'It was a seemingly casual conversation where a couple of friends sought some life advice and I gave it. It did not occur to me that they wanted false assurances, not straightforward advice. They did not like what I said. They twisted my words, and I ended up with no friends in the vicinity for two years. They stopped coming home or calling.'

Malini and her husband had hosted that bunch of friends every weekend for years, and were kicked out of their lives suddenly. It left them devastated and questioning their own trust in people. In the dead of night she would cry a million tears into her pillow after tucking her kids into bed. For them, she had to put up a brave front. 'My kids got bullied for no reason in a couple of those gatherings. They had no right to hurt my kids.'

Malini's blog posts continued in the thick of trauma. Her blog became her oxygen. She had reason to pat herself for starting it.

The blog journey had its ups and downs too. Somebody plagiarized entire posts from her blog and other food blogs to spike traffic and earn ad money, for instance. 'Some people blog to get famous. They want recognition. I did it for myself. The pictures of my earliest posts were not even aligned properly. A blogger friend who was pregnant then helped me sort out the blog. She walked me through the process over a two-hour online chat, taught me to post pictures and showed me how to take pictures of the dishes I cooked,' says Malini.

Her blog has now reached a plateau. 'I cannot tweak recipes and present them as new for the sake of blogging. I know girls who post for the sake of SEO, not passion for food. These days, I post only when I make something new,' she says.

Is it merely an interest in the kitchen that drives visa wives to start food blogs? Or does cooking in an American kitchen nudge them in the direction? Indian cuisine is not as popular in America as Chinese, Thai, Italian and Mexican. Is it about fewer restaurants giving *desi khaana* outside home in American towns?

There are plenty of Indian restaurants in New York, California, Texas and Illinois, where a large chunk of the Indian population is concentrated. More Indians means more Indian restaurants. If you are stuck in a state with no Indian cuisine restaurants for a few hundred miles, you will crave Indian cuisine. A sightseeing trip to New York will make you want to rush to desi eateries. Food is not about satiating hunger. Today, food has leapt from the modest, dingy, coal-stove kitchens to fancy plate canvases and become art.

A spoonful of a piece of pie can induce flavours of not just moist chocolate filling, but the tangy surprise of tamarind when it melts in your mouth. Chef Vikas Khanna likens Indian food to memory, to nostalgia, like food from anywhere in the world can be.

A Canadian woman celebrating her eighty-fifth birthday at Vikas Khanna's flagship restaurant, Junoon, broke into tears once. She had just tasted *wadiyan* that he made using a dehydrator. The crunchies reminded her of her childhood in Punjab. She had lived in Canada for sixty years without ever going to a restaurant.

'Indian food is a strong part of memory for women when they come, so they want to recreate it,' Vikas Khanna told me when I met him in 2015. 'Their initial phone calls are about cooking. When they were in India they never bothered, because it was easily available in plenty. It's like the sun. You do not bother if the sun is going to be up tomorrow morning. But you need it every day. It is interesting how behaviour changes. When they were in India, they probably never went to the kitchen to learn how to make dal or pakodas. In America, the need for authentic Indian food makes itself felt very strongly indeed.'

With blogging, Vikas feels that women have the opportunity to express themselves better. 'They are not bound by too many (limitations of financials). They can be free when they write.'

When an individual loses his or her basic support system with one journey, it is but natural that such an individual latches on to available options for support. It may be to survive the phase, to get a grip on the new culture, or simply stay sane on a day you are tempted to count the fibres in your carpet.

Vikas loves how Indian women post simple recipes online, the process eased by smartphones and videos. 'In America, accessibility is high. Accessibility has reached out to women and they have tools.'

Cooking, he says, gives people a sense of security. 'Cooking means freedom. It's a freedom of thought, that you are not dependent. Michael Pollan, a top psychiatrist of food, says that less people indulge in cooking in America because of two primary reasons: (1) people don't have time, and (2) in America, there are many options available to spend your evenings; hence, cooking evening meals becomes a choice because most people like to go out and eat there itself. For people who don't travel much, don't have a driver's licence, who are stuck at home, cooking becomes one of the primary ways of spending evenings, and cooking shows become a delight.'

It is also easier in the US to find ingredients to experiment with different cuisines. Food blogging is a rage across the globe. In America, it acquires a global twist, with the possibility of the creative blending of ingredients from different cuisines. Some successful food bloggers take their ventures to the next level by turning into entrepreneurs. Some monetize their blogs through advertisements, though a visa wife would seldom brave it. She may blog till the Employment Authorization Document status comes through in the Green Card process, or the Green Card is in hand.

Often, husbands are encouraging when the wives decide to blog about food. Would they be as comfortable if she were to blog about world politics and policy? Not sure. They freak out if she gives an interview about her life to publications. What if she says something that jeopardizes their stay? What if she is not supposed to talk at all? Why take the risk?

Though food blogging might be the most popular, visa wives blog about a range of other subjects as well: travel in the US, their lives as visa wives, home and décor, design, crafts, kids and so on.

For three years after I got married, I posted actively on a personal blog. I was in Chennai and every day was a mountain that needed climbing. It was when the wait for the husband to come back from work was the longest, tinged with the grief of losing out on a profession that was like the oxygen I needed to survive. Umpteen medicine cartons lying by my bed were what turned me to crafts.

I made bookmarks, dug through my cousin's stash of tourism brochures for recyclable pictures, re-purposed used and discarded household items and started gifting them to visitors. A few months after arriving in the US, my craft blog was born in the middle of another phase of copious tears.

It was probably the best thing that happened during those mad months. It helped me connect with others who were bloggers. I was in the thick of post-miscarriage blues when Vikas Khanna organized a bloggers' meet at his plush Manhattan restaurant. My husband gave me that helpful nudge when I was wondering whether I should go. Later, a girl I met there sent me home-made lip balm and a handmade coat brooch. Ever received a gift from someone you met just once? Someone you cannot be useful to? It's a little child in us that dances on seeing a handmade gift in the post. 'You need to meet strangers now. That's your therapy,' she suggested. This friend just flitted into my life, a gust of fresh air in the vacuum of my social life.

Vidya Nair and her husband bought a home in Virginia after moving from their long-time base—New Jersey. The new house became their new DIY project, to make it 'home'. She decided to put their project, their efforts at home décor and DIY projects online. Her home was not what drew her to blogging for a start. Her own love for cooking and constant following up on other food blogs gave her courage. She loved cooking, and cuisine experiments. She speaks on the lines of Vikas Khanna's observations. 'Out here, you get ingredients like chopped vegetables, which make cooking easy. Also, you don't have any help in the kitchen. If you are left alone, and you have easy access to food-related stuff, it becomes easier to be creative. I started cooking what I knew and then started experimenting. My husband and I explored all the other cuisines that are available here. We got curious and said, "Let's make this; let's make that." I followed the same pattern as the other bloggers do. It is interesting. Now I see lots of fusion dishes.'

By the time Vidya decided to blog, she was already a US citizen, far ahead of the time when she had arrived as a newlywed visa wife fifteen years ago. 'I became a good cook in the first two years. And I cooked a lot for our friends who came over,' she muses. In a way, the seed for blogging was sown in her heart then.

She reflects on the journey that should have begun in 2005, when she was still taking baby steps to prepare for her life in the US. 'I used to share a lot of recipes with friends. So my friend said, "Why don't you start a blog?" I thought too, "Why don't I start a blog?" But what deterred me was that I don't cook by measure but by instinct. For cooking blogs, you must be specific about measures. How could I share that online? It would look vague for others to try out my recipes.'

Whatsurhomestory is the crisp name for her home blog. It struck a chord in the online world where Vidya's positioning as a desi blogger adhering to mainstream US interior style and at the same time incorporating the Indian element put her in a creative niche of sorts.

It shocked her family when after two years of backbreaking work on her blog, with no difference in its traffic, Vidya, who got laid off from her job, decided to make her blog her new career. This was in 2014. 'They place high priority on the security of a full-time job, considering we have two kids. For weeks, my parents prayed that I change my mind.'

Something of the sort has been tried out by women in India too, and many have gone ahead to taste success. But Vidya and her husband live in Virginia, and not far from the country's capital—one of the most expensive areas to live in. Vidya persisted for three months, using her time away from full-time employment to promote her blog. She attended conferences where bloggers met. 'At one such conference in Atlanta, I was the only Indian home blogger. It was good because people remembered me instantly after that!'

For two years, she blogged from home and did not connect much with bloggers in person. When she connected with some American bloggers online for advice to improve traffic, they suggested she start a food section. It was such in-person networking that gave her exposure, and put her in touch with groups that offered support on several aspects of blogging.

'A lot of the bloggers are moms who quit work and find time on hand when they are home with kids. They start a blog and network from the word go. You will notice that many home blogs in the US have a bit about parenting too. And most of us go through issues with kids. There is an instant connect when you share your hard times with people. Going to conferences helped a lot. When you take away all these regional and minor differences, we have kids and families. So that bond is there irrespective of the colour of your skin or where you come from. It's just women going through a similar phase of life who connect. You share the bond of being entrepreneur women. A lot of people, contrary to.what I was expecting, are very welcoming.'

'Mommy bloggers' is a trend in the US, just as 'desi food blogging' is a trend among Indians. In it, Vidya found a new world of possibilities. Her style is more 'mainstream'—in the American décor sense, no doubt. Her natural choice was warm colour palettes, unlike American home bloggers who preferred cool colour palettes. 'That is where I come from. I cannot change that part of me.' Vidya also painstakingly sources décor items from her trips to India. Yet, her sense of style is not anywhere near that of other Indian home bloggers in the US.

'When you visit some desi homes here, of talented desi bloggers, it is nostalgia unlimited. It is like a trip to India,' says Vidya. 'A blogger friend told me once, "If you do not fit into the tribe, form your own tribe."'

Vidya discovered through the three months of networking and promoting the blog that she was not able to get through her home DIY projects, thanks to the blog turning into her full-time occupation. 'It took the pleasure out of the whole blogging bit. I realized that I will love doing it when I have a job in hand,' she says. From blogging five days a week, she cut down to three days a week. She and her husband made the blog an LLC (Limited Liability Company).

Often, it takes an individual a journey in person, to a new space, to unlock fresh ideas. That new space could simply be a home, office, village, city, country or continent. It takes a physical journey to delve within. It takes the mundane of elsewhere to appreciate the mundane of back home.

An intercontinental move throws this in your face. It jolts you. The need to share, talk or express fuels your search for a space, a platform. The blogging world, social media and the Internet become your platform to adapt.

Thousands of bloggers like Vidya, Nivedita, Malini, Jayasri and Shivani find their chatting nook in the virtual space. Blogs, food and otherwise, become aids to assimilation in their alien culture.

14

Stay Healthy, or Get Trapped

Rekha found her neighbour, Rani, sobbing and looking dishevelled and distraught. She had rushed to her home after hearing that hot milk had fallen on Rani's four-year-old daughter.

Between sobs, Rani recounted the incident. Post-dinner, she had heated a bowl of milk for her little girls. Her elder one, Shika, and younger two-year-old, Siya, were playing with their father in the open-plan living room. Unpredictable as kids are, Shika ran to her mom suddenly. Rani was holding the bowl of milk, about to pour it into glasses. Hot milk spilled on Shika.

They called 911 and Shika was rushed to the nearest hospital. In shock, the couple could do nothing more than cry. They were unable to take any procedural instructions from the staff. Kant, Rani's husband, had called his boss and a friend who came and helped fill up forms and insurance details. What followed in the next two weeks was so terrifying that acquaintances who had little to do with their lives could not help but pray that a similar fate befall no one in the world.

After being administered emergency first aid, Shika was shifted to another hospital, the best in their 100-mile radius, to be treated for upper-body burns. At four, she was the youngest patient in the hospital's ICU.

For the couple, it was the longest night of their lives. Their baby was declared out of danger after preliminary treatment, but she was in immense pain. She begged to go home. Rani stood by her bedside day and night. For the next two weeks, Shika screamed in agony, and lost her appetite.

Would she survive? Would she be able to lead a normal life? Did the burns hurt her organs? How could we do this? Rani blamed herself. Kant blamed himself. They could not drink a drop of water, or eat a morsel of food.

The couple had no family in the country. They were at the mercy of friends. Not everyone was in a position to put their work aside and stay at the hospital. Their two-year-old needed to be cared for, too. Over the next few days, the couple stayed at the hospital while their younger one was taken in by friends. Some friends brought food to the hospital, but the parents found themselves unable to eat while their baby was in such pain.

Kant got a call from Child Services, scaring them even more. They would be investigated for negligence. 'Will they take our baby away?' It was the biggest fear gnawing at them.

The authorities talked to their friends and neighbours. Inquiries were discreet. The couple told the truth when the time came.

About ten days later, Rani, who was by Shika's bedside, got another call. Her younger one, Siya, who was at a friend's home, had accidentally injured her hand on broken glass. The friend quickly called 911 and rushed her to the nearest hospital. A while later, her husband rushed to his little one, wondering what was happening to them.

Rani asked a friend to stay with Shika that night and rushed to the children's hospital where Siya was. The glass had cut through a nerve on Siya's tiny hand, requiring surgery. The following morning, Kant's boss organized an emergency meeting with his superiors and colleagues to figure out how the family could be helped in this crisis. Transporting colleagues and friends who were helping with care-giving, dropping off food and shuttling between the two hospitals where the kids were admitted, were the main issues. Some of them had no cars, and had to rely on others for a ride to the hospitals. Colleagues were assigned to take turns doing the various chores they had determined.

Siya was discharged after surgery the same evening as Shika. The hospitals were far apart, separated by an hour's journey through Philadelphia city and its traffic. One of Kant's bosses helped transport the family back home, an ordeal that finally ended at midnight.

The next few months were about painful recovery. Shika had to be kept away from sunlight, which meant no playing with friends outdoors. Siya had to be given equal attention. Both needed endless doctors' visits for follow-ups. Exhaustion was an understatement for the couple. They had no time to cook. Their neighbour, an Indian and a new mother, made sure to cook for them for about a month. They barely had time to eat. The time their kids were asleep was all they had to breathe.

Kant could not report to work for a while. His ratings suffered. Bosses, while sympathetic to his situation, would not budge when it came to performance reviews.

When the children were out of hospital, the authorities paid them a visit to ascertain details. 'The police came as well. They asked us lots of questions about what happened, how it happened, and so on. We hid nothing from them.' The couple was thankfully spared.

Their original medical bills ran to about $70,000, inclusive of hospital care, doctors' visits and medicines. The family's insurance policy covered 80 per cent of the costs. This meant that they ended up paying approximately $20,000 from their pocket, staggering the payments over the following year. 'Siya's bills were more,' says Rani, 'about $30,000 because of surgery. When you calculate in rupees, the bills went up to Rs 1 crore.'

A couple of years on, Shrinivas Narayan, another techie who had moved to the area, faced a similar situation.

'My wife was doing a certification and had an exam the following day. I had reached home before her and made some tea. I offered it to our nanny too, who was watching TV with my twenty-month-old daughter. My wife and I were talking in the kitchen when our nanny came to talk to us, leaving her teacup on the dining table. It was hardly two or three seconds, but long enough for my daughter to pull at the cup. The hot tea fell on her and caused her dress to stick to her body. She suffered burns from the neck to the belly button,' says Shrinivas.

'I pulled her clothes off and poured water over her, followed by honey. We wrapped her in a towel and rushed her to the nearest hospital in our car.' The toddler got first aid and was sent by an ambulance to another hospital an hour away to be treated for burns. Unlike Shika, who had to remain in the hospital for two full weeks, his daughter was discharged the same day.

Parenting is difficult. When children go through such accidents, guilt compounds parents' misery. Quick thinking on Shrinivas's part helped.

For the two families, 911 was a saviour. The hospitals that they went to wasted no time waiting for the families to pay up an advance, which is a commonplace practice in hospitals in Indian cities. Bills began arriving a few weeks after hospitalization. What most newly arrived families don't know is that healthcare is not a basic right in the US. The key to your access to healthcare in the US is a great health insurance package.

~

High-skilled arrivals employed by firms on H1, L1 and other work visas are provided insurance coverage, which is part-paid by the employer. Insurance packages, however, vary depending on where the visa-holder is employed.

The US has the highest per capita healthcare spending in the world. But access to it is not easy. A chunk of the population still cannot walk into a hospital and get treatment without insurance. Private insurance is the biggest source of health insurance coverage for people younger than sixty-five years of age. People also access healthcare through public or social insurance and private payment.

Medicare is a form of public or social insurance. Medicare is a government health programme, aimed at people aged sixty-five years or older, and for people with certain types of renal diseases. In addition, the country has Medicaid, which is a welfare programme and not insurance, meant for children of the low-income group and their caretakers. These two programmes are often misunderstood for their coverage.

In any case, an average Indian high-skilled worker and his or her family are given some form of private insurance through employer sponsorship. Private insurance can also be purchased individually, but such policies are expensive and come with limited coverage. Self-employed people, and people who work in industries such as mining or fishing where insurance is difficult to get, usually have to get individual policies.

Group insurance, the other word to understand employer-sponsored health insurance packages through private companies, is less expensive. It works on 'co-pay', which actually means that the costs of a visit, service, medicine and so on are shared by employer and beneficiary. India has such health insurance too. But coverage is limited to in-patient care. In America, outpatient care is covered under health insurance.

Healthcare reform experts note that, of late, employers have started shifting a greater proportion of these insurance costs to employees. If you are a seasonal worker or part-time worker, it is unlikely that you will get good insurance coverage. Similarly, small firms that have less than twenty-five employees may not offer insurance.

In case of private insurance, if you pay a high premium, your healthcare costs can come down. A low premium policy means you end up spending more. It is because the 'deductible cost' is low on a high-premium policy. For instance, if the deductible cost for your policy is $2000, you end up paying costs up to $2000. Beyond that, the bills are borne by your insurance company. Imagine if the policy has a deductible of $10,000. It would mean that the individual pays $10,000 out of his or her pocket. Such a high deductible would likely scare you away from surgeries. If you need a surgical procedure that would cost about $3000, for instance, you would end up paying the entire cost from your pocket. It would also mean that you must save up $10,000 for medical emergencies at any given time.

∼

Archana suffered from the Autoimmune Crohn's Disease as she grew up in Bengaluru, even though it was not diagnosed. Complications from the disease did not prevent her from studying. She finished her bachelor's in computer applications and did additional training at other institutes before applying for jobs. She was keen on pursuing her master's. During a training session, she met a handsome instructor, Krishna. They became friends and he helped her with her course. After the course ended, she began MS in computer science through her company's tie-up with a reputed university. She stayed in touch with Krishna and he soon made it clear that she was not just his 'friend'. Archana realized that she was in love with him too. She told him about her illness. Krishna was shaken but was in love with the frail girl with sparkling eyes who made his heart dance.

Their courtship lasted six long years. Her disease would flare up from time to time. When the time came for her parents and his mother to consent to their marriage, Krishna decided not to reveal her condition to his family. He moved to the US, and he and Archana were married during a trip home. She put on a brave front, even though she was suffering from severe cramps during the wedding. The three nights she stayed at Krishna's place after the wedding were hell, when even minuscule amounts of fibrous food would cause her severe pain in the gut.

That was in 2008. Archana applied for an H1B visa, which she got with great difficulty because of the economic downturn.

In the US, the couple sought out doctors to address her condition. A doctor performed a capsule endoscopy on her, in spite of her informing him that her food pipe was inflamed. 'He messed up. I could not swallow the capsule that usually has a tiny camera attached for a start. He put me on anaesthesia and pushed it down. The capsule that must be expelled from the body got stuck

inside. When he realized his folly, he was harsh with us.'
The camera had to be removed surgically after a few days,
after taking into account her health history.

To this day, Archana and Krishna feel they should
have sued that surgeon. But then, the couple was new
to the US. Archana had another major surgery in 2012,
during which doctors cut parts of her small intestine to
remove fistula. 'Before I was wheeled into that surgery,
the surgeon simply told me, "We don't know what will
happen on the operation table." He was implying that I
might die. It broke me. Krishna couldn't take it either.
We thought it was blunt of him to talk that way, but that
is how it is here. He looked tense too.' Krishna broke
down, as did Archana's brother who was visiting.

Archana survived the surgery. During her painful
recovery, Krishna played nurse, caregiver and soulmate.
He spent several nights on the hospital couch. Once on
the recovery path, Archana made radical changes to her
lifestyle. She stopped working. She researched foods that
would suit her and has stuck to home-cooked food ever
since. She joined yoga classes, and walks a minimum of
twenty minutes a day.

Her last surgery cost them a mere $100 because of a
high-premium insurance between $1000 and $1500 per
month. 'High-premium insurance plans are relative. They
can vary from company to company—where you work,
and the company providing insurance,' says Krishna.
Whenever on the lookout for a job, Krishna's primary
concern was insurance. The two opted for companies
with the best insurance plans.

The couple's search for the right doctors has not ended, though. 'Sometimes, the best doctor might not work for us. Sometimes, people may give you bad reviews of a doctor because he is too blunt. But he might be the one whose approach would work,' says Krishna.

Archana was misdiagnosed in India, but had her own troubles with treatment in the US. 'If only I was diagnosed and treated properly early on, I would have suffered less,' she rues.

In India, people prefer sugar-coated responses from doctors. If a family member suffers from a terminal illness, another family member may not want the patient to know. That's something a doctor in the US is unlikely to understand where it is considered a doctor's duty to tell the patient about their condition and treatment. Fear of litigation influences a lot of decisions too.

In the US, it is a popular belief that Asians are a lot healthier than Americans, which is a myth. When it comes to diseases, Indians have their own set of prevalent issues.

~

What about other life events, like pregnancy and childbirth?

Shirley Raval was in the fifth month of her second pregnancy when, during a routine check-up, her ultrasonologist noticed something wrong. 'He asked us to abort the baby as it was not growing.' Shirley and her husband refused. 'It was not for him to decide whether we should have the baby or not. When we complained about him to our gynaecologist and requested a change of ultrasonologist, she did not agree, so we got the records transferred to another hospital.'

'My gynaecologist called me up when I was alone at home. She said horrible things like my baby would be born deformed, that the baby would not have a normal life, that it would not survive its first year. I was highly emotional,' Shirley's voice quivers when she relives that phone call. 'I wept on the phone when she said this. But she went on. It felt like she was upset about losing a case. When we make a decision about our child, they must respect it.'

Shirley's case was transferred to a hospital that did not believe in abortions. She was placed under the direct care of the head of the department of gynaecology. She went through ultrasounds thrice a week. Her days were spent in the hospital for the most part. Till the seventh month, her baby weighed only 2 pounds. She was given steroids, too, not usually given to pregnant women.

Why was the baby not growing? They were following instructions to the letter!

Shirley, her family and friends prayed hard for a miracle at temples and churches. Endless tests, ultrasounds and medications later, in the eighth month, Shirley's baby suddenly began to gain weight. Doctors stopped her steroids.

On the designated day, Shirley landed at her hospital for a caesarean, only to find a crowd of pregnant women there. A storm was predicted, and all women who were close to term had showed up. In the middle of that chaos, on a night when sixty babies were delivered in that hospital, Shirley's tiny bundle of joy, a baby girl, was born. Shirley and her husband were ecstatic. Their friends were overjoyed. Hers was a miracle baby.

And soon it was time for the bills, which should have scared them normally. 'We had a good insurance plan thankfully,' she says.

After her first delivery, they were handed a bill of around $25,000 for her treatment and $10,000 for the postnatal care. 'Our insurance company paid only $10,000 and washed its hands off the rest. It did not bargain further with the hospital to bring the bills down, the way such companies normally do. It was left to me to call the hospital to cut down on the $25,000. After a lot of bargaining and pleading, they asked me to pay $5000 on the bill of $25,000 and $2000 on the bill of $10,000.' Shirley's total bill stood at $7000 for the first child's delivery.

Due to the complications in her second delivery, the bills came to $135,000 for the ICU alone. Doctor's charges were separate. 'Usually, for caesarean cases, the charges are $6000,' said Shirley. 'Since we did so many ultrasounds, our charges increased. Weekly fees for these ultrasounds were in the range of $1000. Every doctor charges $500–$600 per visit.'

This time, the couple got lucky. They had a policy where they had to pay $2000, and the rest would be borne by the insurance company. In other words, their deductible amount on the insurance was $2000.

If you have infertility problems, you will be referred to fertility specialists. Not all fertility treatments are covered by insurance companies. When a friend remarks that his insurance firm allowed four in-vitro fertilization (IVF) attempts, you can feel that twinge of envy in your heart. 'Wish we had such insurance!' It hits you hard especially if your struggle to have your own baby has stretched through years, and with happy baby arrivals all around you.

Should a visa wife in the US face trouble with fertility, she often scours the list of available lady gynaecologists with an Indian name in the vicinity before even checking if that doctor is part of her spouse's insurance network, or if the doctor's office accepts the insurance package she has. An Indian doctor can represent a 'comfort zone' that a visa wife craves for in an alien land.

Certain diagnostic tests, for instance, can be extremely painful. Gynaecologists, too, ask for information differently than back·home. Instead of 'Are you married?' they will ask 'Are you sexually active?' You may not expect a direct question of the sort. But do expect your gynaecologist or fertility specialist to be more forthright in discussing the intimate details necessary for your treatment. During your treatment, expect calls that say, 'The doctor has ordered you to have sex,' after a set of blood tests and ovulation shots. Some women find themselves less hesitant to discuss their personal health details with a male fertility specialist in the new place, while in India they would insist on the specialist having to be a woman.

It may not help that you are unaware of the nuances of this new system. You may never have, for instance, done a pap smear test in India. In the US, it is a norm to do it regularly.

When Suja Kamal first went to see a gynaecologist, an assistant called her in. The girl checked her weight, blood pressure and height, and asked her to change into a tissue-paper gown after undressing. Suja did not quite get it. 'Undress fully?' she asked the girl.

'Yeah, your panties too.'

Suja was flabbergasted. None of the gynaecologists in India had ever demanded something like this. She felt her palms go cold. The tissue paper gown barely covered her body. The clinic's labour seat type chair was also different from back in India.

Her doctor walked in, and through the initial small talk of health history, quickly did a breast exam and pap smear. For a normal doctor visit in the US, it was nothing different from what the doctors or their staff would do for any woman patient. Suja's husband looked away. The experience unsettled Suja and threw up questions in her head that she was too embarrassed to discuss with her husband, let alone the doctor.

Dr Annapurna Ramanarayanan, a gynaecologist who has seen numerous patients like Suja, notes that as a doctor, she makes extra effort to make women who arrive from India feel comfortable on their first visit.

'I do not want them to leave my office feeling like it was a horrible experience. I speak many languages—Tamil, Malayalam, Marathi, Gujarati, Telugu. That helps a lot. New Jersey has a huge Telugu population. Indian women visiting a gynaecologist for the first time are all married women. Not all of them have had a pap smear test before. They are all educated, but not all of them speak good English.'

Talking about the awkward experience that women go through at clinics in the US, she says, 'When given a gown, they do not know what to do with it. They sit in there (in the examination room) with the gown. For many, it is their first-ever visit to a gynaecologist in the US.'

According to data collected by the Centers for Disease Control and Prevention (US), in 2010, Asian American women above eighteen years of age were the least likely to have had a pap test, compared to non-Hispanic White, non-Hispanic Black, Hispanic/Latino and American Indian/Alaska Native women.

For an Indian woman in the US, the choice is difficult. Should she go to the better doctor, or the one she feels comfortable with, thanks to his or her ability to understand Indian nuances? How does one get to know about the credibility of a doctor? Does one rely on Internet ratings alone? Can one get lucky enough to meet an Indian doctor on the first visit—someone your spouse's insurance company has on its network? What if we have no friends who can tell us which doctor is friendlier? The trial-and-error experience of visiting doctors can stress one out.

Unlike in India, you cannot just walk into a doctor's clinic. You are almost always asked to mention who your 'family physician' or general physician is to the insurance company, with relevant identification. It is left to you to scour the Internet for someone you are comfortable with, who is in your five-mile radius and so on.

Usually, one needs to wait to meet a doctor, unless it is an emergency.

'For my baby son, they would say "You can come in by 2 p.m.", which is fine, when I call in the morning. But if he has a fever below 100 degrees Fahrenheit, they ask me to wait it out,' says Bindhu. 'The wait can be for as long as three days, which is hard. When it happened, it was difficult to keep my son's fever under check. You are not used to it in India. It is right on the part of the doctors, because they do not want to give the kids major doses of antibiotics. It is a lesson I learnt through the system here. And it is a good thing.'

Doctor's appointments usually take time—between a few hours to a few weeks. For medical emergencies, there is always 911—like in the case of Rani and Kant, who did not have the scope to wait, and didn't need to spend a minute more figuring out which hospital they had to rush their daughter to, because they simply called 911. Children are taught to use the number for emergencies of all kinds.

If you need urgent medical attention, an option is to head to the Urgent Care centres that are nearest to your home. Parents of little children often opt for such care when specialist appointments are not easy to come by.

One night, Bindhu's three-year-old daughter developed stomach flu. She vomited continuously from 9 p.m. onwards. By midnight, she was dehydrated and weak.

Bindhu and her husband panicked. They rushed her to an urgent care centre.

'They gave her a tablet to stop the vomiting. We waited half an hour. After the vomiting stopped, we could give her food,' says Bindhu. Her daughter felt drained, but better. Bindhu paid $100 co-pay, which is way above the $15 she normally paid at clinics. Imagine the bill if you are uninsured.

During my own fertility treatment, our specialist prescribed ovulation shots that were to be self-administered. The clinic's nurses helped on workdays and gave me the shots. The days they were closed, we were forced to visit an urgent care centre, where we had to pay $100 for each injection. The doctor showed my husband how to give me the shot. A month later, the bills of about $600 arrived. My husband threw a fit. When you need an injection of such a kind in India, you may go to the nearest clinic or neighbourhood nursing home, who might charge between Rs 10 and Rs 100. But $600 can make up most of the monthly pay of an employee in the US. It is not an amount anyone would want to pay just for an injection.

If there is a pressing emergency, you can also visit the emergency room. That's the welcoming bit about the US healthcare system. 'Nobody can deny you healthcare. You go to the emergency room where you might have to wait for a while. But if it is a serious case, they attend to you immediately. They ask for your insurance card. If you don't have it, you will still be treated. They have to treat you,' says radiation oncologist Dr Lakshmi Narayan, whose practice in oncology spans several years in the States and who now practises in India.

The Emergency Medical Treatment and Active Labor Act (EMTALA), 1986, stipulates that hospitals accept patients who use Medicaid and Medicare. It also requires that hospitals not turn away patients until they have been checked for emergency health conditions. The law requires that emergency rooms treat patients who go there even if they are aware they cannot pay up, or do not have insurance. The legal responsibility to pay bills, of course, lies with the patients.

Says Leigh Kamore Haynes, a representative of the Global Steering Council of People's Health Movement, a global public health advocacy organization, 'Emergency rooms do try to turn people away. According to the law, patients cannot be required to show insurance documents before being admitted at the emergency room. They cannot deny treatment based on the insurance details, but they try to. If a person is uninformed, a staffer can simply say, "Oh, I cannot get the emergency clear" when you do not have insurance, and you may be forced to go away.'

The average waiting time at emergency rooms, according to Centers for Disease Control and Prevention, was thirty minutes in 2014, while the average treatment time was ninety minutes. This, according to some, might be a conservative estimate when the crowds surge. It is a common belief that waiting time across US emergency rooms is on the rise. Waiting time at the emergency rooms alone can scare off patients with less persistent health issues.

It's why Lokesh Sharma got the shock of his life when he visited the emergency room of the main hospital in Stamford, Connecticut, one morning. He had woken up with a stiff arm and shoulder. His wait time was five minutes. 'Had I gone in the afternoon or night, the wait time would have been longer. They did an x-ray, gave me steroids and painkillers for three days, and I was good to go,' he says.

Comparatively, in India, patients are seldom protected by laws that prevent hospitals from turning them away. Hospitals withhold treatment till the family arranges the money, especially if they are super-speciality hospitals dealing with emergency care.

The two countries have their own complications to deal with. Even so, Leigh Kamore is critical of the US healthcare system. 'It is somewhat antiquated and that's me being nice. It lags behind compared to the rest of the world. It is expensive, it is private. There is a major problem of access from a right-to-health standpoint. People get denied their right to health because they cannot access care or cannot afford it. They are denied healthcare at primary care level because there are not many primary care clinics. Many other countries focus on primary and preventive care. In the US, we are more of a curative system. People get sick, we take care of them. I want to use the word medical. It is medically focused, not necessarily holistic.'

Watch prime-time television in the US on any given day, and you will find ads for certain medications being sold aggressively by pharmaceutical companies, with the words 'ask your doctor'.

'What do they mean by "ask your doctor"?' a friend asked, irritated. 'If the doctor knows that the medicine works, he or she will prescribe it anyway. Are they pressurizing doctors through patients? Are they trying to create a market for the medicine?'

The Patient Protection and Affordable Care Act, popularly dubbed 'Obamacare', aims to expand insurance coverage among the uninsured population of the US, increase benefits and lower costs for consumers, increase funding for public health and prevention of diseases, and bring more people under the coverage of the government medical welfare programmes—Medicaid and Medicare.[14]

From the perspective of a newcomer in the US, one might wonder aloud, 'Is insurance the answer to access to healthcare? Can there not be another approach to health and wellness? Will I be encouraged, as a new arrival, for instance, to seek psychological help without having to deal with the stigma of it? Unless equipped emotionally to deal with transcontinental relocation of this sort, women have a tough time dealing with the trauma. So how about providing incentives for mental health too?'[15]

Women are not even aware if mental health redressal can be covered by insurance. Leigh Kamore says that insurance programmes usually cover only ten to twelve visits to the psychiatrist in a year.

Anxiety and depression are some of the issues commonly faced by immigrant women. Domestic violence also is a huge issue, with women suffering from the 'battered wife syndrome', where women stay with husbands who abuse them believing that they deserve the harsh treatment or that they brought it on themselves.

Indian women seek psychological help only if it manifests as physical health issues. Sarika was hospitalized for a physical emergency, and was told by doctors she had post-traumatic stress disorder (PTSD).

Healthcare in America is expensive, no doubt. And that applies to insurance premiums too. Depending on the plan, an average family spends between $100 and $1000 as premium per month. In my own case, I did not recognize symptoms of depression. I suffered from physical ailments and thought hormones had brought on my depression. I worried about the money my husband had to spend on my health. We wanted to clear our debts. So was my health a burden for him?

'Don't worry about it. Just get better,' was the reassurance I was handed frequently.

In the end, the challenge for new arrivals is to accept the new healthcare system with its merits and minuses. It is important to be assertive when the need arises, and accept your situation when necessary. And that is a tightrope walk.

15

The Agony

When you boarded the flight, you had a vague idea you would miss important events in your family. You accepted it. When the events actually happen, though, you hate your American life because it tore you away from the beehive of your loved ones and your life back home.

You want to be home, but cannot be. You want to be with your parents, siblings, cousins and friends, but visa restrictions and job uncertainties will not let you board that flight back home. The worst time to be stuck in your American home is when a wedding in India happens oblivious to your absence. You wonder if coming to the US was the right decision after all. You crave for those words of comfort from your family—'it's okay'. You want to be part of the cacophony, the gossip, the endless discussions about décor, the chaos, wedding clothes, jewellery, the fun, the shopping.

'Why aren't you coming? You can try *na*!' You heard that a hundred times from aunts, cousins, the bride or groom, uncles, grannies in the run-up to the wedding. You are killing yourself for 'not being there', for not helping out with the wedding. How do you explain that your visa status is, for the moment, only a Homeland Security-validated one, and that you'd have to risk it if you were to go to India, or that your husband landed a project that may end soon?

It is not as if India stopped living in your absence. Births, weddings, thread ceremonies, tonsuring ceremonies, graduations, house-warming parties, *arangetrams* (first on-stage dance performance, usually Bharatnatyam, Kuchipudi, etc.)–should they stop just because you took a flight of fancy to America?

'Do they no longer need me in their life?' The American home's isolation fuels your fear of losing your loved ones to distance. You cannot grab that phone to cry out to the husband. Do walls have feelings? Will they lend a patient ear? Do the windows and blinds, and that parking lot outside full of cars, know the screams of agony within? Does that tree outside the window, with its florescent summer leaves, care? 'What if some mad neighbour hears me crying and calls 911?' You shut up. And maybe grab the TV remote to mute the volcano that is erupting inside you.

When D-day arrives, you hound your phone-wielding cousins at the venue to hear the noise, the *nadaswarams* (the music of the wedding drums). You go a step further and relay it live on your phone speaker mode to another cousin in another country, via video chat.

Veena Samarth, who had studied at a residential school a few hours from home, had always missed such family events. It helped her develop a sense of detachment about family events. After a point, they did not really matter, because she had ceased to be part of the live network in India. She built a network of her own in the US, and the necessary connect with her siblings and parents.

Yet, she cannot forget the day she saw her parents for the first time at the airport, three years after she had left. In the pre-video-chat years, it was phone conversations that kept them connected. 'They looked older!' she says, remembering the shock she felt then. 'They had visible grey hair unlike before. I had knots in my stomach. I saw a marked difference in the way they walked. We went for a hike, like we always had, to hilltops in Karnataka. This time, they said they had to be careful. Of course, they did better than any of us. Still, that they had to think twice was bad.'

If missing a wedding is emotional torture, what about missing the death of a loved one, not being able to say goodbye and, worse, not being able to attend their funeral? When such things happen, the futility of the 'dollar pursuit' becomes apparent.

A month and a half after her parents had left after their visit, Aparna Raghu's in-laws came by to be with their grandchild. It was a breather when another set of elders arrived. She cleaned up her home and got busy playing host the day they arrived. Her in-laws were still unpacking their suitcases. 'In the absence of help, I struggled with my baby. I could not leave him alone for even two minutes to go and take a quick shower. I had gone crazy and was fighting a great deal with my husband. One morning, he got up an hour earlier. I thought he was doing his office work. I was too exhausted to be bothered.

'Some time later, he woke me up and took me to the pooja room. I was sleepy. He smeared some kumkum on my forehead and said, 'Be strong. I'm going to tell you something. Uncle (my father) met with an accident.' It took me a full two minutes to even understand what he was saying.'

The next few minutes were a haze for Aparna. 'He said that my sister had called to inform him about my dad's death in a road accident. I broke down in sobs. No, it could not be. Not my dad! My dad was "young and energetic", as he would always say. He was in great health. Why him?'

Tears flowed incessantly, and she did not want to waste any time getting home. It hit the couple then that their newborn son did not have a passport yet. Her husband frantically searched the Internet for a way out. At about 8.30 a.m., they rushed to the US consulate with their baby, a US citizen. She requested them for a passport on emergency basis. The officials were helpful, and agreed to give a passport the same day. Still, there was paperwork involved. The hospital birth certificate validity period of ninety days had expired. They went back to the hospital for another one. By the time the process got over, it was 3.30 p.m. Their next hurdle was the Indian embassy for a visa for the baby. Her sister had booked a 5 p.m. flight to get her home to Bengaluru.

At the Indian embassy, they discovered that their American baby needed a Person of Indian Origin card or visa. But even if the officials were cooperative enough, they would not be able to get it immediately. It was closing time at the embassy. She could manage to get her visa only the next day. The funeral would be over by then. Her grieving mother forbade her from visiting India right away.

It did not help when her in-laws said that should she travel for the funeral, they would travel back with her, as they had come all the way 'only for the baby'.

Her husband's H1 visa would expire soon. 'There was every chance that if I were to travel home, I would get stuck there with my child till the visa got sorted. He was willing to risk that for my sake. But my mom and others did not want me to see my dad's body. By then I lost any sense of feeling, to even decide what to pack in my suitcase.' Aparna gave in, and stayed back.

'I asked my cousin to video the rituals to me. It was late at night here in Dallas and I had put my baby to sleep. I was in a daze. I had to smile and play with my son to keep him happy through the day. I could not accept what happened. By then my tears had dried up. I watched people on the video cry. But it was so far away. I kept telling myself that he was still around.'

With death comes a heart-breaking finality, the reality that one will not see a loved one any more. When a loved one is sick back home, you worry yourself to death and resort to online shopping and monitoring via phone calls to make things easier for them. However, no amount of online shopping for your folks can replace your presence. You know it as much as they feel it. You hope they have adequate support in the form of friends and relatives to keep tabs on them. You wonder if you must make that call to an old friend and beg him or her to visit them. Soon, your day centres on that phone call you make back home. You watch for how they sound, how tired, the quiver in their voice, the panting . . . is your loved one putting up an 'I am all right' show on the phone? Why won't they fix the web-cam so we can chat? How those few minutes with your parent in India go become markers for how the rest of your day goes in your American home.

When Sathya discovered that her father had been diagnosed with cancer, she was distraught. 'I can't breathe. I need to go to my dad,' she gasped one night. It was another bout of crying all day. Her dad was on one of his daily visits to the hospital. In a week's time, she was on a flight to India.

Neha disembarked from a joyful cruise ride with her daughter a few months after her dog died of cancer. It was a welcome break for the family after the gut-wrenching battle they saw their pet fight. For her four-year-old daughter who was still reeling from the loss of her friend, the cruise was a healer. Neha stepped off the ship and called her sister, and got the news that her mother had developed breast cancer. Doctors feared it had spread to her skin, prompting them to put her on chemotherapy instantly. It was not the kind of news she expected after a vacation.

Every year, her parents stayed with her for about four months. The news hit Neha hard. Why would something of this sort happen to someone who was in perfect health? The urgency of treatment options they had to pursue, and the need to stand by her family, pushed Neha to gather herself. She put off dealing with the shock for later, and geared up to check on her parents every single day, tracked her mother's treatment, medication, options available and connected them with their granddaughter more closely. The fact that her father was around to care for her mother, with relatives taking turns to stay by her side, was a help.

~

It's morning in the US—and evening in India. You wake up with a jerk and realize you need to call your parents in Chennai. NOW. The call will, however, simply not go through. You try the numbers of other relatives . . . no luck. You then check Facebook for unusual status updates. You browse through the news online. The images on the screen leave you terrified. No! This cannot be happening! You try to send out messages on WhatsApp, to friends in the neighbourhood. A family friend living a few kilometres away from your parents responds, but says stepping out is difficult. There is water everywhere. He got lucky he lived on the first floor, but they are marooned.

You fear the worst, because your aged parents live on the ground floor. They battle their old age and health problems with aplomb. But this is a disaster.

No point fuming. You pack your suitcase. You are not thinking. You try to stay sane. Wind up chores at home and figure out how to head to the nearest airport, all the while restlessly checking the news again and again. That's when you spot pictures of Chennai's airport—under water, and a submerged plane on the tarmac.

Twenty-four hours later, there is still no contact with parents. Thanks to an angel from a neighbourhood store, who waded through floodwaters to check on them, you know they are safe. Do your parents have water? Both have health problems. Do they have food? Has water entered the house? Every other home on that street is flooded.

You get messages—of a woman who needs help because her mother has passed away and there is no one to help move the body, of a pregnant woman who may go into labour any time. Stories of courage also pour in. Stories of despair. Stories of hope.

It's the worst of times that bring out the real nature of people. In two days, complete strangers on Facebook turned Samaritans..You do not know what is happening out there, but updates from various suburbs of Chennai fly in by the minute. Water has reached the second floor of buildings in areas adjoining the Adyar River. Zones along the Cooum River are not in a good condition either.

Shopping groups you followed on social media turned into rescue and relief groups. An actor jumped into the rescue relief mode after his own home and studios got flooded. Among those sharing information on social media are friends and strangers—from Singapore, Australia, London and many other parts of the world. On the ground, people went the extra mile to help others out.

And then came in reports of local thugs either looting relief material, or preventing distribution.

So while politicians in that city have gone missing, you know that everyone is helping themselves and others.

This is when you reflect on what happens in America when such a disaster strikes. When Hurricane Sandy struck in 2012, warnings were issued a few days in advance. People went on a shopping frenzy for water and emergency supplies. Evacuations along the coast were on in full swing. Authorities asked people to settle in, or head to safer zones in advance. Friends came forward to offer support and take people in.

Alongside all that, there were reports of sporadic looting in empty homes in flood zones. People living on the coast continue to reel under the effects of that one night. But the administration was present. At Chennai, people had to mobilize themselves. Armed forces stepped in. People from other cities drove down to the city with supplies.

Some rescue volunteers blamed those living abroad making check-on-elders requests for not being there. Guilt is inevitable. Natural disasters do not have a roster. They strike, anywhere, any time.

At Chennai, your folks were too calm when you warned them ahead of the rains. 'After all, it is rain!' No one saw such rain before.

What gives one hope? Your parents took a family in during those crucial flood days. They cooked food and distributed it to other victims at relief centres. Pictures of mosques and temples opening their doors to families . . .

Really, what is the purpose of human life? Why do disasters happen? Why so much grief in the world?

'I don't know how they manage to do it—skipping the funeral of a parent,' a friend remarked during one of those visa conversations, about H1B visa holders not wanting to risk their jobs by going to India and face another US consulate interview, even when a parent dies. Such conversations also revolve around 'married bachelors' who leave family and kids behind to earn and save, and become all too reluctant to bring their family over as it would hit their dollar-saving goals. It's usual among dinner conversations to run down such people who are seen as being less responsible towards their wife and children.

Yet, for a country with a highly aspirational middle class, and the huge struggle to escape poverty, expats face life-defining moments. It's hard to judge. The enormity of financial crises in their families, the compulsions they face, might all be important enough for them to make the decisions that they do.

In the highly networked social setup back home, you are part of a whole. You are not independent. The network around you supersedes your sense of self. Some friends I speak to contest this. 'Are we not moving towards a more individualistic existence? We do not talk to our own neighbours these days, and keep a safe distance from relatives!'

Still, an American child is taught independence from the time it is in the cradle. What does being uprooted from the comfort of your family mean when you go through illnesses or traumatic events? You have no choice but to depend on strangers and friends—whoever you are. Your family is far far away. If you choose your 'great new life' over family, be prepared to face flak for life. It is unlikely that in the deep recesses of your heart, you forgive yourself either, unless it is a genuine visa predicament or unless your family back in India is willing to stand by you.

Here is my own tale of tears:

'Don't go, I'll protect you,' I bawled away in the gnawing whiteness of my new bedroom in New Jersey. It had been two weeks since we had moved from Delaware to Central New Jersey—not a great distance at all—two and a half hours away by road, but an attitudinal and cultural shift for us, who had grown comfortable with life in a small state. The day before we left Delaware was when my husband and I discovered that we were going to be parents. It was a heady feeling. I had finally conceived! 'It could be a pregnancy, or a pregnancy on its way out,' the gynaecologist warned us. I did not heed her words.

For ten days after that joyous visit to the doctor, we were stuck in a hotel sponsored by my husband's new client firm in Central Jersey. I thanked heaven for a friend there who guided us to her family gynaecologist. We rushed to the clinic at Somerset.

'You need some iron tablets,' she said. I told her how my constipation and gastric pains flared up with those. She said these were not so bad. They would do no harm.

But kill me they did. Over the next ten days, we did the mandatory Human Chorionic Gonadotropin hormone tests (HCG or pregnancy hormone test). The first test threw up 14 as the result. 'It's supposed to multiply. It's not exactly going forward,' our gynaecologist phoned in from Delaware. Go up they did—the numbers. Multiply they did not. 'Low HCG, pregnancy on its way out,' my New Jersey doctor called. What exactly should I do to multiply that hormone count?

'A tissue.' That is what they all called it. It was not a foetus. It was my baby. In my head, I fought them all a lot for not using the 'pregnant' word. And then one afternoon, I rolled in pain, probably from the iron tablets.

'Don't go, don't go . . . ' I cursed myself for listening to the gynaecologist and gulping those tablets while I cried out to my baby. I fell from the bed, and shrieked into the empty room. My husband was away at his new office, trying to adjust to the new project.

Guilt prevented me from making that call to my husband for help. I gave up after an hour—and simply sobbed to him between hiccups and half-breaths, unable to say a word. He rushed home in a cab.

When he walked in that door, he knew the worst was over. My bout of gastric had eased. I was still on the bed, exhausted. I managed a meek half-smile. We headed to the clinic at Somerset. 'Something's not right,' I swallowed a lump, gulped my tears and said to him, running my hand over the belly. He held my hand.

'You've had a miscarriage. We need to see if you need a clean-up of the uterus. I will send you to get an ultrasound.' She was eighty—my gynaecologist. Her voice sobered at the word 'miscarriage'. She left the room, barely answering a question or two. We knew what she was to say, didn't we?

A day or two later, we went for that ultrasound. They thrust a rod inside, where my baby should have been—machines and their rods have no feelings. People who use them care little too. They looked for residual tissue for a clean-up. It was my baby's home! Was it the coldness of it all that crushed my being? I broke down on that table by the machine. A rod went into my baby's nest—a rod!

On the ride home, I watched big cotton clouds on the blue sky and searched for my precious, tears dry by now. I was confused. 'Should I feel something? What just happened?'

Over the next few months, I battled enormous fatigue, and my body's refusal to get better so that we could start planning another baby. I went overboard with ovulation kits and pregnancy tests, fought with my hubby over little things and begged God to give my baby back. On other days, we rationalized that God probably decided to spare the baby some trauma.

Such immense grief can isolate your husband and you even more in a new town, where everyone is a stranger for a start. Your neighbours are making attempts to get to know you. Your husband is still adjusting to the new workplace and is dependent on colleagues for a ride to work and back home. What helps? In our case, it was taking the first step to reach out. We talked about it to a couple of close friends.

Friends, who extend their hand in an alien land, are really your family that providence brought you. The friend who connected me with the New Jersey gynaecologist had an eight-month-old baby, and was a welcome break in all the gloom. She made me hold the little one, watch his toothless smile, kiss him and cuddle him—priceless moments that helped me forget the pain for a while. My childhood friend drove for five hours with her family to stay with me over the weekend and let me play with her darling daughter. I painted the six-year-old's nails, taught her craft, took her to the nearest beach and cried after they left.

We could not bear the thought of being alone at home. We ran off to friends and neighbours at Delaware, spending time with their kids. They hosted dinners for us, and made us laugh. We played with their toddlers who jumped into our arms from atop couches, and held them to the ceiling as they tried to touch the roof.

What makes those who were complete strangers till recently bring us comfort in our sorrow? If we are destined to grief, we are probably destined to find succour too. We learn to value the worth of human beings. Juxtaposed against an individualistic culture, we form our own networks, of friends, of extended family, if possible. Grief strikes without warning. It leaves you with lessons. Grief in an alien country leaves you numb, at times grappling to hold on to yourself.

Sathya and her husband were at a crossroads. Their latest round of fertility treatments was had just been completed, with no results. Adoption was on Sathya's mind, but her husband hesitated. He wanted their first to be a biological child. Every now and then, exhausted with fertility treatments, they would say, 'Wish we could adopt.' When they had moved to the US, they were not aware that they could only adopt a child in India and take it to the US if they spent two years with the child in India. Only then would the child be allowed into the new country as a dependent.

Sathya hoped she could adopt a child from the US. Her husband was not sure. Their non-resident status, combined with the fact that they were not yet Lawful Permanent Residents or Green Card holders, made him jittery.

Sathya sometimes lost her cool and blamed him for getting hung up about a biological child in India. 'We could have been parents by now,' she sobbed. On other days, they hoped for miracles—getting pregnant, or some such miracle that would bring a baby to them.

Sathya had, on a trip to India, made a donation at an orphanage. She was introduced to their youngest inmate, an eight-month-old baby. Sathya's heart melted. She inquired if the baby was available for adoption, knowing what it would imply for her and her husband. 'She has a prospective family already. They've built a home for her and are waiting for the legal process to be completed,' said the manager.

'We made enquiries about adopting children in the US too, and lost hope,' Sathya's friend told her. 'They prefer giving the kids to citizens. They prefer a particular style of upbringing for the child. Sometimes, the biological mothers are keen on the same religion too.'

Sathya was tired. She had no legal status other than that of an H1B worker's wife. Her documents listed her as

a 'resident alien'. Was she so alien that motherhood had
to elude her, not just because of her biological situation
but due to ill health and insensitive laws? She had no
identity other than being a homemaker.

'Let's pursue surrogacy in India,' suggested Surya.
She had been dead against it all along. The very thought
of paying another woman to carry her child sank her in
guilt. And why surrogacy when thousands of kids were
out there and in need of a family, a home?

She realized it was a lost battle.

'Let's do it.'

16

Bringing Up Babies

As my husband and I went through enormous emotional upheavals during our efforts to become parents, our friends with kids would often say, 'Do not worry. Enjoy what you have now.' It is one of those conversations that automatically turn to how difficult it is to bring up children in America. Our friends are busy helping their children excel in academics, enrolling them in math classes, preparing them for careers in medicine and engineering.

Parenting in a land where one hears of guns and violence every other day, where there is teen bullying and a high premium on child safety, has to be tough. Especially since one is away from the networked support systems of India. The risk of losing your child to negligence charges is also high in the US. It's what makes you cautious even before you become a parent in the new country. It makes

you chide a friend who might spank her child by saying,
'If you do this in America, they will jail you.'

Spank your child and you pay dearly if the child is hurt.
For parents from India who come on work visas, their
own identity troubles play a major part in parenting their
children. Bringing up babies can become a burgeoning
war of cultures.

In India, a child is conditioned to depend on
the mother. In the US, it is about independence and
individuation, which is taught from the cradle. Women
who leave everything to start their lives in the US find it
hard to reconcile these two diverse ideas of parenting.

On the one hand, they must uphold the culture and
values they grew up with. They are unfairly expected to
uphold them through practice, and their performance is
judged according to the yardstick of their own children.
On the other hand is their struggle to accept local
parenting styles, the rules of the land, and protect their
children while coping with their assimilation hiccups.

The gap between two cultures becomes apparent right
from the start. During pregnancy, for instance, abortion
is a contentious issue. Different states of the US have
different laws pertaining to abortion, although it is legal in
the early stages of pregnancy. The issue is more complex
than in India. In the US, the pro-life, pro-choice debates
rage in political circles, unlike in India, where abortion is
not up for political debate. The consequences of either
choice—to abort or not—are grave. India has a law in
place permitting abortions—the Medical Termination of
Pregnancies Act (MTPA). The law is often misused for

sex-selective abortions, which are rampant, leading to a silent genocide of female foetuses. The large-scale genocide is what prompted the passing of Pre-Conception Pre-Natal Diagnostic Techniques Act (PCPNDT Act). Revealing the sex of a baby during pregnancy is now a crime in India. But it is not unusual for Indian couples in the US to do it.

Indian beliefs about pregnancy and childbirth are different. Visa wives on the H4s, L2s and F2s may want to adhere to the American system of prenatal and postnatal care. But Indian families, consisting of a host of elders and relatives, have other ideas, often traditional, that include tried and tested home remedies, and sometimes superstition as well. When the husband's mother controls the daughter-in-law's activities and diet during pregnancy from across the seas, things can go awry.

Vanitha recalls the horrors that her own friends went through during their nine months.

'A friend had a lump in her breast. Another had kidney stones. As for my husband, he was very stubborn. He did not let anyone from India to come and take care of me. He did not let me go to India either. He had his reasons. But I suffered.'

Vanitha's husband's PhD thesis defence was coming up. The couple hoped their baby would arrive after the event. But she went into labour the day before. Her husband called his professor to let him know he would not be able to make it. To make matters worse, Vanitha did not know how to 'push' during the labour, the way

American women mostly do. For the longest time, the baby's head did not crown. The resident doctors, nurses and the gynaecologist present to help deliver the baby were in a fix. They had to call in the head of the department who performed an incision for the head to crown. It turned out her baby's head was bigger than expected. Through the ordeal, Vanitha went through not just pain, but emotional upheaval as well. She was helpless. She wanted her parents every minute. She doubted if she would make it and prayed her baby would be all right, even if she did not survive.

When she got pregnant with her second child, she had just completed her post-graduation in the US. 'My in-laws wanted a boy. They would not understand that nothing was in my hands, my husband's hands, or their hands. They harassed me on the phone, and blamed me for not doing something so that a boy was born. They took my horoscope around to find out if the baby will be a boy. '

Women like her also have to counter beliefs related to 'pollution' or 'impurities' post childbirth. Elderly women in the household decide what the pregnant woman must or must not consume, when the baby must be given a bath, whether the baby should be wrapped with diapers or not, when to name the baby and so on. Often, this advice can clash with practices prevalent in the US and the necessity to adhere to them.

The differences play out even more once the child is born. It could begin with how sleeping with your newborn or co-bedding is not encouraged, although room-sharing for infants is. The American Academy of Pediatrics insists that parents and the baby sleep on separate surfaces, in its policy statement about Sudden Infant Death Syndrome prevention. The concern is that babies might be asphyxiated while bed-sharing. In cases of infant deaths where the parent was intoxicated while bed-sharing, the parents get prosecuted for manslaughter.[16]

When Rani and Kant met doctors and paediatricians in the aftermath of their children's accidents, they faced a barrage of advice, often in the form of chiding.

'I was asked why I had to boil milk that night in the first place. The doctor insisted that the child must sleep away from us, and that we should not rush to the child when she cries at night. How can that be? How can a mother not comfort a baby? The child should learn to be independent. She said once the baby turned four months old, we should start keeping her away from us.'

Rani and Kant lived in a one-bedroom apartment. They could not fathom the concept of space when their friends told them that if they had two children, they should shift to a two-bedroom home. They were told that each individual should ideally get 150 square feet of space in a home.

Indian mothers are rattled when their children start showing their preference to do things on their own and in their own style. Pooja was surprised when her baby insisted on holding a spoon and feeding himself. Her son learnt to be self-reliant at his day-care centre where they were taught to eat on their own, and to even wash their hands by themselves soon enough. Even before he could speak full words, her baby boy learnt to say 'tha' for 'thank you' when he received a gift.

Rupashree liked how her three-year-old was taught 'serious things through play' at his day care. As a mother, she has had reason to fear for his safety, thanks to the endless reports of gun-violence. The tragic shooting at Sandy Hook Elementary School in Connecticut in 2012 only escalated the fears of parents like her. It is not as if safety standards are any better in India. There are plenty of reports of children being subjected to abuse, kidnappings and the like all the time.

'They want kids to be physically fit,' says Rupashree. 'They are taught 'hand and eye coordination improvement' with activities like fixing beads to strings and ball throwing. They teach small muscle movement and big muscle movement. They observe each child and teach accordingly. They are very concerned about safety. They do not insist on learning alphabets soon. I teach him the alphabet at home. I want to get back to India soon; otherwise, catching up with the academics there will be tough for him.'

Safety of children is something taken seriously not just at school, but during travel as well. Which is why 'child restraints' in the car or 'baby car seats' are a must for infants, just as 'booster seats' are for older children. And they dictate the parents' ability to socialize or not among a lot of other considerations.

'My daughter will not stay in the car seat for long. Travelling to your place will be difficult,' said a friend who lives six hours away. Vanitha says her family had to forgo road trips, a norm in America, for many years, because their younger one hated the car seat. Your child may start bawling in the car, but if the car is on the move, you should not take the baby out of the car seat. You need to drive your car to a stop or the nearest available parking space to calm the baby down, check the angle of the seat, its harnesses and so on.

~

Vanitha also talks about how it is a huge challenge for Indian parents to impart values to children without raising a hand when they err. In America, corporal punishment at home is legal. But if that punishment hurts the child physically, it constitutes abuse. Definitions of what constitutes an injury are fluid, making it a difficult provision to conform to without erring. Parents get investigated if they are reported.[17]

During one of our dinners, a friend narrated an incident he had heard. A boy who was spanked by his parents every once in a while for his antics dialled 911 after one such beating. The cops turned up instantly. They questioned the couple who downplayed the spanking. The cops did not take the boy away, but the parents were under watch. They would get a surprise visit by the concerned police officer every once in a while. The child felt empowered enough, and each time they wanted to discipline him, he would threaten them with a promise to tell the officer.

The couple got fed up of being watched for what they thought was their duty, and getting reported by their own child. Without revealing their intentions, they left the country for good. The child thought they were going to India for a vacation. The father was so furious that once they reached the airport in India, he spanked the child to his heart's content.

The narration of this incident triggered that evening's conversation. Questions were plenty.

'How do we discipline kids at all without giving them a spank or two once in a while?'

'Our own parents did a good job of disciplining us and we still love them. Children must be made to obey their parents.'

'Is it possible to instil values without raising a hand?'

The group that discussed these issues comprised young Indians, anxious about parenting their children in the US.

The United Nations Convention on the Rights of Child, 1989, bans all forms of violence against children.[18] It focuses on a child's right to survival, development, protection against abuse, neglect and exploitation. It also addresses education of children, healthcare, juvenile justice and the rights of children with disabilities. The United States is not party to the convention for various reasons,[19] while India is party to it. Some in the US feel it may deprive parental rights to discipline the child, or to opt out of sex education. In India, the problem is enforcement of laws of child welfare.

It matters, for Indian parents in the US, to adhere to the law rather than hold tight to the beliefs they grew up with. There are many alternatives to spanking.

Indian parents need to understand that as opposed to the Indian social belief that places greater importance on family, America prioritizes individual freedom. A guide authored by the Coalition for Asian American Children and Families (CACF) and published by lawhelpny.org notes that the American government strictly enforces laws against child abuse and neglect. 'These laws are meant to protect the safety of children, even if the parents do not mean to hurt the children. You need to understand how the American laws affect how you raise your children and you may have to learn new ways to discipline your children.'[20]

Organizations and experts involved in the field of child welfare and care have always said spanking hurts the child in the long term. The Academy of American Pediatrics strongly opposes spanking.[21] According to the American Psychological Association:

[R]esearch has shown that to a considerable extent children learn by imitating the behaviour of adults, especially those they are dependent upon; and the use of corporal punishment by adults having authority over children is likely to train children to use physical violence to control behaviour rather than rational persuasion, education, and intelligent forms of both positive and negative reinforcement.[22]

Mothers who have young children would therefore benefit from not just learning the laws related to children and their upbringing in the new country, but also by connecting with advocacy groups that could guide them appropriately.

It is not just spanking and discipline that bothers Indian families who are trying to understand the behaviour and civil norms of people around them and figure out 'where to draw the line' and 'what degree of freedom' to allow their children. Sometimes a minor inconvenience can become magnified, thereby unsettling mothers.

Alice and her husband, Paul, moved to a two-bedroom apartment in Maryland with no inkling that their year's stay there would be a nightmare. Their seven-year-old daughter was a happy child, excited about little things and prancing about all day. Within two months of moving into the apartment, which was only a stopgap arrangement, their neighbour from the apartment downstairs arrived at their doorstep, complaining of noise.

'It was a structural problem because the building had paper-thin walls and flooring. That neighbour used to complain about whoever lived in that apartment. We learnt that it was the reason the owner of the apartment moved out and rented it. They were an old couple who went to bed around 8 p.m.—while we entered our house at 7.40 p.m. after a long day out. They complained to us first, then to the owner, who they wanted to fix a thick carpet to the floor. It was a wooden floor, which amplified the noise. To add to it, my daughter was learning to tap dance those days.'

Her daughter could not practise her tap dance at home. Every few minutes, the mother would remind her not to stomp around. 'She is a jumpy person. Asking her to watch herself was difficult.' The family kept a low profile, but got tired of doing it for the few hours they were home in a day. Alice laid carpets around the house. One day, they found a written complaint on their door. The neighbour had complained to the apartment management.

'The owner merely put up a display of taking measurements to fix a carpet,' says Alice. 'But he did not get a carpet fixed as "it reduces property value".'

Once, the neighbour complained of noise after the child went to sleep because Alice's husband would walk with a heavy step. Soon, they heard their owner was being sued for the noise. Their ordeal lasted several months. When they heard the old neighbour and her husband had gone away on vacation, they were relieved. But by then they had put up with enough, and were looking for another home where their child could jump around without fear.

Alpana Gautam moved to an apartment community in Missouri from Gurgaon. Her three-year-old son would hop on the apartment stairs every time they got in or out, causing thuds on the wooden stairs. He would also scream in excitement. One of their neighbours would get annoyed. Every time he spotted them, he would pass remarks like, 'You got to be careful with the boy, lady!' She tried making light of it. She thought she would get friendly with him and calm him down. One day he told her, 'I am a lawyer!' His tone was authoritative, and more or less seemed to warn her, 'Do not mess with me.'

Alpana had wanted to make friends with her neighbours irrespective of who they were. She begged her husband to find another apartment, even if it was in the same community. Although the community had Indians, she did not have Indian neighbours in her building. At

the park, she told her friends who were moms not to
think of moving into her building even if they loved that
stretch. Constant fear of doing something wrong and
getting caught by a watchful neighbour was getting to her.

She, like most mothers, wanted the best for her child.
She wanted him to assimilate well, while keeping his
Indian values intact. That was her dream. That was the
dream of her peers.

Being judged as a parent is a universal fear. Among
other things, Vidya finds the possibility that the children
may succumb to peer pressure worrying. 'I'm just going
with the flow. Frankly speaking, there is no tutorial to
teach you about this. A lot of things that worked for us do
not work for our kids,' she says.

Moulding a child depends a lot on his/her personality.
'My two kids have varying preferences. My son is
comfortable around Indian children. He gets along with
other children too, but if you ask me his preference, I'd
say he would rather associate with desi kids. My daughter
is different. She gets along well with non-Indian kids.'

Vidya's children are a year or two away from teenage.
She is left figuring out the why of the difference between
them. 'We are treating them the same way. What's
different? We tell my son he should mingle more with
non-Indian kids. And tell our daughter she should get
along with Indian children too.'

She prefers a liberal approach to parenting. 'I notice
something among a large chunk of Indian parents
who have arrived in recent years here (in Virginia).
Schools have family education classes, and send out

permission letters to parents saying, "We will teach this (puberty-related classes). If you want a detailed report, send us a note, and we will give you a copy. Please give us permission so the kids can attend the class." A lot of Indian parents opt out. Many do not. The schools start these lessons in fourth grade—starting with personal hygiene. It was not so before. I would rather they learn about it from someone in the position of a teacher than from their friends. Children understand well. They would trust a teacher more. Maybe parents think their children are too young to learn about puberty.'

Traditional beliefs play a big role. Or it could be the fear of over-exposure to the American lifestyle too early. Sometimes, parents fear their children might not learn to speak Indian languages at all. It prompts them to speak to their children in their mother tongue.

'I know she will pick up English quickly once she goes to day care,' said the mother of a three-year-old to me. We were discussing how the baby managed to speak her mother tongue so well. This mother had been to India for a few months.

Kamalini Sundar makes sure that her two children attend Bhagavad Gita classes and learn shlokas and whatever necessary from their culture. 'They can be whatever they want to be when they grow up. That was the way my parents brought me up. And that is the way I would want to bring them up. But I would like to expose them to a lot of things so that they make the decision for themselves.'

Vanitha prefers such an attitude for her daughters too. Her older daughter is in her teens. She and her husband go through their struggles, but she does not want her daughters leading a dual life. 'I have seen ABCDs (American born confused desis). They say something at home and have to do something else outside.' That is why it bewilders her when her husband wants his daughters to go to school with plaited hair and wearing bindi and flowers. She cannot imagine subjecting her daughters to the taunts of their peers.

Vanitha's parents, who compared Indian schooling to the American system, felt her kids were not learning enough. It bothered her enough to make her approach their teachers. 'A teacher told me, "We teach kids to be inquisitive and interested in learning." Her words assured me that my children will be fine in academics.'

She has not decided to push her children towards any particular profession. 'In India, parents plan their children's future. Here, the kids plan for themselves. We are worried our kids will make the same mistakes as we did. We tend to not give them a chance to make mistakes and learn from them. Among my friends, most children are doctors. We have a fascination for doctors, unlike Americans.'

Vanitha worries if her kids will be judged by relatives for wearing 'American' clothes. She had reason to fume, however, when her daughter was subjected to untouchability during her periods by her visiting mother-in-law. Vanitha had to put up with their whims because her in-laws had made the trip after many years. Her daughter, who was then thirteen, was annoyed.

'My grandma always kept telling me what to wear, how to wear it. I would have to sit and sleep in the basement during my periods. I felt lonely out there. I was not allowed to sleep on my bed. I could not do anything for myself. I complained to my dad. He said it was "tradition" and that they would go away soon. I missed them when they left, but then I did not have to worry about what I *had to* do any longer.'

Vanitha would have to wash her daughter's bedding every day before she could bathe. When the orthodox elderly have their say, identity issues become a war of emotions and personal beliefs pitted against notions of duty and sacrifice.

Kamalini lives in a joint family at Pittsburgh, and finds her in-laws' help with her children an immense source of support. She'd rather have them look after her children than a stranger. Like every other visa wife who arrived from India and had to build a life for herself, Kamalini is worried for her children. 'What if they get into drugs or other bad stuff? Gun violence in schools is also a concern. But such fears persist in India too. I make it a point to teach them about Indian culture. They pick up bad stuff so easily. You need to constantly tell them what is right and what is wrong. There is a need to coach them non-stop.'

Her children are toddlers. She knows the 'bad influence' anxieties can rest for a while. Her current parental stress is focused on the safety of her kids while they play.

Darshana Apte, mother of a twelve-year-old boy, feels stifled even as she negotiates her daily battles in the US. 'My husband's family is here. My mother-in-law travels twice a year to be with us. She is controlling and dominating. Even recently, during my son's thread ceremony, she picked a fight with me. When my son was a baby, she insisted that my husband not change his diapers or feed him. She would bring these things up when my husband was not around.'

Darshana's post-partum depression coincided with grief over her mother's death, who had passed away before her child's birth. It took a toll on her health. She constantly resisted her mother-in-law's desire to control her son's upbringing. Her feeling of enslavement grows when her mother-in-law invites people over to her house every week, every day at times. 'I end up having to do the cleaning. My husband's family has free passage. They treat my house like a dharamshala.'

The pressure to host people, and being branded by relatives as the one 'with attitude', left Darshana depressed and with little time for her child. Mothers like her find themselves walking a tightrope as their children grow into their teens. Sometimes, she wonders what her life would have been like if she did not try so hard to be the 'good bahu', and if her mother-in-law did not visit them in the US so often.

17

When Relatives Visit

Walk in to the arrival lounges of international airports across the country, and you might occasionally spot a woman decked in warm-coloured desi clothes, standing demurely beside her husband in his Western casuals. She may have bindi and sindoor, maybe even bangles, and a mangalsutra dangling prominently from her neck. It is time to impress the mother-in-law.

Bouquets nestle in the arms of other anxious couples, families and sometimes friends. From across the interiors of these airports, some pickles, sweets and chutney podis get lucky enough to dodge the prying eyes of the Transport Security Administration, and find their way to Indian homes in the US, amid squeals of delight at the much-craved-for mother's recipes. The elders, or parents, have arrived, sending their offspring into bursts of happiness.

A ticket for an Indian guy on a work visa is also a ticket to fulfil the American visit dream of his parents.

Setting foot in America feels like an achievement for such parents who might have faced pointed queries by peers, such as, 'So when are you going to meet your son?' or 'Have they not called you over yet?'

Many parents arrive in time for the birth of their grandchildren. Many arrive to kick off a custom of six months' stay over the following years on a visitors' visa. Six months is the maximum they can stay, after which they must leave the country before they can apply for their visa again. An extension of stay for another six months can be requested if the elderly person has met with an accident, suffered injury or has a health emergency. They just need to apply with sufficient evidence to the authorities.

A visit by elderly relatives is usually fraught with all the tears and triumph, risk and surety you can normally expect in any Indian household. They bring with them the warmth of parental love and nurturing, and give their own selves a reason to swell in pride and happiness for making it overseas. They also bring with them decades of conditioning shaped by religious practices, beliefs, prejudices and pragmatism. The truth is that their children who arrived on work visas or dependent visas took their time to adjust to the alien culture. Their parents, with their decades of cultural conditioning and generational differences, come bearing their own fears and biases.

For the offspring, it is not just apprehensions about their parents being able to adjust to the local culture, but also concerns that they should not have any major health issues—be it because of the change in climate or their own physical disposition.

If it is the husband's parents coming over, he makes panic-stricken calls to friends asking for tips to survive the 'stuck between wife and mother' situation. Their wives might pass on their shopping lists to their in-laws, and hope they do not fuss about bringing too much stuff with them. Often, hoping to please their mothers-in-law, and because they don't want to be known as 'complainers', women do not openly talk about them. Their husbands, too, stress on the 'do not react to jibes' part, and expressly hope their wives earn a 'good bahu' tag during the visit.

Visa wives do taste a sense of freedom in the US despite their precarious 'no-job' status. Visits from the in-laws often put these women back in the life of up-close scrutiny and 24/7 responsibilities that they had left behind.

During our early days in the US, we spotted an elderly woman in the community. She was saree-clad, wrapped in warm clothing and would go for a walk twice a day. A few days later, we spotted her son and his wife arguing outside their home under a tree. They probably had nowhere to go. The wife was agitated, her gestures showing she had had enough. The husband was trying to calm her down. 'It's a saas-bahu story,' my husband dismissed the sight. 'Probably their apartment is small, or they cannot fight in front of his mother.'

On another day, a friend's elderly father, who had come visiting, told me, 'My friend and his wife come here often to be with their son. And their daughter-in-law does not allow his wife to cook. She won't let them use her kitchen! My friend does not like coming to the US, but his wife always wants to see their son.'

Was the daughter-in-law possessive about her kitchen? Was she being rude to them when she refused use of her kitchen or did she want to protect herself from taunts that she made her mother-in-law work in the kitchen?

My friend's dad did not mention if the elderly couple was being starved. If they were, he would surely mention it. It was obvious that there were differences between the visitors and their daughter-in-law, and she was certainly not playing the sacrificial and duty-bound bahu role.

When elders visit, the grandchildren enjoy the most. But there is a vast difference between a visit from a girl's parents and her in-laws. Visitor arrival months are sometimes happy, sometimes sad, and almost always stressful.

Aamani had had bitter experiences with her in-laws before she came to the US. But she did not hesitate to invite them over. She had her fears but hoped things would improve during her in-laws' visit. Her husband and she decided to shift to a larger apartment, mainly because, like many other apartment communities, their management would not encourage more than two people and a small child in a small apartment. The couple found an apartment where the elderly couple would have more room, areas around to walk in and some Indians to make friends with.

Aamani wanted her parents to visit too, but it was simply not acceptable for her to express such a wish. It had to be her husband's parents who visited first. She knew that once her in-laws came and left, she would have the liberty to bring her parents over. Booking their tickets, necessary medical follow-ups before the journey, the visa interview, visitors' insurance and booking travel tickets for touring the country were all done by Aamani and Sreenivas Rai. The process kept them on their toes.

Intent on studying further, Aamani was busy preparing for TOEFL (Test of English as a Foreign Language) and GRE (Graduate Record Examinations) in the run-up to the in-laws' arrival. She was not sure how she would be able to concentrate on her studies with her in-laws around. She was an active homemaker and cook. Their presence would demand more work from her.

They moved into their new apartment in a better neighbourhood after the elders arrived. When the time came to get a new bed for the master bedroom and arrange the guest room, her mother-in-law insisted that she get the master bedroom for the duration of their stay. Aamani was angry but could not protest. As for the mother-in-law, she was not willing to let go of her position of authority.

Aamani's life became hectic. Before her in-laws' arrival, Sreenivas split the kitchen chores with her. With his parents' arrival, he stopped. His mother would not hear of him working around the kitchen. Aamani was expected to wake up long before everyone and get the kitchen started. She was keeping late hours because of her exam preparations and applications to local universities. But that was not an excuse that would work with her mother-in-law.

When she chatted with her mother-in-law, Aamani expressed her views as well. At one point, when the mother complained about Sreenivas, Aamani added her bit too.

The mother was irked. How dare this girl complain about 'my son'? Soon, Aamani found herself recounting her woes to friends. 'Why does she have one rule for me and another for herself?'

Differences between Aamani, her husband and his parents were stark, even if they were from the same caste and clan. Sreenivas and Aamani practised meatless days on certain days of the week, while the parents did so on other days. Her mother-in-law insisted on meat being cooked on days that were meatless for the young couple. If Aamani and Sreenivas had an argument about something, her in-laws always thought she was wrong. They would not intervene, but would complain later. Soon, Sreenivas faced a list of complaints against his wife nearly every day.

'How much dowry did you give your husband?' her mother-in-law would ask friends of the couple who came visiting, hoping to hear a higher figure than that paid by Aamani's parents. It put Aamani in a spot.

'She tells her relatives she made a mistake by choosing me. She does that in a loud voice, even if I am present in the room. What more should I do to please her?' Aamani cried to a friend. That morning, she had woken up after a late-night research session and coordination for their upcoming trip to California. She got up later than usual, and walked into the kitchen without bathing first—sacrilege, in her mother-in-law's book, who sent her back for a bath. Arguments ensued. She wanted to fight with her mother-in-law but quietened down for her husband's sake.

Aamani hardly had any time to prepare for her exams and, as a result, could not score well in her GRE. Her hopes of getting into a good university were dashed. She had to opt for a regional university instead. She knew her mother-in-law was unhappy about Sreenivas spending on her master's degree. But, if the girl would bring in a salary packet every month, after everything, it might help, she thought. She did give her bahu the silent treatment for a day or two in any case.

Sreenivas looked up to his mother as a role model. He thought his dad was a deadbeat, who spent more time among relatives than with his family. His mother had struggled with her own job as a teacher, saved every penny and educated him. She had made many sacrifices while bringing him up, and he would never be able to repay that. He wanted respect for her even if she was wrong.

Even so, he hoped to placate his mother by pushing his wife to be more active in cooking, housekeeping, hosting and so on. His logic was that they could always repair their relationship later even if things went wrong. But his parents going back to India unhappy was simply not acceptable to him.

A common difference that crops up when elders visit is regarding food and cooking habits. Many Indian families continue to cook traditional food, but also adapt partly to food from fast-food restaurants, and enjoy other cuisines available in abundance in America. Fast-food chain restaurants are not a healthy idea. But when they are the only option left during a five-hour drive from your home, it makes sense to grab a salad or a sandwich.

It's something elderly relatives from India find difficult to adjust to, used as they are to a lifestyle of three meals a day and a snack. So Ravali Vishwanath, a homemaker with visiting in-laws, had to cook six meals for a two-day trip from her San Francisco home to Los Angeles. She did so for every weekend trip they went on, every time they set foot outside home. Her children, a son and daughter, had their own food preferences, though.

Kanika Desai found a solution to the problem by simply carrying her electric rice cooker over to tourist spots that she and her husband would take the in-laws to. She would tuck away rice, dals, vegetables and some spices in travel-size containers in their car trunk. Several months before their arrival, she had scouted endlessly for deals on hotels with kitchenettes. On the day of travel, she would carry a jug of milk too for coffee and tea. Her husband and she were used to creamer sachets and pods to add to their coffee at cafes. Her in-laws were still reeling under the shock of seeing mug-sized paper glasses that held as much coffee as a bowlful of rasam. At the hotel-with-kitchen, the seniors were served piping hot meals with curries. They were impressed. All their food-related apprehensions were laid to rest.

Still others find the lack of activity and bustle in smaller towns a torture. On most days, an average retiree in Mumbai, for instance, would want to walk to the vegetable vendor near home, or hop into an autorickshaw to the nearest temple. The *vada-pav* peddler, the traffic in their neighbourhoods, sounds, smells and noise are integral to their daily lives, even if they detest the chaos.

'There is no one outside the house. No animals, no people, no vehicles not even birds,' complained an elderly gentleman from Mumbai to his relatives when he came visiting. His biggest grouse was that there were no shops within a ten-minute walking distance. He was in the habit of downing a cup of tea at the neighbourhood *vada-pav* shop while on his evening stroll. At his son's Virginia apartment, it took him ten minutes to reach the apartment community's entrance. And a walk of another mile and a half to reach the nearest store. Soon, he grew restless and began to look for excuses to cut short his visit.

'Shift to New York City—I will come again,' a Connecticut-based son was told by his father when he invited him over for a stay the second time. This gentleman was in the habit of visiting temples in his Mylapore neighbourhood in Chennai. He liked to walk to a park where he met up with elderly friends. His son's home was a one-bedroom apartment, while he was used to a three-bedroom house. His son was still going through the uncertain-about-projects phase. He could not obviously ask the youngster to move from a one-bedroom apartment to a two-bedroom one. It was hard to be in such close proximity with their daughter-in-law for him and his wife.

Project uncertainty had prompted their son to book their tickets in early spring, when the northeast's winter was still phasing out, and when a couple of snow showers still dotted the weather transition. The gentleman hated that his hands would freeze whenever he stepped out for a smoke.

Some families continue to live in one-bedroom apartments for years after they arrive. When elders come to visit, a makeshift bed or mattress pops up in the living room, to which the elders are confined. The bedroom exists, but the elders may keep to themselves for propriety's sake.

Elders who might be accustomed to larger living spaces in India find it tough to adjust in a smaller space in the US. Add to it the lack of mobility that the new place imposes, because of poor public transport, and they feel imprisoned. Their day then becomes a perennial wait for the car-driving member to return, so they may be able to step out, even if for a five-minute drive.

'The biggest challenge during my parents' stay was to keep them entertained,' says Ria George who had just started working in Missouri when her parents visited her. On their earlier visit, she was still a visa wife, going through her share of trauma. By now, she had a two-year-old daughter, had done several community college courses and finally found a job befitting her profile. The EAD stage on her husband's Permanent Residency process allowed her to work.

'My mom would be busy with my daughter all day. So she was less of a challenge. My dad would rest all day and get bored. As soon as I got back from a hard day of work, I would have to take him to the library. There was no place close enough for him to walk to. They were completely dependent on me. I completely understood his situation, but for me it was physically draining. Work for me was a forty-five-minute drive one way.'

Some elderly people find their US stay wonderful, while others find it bittersweet. For the visa wives, such visits often alter relationships. Take the case of Ravali. 'My attitude towards my husband and in-laws changed. They can be sneaky. I cannot really blame my husband, but he should have been confident that I would take care of his parents. For all the years that I lived with him, I prioritized his needs over mine. After my in-laws left, I realized what they and my husband truly thought of me. It was an eye-opener.'

Ravali, who had earlier called up her in-laws once a week, stopped doing so. She felt her husband was 'managing her' rather than being a supportive partner. 'All those years, they kept saying they struggled to bring their son up and sacrificed for him. I had cared. Now I do not.'

Not without reason. Serving them leftovers for dinner, even using idli batter from breakfast in the evening, was not allowed. She would have to wash her hair every day during her periods so she could enter the kitchen and cook. She admits she started yelling at her husband during their stay, unable to stand the harassment. 'My husband thought I was insulting them, because after all those years of keeping quiet, I started voicing my feelings. I had to let my frustration out. My husband later admitted that his mother had been stubborn.' Ravali says she started practising detachment from people around her after that disastrous visit.

Madhuri, on the other hand, found an ally in her mother-in-law. 'At her age, she is so energetic it can put someone like me to shame. She does multiple things in a wink. I have lots to learn on that front.'

Sometimes, the dependent wife might have a wonderful relationship with her in-laws during their visit but relatives in the vicinity might cause misunderstandings.

Sangeetha Kannan was pregnant when she requested her parents to visit during the crucial third trimester. She had not waited for long after getting married to assimilate into her new life. She had enrolled herself in an MS programme and was in the thick of her assignments when she got pregnant. She had been keen on having a baby because she thought her husband and she were at the right age to have children.

Her parents could not make it so her in-laws pitched in. Her mother-in-law, a soft-spoken woman, doted on the mother-to-be and took care of her needs just as Sangeetha's own mother would. She got tired, though, when another elderly relative dropped by regularly and put her on the defensive by expecting her to cook. Sangeetha was in the final term of her pregnancy, and cried bitterly from the exhaustion and jibes.

Her in-laws' visit had to be cut short because of her mother-in-law's ill health. With their visitor's health insurance failing to cover her expenses, they had to foot sky-high medical bills. Visitors to the US are not eligible for medical insurance coverage the way people on work visas, their families, citizens and permanent residents are.

So the in-laws thought it more feasible to proceed with treatment back in India.

The trouble with visitors' health insurance is either the lack of coverage for pre-existing conditions, or not qualifying for insurance plans at all in case of diseases like cancer. This applies even if a concerned elder has completed his or her treatment in India. In the case of diabetics, or those with renal ailments, the premium may go up. It is essential that families who bring their elders do thorough research and opt for the best policies available.

Visitors' health insurance largely falls under basic plans or limited plans with their low-cost premium and the comprehensive coverage plans that cover about 70–80 per cent of costs up to the first $5000 on a policy and 100 per cent beyond that. Comprehensive plans involve more benefits, and cover acute onset of pre-existing conditions. Usually, things like preventive care, cosmetic procedures and dental work that are not related to accidents or emergency are excluded from coverage in such plans.

Often the health of elders is a huge gamble for families, partly because of the high costs of healthcare involved. In extreme cases, families are left to accept cruel twists of destiny, like Shrinivas and Seetha.

Shrinivas brought his mother, a practising pharmacist, and his father, a diabetic, to the US so that they could spend time with his six-month-old baby. For a few weeks, the family had a great time. It was the end of summer. Seetha and Shrinivas did not worry much. They made sure to take them to temples nearby, attended get-togethers among friends, performed some special poojas at home and visited must-see places that dotted the east coast.

One evening, Seetha's mother-in-law called up Shrinivas in a panic. He called 911 and rushed home. His father had been asleep in the bedroom, when his mother went in and found fluid oozing from his mouth. She asked him to get up but he did not respond. By the time the paramedics arrived, it was too late. They tried CPR and failed.

The family was mystified. He had been healthy, had his lunch on time, played with their baby and, for a change, talked to their child's nanny too. What could have happened? For the next two hours, the police and a medical examiner asked them questions to ascertain whether the death was natural. They took the phone number of the deceased's doctor in India. The authorities were polite, and asked them whether they wanted the funeral in India or locally.

Through the tears and shock, his mother decided to perform the cremation in the US. If the body had to be transported to India, they would have to perform an autopsy. They checked the family's religion, and gave the reference of a funeral home. The funeral home had a webcam through which the funeral could be relayed back to their relatives in India.

It was the toughest for the son, who had been eager to show his father the country. He did not want to claim the insurance policy his parents had purchased from India before travelling to the US. The funeral cost him $5000 and rituals another $15,000. He had fortunately saved up money over time. And now, he used it all up. For long, the family tried to come to terms with the tragedy. What went wrong?

'It was November when my father died. The weather might be one of the reasons for his demise. Apparently, strokes are a big risk among the elderly in cold weather. Even though it was not winter, they are used to tropical weather, so it probably affected him,' says Shrinivas.

The sudden death shook not just him and his family, but their friends and acquaintances. Most of them resolved not to bring elderly parents over after the month of October.

Not every family faces such tragedies upon the arrival of elders. There are families where the arrival of elders is stress-free, happy and fun. It is a matter of understanding, and accepting, that not everything is under one's control.

18

Uncertain Visas

You might have heard how work visas can get exploitative in the new country. But you truly understand the turmoil that work visa vulnerability puts you in only when you actually experience it. The tenure of a standard non-immigrant visa like H1B is six years. The permit for the individual's stay in the US is not granted for the entire period of six years at a stretch. If you are a skilled worker, you might get a valid visa for one year too, and would need to get it extended from time to time.

Not every on-site posting is one that might last over a year or two. Your spouse or you might be told by the company that 'this is the only project available. Take it. If things work out, you might be retained. Otherwise you can find other projects.'

The on-site client company then plays god. You thought you could make it for nine months. Three months on, 'market compulsion', 'large-scale downsizing' and other such phrases can send you back home.

'My colleague was good at his job. But to terminate his services, they sent the security personnel to his desk, and escorted him out. They would not even let him collect his things.'

Once a client company decides to terminate your role in the project, you will need to fall back on your India-based employer company to be assigned to another project. This is time-bound. Usually, companies allow their employees to stay on for a few weeks after termination. These weeks can be a drain, emotionally and practically.

Says Sailu Balakrishna, whose husband has made such moves five times in two years, 'When it happens the first time, you get tense. You do not know how the process works. By the second time, you get used to it. If you have made up your mind to go back to India after a while, you view this as a chance to live abroad. But if you want to stay on, your peace of mind is impacted. We are usually unhappy with the companies. They project some tenure which may be long and push us out too early. Sometimes, they stand by their word. It is all right if the tenure is shortened or extended by a month. But when they say they will keep him for eight months and turn him out in four and a half, we feel cheated. Usually, it is unlikely that you will get the next assignment in the same state. Even if another project is assigned, uncertainty looms ahead.'

The worst part, she says, is how a lot of hopes get pinned on the boss and his or her willingness to do the needful for the worker. Negotiating the corporate system, replete with its hierarchy and delays, is akin to climbing a steep hill.

'If the manager is good, he can keep you on the bench for three months in case he foresees a project. He has to assure your Indian company, and if the human resources department agrees, they can keep extending the time while you get paid your salary. We have seen families who have got paid by their companies for three months with no work, because at times they do not want to move out of that particular city or town, mainly when kids are involved.'

What happens when you are given the pink slip from the client company? What does it do to not just the H1B visa holder, but also the woman who has left everything behind and joined him in the hope of a new life? Pink-slip fears and nightmares of H1B holders can affect families greatly.

Who gets to stay on and who doesn't? How do people fight their circumstances?

Kripakar Nath and his wife were both working on their respective H1B visas when her visa was rejected. The only option was to convert her visa to an H4 if she were to continue living in the same town. Misfortune played its cards. In the same week, Kripakar's office laid him off. He was forced to make a decision on whether to stay on or move back to India.

A key factor for them was their five-year-old son and his schooling. Kripakar did not want to jeopardize his son's chance of staying on in the US, and so sent his wife and child to live in India for a while. Meanwhile, he vacated his home, put their furniture in storage and moved in with some bachelor colleagues.

He constantly tried looking out for other assignments through his Indian company, but also kept in touch with the boss who had given him the pink slip. It took him some months and efforts with his old boss to get back into the same office on a new assignment. It played havoc on their family life in the bargain. Kripakar's wife continued working in India, and was dependent on her own parents for support in taking care of her child.

Should a new assignment be allotted in another state within the US, it is likely that families might choose to stay on in their locations for the sake of their child's schooling till such time as the spouse settles down in his new assignment. Such moves transform transcontinental nomads to intra-country nomads of the IT workforce. Such a life might make sense for those who are backpackers at heart. For the ones seeking stability and a sense of settling down, it is hell.

Consider this, a typical transition day for an H1B holder. Sailu's husband, Anuj, was on the verge of finishing his current project in Texas—the project he was sent to the US for. With a whole two months of uncertainty, the two were very worried.

Inside Sailu's troubled head, a storm was brewing. 'Why is he not being aggressive? Why does he take anything anyone says at face value? Why does he trust people blindly?' She wanted the American dream to work. But was this really that dream?

Their future was hanging in the air. Here she was, having left her own job, to support him through the

transition, hoping against hope that he would land a
long-term assignment soon. And yet, her own sacrifice of
her career seemed to be mocking her.

She took tired steps into the kitchen to get breakfast
ready—and stared at the spartan plastic canisters with
half-finished grocery supplies. 'Have to finish these before
we move back to India.'

She let out a loud sigh. 'Or not.'

It was obvious that she did not want to go back. Anuj
did not want to go back either. Neither of them was sure
how desperately the other wanted to stay on in the US. 'If
things don't work out, come back. You can make money
in India too,' his mother had told him the previous
night. From what he had said in response, Sailu was sure
he sought solace in returning home, to the comforting
proximity of his parents.

From the kitchen, she heard him talk to his boss.
She knew his manager was giving him false assurances.
The end of the project was days away. Anuj's profile was
up on the intranet site of his company in the 'resources
available' section. Calls that initially came in were for the
north—Seattle. He was keen on taking it up, though the
thought of a harsh winter scared him.

'Wait for a better project that does justice to your
technical capabilities. This one is a diversion from your
profile,' suggested his manager. An entire week after
Anuj heeded that piece of advice, they were left with
conversations that ended with no return calls, possible
'client interviews' and no other project availability. Each
time he responded to any calls, Sailu was immediately

on the Internet searching out those places—Minnesota, Arizona, Tennessee.

'Hurry up. Once Thanksgiving arrives, no one in your company will be in the mood to work or assign projects. Grab what you get,' Anuj's friend from Philadelphia told him. Anuj felt sandwiched between the 'go, get it now' pressures of his near ones, and the non-committal attitude of his boss. 'What if it's destiny for me to go back to India? What will these company guys think of me if I keep going after them for my work? It's not right to disturb people . . . '

Sailu was enraged. She felt the urge to chat with his bosses directly and ask them what was happening. She had experience in IT too, and understanding of the way bosses and systems work. It was a game she knew like the back of her hand. She had grasped the jobs game in the US economy too very quickly.

Soon it was Thanksgiving, the holiday weekend when company bigwigs would be away with families feasting on turkey or shopping. 'We have a project in Arizona. You are a good fit, but the client will need to interview you,' said an HR representative from his company. An interview with the client always takes some scheduling. The couple knew this would take a few days. They had to take a call on vacating their Houston apartment.

Sailu had taken pains to assimilate in their Houston neighbourhood. She made a bunch of friends among the Indians out there. For the first time in her life, she felt uninhibited about exercising in her neighbourhood gym. Women would send their kids off to school and spend an hour or two at the gym every morning, giving them a break from the daily chores. They had even planned a trip together soon—with all the families.

It had hardly been a few months. She had sacrificed her own career—for what? This 'now here, now gone' situation?

Should she call up her own boss at the Indian company and check if there were vacancies? After all, her boss had assured her she would have no trouble getting hired again in that company should she decide to get back to India soon.

Such a situation is not confined to those with work visas alone. A decade ago, when Sonal Chauhan's husband was done with his PhD on the F1 visa, after years of being in a postdoctoral researcher's position at his university, he tried getting a teaching position. He was told that someone else had already been shortlisted for the position. It hit him hard. Her husband had pinned his hopes on the university. Dejected, he decided to go back to India and began to apply for jobs in universities there.

Sonal faced the biggest dilemma a mother could face. Her children, aged ten and nine, were both US citizens. Her elder daughter, who had visited India a few times, complained of the weather being hot and humid, and the studies involving a lot of stress. Sonal was sure that if they moved with the kids to India, the kids would insist on returning even after the initial hiccups. What would happen to her under such circumstances? Being citizens, her children would get a free passage back to the US. She was still on the F2 visa, having completed her master's in science (MS) the year before. Her own search for employment had yielded no results.

Sonal and her husband decided to ship some of their important items to India. Her husband had found a position at a university in Kerala. She felt helpless. A battle of emotions raged within her. The proximity with her parents was a welcoming thought. But going back to another city in the country she had left behind over a decade ago, to a culture she was not quite up to date with after all these years, having to adjust to a language she did not know, were all too much to put up with. That they would have to move lock, stock and barrel to a place that felt more like a dot on the map was tough.

How would the kids cope? It was not as if the Indian university would pay him well. Their relatives told them that his Indian salary would merely help them cover half the monthly expenses for the lifestyle they led. All that they had worked for had amounted to nothing.

'We had hoped our in-laws would move in with us in Kerala. They refused, saying it was too far for them,' she says.

Her husband did not give up his search for positions locally. The uncertainty of his employment dragged on—not for weeks, but for a whole six months. Each day, she researched her would-be city in Kerala and figured out the schools, stores, transportation and hospitals in the city. She tried to prepare her kids for the move too, albeit slowly. Her children were disappointed. They would have to give up their school, their friends, their city.

Slowly, though, Sonal learnt to accept the compromises they would have to make for a lifestyle on a lower salary in

India. She knew that cutting corners would help. After all those years, she would become a hidden immigrant in the same country she grew up. She was willing to risk it. Her husband was eager to go back.

One morning, her husband called with some news. 'The other guy did not clear the position,' he said, adding that his university had offered him the job. For Sonal, it was too much to take. In her head, she was already in Kerala. She asked him not to take it. A few minutes later, he called back, saying he had accepted the offer. Moments later, she was sobbing into her pillow. She did not know if she should be angry with her husband for not heeding her words, or happy because they could now stay back.

Sometimes, decisions by companies can take weeks. Sometimes, they can decide to let go of the H1B holder who may be a 'contractor', and he may be left with no payslips to apply for a transfer of his visa to another company. Often, the insensitivity of the whole process drives couples to the edge.

Sathya and her husband were in the US for about eight months. He had been brought over by his current project managers with the promise of employment for a whole year. Surya had been hoping to find something in the following month or two, when his bosses gave him the 'let go'.

For the last few months, she had seen his confidence take a blow. 'They micro-manage. They do not let you work,' he complained to her every day, and spoke of how, in a country where people did not really work beyond 5 p.m., his bosses would harass employees at odd hours for office work. He was expected to be in the good books of his bosses, to survive, by feigning obedience, like in India. He did not bow down to their demands. The result was daily threats of, 'Do you want to go back to India?' or 'Why are you so lethargic?'

Sathya and Surya had somewhat settled down into their new life when his bosses told him he would be out of his project in about two weeks. He felt cheated. Eight months ago, he had refused to join the project from India. He knew the work culture was not great. But his boss at the Indian parent company had assured him something else would work out once he landed in the US. Of late, Sathya's health was not doing great either. She was unusually tired. It was time for a doctor's visit.

The couple was devastated. Her parents wondered what happened that she had to return to India in such a short while. They were happy their daughter would be home though. His parents, who were postponing their own trip to the US, were shocked.

The two had just set up home with difficulty—a sofa, TV, laptop, a bed for their bedroom, an old dining table, a kitchen they were slowly buying things for, winter clothes and shoes.

They were forced to send word out through friends that their items were up for sale. Her husband had not got a driver's licence yet. So buying a car had been out of the question. For the moment, it was one item less on the list of things they had to give away. When prospective buyers came to survey their belongings, Sathya felt a pang of pain.

They were not random items that were lifeless. They represented the hard work and sweat that had gone into picking them up and turning them into crucial constituents of their home. Still, they could not carry these items to India all the way from here. For friends of friends, these were cheap deals, as good as free. When they were busy surveying the goodies lined up on the floor of her living room, Sathya felt the urge to scream. She realized in a second that the visitors were actually doing her and her husband a favour by agreeing to buy up stuff.

Over three weeks, the couple travelled to places they had never dreamt of going to. They met friends, attended birthdays, threw away items they could not sell or give away and asked for help in finding jobs. Sathya was exhausted—from the travel and the uncertainty. They noticed that although people genuinely wanted to help, they would never do so at the cost of jeopardizing their own standing with their respective companies.

Time was ticking by. Three days before their impending return to India, her husband received an interview call from a client listed with his Indian company. They were looking for a profile matching his. It was a two and a half hour journey to a remote town and he did not know how to reach there. He called up the interview team for directions.

The interview went well. They were impressed by his work experience. He requested the interviewing project manager to take a call on his position as soon as possible, because his future in the US was hanging by a thread. He was barely forty-eight hours away from a flight back to India. On his way out, he noticed the next candidate, a woman whose husband worked in the same company.

'Oh no! Looks like I will not get it,' he thought, his hopes dashed.

That night, Sathya was trying to get some of the packing done. After a while, she collapsed on the sofa. The anxiety was killing her. She was confused about what to pack. If the decision was final, it would be so much easier. 'Go back' and she would throw away most of the stuff into the trash bin. 'Stay' and she would rearrange things back in the closets.

'It's not like I mind going back. It is just that I feel a sense of incompleteness. We were supposed to achieve a few things here,' she had told her husband the previous evening.

He agreed. He had to give that interview one last shot.

'It went well. Only hope they say yes by tomorrow,' he told Sathya before he called up his Indian boss.

By late next morning, they were a bundle of nerves. She had no heart to enter the kitchen, leave alone stir up something to eat. He was pacing up and down in the living room that was strewn with cardboard boxes and half-filled suitcases. Unable to take it any longer, he called his boss in India. 'My suitcases are lying open. I have a flight back to India in less than twenty-four hours. Tell me something. Did they at least give you a hint about whether I will stay or not? What do I do?'

His boss was equally clueless. It was post noon when he got off the phone. He called up the firm that had interviewed him, who told him a meeting was on to make the decision. His hands had gone cold. Half an hour later, when he refreshed his e-mail page, he saw a one-liner.

'Welcome on board,' said the email from his prospective new boss.

What?! He re-read the mail, double-checking the ID it came from and the sender's name to be sure. He was in. He ran to Sathya. They hugged each other, feeling a bit numb. Were they actually staying back? So they no longer had to check into a hotel in Chennai. They had to check into a hotel in the new town he would be working. They had to call up their parents. They were both tired and just wanted to sleep for a while.

What Sathya and Surya went through is a routine that repeats every now and then in the homes of thousands of non-immigrant workers all over the US. Some families become experts at it, having to move every two years or so with bag, baggage, home and hearth to other cities. They might shift from New York to Denver, spanning the dramatic change from Eastern Time to Mountain Time, for instance. Or from California to Georgia, over the deserts and plains, from the West Coast to the East Coast. Each shift brings with it new challenges and the humongous task of having to forge new friendships, adjust to a new life and more. Sometimes, families welcome the change between cities, based on the cost of living, local environment, health and other factors.

Azhagi Kumar and her husband, Saravanan, had moved from Bengaluru to the Chicago area a few years ago. She arrived as a bride and went through her own problems trying to adjust to the extreme cold during winter. Saravanan's one-hour drive to work every day left him drained. Pressures at work apart, he suffered from severe backaches. He was not sure if it was the cold weather or his long drive to and from work. Azhagi was helpless. They had a toddler who needed attention all the time. At times, she was tempted to convince him to move back to India. They would both be closer to their parents and she might be able to renew her career prospects too.

Saravanan checked out the possibility of moving to warmer places within the US. They found Florida, with its tropical climate, to be the most suitable. Saravanan began looking for prospective jobs there. A few months later, they moved to Tampa in Florida. Though Saravanan's back woes did not vanish, he did feel a lot better there than in the mid-west.

In the case of Rani and Kant, Kant's bosses had become somewhat hostile after his work-from-home days increased after his daughters' accidents. His Indian company was not willing to renew his visa either. Kant was left with no choice but to return to India. It was a bit difficult for him to digest. Had the health of his children not suffered, he would probably have done a lot better at work. Had his bosses been more understanding, they might have recommended continuing his employment. Why his Indian company did not want to apply for his visa renewal, he simply did not know. He was told it was a management decision that was affected by projects with other US-based and European companies.

Their children were still healing from their injuries the previous year. Rani was relieved. She was unhappy about having to leave the way they did, but she was extremely attached to her family in Patna. Having to live away from them had been torturous for her. She never wanted to relive the past year ever again. Kant had to report to his Gurgaon office upon return to India. Having lived in Gurgaon before, Rani thought it would be easier to assimilate back into the fold.

They were allowed a few weeks to pack up for good. It meant breaking the rental lease of the apartment before their tenure was over. Kant produced a letter from his office stating his services were not required in the company, and the apartment management relented. Their suitcases were packed with their children's clothes , aside from gifts for relatives. An important addition to their luggage was a stuffed life-sized Minnie Mouse doll that they had bought for their girls during those hellish months. The hug-toy was an inseparable friend for their kids, and seemed to have played a role in their healing.

Sailu says that the way bosses deal with their employees makes a big difference in determining the lives of families that move to the US based on their non-immigrant work visas. 'If there are kids involved, you need to be in the good books of your manager. If you are a first-timer, though, managers are not in the least bothered about your needs. If they want, they can relocate you within an hour. The way they inform you is also insensitive. Most times, they inform you a day or a few hours before relieving you from the project.'

Sailu finds her situation a lot better than families of other H1B workers who do not as much as get paid when they are thrown out of projects. 'A close friend had to find a job as soon as he was fired. He was not getting paid a salary by the employers, which meant he would not get the pay-stubs necessary to produce to the authorities for an extension of the visa. If a person is a contractor for a company here, he must leave the country immediately.'

Sometimes, the uncertainty factor is not limited to the macro-economic HR decisions by large companies. It boils down to the life struggles of women and their spouses. It relates to family events—big and small, good and bad—back home in India.

Aruna had settled well into her American life at Pittsburgh, soaking in its hilly magnanimity and falling in love with the 'City of Bridges' every day. 'I could not find employment after my graduate school studies. It is great to volunteer for a while. But I had been in grad school, so I wanted a job. It may have been an impulsive decision in hindsight. My cousin was getting married and I was feeling restless about not being in India. My brother, who was in the US, was going through a difficult patch. It was a confluence of factors. Even the day we left, my husband said, "I hope you are sure about this!"'

Since her return to India, Aruna has played the role of a caregiver in her family, to ailing near ones, and moved into the field of social innovation. It was a huge effort to readjust to life in Bengaluru. Her perseverance has paid off.

For many others, it could be about the lack of support in the new country, poor health of elders back home, or job prospects not looking up in their land of dreams. Their own long journeys towards becoming Lawful Permanent Residents that stretch to a decade and beyond prompt their return in many cases.

Rarely, it is about itchy feet. Either way, uncertainty rules.

19

Studying in the US

'You can always study there.'

Gita Shankar looked at Ajay Sivan with renewed interest when he said these words. Gita had not been interested in the alliance from the time his 'biodata' had been thrust on her. She had wanted to study. She had done her BA, not a post-graduation, but she hoped to finish her MA before getting married. She was merely being courteous when she agreed to meet him. She was waiting for a definite reason to say 'no'.

All the brouhaha about this 'America *sambandham*' was getting on her nerves. He was not a god who had descended by her backyard well! She watched squirrels and crows fight for a handful of rice scattered on the compound wall as she listened to this man speak. A normal guy with an 'IT' tag, worse, the 'America *maapizhai*' (bridegroom) tag. Thankfully, he was not putting on any airs.

Ajay was a Chennai-bred man who was looking for a traditional homemaker who would cook and clean for him. He wanted a 'homely girl', not an emancipated one. His colleagues were chasing engineer alliances, but he knew what he wanted. The last few trips had revealed to him that there were no girls who wanted to ditch their studies and turn caregivers for their men. He resigned himself to the idea of letting her study if she wanted. 'You can do your post-graduation in the US. And then we can come back,' he told her.

No groom had told her this. The other men were only interested in her cooking skills, cleaning skills and determining if she was 'cultured' enough. The thought of studying further was the clincher. Gita warmed up to the guy. Ajay's nephew came by to check on them. 'What are you doing here?' the five-year-old demanded. Ajay knew the bunch of relatives inside the house were playing chaperone. 'I'm talking to aunty,' he said. Gita smiled. 'What are you talking about?' Ajay feigned an excuse and sent the kid away.

'I am not keen on working, but I definitely wish to study,' said Gita. He asked her about her interests other than studies. In the next few minutes, while their families waited, Gita and Ajay exchanged numbers. They would need a day or two to make up their minds, probably another conversation, but something clicked between them.

Grooms living in the US sometimes throw in these phrases during 'girl meeting' trips to India, when they know it is difficult to find women who would want to leave their careers behind. It is a saleable carrot for prospective brides who may not otherwise be inclined to accept the match. It works in the case of young brides who may be persuaded by their families to say 'yes' when their version of a 'good alliance' turns up.

Sometimes, a husband might suggest the option to his wife a few years into the marriage too, in the hope that she will not fuss much about his sojourn 'on-site' or about joining him.

A bunch of Gita's schoolmates had moved on to the traditionally lucrative careers of engineering and medicine. Her parents could afford neither. Gita joined an arts college instead. What she was not prepared for was the fact that her three-year degree meant nothing in the US. Many women who have spent their lives acquiring their Indian degrees, and sweated it out at internships and jobs, are in for a rude shock when they arrive in the US hoping to find work and work permits. Their bachelor college degrees that span three years of study in Indian universities are not valid in many American universities. In the case of eligibility for the H1B visa, a three-year degree and additional work experience are good enough for the USCIS.

For pursuing post-graduation in the US, four- and five-year courses such as engineering and medicine are recognized. Some US universities do recognize three-year degrees, subject to evaluation by the World Education Services and sometimes with the student's acquisition of additional course credits. Persistent search among universities across the country turns into a huge task for the visa wife. If you wish to join a particular college, you will need to check with its admission department individually.

For many Indian men who want a double-income household, the search gets concentrated on engineer and medicine background brides alone. In short, women who qualify enough to cook their meals, rear their children *and* get them an additional salary packet. When Sairam met Sarika, the clincher was that this girl, from the same caste as him, was an engineer. The conversation did not come up during their video-chat 'boy meets girl' ritual. Too many cousins from her family jumped in to converse with the US groom. He had originally wanted a doctor bride but found that Indian girls who were doctors in the US preferred doctor husbands, not engineers. He wanted a homely girl but also someone who had the qualifications necessary to get a job, or find a sponsor for an H1B visa after she came.

In the hope of getting their daughters married to US-based grooms, some Indian parents do not wait for the right 'alliance' to turn up. They sponsor the education of their daughters for an American master's programme.

In many upper middle class homes of India, the clamour runs strong for an MBA or MCA, which will get daughters NRI husbands.

'You can always study in the US.' When a prospective US groom says this, it might mean, 'You shall not sit idle at home. You shall study, work and earn us that monthly packet', or 'Am saying it just in case you are keen on not sitting at home. Not sure if I can sponsor it, though', or still better, 'See, I'm being a benevolent husband, willing to sponsor your master's!' For most part, it feels like a practical solution to avoid heartache in the marriage, as in the case of Ajay and Gita.

It might not mean anything either, like in the case of Sathya.

When Sathya came to the US, she flew to a dot on the global map. Soon she realized she might begin to feel sub-human if she did nothing for herself. She began to browse online for available courses in the vicinity. Her interest was in the media and arts. She wrote to an arts institute for fee details so she could prepare herself and join. She was not looking for a master's degree. She was keen on learning painting, even if it was a short-term course. The brochures arrived, and the fee ran up to $8000 for a six-month course. She was taken aback. The figures went into lakhs of rupees in Indian currency. She was scared to broach the subject with her husband, even if he had mentioned in passing before they made their decision—'You can always study'. Other details rattled her too—the brochure listed details for credit and non-credit courses. She wondered what they were, until the Internet revealed that US universities have a system of accumulating a specific number of credits for the subjects of study, to be eligible for the degree certificate.

One day, Surya chanced upon the brochures and questioned her, 'Did you see the amount they are charging?' His tone was nearly accusatory. She did not say anything. Deep down, she resented him. She felt a mild sense of betrayal. The first months in their new home

had unsettled her enough. She badly needed a dollop of
self-esteem. After all, he did say those words about
studying in America. Did he mean anything when he had
said that? Was it her fault that the fee was so high?

For a few days, she agonized over his over-zealous
effort to save every dollar to clear his debts. 'He should
have cleared them long back, much before we got married,
not now,' she thought to herself. His remark made it
evident that he did not want to sponsor her education.
She was willing to let go of her own career and he was
only bothered about clearing debts. What about her need
for validity in the new country? What about her need to
meet people, and gain confidence?

She checked out the community colleges in the area
and found that reaching by bus in the harsh winter would
be difficult. What if he said no to community colleges
too? What if a community college fee proved too much
for him? Sathya stopped researching universities online.
In reality, his one sentence had sealed it all. He never
showed interest in her studies. He probably suggested the
studies part only so she would agree to leave India for
him. Her resentment slowly morphed into despair.

Neha was clear she wanted to study when she moved to
the US. She had saved up money through her stint in the
Middle East but had had to spend it on her wedding. She
had a BA and a post-graduate diploma in her kitty, along
with another course in computer science through a private
institution. 'It should amount to something,' she thought.

'When I went to these universities, they told me my
three-year degree would amount to nothing. If I had to

study further at all, I would have to repeat my graduation. No post-graduation for me. University after university told me that. I got fed up.'

Neha decided to forgo her hopes for a master's altogether. She focused instead on vocational courses through community colleges.

Community colleges, or city colleges, in the US are primarily two-year public institutions of higher education. These colleges are a popular alternative to completing the first two years of a bachelor's degree. Credits from these . colleges can be transferred after two years for students to complete their bachelor's degree at universities. As a visa wife, you do not need to procure the F1 student visa to pursue courses in a community college. Moreover, it is likely that you will become eligible for a lesser fee at the college after one year of staying in that city, which gives you the status of a 'resident'. However, studying at a community college does not entitle international students to the OPT period, the one-year period available to F1 visa holders to work without an H1B permit after their course.

The advantage of community colleges is that they are more affordable.[23] Community colleges have a wide range of courses—not just associate degrees and certificate courses, but those focused on personal development and languages too. For women seeking to assimilate into the new country's culture and ethos, enrolling in such colleges becomes a good way to do so.

Neha did courses in project management offered by her local college, and waited desperately for her husband's

Permanent Residence journey to reach the stage where she could obtain the EAD.

Women also pursue courses in subjects such as cooking and defensive driving, among others. When Sarika returned from India after therapy, she kept herself busy with visits to the nearest temple, its special poojas and events. A few weeks on, Sairam and Sarika began attending events related to employment opportunities in their area. They had run-ins with shady consultancies waiting to rip them off.

Sairam gently suggested she start exploring requirements for admissions in universities. 'I am not interested in studies. I want to work. Why did I spend so many years studying? Only to get back to studies here?' Sarika fumed.

She did not mind a low-paying job at a consultancy run by fellow Indians though. Arguments ensued between the couple. Things came to a boiling point one day. A consultant they were in touch with had a phone conversation with Sarika in Sairam's absence, and took details of his date of birth from her.

When Sairam found out, he was livid. 'They are out to loot us. You can't give my details to anyone just like that. They're confidential!'

Sarika realized that noticing her zeal to work and her husband's reluctance to break away from rules, the consultant was trying to play them against each other. Added to it was the fact that the couple was still easing into their relationship after a turbulent start. Sairam called the job consultant and questioned him.

'Why do you need my date of birth? What are you going to do with it?'

'We are only collecting details of our prospective employees. She can come and train our people.'

'Why do you need my birth details for that?'

'We will not misuse it. Do not worry.'

Sairam gave him an earful and hung up. For the next month and more, any message or e-mail about credit card transactions would send him into a tizzy. He alerted his bank about possible fraudulent transactions. Their friends explained how the SSN, address, date of birth and other such details are confidential information in the US, unlike in India, and can be used by conmen to obtain new debit cards, credit cards and empty your bank accounts. The experience prompted Sarika to try her hand at further studies . Her preparations for the GRE began. She decided to enrol in the MS Information Systems Technology course, with which she could get a job in the IT industry.

The cost of higher education in the US can be a prohibitive factor for women who want to continue to study. Consider this. To pay for her GRE, Madhusmita Bora took up ushering jobs at film festivals and exhibitions in Delhi. She was born into a political family and decided to study in the US against her family's wishes. She wanted to eventually join her fiancé in the US where he was studying at another university. Ahead of her arrival at a Chicago university in 1999, she successfully managed to get student loans.

'I paid off my student loans this month,' she said when we met for the interview in 2014. It was a huge milestone for her. Students often begin their work lives steeped in debt, and clearing these takes years. Madhusmita's journey towards self-sufficiency was not easy. She considers herself fortunate because the dean of another institution in Chicago, who was from her home city of Tezpur, co-signed her student loan. For the first three months after her arrival, her roommate supported her financially because the loan money had not begun to come through. Madhusmita eventually found a job at the college library to fund her expenses.

Just how much can an average master's degree cost? Says Aruna, whose spouse sponsored her studies, 'We paid $28,000 out of our pocket, which was half the tuition fee. For the rest, I got a scholarship. I paid the money semester by semester. It was $14,000 per year which came to $7,000 for six months. Once the scholarship came through, we decided it would not be worth letting it go.'

The partial scholarship helped Aruna go for her master's programme in international development. That was not all. She had a master's degree from Madurai Kamaraj University as well as work experience in India. When she moved to Pittsburgh, she braved the harsh winter and enrolled as a volunteer in the city's Carnegie Museum for three months, and later with other non-profits. The experience helped her connect with people and the city.

'The CEO/MD of one such non-profit wrote me a letter of recommendation. I would attend a lot of lectures. I wanted visibility when my application went to the university. Education in the US is all about a well-rounded experience.'

It is why the process of getting admission can be daunting. Vijaya Shetty decided to give a shot at an F1 visa when her repeated attempts to arrive on an H1B visa failed in the lottery system and left her devastated. Her fiancé was doing his master's at Iowa State University then, and suggested she join him on an F2 visa. She could also explore the MBA programme at his university.

By then, her H1B petition had been filed and there was still time for the results on the lottery for her visa to come through.

The couple explored the option of him returning to India, which was another whole year away. She started researching for MBA programmes in US universities by June that year.

'I found that the application deadlines were September and October for the first round of admissions. The second round happens in January and February, and the third in March. I was hardly two months away from the application deadline. If I missed it, I would not be able to make it for the following year's admissions. And to get an MBA admission, I had to appear for the GMAT (Graduate Management Admission Test). I decided to not risk it and apply in the following January.'

She prepared for GMAT, cutting her sleep time to five hours a night. She did not quit her job. After three months, she gave the test. Each university required different essays.

'One school would ask about teamwork, another about leadership and challenges with professional career and family. My GMAT scores were neither impressive nor disappointing. They did not make me a top choice unless I had a good essay. My application needed to be stellar to make it into the top MBA programmes. It meant that I had to spend a lot more time on the essays. I wrote my essays, and got them reviewed by friends and my fiancé. I found people in business schools and also researched through blogs. I found some current students to review my essays before I submitted them. I applied to six schools in all.'

Vijaya faced a tricky situation when it came to letters of recommendation. She could not tell her colleagues she was thinking of leaving, so she had to request people to write the recommendations in confidence. She had to do the interviews on phone and video chat.

When she was selected in three universities, she had to quickly make up her mind and choose one. Next was the bit about finances. Her MBA education alone would cost her $124,000 (INR 60,00,000) over two years. She had to procure a student loan.

'I was not eligible for financial aid as I applied in the second January round. I had a sleek chance of getting any financial scholarship. I had to discuss with my parents and convince them of the value of getting an MBA at such a high price.' Vijaya succeeded and went for her F1 visa interview two months before her wedding.

'A husband may or may not be able to afford his wife's education,' says Pooja, who opted to study after her arrival in the US as an H4 bride. 'In many cases, there are family circumstances to consider—expenses if you have kids, healthcare, debts, if their income is less, for instance, or if they have a new home and are paying mortgage. Also, those who have finished their master's in India might not want to repeat their master's here.'

Like Vijaya, Sarika and Pooja too applied for student loans for their MS. The costs of their courses added up to $30,000 by the time they finished. Before Sarika's course began, though, she was evaluated for English language skills by her university, in spite of having cleared her TOEFL. They insisted that she do a bridge course of about six sessions spread over six weeks, before beginning her MS programme.

Latha's husband, Ravi, was teaching at a North Carolina university when she decided to pursue her MS. He had finished his PhD and was on an H1B visa while she was on an H4. The catch was that their income was not sufficient to fund her studies. Latha did not give up. She studied hard and scored well in her GRE and TOEFL exams.

'I had perfect TOEFL and GRE scores. I also took a job as a teaching assistant at my school of study and got a scholarship, which virtually took care of my tuition and other fees. I was already a mother. And we were barely making any money then. Towards the end of my MS, I became pregnant again. This delayed my graduation by two more years.'

GRE and TOEFL scores might be benchmarks that many universities accept. But a lot of them do their own internal evaluation of the student's capabilities in articulation, overall personality and ability to bring diversity and talent to the campus.

Sarika and Pooja stuck to universities closer to home, since living away from their spouses would have made things difficult. They worked towards their university admissions months after they arrived. Not so for Vijaya and Madhusmita, who already had their admission letters in hand before they boarded their flights to the US.

Madhusmita endured the separation from her fiancé for years after she arrived on her F1 visa. Vijaya was fortunate that her fiancé eventually found a job in the same city as her university. The couple had all the reason to thank their stars, because his job opportunity came ahead of their wedding. They would not have to worry about her living in a dorm and his checking in with bachelor colleagues in another city.

Many women are unable to take a call on pursuing their studies in the US, partly because of the unpredictable nature of their spouse's postings. If your spouse gets posted to a different project and city every few months or after one year, it puts you in a fix.

Pooja was still pursuing her two-year MS when she got pregnant. She took it in her stride, confident that motherhood would go alongside her studies. As her pregnancy progressed, though, she took a break for a semester and restarted her course work once her baby boy was a few months old.

When the time came for the OPT period, Sarika found a job in a city four hours away. She tried hard to find a job fitting her profile in their vicinity, but when the opportunity arrived, she had no option but to grab it.

When Latha's OPT period ended, her company shut down. She was left struggling to find a new job during the recession of 2007-09. She has been trying hard for placements since.

Neha's experience, which spanned not just media, but also computer software and her own courses in project management, landed her a position as a project manager eventually. She does not regret her associate degree programmes. They helped her fetch jobs when she became eligible to work.

20

First Steps, Baby Steps

The hardest part of assimilating into a new environment, and in the case of visa wives, the new country, is the first step. But first steps set the pace.

I'll take Radha's example. Her calls to India were dampeners to her spirit. Her folks were too engrossed in their own lives. She cried bitterly about it, but the endless woes of her first few weeks in Seattle taught her something. She had a choice between not doing anything except wallowing in the misery of not having her family around, and making the mountainous climb to adjust to the new place. She needed someone to talk to.

Should she put on her walking shoes and step out? What would the new place make of her? It had stopped raining for a while. She peered into the doorway closet that her husband called the 'entryway' and pulled out her raincoat.

Radha had read a lot about those umpteen Seattle institutions—Amazon, Starbucks, Nordstrom,

Microsoft. She was not interested as yet in checking them out. That sort of a journey would be too much. 'Maybe these shoes will get wet on those sidewalks,' her excuse nearly prompted her to slump back on to the couch. Shaking her head to clear her thoughts, she wore her shoes. And felt something familiar with the way they splattered the collected water on the sidewalk when she walked. The sky was clear, the air cool and the sunshine welcome.

'An Indian woman clad in salwar-kameez was out on her walk too. When the time came for eye contact, she turned away.' Radha had hoped for some conversation. A tear escaped her eye. To her surprise, some elderly Americans who were out on their walk smiled at her. 'Good afternoon,' one of them greeted her. Radha smiled and returned the greeting—and eased a little. She tried to step out more in the days to come. The little steps of coping with an alien space had begun. She knew her road to days of no tears was a long one.

Women who have tried hard to integrate into their lives in the US after the initial honeymoon phase has worn off can feel battle-scarred when their initial experiences are bad.

'Women have the ability to look for defence mechanisms. They can hold on to something that keeps them going when everything else fails,' remarked a friend during discussions about long-suffering women in bad marriages in India. Probably, that is what helps many women steer through the toughest years of their lives—the first few years of their stay in the US.

It may feel odd to few people, but talking of first steps, window shopping and browsing at bookstores worked for some women.

Mercy was newly married to an American when she arrived in Oregon. Just how did she adapt to the local ethos? She had her American family to guide her through her initial anxiety.

'I loved, loved and loved the fact—and cannot stress this enough—that you go to the mall, walk into any store and try millions of clothes. Nobody stares or gives you a look wondering if you are going to buy that product or are just wasting time.'

Mercy has strong Goan roots. It was a big move, leaving her close-knit family behind and taking a flight to be a homemaker in the US. Oregon, like Goa, offered the comfort and familiarity of a coastal state. Still, it was very different from the dreamy Goan landscape with its thousands of coconut trees, backwaters, churches and the Mandovi river. She could not spot coconut palms. The houses too were very different from Goan homes that were an architectural fusion of European styles and Indian needs.

'It takes two years to become one with the country here,' she said. Mercy did not wait long to venture out of her home. She walked out the slope of her street and headed to the stores.

'After my husband left for work, I went to the malls and walked around and tried new things like clothes and cosmetics. I loved going everywhere by myself. My favourite spots were flea markets and farmers' markets. Even today, I feel more at ease and free when I go by myself without any hindrance. There is lot to explore in America if you want to experience and learn.'

Mercy's real sense of belonging came in the stores. 'Irrespective of the size of the store or your pockets, they treat you the same. They truly understand the concept that the customer is the king. If you are not satisfied, you can return the product even after a month as long as you have its receipt.' Mercy's strength was her refusal to be cowed down by the newness of it all.

Shirley, who moved to Kearny City in New Jersey when she and her husband first arrived, soon fell into the loneliness cauldron.

'Even at my church, there were no Indians. They were mostly Americans. People did wish you. They said their "Hi, how are you?", but they did not invite you home as quickly as Indians would,' she says. 'We know an American family well through common friends. They are great friends, but we do not visit each other. We only talk · on the phone.'

Shirley used the unusually good transportation system in her new city. 'I would take a bus from my apartment community to the Elizabeth Mall. I love malls! I would go to the mall, eat and come back by evening. My husband was happy. I would find something new at the mall every day. I would check out every shop. I would not spare even the cutlery shops. Surprisingly, the store keepers never got familiar with me, even though I visited those stores so much! I bet no one missed me when I stopped going there. Bus conductors got familiar with me though. They would say hi.'

Shirley was not a shopper. She loved checking out new products and that was that. Eventually, Shirley and her husband moved to another town in Central Jersey. She found a church where the priest was of Indian origin. He put her in touch with some of the members who invited her and her husband home. Soon, she found herself a huge network of friends.

'I look for some level of maturity in making friends. My friends are from all over India—Punjab, Delhi, four are from the south, then there are those from Mumbai, Bengaluru, one friend is from Assam.' Shirley soon discovered a potluck trend among Indian families in the US. For her, it is an extension of her years in Mumbai.

'Mumbai has train groups, people who gang up with each other during their local train commute to work. Like that, we have 'pot luck' groups! Everyone somehow gets into a group! We too got into groups. I would wonder why people were giving 'Save the dates' so much in advance here. It is because if you organize a pot luck on the day of some other group's pot luck, there is a chance people may not turn up!'

Pot lucks are a way of networking among Indians. For the women and their spouses who are FOB (fresh off the boat), being part of a bunch of friends can be a great start to acculturate.

Says Rupashree, who found her anxieties of motherhood ease a bit with pot lucks organized by the wives of her husband's colleagues, 'It is good to meet people regularly. In India, we are busy with our family on a day-to-day basis. Out here, our friends are our family.

And potluck lunches and dinners are a great way to celebrate festivals and other events. My own friends' circle improved when we started pot lucks in our apartment community.'

Sathya found it taxing to talk to people. The once sociable girl who had made friends in a jiffy found herself struggling to initiate conversations in her new setup. Her husband Surya was scared because he did not want to get into trouble with anyone or anything, lest he be sent back home. Workplace woes added to his insecurities.

'Be careful what you do,' he would chant. Sathya knew that to actually make friends, she had to muster courage. A chat with an American neighbour, for instance, would get her excited. She would eagerly tell Surya about it in the evening, and his questions would point at 'if the neighbour was trustworthy' or 'was the neighbour as unfriendly as the other rude guy'.

Sathya was dependent on her husband for her survival in the new country. The thought of hopping on to a bus did occur to her. But that Surya spoke in two voices did not help. Sometimes he would urge her to step out, ask her to meet new acquaintances in the neighbourhood. But most of the time he would urge caution, which would put her off.

As someone who was in the workforce before she took the flight to Pittsburgh, Aruna preferred to use money from her bank deposits in the initial months of marriage. She did not want to depend on her husband, despite the new status. The change in marital status did not give her a sense of insecurity, nor did Pittsburgh frighten her with its unfamiliarity.

Aruna's apartment community had a bus stop with regular bus services. 'The bus ride was liberating. There was a bus once in every 15–20 minutes, which was a luxury. My hubby gave me a printed bus schedule and map on my first ride. I told him I would go out to discover the place. Pittsburgh is very different from New York.'

The city was not spread out in blocks the way Manhattan was. Its terrain fascinated her. How could an entire city thrive between hills? The bridges, the seamless traffic, picturesque downtown that stood at the confluence of two rivers, co-existence of the city's heritage and its modern skyscrapers . . . they left Aruna besotted.

Her volunteering months at the Carnegie museums brought her face to face with American women who were curious about where she came from. 'I was the only person in my age group at the museums. They wanted to know my story. Other volunteers there were protective about me. What was life like for immigrants, for instance? How can we even sit on a plane and ride for so long? That is where my love for connecting with people of different countries bloomed.'

Aruna found from people that the city had a lot of free events to attend. 'Suddenly, all the people who are likely to judge you are not around you. I had been to all kinds of places and events at the university in Pittsburgh, even for things I did not know about. That was my way of claiming the city. I get very defensive when people say,

'Oh Pittsburgh? What is there to see? Only museums and temples.' I acquired that fierce sense of loyalty, and freedom to meet friends.' Aruna soon joined non-profits that worked towards diaspora communities and connected with a whole other set of people.

When Neha landed in Missouri, she too had left behind a job and arrived as a bride still stunned by the idea of having to cook and clean for her husband. Three months into her new life, she put her foot down and said she wanted a dog. Her husband was keen on living in the US for the long term, so there was no scope of the trouble of a transcontinental shift for a pet. 'He was reluctant to make a commitment,' says Neha today. If she were in such a situation in India and married to the same man, she would probably have given in to his point of view—about the inconvenience a pet would cause, about the expenses involved and the enormous responsibility. Pet care in the US is big in terms of industry and laws. The country has pet insurance too. For Neha, it was about staying firm about her need for companionship. Her husband liked pets too. His family had a dog back in Chennai.

She stuck to her demand. 'We went to the pet store to just have a look at the animals. And found our puppy soon enough. As soon as she saw us, she came closer, wanting to be petted. We fell for her immediately—and brought her home. Our dog was my coping mechanism. I used to take her on ten walks a day and train her. I would play with her and feed her. I can easily say the reason I stayed married is our dog.'

Neha and her husband have had their share of memorable experiences with their pet. Before every India trip, the couple would have to drop their pet off at her sister's place in Atlanta and pick her up on return. Regular trips to the vet were a must. Neha also credits her family's outdoorsy lifestyle to their dog. 'Many Indians I know are reluctant to have pets such as dogs. They find it too much of a bother. We had no such qualms. The advantage in the US is that you have pet-friendly hotels when you travel,' says Neha.

Pooja spent her first two months after a stressful wedding and move, setting up home, but nothing much else. She took up art and craft projects around home, and learnt about her new town. Her friends suggested she do newer courses and certifications in her field. After a point, she felt she was wasting her time on hobbies and DIY home decor.

Two months into her arrival, her husband took her to an event organized by an Indian association, a Bharatnatyam performance included. Pooja was surprised that her husband, who was not the kind to attend cultural events, accompanied her. After the event, he approached the dancer and discovered that she taught dance. He took her number, and Pooja called her without second thought.

Pooja had learnt Bharatnatyam in her childhood, but lost touch in the pursuit of a career. 'I did not have any inhibitions in learning from a new teacher because Bharatnatyam is something you learn a great deal on your own,' says Pooja. Soon, she started enrolling for performances. When she took stage for a group performance in her classical dance costume, kohl lines and jewellery shimmering on her face, she felt one with her dance all over.

Sarika was a qualified engineer. One of the things that shocked her when she moved newly to her community was how the woman who did her eyebrows at her home was earning her extra income through these basic beauty services. That woman was a qualified engineer too. Instead of worrying about where her qualifications would take her, Sarika's beautician did a course during one of her India trips, and started providing services to friends and acquaintances. She found that her new country had a different approach towards labour. She did not have to look at such jobs as lower in hierarchy compared to the hi-tech job in a company cubicle.

Sarika's own massage to the soul worked through her religious rituals at the temple, which found her many friends. She learnt about the families that help fund the temple, their long journey towards establishing themselves in the new homeland and their effort to stay connected to all things Indian.

During one such temple event, she realized she could contribute to the temple's charity box in her own way. The temple was holding a mini-carnival during an annual event. They would set up stalls, and those who wished to contribute could provide services or conduct games on tickets, and donate the money to the temple. Sarika was good at the ubiquitous desi mehndi, a craze among those outside India, Americans included. Sarika decided to set up a stall of mehndi art and nail art for children. She had about twenty mehndi cones that she had brought from India, and a bunch of nail paints with nail stickers.

At her stall, eager kids lined up for their mehndi hands. Hand after little hand came forward while Sarika squeezed the mehndi cones away, now wiping the tips clean on a white tissue, now gently tilting.

By the time the carnival came to a close, Sarika's neck and back were hurting badly, but she was happy. She and Sairam collected the currency from their cash box and deposited it at the temple office. Sarika's contentment was profound.

Four months after she first went to the community beautician, Sathya found to her shock that the beautician, who she was finally growing comfortable with, would be leaving the apartment community soon.

'You can come to my new place,' said the woman.

'Where is it and how far is it from here?'

'Twenty-five minutes.'

What? Twenty-five minutes for some grooming, when they were still have-nots without a car! Sathya could not dream of burning $50 on a taxi ride to her place either. She called her childhood friend in another city for advice.

'*Yahaan pe toh sab kuch khud karna padta hai re* (we need to do everything on our own here),' said her friend, and suggested brands of waxing strips for her to wax her body and face by herself.

When Surya hitched a pharmacy ride for her medicines, she asked him to pick up boxes of waxing strips as well. When the strips did not warm up between her palms, Sathya filled her plastic mug with hot water, dipped the strips, melting the wax between them, cut them to the shape of a bow to fit above and below her brows and pulled in the opposite direction of her hair growth. She screamed from the pain, but it worked. Despite the sting, Sathya felt she had achieved something—self-dependence.

Sathya also had a weakness—for craft supplies. She thought she was a sensible shopper, taking her time through each aisle at the grocery store. Surya hated her leisurely attitude towards shopping. He thought she spent beyond his designated budget, although he was not sure what his budget was. The couple fought after shopping trips. Sathya forbade him from following her in shopping aisles. He refused to back down.

What was the use of having a car if he was behaving this way, not even letting her shop in peace? She felt stifled. After a bad fight, she packed her bags but then decided to give it one last chance. She demanded pocket money for herself—money that he would ask no questions whatsoever about. Surya was sceptical. Was he not taking good care of her? Why was she being unreasonable?

'But is it not for us that I am saving? My money is our money,' he protested.

'I am not asking for half your salary,' she retorted.

Surya relented. A few months later, Sathya suggested the approach to her friends too. Surya protested again.

'Why are you spoiling their relationship?'

Sathya's friend reasoned with Surya. 'It is not as if we would go around throwing money away. We would want to buy a few things for our parents in India, which we wish to do without worrying about the budget. We may do charity, or keep it aside as savings. Why are you so afraid?'

Surya was silent. He got the point.

After one of their money fights once about shopping, Surya stopped taking her to grocery stores. Sathya dug into pocket money from previous months to buy herself a membership on an online shopping site. She did not wait for his nod as she would have done before. He would have said no anyway. She informed him afterwards.

'It's 100 dollars!' he yelled.

'Yes, but it will save you many hundreds. I will not end up buying ten items from the craft store when we go there for a mere tool.'

Her purchases would be focused, she pointed out, and not compulsive. Soon, it was Surya who realized the benefit of Internet shopping. He did not have to go shopping with her. Soon, he found himself ordering gadgets, phones, tablets, batteries, clothes. Online shopping played peacemaker between them.

21

Turmoil at Home

'So, how much dowry did you pay?'

It was a question from a mother-in-law to her daughter-in-law's friend at a get-together in America, and not a sequence in a desi saas-bahu soap. If you think such a question is gross, wait till you go for a walk in the summer around your neighbourhood, encounter respectable seniors who you make conversation with out of courtesy, and get asked questions about how much gold your parents gave at your wedding, where the wedding was conducted, how much your parents spent, how much property they own, did your father give any property to the groom and so on.

In the case of this mother-in-law who asked her bahu's friend about dowry, the reply was, 'If my husband, or his parents had done anything of that sort, I would have thrown them in jail.'

The mother-in-law hated her daughter-in-law's forthrightness, and thought the girl was 'too dark' for her 'better' coloured boy. She was smarting after close relatives said her boy could have landed a 'better deal'. The bahu in question would be crushed by the insult, realizing she would never be the 'ideal' one. Her husband's mother would always try to 'put her in place'.

What makes men unabashedly place a price on their own heads?

Many H1B visa holders expect a dowry despite the outrage such a demand might spark. Some simply opt for expensive weddings to be paid for by the girls' parents, instead of asking for cash or material goods. While dowry may really refer to a financial transaction, a lot of emphasis is laid on grand weddings acquiring a cinematic scale these days.

'It's a real shame that such practices (dowry) still flourish in India. Unless the brides, grooms and parents on both sides join efforts to fight this harmful practice, it'll continue,' says Manisha Roy. 'Unless young women themselves rebel against this practice and their parents cooperate, this outmoded and potentially dangerous custom is not going to change. I am appalled by the expenses in a wedding nowadays in middle-class families in India. Why don't the grooms and brides object?'

Incidentally, NRI grooms command their own scale of weddings in India. They are all about candid photography, designer clothes, pre-wedding video shoots, glamour events that were not traditionally a part of the region's rituals and expensive destinations such as resorts and hotels in fancy touristy places.

Do these things actually translate into a blissful wedded life? Do they guarantee respect between partners? Does a designer wedding in India mean the woman will be treated like a queen by her NRI groom?

Charan, a soft-spoken engineer married to another, says, 'When I got married, I decided against a dowry. During my first face-to-face meeting (after two video-chat sessions) with the girl and her parents, I told them as much.' He was an H1B visa worker at the time whose education in an American university had been an uphill task financially for his parents.

'All I wanted was that my parents be treated with respect. When I went home after that first meeting, everyone began pressurizing me to ask for at least a token amount in the name of dowry, because they felt that otherwise the girl's family would treat us like dirt. I have seen that happen in my own family. An uncle who had not taken dowry would get less respect from his in-laws than others who had.'

It is difficult to understand Charan's justification of dowry as an instrument for getting 'respect'. Does dowry not represent a way of gaining control over a woman's life? The need to control her is passed from parents to their son. And aggression, emotional abuse and physical violence become ways in which this control is enforced.

People such as Charan, who believe in the institution of dowry, are also amazed that domestic violence exists as much in the US as it does in India. 'Really? Does it happen here?' asked my schoolmate who lived in the US earlier and visits once in a while. 'Men from India who come here are educated, right? Why would they resort to domestic violence?' To him, domestic violence and the US were not words that match.

Control is always an issue, says Joseline Kirkendoll, acting executive director at Kiran, Inc., a North Carolina-based organization that helps South Asian women, men and children suffering from domestic violence. She talks of the common thread in a lot of cases her organization handles. 'When you bring in a new spouse from another country, in many cases after an arranged marriage, there is a tendency among men to feel, "I am in control. I am the provider. I am in charge."' This view is echoed by Gouri Banerjee, co-founder and board president, Saheli, Support for South Asian Women in Boston.

About 40 per cent of women in the South Asian community are subjected to violence, according to a 2002 study on intimate partner violence in the Greater Boston area. The study called for culturally tailored domestic violence services for South Asian women.[24] Says Gouri, 'For Indian men who have grown up watching their fathers, uncles and other men exert control, the need to control is strong. Indian men who come to the US and go back to get married do not realize that a lot of things have changed back home, and women have come a long way. In today's setup, women want to be equal partners, while men want a 75–25 power equation.'

How does control work in the lives of those who arrive on dependent visas? For starters, it's the visas themselves which make them reliant on the skilled worker visas of their spouses and are rightly known as 'dependent' visas.

If your visa becomes 'out of status' the minute you cease to be the skilled worker's spouse, it puts the skilled worker in a position of power.

A study observed that 'immigration policies that prevent women on spousal visas from working and petitioning to change their status increase women's vulnerability to partner abuse.'[25]

Most H4 visa wives either never had jobs before they came to the US, or had to quit them to join their husbands in the US. H1B spouses turn providers by default, taking on not just added responsibilities to run the household, but also the sense of authority and one-upmanship that comes with being the sole breadwinner.

Spousal violence is rampant in India. In the US, the absence of their immediate family's support complicates the woman's or dependent spouse's position. Families, including parents and friends who form their support system, often have no idea of the visa wife's woes because of the tendency among South Asian women to tolerate high levels of abuse before they speak up. Even if parents learn of their daughter's situation, they tend to advise her to 'stay put in the marriage', shutting her up further.

In a study of sixty-two battered women, twenty of whom were South Asian, it was noted that when it came to reporting violence to family, 'following disclosure, South Asian women were significantly more likely to be advised by family members "to stay in the marriage" than other groups of women.'[26]

In the US, organizations that work for the welfare of women and families facing domestic violence address the needs of people from all South Asian countries and not just India, because of cultural similarities. They work towards inclusive support systems that are culturally sensitive to the needs of women, and sometimes men too, from these countries.

Based on the several cases that Saheli has handled, Gouri Banerjee states that 80 per cent of the clients who approach them are from India. Women from other countries report domestic violence too—10 per cent of them are from Bangladesh, 5 per cent from Pakistan and 5 per cent from Nepal, Bhutan and other countries of the Indian subcontinent.

She notes that the numbers of reported domestic violence cases have risen significantly, with younger women reporting more frequently than older women. The kinds of abuse Gouri sees in South Asian families is emotional and physical, and includes abandonment by the spouse where there is no physical attraction for the couple to hold on to, control and financial issues, and interference by in-laws where they live in the US.

'In most cases, the husband takes away the wife's passport and visa. The victims should go through the process of petitioning, which is easier for permanent residents or people with an immigrant status. In such cases, we can write to a city mayor and say "she lived here for these many number of years". In the case of H4 visas, this is very difficult. Many times we ask them to file for divorce in India. Laws in the US are not friendly to women who do not have the papers. Even relatives who live here are reluctant to help in such matters.'

Gouri points out that documentation of violence helps women.

Lack of awareness of violence, the ability to recognize it as violence in the first place, means the victim will downplay it. The woman would not want to be labelled negatively, to which is added the tendency of everyone around to shame the woman when her man abuses her. Violence need not be physical. Emotional abuse can kill too—by spouse or extended family.

Aisha was a distressed mother from the Bay Area who was struggling with her in-laws. They lived with her and her husband for six months a year, and ruled their lives. She wanted to cuddle her boy, tell him stories, teach him, play with him and be a mother in the real sense. Instead, she was kept busy cooking, cleaning and serving others all the time. Aisha had wanted to be a stay-at-home mom for a while. Her presence at home did not guarantee her being allowed to enjoy her motherhood.

When Aisha got an opportunity to visit her parents once, she was overwhelmed. She was finally getting to be with her child. She did not think she was facing domestic violence or emotional abuse. She cried to her friend, 'My in-laws treat me like a maid.'

If women like Aisha muster the courage to speak out to friends and family, chances are they might turn around and say, she must have done something to invite it. Such cornering would make someone like her, who has already been suffering, internalize blame. Shame is a catalyst for a woman's silence.

The United States witnessed a considerable influx of Indians after the Luce-Celler Act of 1946 restored naturalization rights for Indian Americans. Asian Indian immigration picked up in the 1960s, gaining momentum in the 1980s. Jungian analyst and writer Manisha Roy recalls that when the immigrant population was smaller in the 1960s and 1970s, 'domestic problems in a small group—even if they existed—were not visible or known. One very important fact about married women who are abused is their silence. They naturally feel ashamed and embarrassed to report domestic strife and violence or even talk to close friends about it. The first time I heard of any kind of domestic violence among the Indian immigrant population was in the 1980s, when I met Professor Shamita Das Dasgupta who started an organization called Manavi in New Jersey to help battered wives. I remember being shocked hearing about it.'

Shamita Das Dasgupta was one of the six women who in 1985 started Manavi, a pioneering effort to address concerns faced by South Asian women in the US. Manavi become the first organization to highlight domestic violence among South Asians at a time when no one else talked about it. Shamita says, 'We see about 400 new cases every year. In 95 per cent of these, the parents are unsupportive. In 5 per cent, they take some responsibility. The prevalent belief that "marriage is the most important thing in the world" is the biggest challenge. We blame mothers-in-law and in-laws. We should blame parents and husbands too. "We do not want you back because someone's marriage is going to be affected" is a common excuse doled out by parents of the girl.'

Shamita also blames the importance given to the notion that women should be liked by their in-laws. As a result, women approach organizations only when the situation becomes unbearable.

When your life is in imminent danger in the US, all you have to do is dial 911 on your phone. Many South Asian women do not know that such calls will actually get them help in the case of domestic violence. And even if they know about it, it is rare for them to actually pick up the phone and make the call. It gets complicated further if the husband's parents are involved or are active perpetrators of the abuse. Often, the thoughts of ending up on the streets or being forced to board a flight back home to an unsupportive family take precedence over safety.

Smitha reluctantly called a women's organization to find out if she could talk to them. She thought she was in a bad relationship, and that the changes that had happened in her life were too dramatic. She did not realize it was domestic violence.

'We were fine till the in-laws came. Now they are here and making my life miserable,' she shared. They were creating situations where the husband and wife fought, she felt, and her husband almost always sided with his parents. Of late, she had started having suicidal thoughts. She did not want to leave the marriage. She just could not cope with her in-laws dictating every minute of her day. Her husband was helpless.

It was similar to what Kala had to go through, except that her husband was no helpless soul. A divorcee, she funded her own engagement and took a leap of faith in shifting from Delhi to Chicago. She thought she had found the right man who would also be a father to her toddler son. She had family support in India, but was willing to give marriage another chance. She enrolled on matrimony websites and was particularly charmed by a man who came across as a straight talker. He made no lofty promises and yet made her feel beautiful. To her relief, he had not been married before, but did not mind her young son and was not worried about how the child would impact their marital life. After three months of dating, she decided to get married to him and embrace a new role as a homemaker in another country.

Her family funded their low-key engagement and registered wedding. His relatives were missing from both occasions. He told her that he and his parents were not on good terms with their extended family. His parents were part of their life, and that was all that mattered. She agreed. After all, his parents, who lived with him in the US, came all the way to India to participate in their wedding. It took her a while to get her visa. Three months after her wedding, she was finally on her way to join her husband in the US.

Two months later, Kala placed a frantic call to 911. The reason for it was not because she was thinking about escaping. She had discovered in the first week of arrival that he was a divorcee and had a child too. What was more horrifying than his lie was that he did not want her as a wife.

Her in-laws and husband made her do all the housework. It slowly dawned on her that they really wanted a maid, a hard find in the US, so they brought one over from India through marriage. She was a wife only on paper. In reality, she was a slave whose job was only to cook and clean the kitchen and home. She was not allowed to talk to her parents or relatives. Her son was not enrolled in a school, but confined to a room with a bunch of toys. She was not allowed to spend time with him. She could not as much as take her son out to play. Her marriage felt like a joke because her 'husband' really behaved like an employer. Their marriage remained unconsummated. The morning when she called 911, she just wanted to talk to someone and make sense of her own situation. She did not feel safe in that home with her son.

The officers who responded to her call found a dishevelled Kala unable to make a decision. They asked her to pack up her belongings. She did so in about half an hour, while cops stood guard in her home. They took the phone numbers of her relatives, called them up and sent her and her son to a cousin's home in Florida. Far from being comforted for what she was going through, Kala was reproached for getting married in a rush. The cousin was not willing to house her. She did not care what Kala would do next. She simply booked tickets for her and her son on the next flight back to India. Kala was helpless, homeless and at the receiving end of her own extended family's ire for being a victim of domestic violence. Her husband's family had hidden her papers and feigned a 'lost' excuse. She called up Homeland Security to figure out where she stood. They suggested she call the domestic violence hotline and approach women's organizations that helped women like her. They also said they could take her to a shelter. Kala's cousin did not want her to check into a shelter from her home.

A few calls by the cousin and other relatives on, Kala found an Indian family that was willing to house them. The mother and son were given bus fare. The moment something changed within her was when she, a staunch vegetarian, was forced to share a beef burger with her son using two dollars change from the ticket.

The next two years saw Kala moving between homes that took her and her son in. Someone who sheltered her for a few days said her dog was not used to strangers and so she had to leave. A kind American woman in her sixties finally took her in. Kala found relief, and family. The elderly lady's local church community accepted Kala, and gave her so much love that she found the strength to fight for herself. A women's organization or non-profit helped her file for papers under the Violence Against Women Act (1994). Kala soon began doing small jobs to support herself, and eventually found a full-time job at a non-profit. She could finally afford to send her son to school.

The biggest shock for Kala was when her relatives living in the US turned their backs on her. For them, her identity as a woman was tied to a successful marriage.

It did not matter that someone had hurt her. Kala was determined to not go back to India. It took not just all her courage, but also the unexpected kindness of strangers, to rebuild her life. A stronger motivation was the thought of providing for her son. Kala's predicament is what frustrates those working in the area of rehabilitating battered women.

What makes men inflict violence—physical or emotional? Does anything change for them when they move to another continent?

Manisha Roy explains the psychology behind it during the transcontinental shift: 'Marital abuse may happen when husbands (especially if they come from patriarchal conservative backgrounds where women had only high school education or no education) feel threatened by their wives' gradual change in having more confidence in their own capacity to earn and becoming less dependent on them. Do not forget that men in all societies grow up to play the role of provider on whom the wife and family depend. A lot of their self-worth comes from playing this role well, and the motivation to do well in their careers comes from that.'

The change in their wives once they arrive in America becomes hard for the men to handle. 'Despite modernization and education, women in India and in many parts of the world grow up with the belief that their husbands will take care of them forever. There is a built-in dependency on both sides, although differently experienced by the two sexes. Indian men grow up being treated as special by their mothers and unconsciously expect that kind of unconditional love and adoration from their wives. This is compounded with the inherited idea of women being the weaker sex that needs to be taken care of, which also necessitates their docility and subservience. After being in the US for a year or so, wives might become emboldened (due to education, job, mass media and watching American women), and husbands do not know how to handle this. Sometimes, they resort to the only thing they are sure about in their quest to be superior to the women—physical strength. These undercurrents become more pronounced because the couple is no longer in the safety net of family and society back home that supported traditional roles.'

Women have come a long way from their 'cook and clean' days. Today's women are astronauts, mechanics, scientists, surgeons and cops too. In India, they have careers and are independent, making strides in various industries. And yet, financially well-off women can go through abuse in marriages too. When women move overseas, some hold on to the 'be good, be sacrificial' notion. Others struggle to accept their new situation. Possible change in the behaviour of their men might empower them to say things to exert greater control in the relationship.

Do women become bolder after coming to the US, thereby posing a threat to their husbands' 'provider psyche', or is it insecurity in men that finds support from their families and encourages abuse?

Sudeepti was a woman who carved her own niche as a publishing industry professional before she got married.

Unassuming and focused on her priorities, she earned respect at the workplace. 'Of all the idiots I had met till then, this person was the most intelligent and focused, and was looking for an independent woman who could be a companion more than anything else. And, of course, we had similar "hobbytual" interests too.'

The wedding was an arranged one, and she abided by her parents' decision to tie the knot with their 'good match' not long after they had met. He was a software industry professional and no red flags came up at any point during background checks in the run-up to her wedding. She took the flight of trust.

Sudeepti set foot in her new home and realized the implications of having married a stranger. She was crushed. Her husband set rules for her from Day One. She discovered that he really did not want an independent woman but a housekeeper. 'During the day, I had to stay at home. I did step out when he took me to shop for groceries and to meet a couple of friends. But these outings ended in arguments because he would give me new rules on how to behave and what to talk about,' she says.

He asked Sudeepti about the money she had carried from India. 'Let us open an account,' he told her. She did not fall for it. She opened a bank account near her home and in her own name. Much later, she discovered that her parents had sent Rs 2 lakh to her husband without her knowledge for 'visa expenses'.

Was it fear of the new place and the role it played on her mind, or the vulnerability that her new situation brought about? She was not sure. From the first week, Sudeepti tried to meet new people. One afternoon, she was so distraught by the things her husband had said that morning that she stepped out into her community garden for a walk. She paced through the lawn, tears streaming down her face. An Indian family noticed her as she walked by.

They invited her over for tea and told her that she would be in trouble if a police car passed by and saw her in the state she was in. They asked her no questions, and asked her to drop by any time she felt low. She felt relieved to know someone cared. They became her friends.

Her husband's need to control her left her so devastated that she felt safer in a neighbour's home than in her own. The advice she received from her mother-in-law constantly was, 'Cook his favourite dishes. Ask him what he needs. Make "sweet" conversation.' In other words, pamper his ego.

Sudeepti did sweet-talk him. His ego bloated. His need to be the boss towered above her need for dignity. His orders became too important to be ignored. When she decided to walk out of her marriage, an aunt asked her to save her parents the 'embarrassment' by staying on and looking for a 'job instead'. It meant society would not accept her return. For a change, Sudeepti's parents stood by her like a rock.

'Come back to India, we are with you,' they told her. And that shut her relatives up.

'I have heard of girls killing themselves because their parents do not support their decision to leave bad marriages. When parents stand by you, everyone else backs off,' says Sudeepti. She obtained her divorce in India, *ex parte*.

'I was level-headed and independent. He could not handle that,' says Sudeepti, years after the divorce. The money her parents had sent him vanished. She is sure the 'safe-keeping' money would have too.

Kala and Sudeepti found themselves imprisoned in a situation that allowed the man's aggression to flourish and expected the woman to be relegated to subservience. And this was in the name of cultural values to be 'upheld' by the woman.

The two decided to walk out early on in their marriages, unlike others who find it difficult to leave violent relationships for years. They did not face physical violence but emotional abuse that killed. They did not wait for the abuse to escalate, unlike most other South Asian women who put up with violence for as long as they can.

Professor Joseph Vandello from University of South Florida's department of psychology, who has researched precarious manhood, gender and aggression extensively, explains why women do not leave violent relationships in general.

Talking about his research on the subject, he says, '[W]e found that women are often reluctant to leave violent relationships, not just because of economic constraints, but because of a notion that part of femininity (particularly in honour cultures) is wrapped in loyalty.'

Joseph notes further, 'The "stand by your man" belief (that phrase comes from a popular old country music song), suggests that a good, strong, honourable woman sticks it out with her man, even in tough times. This runs counter to more individualistic and feminist notions of womanhood which would argue that a strong woman should leave her abusive partner. The point being that, in many cultural contexts, a woman who stays in an abusive relationship is not necessarily seen as weak or foolish. Sacrifice and loyalty are strong feminine values in many cultures.'

In 2014, Joseph Vandello talked about precarious manhood in a symposium on mental health awareness conducted by Saheli, Boston, with focus on domestic violence, as its keynote speaker. The symposium was titled 'Yes, it's OK to talk'.

The symposium discussed at length the need to address mental health and domestic violence and the lack of ethnic-sensitive redressal systems for South Asian women. It also discussed the need for first responders such as physicians to watch out for evidence of bodily harm, such as genito-urinary problems among women as a result of sexual violence, low birth-weight babies because of battering during pregnancy, cuts, bruises, broken bones, injuries to ears, eating disorders, post-traumatic stress, bowel irritability and so on.

'Often, the only time that domestic violence victims are allowed to leave their homes is when they have health problems,' said Internal Medicine specialist Dr Manju Sheth at the event.

'Physical symptoms are more legitimized by the community,' said Diya Kallivayalil, psychologist at Cambridge Health Alliance, who was also a speaker at the symposium organized by Saheli.

South Asians in the US have negative impressions of psychological counselling and under-utilize mental healthcare provisions. There is the 'model minority myth' where many members have achieved success in [the] US according to their peers and so they want to project a positive image to the outside world. There is cultural proscription that inhibits people from sharing.

The need for parents to bring up sons who respect women was a unanimous standpoint among those who spoke that day.

Joseph Vandello, while talking about 'precarious manhood', said there was a need to 'socialize our boys to understand that an honourable man protects his family and does not harm his family'. He also talked about the need to allow men to express anxieties and vulnerabilities. 'Silence is an endorsement. Unlike womanhood, "manhood" is easily threatened and, in several cultures, is "earned" through rites of passage, and men might use risky behaviour and aggression as means of restoring manhood status,' he explained.

Vandello continues, 'I don't think there are any easy solutions to the problem of domestic violence. Most of the headway in raising cultural awareness has been led by women's organizations and feminists. And this is great, but it frames the issue as a "women's issue" rather than a problem of men. So, I think what is needed is strong male leadership and visible men's groups opening a dialogue about how we need to change cultural norms about masculinity that give rise to acceptance of domestic violence, objectification of women, rape culture, etc. (Note also that the problem isn't just "domestic violence" but a broader issue of men's control and objectification of women, that leads to a host of problems.) I think men are likelier to listen to other men. So, men need to be more vocal about standing up to negative and harmful male cultural norms.'

Perhaps, this is the reason that some organizations have started programmes with the organization Men Against Violence. Saheli, Boston, has such a programme. The general discourse around violence is centred on women because a majority of women are victims and men the perpetrators. When violence assumes expressions rooted in patriarchal values often not considered 'violence' by many women, interventions can become complicated.

Consider this: An Indian woman, into her fifth month of pregnancy, goes to her gynaecologist in an American city and asks the sex of her baby. Her past two pregnancies resulted in termination because the foetus was female. Sex-selective abortions are a crime in India. What happens when the husband insists on having a boy and presses his wife to abort female foetuses? And the woman complies, and does not view it as abuse? She is simply being a 'good wife'. Sex selection is rampant in Korean and Indian families of America.[27]

Or, the woman has gone to India in the fifth month, and considers returning by her seventh month. She goes to meet a gynaecologist in India in the meanwhile with the husband. Just before they head back to the US, the couple asks their Indian gynaecologist to reveal the sex of the baby so they can buy the 'right clothes' and decorations for the nursery.

The gynaecologist hints in a gesture, skirting the Indian Pre-Conception Pre-Natal Diagnostic Techniques Act to prevent sex-selective abortions. The couple is elated. Thankfully, their relatives do not seem displeased that it is a girl. But, a baby girl 'will need gold', and so begins the coercion. Veiled queries crop up in conversations about things the couple plan to do to secure her future, if the would-be mother's parents will buy gold ornaments for her and so on. The expectant mother is distraught and feels betrayed.

Your conversation with a visiting 'aunty'—the mother-in-law of an acquaintance—goes like this:

'Do you have kids?'

'No, aunty, not yet.'

'How many years since marriage?'

'Five years.'

'Are you taking treatment?'

'Yes.'

'Who is the doctor?'

You wonder why she needs the name of your doctor, but you tell her anyway.

'Did your doctor not suggest IVF (in-vitro fertilization)? I pushed my daughter-in-law to get IVF. Now she is pregnant. My relative's daughter did not have babies. They got IVF. She was to have triplets, but they got one removed. And now she is happy with two babies.' The next few minutes, she badgers you with an unwanted IVF ad.

'Go to India. It is expensive here. For the money you spend in the US, you can get two or three cycles done in India,' she continues.

The mother-in-law has no qualms boasting about how she harassed her bahu into getting an IVF treatment. She makes it look like it was the best thing she did. What will happen if the grandchild happens to be a girl? You cannot help but shudder.

Often, the cycle of violence begins long before women set foot on American soil. Several Indian men who arrive on US shores to fulfil their ambitions do not necessarily leave behind core evil beliefs such as dowry. If they do evolve into people who do not believe in them any more, they remain vulnerable to familial pressure and coercion.

What are the measures a woman can take to keep herself safe? How does she exit an abusive marriage in the US, especially if she is a 'resident alien'? Are there things a woman can do for her well-being irrespective of the health of her marriage? And her status as an immigrant?

'It is important to remember that help is available if you want to leave an abusive relationship,' says Kala from her own experience. 'Leave copies of your paperwork with your parents. If you have an option for SSN (which dependent visa spouses usually do not), get it. When you come to the US, research a lot. Be respectful of the local culture.'

Shamita emphasizes that given an opportunity to work, Indian women should get out of 'class issues' in their perception of jobs. In the US, it is normal to work at the cash counter of a cafe, or be a book-keeper at the local library.

At a personal level, support groups insist on women getting out of their comfort zones from the beginning, to make a concerted effort to assimilate. Says Shamita, 'A lot of times, the issue South Asian communities face is that unless they are facing a problem and it is a crisis, they hardly seek help. They wait till the last minute. Most of the time, women don't want to come out. They should make friends, do things they enjoy. First of all, upper-class South Asian women are privileged. They get overwhelmed with, "Oh, I have to do this, I have to do that . . .". Be ready to work hard. Go out, make friends. They should volunteer, go to the library, engage with communities. We do not teach this to kids in South Asia. We do not teach them to engage with people in the community. If you are going to stay at home and be totally dependent on the husband for emotional support, there will be problems. He is out for twelve hours a day every day.'

On a similar note, Sudeepti gives her share of advice on 'quickie NRI' marriages. 'I would advise any girl to avoid a quickie NRI marriage, where the guy comes to the country for a few weeks to get married without any option of a courtship period. Before you know it, you are married, he is off and you join him. You actually "meet" the person for the first time in his home that is foreign to you. While this precaution can't be avoided, I would recommend the girl to start exploring her environment immediately, within a week or two of landing and settling down. Know the area, the commercial spaces nearby, the neighbours. Introduce yourself to some. Even start talking of the possibility of working or studying some time soon and generally exploring options along these lines.'

Sudeepti warns against handing over all your money to the partner. 'Insist on your own single-owner bank account, not a joint one. If it comes to a stage where you need to get out, you can buy yourself a plane ticket overnight.'

Unlike Sudeepti's case, abuse can occur over a period of time. When you explore websites of organizations that can help, it is possible that the perpetrator monitors your computer usage. Domestic violence helpline websites provide safety measures that one can take, such as calling the helpline up from a neighbour's phone or trusted friend's phone rather than the home phone, opting for calling up rather than mailing, which can be susceptible to hacking, keeping a set of documents with friends, practising escape routes, keeping a 'leaving bag' with key documents and basic necessities, among other essentials.

These are practical measures that women need to take. Other than the safety measures, experts do point out to the need for making efforts to connect with others.

'The woman needs to keep a line of communication open. What is lacking is 'confidence-building' for the woman. That confidence will help her in any country. The trouble with a lot of women is that once they get married, the new family becomes their whole family,' says Geeta Menon, secretary of Stree Jagruthi Samithi in Bengaluru. Geeta has worked extensively on women's issues. 'They don't even keep in touch with old friends. It is essential to keep past relationships steady. They come in handy during situations when they are needed.' Geeta points in the direction of a woman putting in efforts to address her own needs too post marriage, instead of giving up all of herself for her new family.

Perhaps, one way abuse can end is for men to understand that exerting control in a relationship is not honourable—it is shameful. It is high time that society accepts that marriage is not everything in a woman's life, that girls have come a long way, and teaches boys to respect women.

As for supportive mechanisms, advocacy and support groups do talk of the dearth in supportive mechanisms that take note of the difference in cultural nuances between Asians and Westerners living in America. Research and advocacy in the last decade has focused in the direction of calling for a better understanding of this.

The National Domestic Violence Hotline website in the United States lists the following tactics that partners use to abuse immigrant victims: isolation or preventing the victim from learning English and communicating with friends or others from their home countries, threats of deportation of the victim, intimidation by destroying legal documents or papers such as passports, resident cards, health insurance and drivers' licences, manipulation regarding citizenship or residency where the abuser withdraws or does not file papers for residency, lying to the victim that they will lose citizenship or residency if they report the violence, economic abuse by getting the victim fired from a job (likely in the case of L2 and J2 women), threatening to hurt children or take them away if police are contacted.

Women on dependent visas of course face added coercion through the control of their expenditure.

Girls like Kala and Sudeepti were fortunate. To this day, they have their tough moments when they remember those nightmarish days. But they take heart in the support they receive.

In the suburbs of an American city, Sapna, who had been married for a few years, wiped her tears after a bout of crying. Her husband took her visiting in-laws out to a temple about forty-five minutes away, and she got those precious couple of hours to cry.

Within a month of their arrival, she was an emotional wreck.

'Have you finished cooking?'

'Why did you wake up so late?'

'Did you clean the toilet?'

'Why did you fry the potatoes? They were supposed to be boiled.'

Or

'Why did you boil the potatoes? We do not like them boiled.'

On another day, they would criticize her parents. She was not well and was walking around gingerly. Her in-laws were miffed. They thought she was acting up to avoid kitchen work. They did not ask her. They complained to their boy later. They were irked further that she was sleeping in their room rather than playing host when she fell sick.

During one of the fights with her husband, he said, 'They will be here a few weeks more and be gone after that. Be good to them. It matters. I do not want you to get a bad name.'

Sapna reached a saturation point. She was on her feet all day. Her back was breaking, and hormones wreaking havoc. She bled heavily. They did not care. She had to be the robot that did not talk, except for asking about their needs and checking on them every hour. How dare this robot fall sick?

'What about my condition by the time they are gone? It's all right that I lose my head and health?'

She wanted to yell at him. He was afraid they would 'hear' their fight and make her the 'bad one'. She wanted to yell at them all. He was silent. She got the message. He just did not want her to react. He would manage her after they left. He would manage her if she tried to kill herself too.

She hated him. Betrayal was an understatement. A man who could not stand up for her to his parents was not capable of being her dream man. She sobbed more, as he looked away.

'I do not care,' she declared. 'I would rather be the bad bahu than put up with this nonsense. What will they do? Bitch about me to all your relatives? To my parents? For talking about how they treat me?'

In her head, she worked out her exit plan should things worsen. She would be out on the streets probably. It steeled her resolve. She would not 'play good' just so they could abuse her more. 'I'll be bad,' she thought grimly.

22

Reinvent, Integrate, Let Go

The first year in the US is when you experience everything with the curiosity of a child. It is also when you watch the dramatic shift in seasons, the silence and the beauty with an inner conflict—of a heart that falls in love with the orderliness, drops of rain softly trickling down the outer surface of glass windows, highways and country roads, trees that follow seasons diligently by shedding their leaves, changing colour, flowering and flourishing.

Feel that pain that nearly strangles you, knowing the price for those fleeting moments of beauty. Your destiny just played tricks on you.

The way to deal with it is to reinvent and let go. When Sarika returned after three months of recovery in India, she learnt driving, visited the temple, networked with friends and eventually signed up for her master's. She worked hard through health complications and completed her course. On the day of her convocation, it was her beloved Sairam who posed proudly with her for photographs. Today, Sarika has found her foothold. She has come a long way, after all, and is poised to enter the IT workforce.

One afternoon, a young woman sat in a cafe along the Hudson, writing a plan for a project that began in her head. She was a Mumbaikar who had been in love with the madness of the city. Out here, by the Hudson, she was busy venting her feelings that needed validation. So lost was she in her writing, and reminiscing about all that she had left behind, that she hardly realized when two hours had gone by.

She looked up at the New York skyline, the gleaming sunshine on Hudson's waters, boats meandering on the waters and the sunlight refracting on the glass of its edifices. It was the Queen's Necklace! She was in Mumbai that moment . . . something ·about that view simply brought Marine Drive, her home, right there in front of her eyes.

Meghna Damani, a married woman with a successful career in India, went through her share of gloom when she arrived in Jersey City. She even contemplated suicide. She looked out of her apartment window on to the Hudson river one day, watching the sun play on its waters. Something in that live scenery set her off.

She decided to speak out. She did not know what would come of it when she picked up her camera and started filming the people and things around her. The visuals slowly took the form of a story. She decided to speak to other women who arrived on H4 visas, to tell their stories. As she puts it in her short film, now well known for its ability to bring out the pathos of visa wives, after a year and a half of trying, a handful of women who had agreed to be filmed, backed out.

Meghna Damani enrolled in a documentary film-making course so she could learn to make her film. 'When no one agreed to be the protagonist of my film, I began filming myself. Was it foolish for me to make this film?'

Meghna was clearly not comfortable making a movie about herself. In the short film—*Hearts Suspended*, she says, 'I wondered why . . . It meant digging into a part of my life that I had shut away. I wanted to believe I was this confident person making a movie about this issue. I did not want to acknowledge all that I had lost—my confidence, my dreams . . . How could I expect these other women to expose their sufferings and failures if I couldn't?'

In the fourteenth minute of *Hearts Suspended*, Meghna is in an argument with her husband about their finances. She wants to attend a film festival elsewhere. He talks of financial constraints. She fights back. He wants her to understand the issue and work out their finances together. 'For the independent career woman that I was, I did not think it was "our" money. I saw it as "his" money,' says Meghna reminiscing about that altercation.

The quarrel ends with him leaving, while she insists on finishing their argument. Her camera pans to the emptiness, peering through the gap between the door and the beige carpet—a single moment symbolizing the devastation that her dependent situation has wreaked on her life. She is left sobbing. It's a situation that plays out a million times in the lives of millions of women within the four walls of their homes, at various times of their lives, especially so with visa wives.

A few minutes on, Meghna relays another discussion. The couple comes to terms with how he is unable to understand the depth of her turmoil in spite of trying hard to. 'My struggle during filming and editing was to bring forth the strength and courage to tell this story because I was still recovering from a dark, depressive state. Telling this story, especially watching the footage of my fight with my husband over and over again, was traumatic. Still, I knew that if I did not tell this story, the suffering would not end for anyone.'

I asked many women about this phase, long after they have moved past their dependency years or have managed to find work. They do not remember much of their trauma. Human minds have the ability to shut out bad past experiences. The hellish years after their arrival constitute a place former visa wives will avoid for life.

Meghna says, 'A lot of people encouraged me not to make this film and that I should feel "lucky" that I had at least been "allowed" to accompany my husband. Maybe I should just accept my situation and work for cash, like an illegal immigrant. I could not come to terms with that because I found it ironic that here I was a person who wants to work in accordance with the law, and have legally entered the country, and am being forced to do something illegal.'

The documentary points in the direction where a woman's success is measured by the success of her marriage and the 'good life' she manages to build for herself. This means no failures—either in her husband's personal and professional life or in her own relationship with him and his family. Should she, as a transplanted human being, suffer in America, she will not have an audience that understands her trauma. Her complaints translate into sympathy for 'the husband who is putting up with her'. Making the film taught Meghna that a lot of other women were going through their challenges and suffering.

When Meghna started showing the film at film festivals, local Americans were surprised.

'Did you know about this when you came (to America)?'

'How come we did not know about this?'

It was in 2007 at the New York Indian Film Festival when such responses from the audience gave Meghna a reason to stand tall, with her head held high. 'I felt proud that I was able to do something about this in my own way. It felt very therapeutic. I felt motivated to get into film-making . . . and it felt like the first step,' says Meghna.

Using the ubiquitous video camera, Meghna found purpose in life and reinvented her existence in the new country. She took a lead in speaking out about the issue when H4 visa woes were not much talked of yet. What helped her cope was joining a Buddhist group. 'Buddhist practice helped me cope on a day-by-day basis. It gave me the courage to share this story that is deeply personal. Developing empathy for people is important and my practice really helped,' she says. Putting herself in others' shoes to understand her own woes better has helped. 'The second part of my film shows that men too struggle in their own way. It is about them making adjustments, dealing with this new person (their bride) coming here, having to deal with her issues and so on.'

Meghna's film contributed its bit to the debate. She has attended summits, advocacy meetings and policy discussions to share her experience. She has also contributed to discussions around the executive action that allows some H4 visa-holder spouses to work.

What is the key to finding your moorings in a land whose culture is far removed from what you grew up with? What can be done to avoid the depression that comes during such transition?

'Hit the ground and get going right away,' says Meghna. Her tips for survival come from her own experiences:

Be proactive. It is easy to feel alone.

Mix with your community and, in addition, with the American community as well.

Be open and flexible.

Quoting from Neuro-linguistic Programming (NLP), she talks about the power of flexibility—'The person with the most flexibility has the most power'.

~

In the summer of 2014, my family and I were visiting Washington DC's Smithsonian Museum of Natural History when I sauntered through its second floor.

The words 'Beyond Bollywood' caught my eye. At the entrance of this exhibition was an all-familiar shelf of shoes—branded ones to traditional *jutis*. For a moment, I wondered if I must take off my shoes to enter the show.

The exhibition opened in April 2014 following a fervent plea for representation by the Indian community. Work on it began in 2008. 'We had to start from scratch,' says Masum Momaya, who curated the show. 'It took us six years to research and collect things for the show.'

The show traced the history of Indians who moved to America in the nineteenth century (Punjabi Sikhs), stereotypes about Indians, their struggle with racist exclusion through the twentieth century, Indians in various spheres of American life, contribution to American society and a host of other facts. Needless to say, Indian visitors were excited. 'Just the fact that something about their community has been put up at the museum makes them very happy. The exhibition does not go into the depth of anything in particular. That (is what) has drawn people in,' says Masum.

The museum finds itself on the must-visit bucket list of most visitors to Washington DC, and gets a footfall count of 10 million a year. 'We want to show this story to everyone, not just Indians. Many visitors have an Indian co-worker, or classmate, someone they went to school with or knew. It is to talk to everyone,' said Masum.

The project was an example of how persistently engaging with the local community works towards greater recognition and acceptance. That's something women on dependent visas can work on—persistent engagement with the local community.

At a personal level, perhaps, when Aruna braved the winter cold of Pittsburgh to simply walk around, feel the air, the hills, monuments and museums, she did not wait for the city to accept her. She let it grow on her. She made friends. She tried to reinvent herself by volunteering, which is greatly valued in America.

Sathya had gone through one of her days of gloom when Surya decided to surprise her with a trip to New York City. Little did she know that her long-awaited dream of watching a show would come true.

On a winter evening with temperatures running as low as -5° C, the couple made it to the city, and walked into New Amsterdam Theater. It was the first time Sathya felt part of an opera-styled theatre. She felt as if she had walked into a renaissance painting. Vines, floral details and murals filled the ceiling.

'What a slice of history!' she thought, as she gaped at the breathtaking detail. She later learnt that the building had had its own share of ups and downs through the decades. In a short while, she noticed that not one seat was left empty in the gallery. It was a big deal for her to have this dream come true. She could not have dreamt it during all those years back in India. Sathya noticed that it was probably a big deal for the Americans too. Many in the gallery were families with kids; many others were elderly people who were busy taking selfies to mark the moment. Soon, the curtain rose.

What followed was a live fantasy she did not expect to see on a normal dais. It was Disney's *Aladdin*. The show stealer was Genie, not Aladdin, and what a way to appear! He emerged from the floor while the smoke filled up the stage. Aladdin's own discovery of the treasure cave, 3D props that moved around the dais to change a setting in a flash, filmy dances . . . Sathya felt it was a Bollywood movie come alive.

Her 'wow' moment came later though, when Aladdin and Jasmine settled on the flying carpet, and the carpet actually flitted in the air on top of the dais, for a whole few minutes. 'How did they just do it? How did they make the carpet fly?' she said aloud. If there were cables to synchronize it, where were they?

When the Genie came back in the end with holiday clothes on, she actually wanted to whistle. Watching the show infused a new energy in her.

Would she have done it back in India? Watch a musical? Perhaps. Most probably, no.

She remembered the time she had gaped in awe at the Grand Canyon a few months before. The pictures did not show much, but when she stood atop the cliff over the Colorado river, she forgot to breathe for a moment. Such was their magnificence. She thought of her long-lasting wish to visit the Himalayas as she spotted a red dot against the Grand Canyon and realized it was a helicopter. It brought home the truth—that we humans are but mere specks in the vastness called the universe.

On their train ride to Manhattan and back, Sathya and Surya found people generally cheerful, unlike on a typical work day. The train driver's announcement was witty, and the ticket collector made small talk when he came by. Sathya peered out of the train window into the night and spotted Manhattan skyline's beautiful city lights, the One World Trade Center towering over the skyscrapers . . . moving farther away. She was tired, and loved it.

'Let's make a donation to a food bank here for our anniversary instead of partying,' Surya suggested to her. She was elated. They had started donating to orphanages back in India. Why not in the US? She had thought about it many times. The first time they spotted homeless people on the streets of Washington DC, they were shocked. She found it heartbreaking to see homeless people, some of them stretched out by a couple of expensive-looking suitcases, reading a book in the biting cold. The country of opportunity had poverty, and there was no doubt about it.

They had to give, to the country they left behind, and to the country that was now their home. She loved both her countries.

A couple of days later, she headed to the library, smiled at the librarian and chatted with the staff as she borrowed books. The library was her haven. A million times she had silently thanked the new country for such amazing hangouts that did not need money. She had described their neatness and welcoming feel to friends back home, and her surprise at finding Gujarati and Hindi books.

All through her trips to the local book paradise, she had found it hard to initiate conversation. She had taken her first step in letting go of her inhibitions that day. 'Let go, let go,' she sang away in her head.

For once, she felt it might be okay to fail.

In her pre-arrival mail to her fellow classmates who introduced themselves on an e-mail list, Madhusmita simply introduced herself and said, 'No hang-ups.'

'I wanted to fit in right away,' says Madhusmita, who found a great roommate. She went through her share of hardships as a student, but a friend as dedicated as her roommate and her own steadfastness helped her survive the first year.

She went on to have a successful career in journalism, and now teaches in Philadelphia. On her invitation, I decide to drop by at a dance show in downtown Philadelphia.

It's spring, and the drive to Philly (as Philadelphia is popularly called) is a pleasant one. The cost of tickets is what surprises us. At $10 a head, we would not mind watching dance shows every week. The venue is the Community Education Center, and the performances are part of the ETC Performance Series.

Worth every penny, in fact a lot more, the modest setting, a small indoor auditorium comes to life with eclectic performances by various groups.

My husband and I rarely went to concerts in Bengaluru, though classical dance performances were part of school life—Bharatanatyam, Kuchipudi, Kathak and the like. I was still dreaming of watching those super-grand musicals, *The Lion King* and *Chicago*, so when a group of graceful young girls, dressed in beautiful green-and-brown ballet costumes, filled the floor, it was magic. Group after group performing contemporary dance made the evening magical. But it was the last performance by Reggie 'Tapman' Myers that caught us off-guard. It was the first time we were watching tap dance too.

Focus lights beamed on the youngster and he tapped away to the beats. So engrossed were we that we did not understand why a part of the crowd suddenly giggled. It turned out that someone had made an entry from the audience door of the hall in a classical Indian dance costume, dancing to the same beats. She took stage alongside the tap dancer. The classical dancer was Madhusmita, dressed in Sattriya dance costume. What followed was a *jugalbandi* of sorts, something the dancers had never tried before.

The classical dancer interpreted tap music and offered her own beauty to the flow, while Reggie tapped away. The two performers were conversing in the language of dance—she with her graceful ode to the Lord, and he with his energetic rhythm. The performance was extempore, a surprise even for the organizers. It was their first-ever attempt at the experiment, straight on the dais.

'It was possible because he is a friend,' said Madhusmita afterwards. The response was so enthusiastic that they decided to repeat their *jugalbandi* at future events. Cross-cultural fusion is a great discovery in one's journey into the deeper nuances of one's own culture. Madhusmita learnt Sattriya at an early age. She continued to stay in touch with the divine Assamese classical dance form through her years in journalism, gradually honing her art. Every year, she makes a pilgrimage to Majuli to soak in its calm. Majuli Island, the largest of all riverine islands known, is the home of Sattriya, rich in wildlife, green cover and fragile, with a plethora of Vaishnavite monasteries.

In Philadelphia, Madhusmita runs the Sattriya Dance Company and teaches the beautiful dance form to students of all nationalities. She also makes efforts to document the dance form.

From the time she set foot in America, Madhusmita focused her energies on assimilation. She did not let go of her roots though. She has actively promoted Sattriya through her teaching, performances with students and creative collaborations.

The first step to integrating oneself into local culture is to accept it, with all the differences that it offers. It is easy to judge a new place, to detest its mundaneness, to scoff at its over-emphasis on privacy. It is easy to fall into the trap of insularity. As a new arrival on a dependent visa, the perceived banality of American landscapes can put you off. But if you train your mind to look beyond the monotony of spaces, you will find the new blessings that the place has to offer.

Thank You

This book was not something I dreamt about writing. It happened. Clichéd as it sounds, the book found me. I wrote it because I needed to rant. I wrote it to validate the feelings and struggle of women like me.

My friend and former colleague Teresa Rehman encouraged me to write a column on my travails as a has-been career woman in my US home, my adjustment struggles in the new country and the childlike wonderment at the landscapes, lifestyle, etc. Thank you, Teresa.

My desire to write a book was largely fuelled by the enormous inclination towards the written word in my family—my grandfathers in particular. My maternal grandfather was a columnist, and a scholar in Telugu and Sanskrit. My paternal grandfather took keen interest in poetry and plays, and devotedly participated in All India Radio contests every week. The real foundation for the book was laid when I was just a child, in my Ammumma's (maternal grandmother) home. This supermom is over ninety years old today, but back then, she was an active homemaker, her household teeming with not just her own children, but also visiting relatives and, in later years, her grandchildren. My summers with cousins at her home have been a great inspiration for my writing. I am in awe of my grandfather who authored many books, but Ammumma was his rock, and ours. She embodies the richness of another era, and love unlimited.

I thank my baby who has motivated me from long before she arrived in this world. My husband Dhinesh has been my support throughout my book journey. He put up with my 'writerly' troubles, played my book-parent, even drove me to different cities in the US to attend meetings and conduct interviews, and supported me in a million ways so that I could simply stay at home to write. My parents and sister have played a constant role in nurturing the writer in me. My parents nurtured me to dream and achieve. And let me be. It's thanks to their understanding and support that I managed to write even when my dad was ill. My sister took an active interest during that phase to help me with research too. I thank my bunch of cousins for helping me observe life at its dramatic best. Thank god for those pre-gadget years! My husband's family has been accommodative enough of a daughter-in-law who is different. A huge thanks goes to them. My teachers at school and college have helped shape my thought process a great deal. I thank them for continuing to inspire me.

My shout-out goes to my colleagues in journalism, and the bunch who turned friends for life, for their frank opinions during discussions related to the book, and giving me invaluable leads. That includes colleagues at the *adda*, the office nook off Infantry Road in Bengaluru, who set me off in the direction of the non-stop pursuit of quality in writing as a way of life.

This book happened because many people helped me steer through the confusing waters of publishing. I thank my literary agent Kanishka Gupta who helped me stay on course during the tough chase-and-write months of *Visa Wives*. Not without reason. Getting people to talk, mostly women, was the most difficult part of this whole journey. Immigrant mindset makes it hard to share experiences. I changed the names of several people who I have quoted in the book for the sake of protecting their privacy. Others were keen on being quoted. In the end, their stories mattered.

I thank the people who shared their stories, and who agreed to do so. I could not include all the interviews I did, but, even if your voice did not make it directly into the text, be assured your inputs made a huge difference to this book. To the women who refused, for whatever reasons, thank you, for helping me learn to empathize.

Some chapters in the book were harder to put together than the others. In terms of research, the one on domestic violence and the safety of Indian and South Asian women living in the US, was tough. Thanks to Manisha Prasad who put me in touch with Saheli from Boston. I thank Saheli, a community-based organization in Boston, and Gouri Banerjee who was of immense help, for their time and inputs. I thank other organizations working in the area of domestic violence too, for sharing information on the subject. I thank the experts in the various fields—healthcare, food, writing and IT—for sharing their expertise.

I thank America for expanding my horizons and teaching me to appreciate things I took for granted back in India, and for some of the values I learnt from a fresh perspective. I thank my friends in the US who have become family, for helping me every step of the way. I thank my home country, India, and the cities that shaped me—Bengaluru, Chennai and Mumbai— for making me who I am today. If this book makes a difference to women who make that crucial 'stay or travel' decision, it will have been worth the effort.

This page also prompts me to look back at those school years when my school, my schoolmates, teachers and that compound under the protective shade of a banyan tree formed my world. I am grateful for the life lessons that dreamy compound offered, as well as for the community life that the neighbourhood I grew up in sheltered me with. A lot goes into the making of a book, and this is where the dedication shown by Mriga Maithel at Penguin Random House matters a great deal. My thanks to her, and to Swati Chopra, for their work on the book. Thank you, Penguin Random House, for making this book a reality.

Notes

1. Caroline Healey Dall, *The Life of Dr. Anandabai Joshee, a Kinswoman of the Pundita Ramabai* (Boston: Roberts Brothers, 1888), retrieved from http://archive.org/ stream/lifeofdranandabai00dalliala#page/n7/mode/2up. Also see Wikipedia, 'Anandi Gopal Joshi', retrieved from https://en.wikipedia.org/wiki/Anandi_Gopal_Joshi.
2. Srirajasekhar Bobby Koritala, 'A Historical Perspective of Americans of Asian Indian Origin, 1790-1997', retrieved from http://www.infinityfoundation.com/mandala/ h_es/h_es_korit_histical.htm.
3. Wilma Mankiller, Gwendolyn Mink, Marysa Navarro, Barbara Smith and Gloria Steinem, eds, *The Reader's Companion to U.S. Women's History, Asian Pacific Women* (New York: Houghton Mifflin, 1998), p. 48.
4. Jie Zong and Jeanne Batalova, 'Indian Immigrants in the United States', *Migration Information Source*, 6 May 2015, retrieved from http://www.migrationpolicy.org/article/ indian-immigrants-united-states.
5. US Census of 2000, 'Population Change by Race and Ethnicity, 1990-2000: USA, California, Southern California, LA County, Orange County, Koreatown', 2 July 2003.

6. Wikipedia, 'Indian Americans', retrieved from https://en.wikipedia.org/wiki/Indian_Americans

7. Sara Ashley O'Brien, 'High-Skilled Visa Applications Hit Record High', CNN Money, 13 April 2015, retrieved from http://money.cnn.com/2015/04/13/technology/h1b-cap-visa/

8. U.S. Citizenship and Immigration Services, 'Petition Filing and Processing Procedures for Form I-140, Immigrant Petition for Alien Worker', last updated 5 June 2014, https://www.uscis.gov/forms/petition-filing-and-processing-procedures-form-i-140-immigrant-petition-alien-worker.

9. Consulate General of the United States, 'Frequently Asked Questions', https://chennai.usconsulate.gov/temporary-visitors/faqs.html#NFNNS

10. Immihelp.com, '221(g) Refusal – U.S. Visa', http://www.immihelp.com/visas/221grefusal/

11. Wikipedia, 'List of United States Cities by Population', retrieved from https://www.census.gov/quickfacts/table/PST045215/00

12. For those looking for more information on apartments and rents in the US, the following links might prove helpful:
    http://www.rentjungle.com/average-rent-in-new-york-rent-trends/
    http://www.immihelp.com/newcomer/apartment-rental-tips.html
    http://www.usa.gov/topics/family-homes/renting.shtml
    http://www.internations.org/usa-expats/guide/16311-housing-accommodation/renting-a-home-in-the-usa-16314/rents-and-rental-agreements-in-the-usa-2

13. Wikipedia, 'Garbage Disposal Unit', retrieved from https://en.wikipedia.org/wiki/Garbage_disposal_unit

14. Chelsea Stanley, 'The Patient Protection and Affordable Care Act: The Latest Obstacle in the Path to Receiving

Complementary and Alternative Health Care?', *Indiana Law Journal* 90, no. 2 (2015): Article 11, retrieved from http://www.repository.law.indiana.edu/cgi/viewcontent. cgi?article=11153&context=ilj

15. Elizabeth Renter, 'Does Your Health Insurance Cover Alternative Medicine?', *U.S. News*, 9 March 2015, retrieved from http://health.usnews.com/health-news/ health-insurance/articles/2015/03/09/does-your-health-insurance-cover-alternative-medicine

16. James S. Kemp, Benjamin Unger, Davida Wilkins, Rose M. Psara, Terrance L. Ledbetter, Michael A. Graham, Mary Case and Bradley T. Thach, 'Unsafe Sleep Practices and an Analysis of Bedsharing among Infants Dying Suddenly and Unexpectedly: Results of a Four-Year, Population-Based, Death-Scene Investigation Study of Sudden Infant Death Syndrome and Related Deaths', *Pediatrics* 106, no. 3 (2000): e41, retrieved from http:// pediatrics.aappublications.org/content/106/3/e41.full

17. Denver Nicks, 'Hitting Your Kids is Legal in All 50 States', *Time*, 17 September 2014, retrieved from http://time. com/3379862/child-abuse/

18. Wikipedia, 'U.S. Ratification of the Convention on the Rights of the Child', retrieved from https://en.wikipedia. org/wiki/U.S._ratification_of_the_Convention_on_the_ Rights_of_the_Child

19. Lawrence J. Cohen and Anthony T. DeBenedet, 'Why Is the U.S. Against Children's Rights?', *Time*, 24 January 2012, retrieved from http://ideas.time.com/2012/01/24/ why-is-the-us-against-childrens-rights/

20. The Coalition for Asian American Children and Families, 'Understanding the Laws on How You Can Discipline Your Children', January 2002, retrieved from http://

www.lawhelpny.org/resource/understanding-the-laws-on-how-you-can-discipl?lang=EN

21. Brendan L. Smith, 'The Case against Spanking', American Psychological Association, Feature, Monitor on Psychology 43, no. 4 (2012): 60, retrieved from http://www.apa.org/monitor/2012/04/spanking.aspx

22. American Psychological Association, 'Corporal Punishment', retrieved from http://www.apa.org/about/policy/corporal-punishment.aspx

23. American Association of Community Colleges, '2014 Fact Sheet', April 2014, retrieved from http://www.aacc.nche.edu/AboutCC/Documents/Facts14_Data_R3.pdf

24. A. Raj and J.G. Silverman, 'Intimate Partner Violence against South Asian Women in Greater Boston', *Journal of the American Medical Women's Association* 57, no. 2 (2002): 111–14, retrieved from http://www.ncbi.nlm.nih.gov/pubmed/11991419

25. A. Raj, J.G. Silverman, J. McCleary-Sills and R. Liu, 'Immigration Policies Increase South Asian Immigrant Women's Vulnerability to Intimate Partner Violence', *Journal of the American Medical Women's Association* 60, no. 1 (2005): 26–32, retrieved from http://www.ncbi.nlm.nih.gov/pubmed/16845767

26. Asian and Pacific Islander Institute on Domestic Violence, 'Fact Sheet: Domestic Violence in South Asian Communities', July 2012, retrieved from http://www.api-gbv.org/files/DVFactSheet-SouthAsian-APIIDV-2012.pdf

27. Sujatha Jesudason and Anat Shenker-Osorio, 'Sex Selection in America: Why It Persists and How We Can Change It', *The Atlantic*, 31 May 2012, retrieved from http://www.theatlantic.com/politics/archive/2012/05/sex-selection-in-america-why-it-persists-and-how-we-can-change-it/257864/

A Note on the Author

Radhika M.B. is a seasoned journalist who has worked with *Tehelka*, *New Indian Express* and the *Deccan Chronicle*. She actively contributed to the setting up of *Tehelka*'s Bengaluru branch in 2004, and its functioning till 2007. She is the consulting editor for the *Thumb Print* e-magazine. She is currently settled in the US and is an active crafter.